THE GREAT
MISTAKE

MARY ROBERTS RINEHART (1876-1958) was the most beloved and bestselling mystery writer in America in the first half of the twentieth century. Born in Pittsburgh, Rinehart trained as a nurse and married a doctor. When a stock market crash sent the young couple into debt, Rinehart leaned on her writing—previously a part-time occupation—to pay the bills. Credited with inventing the phrase, "The butler did it"—a phrase she never actually wrote—Rinehart is often called an American Agatha Christie, even though she was much more popular during her heyday.

OTTO PENZLER, the creator of American Mystery Classics, is also the founder of the Mysterious Press (1975); Mysterious-Press.com (2011), an electronic-book publishing company; and New York City's Mysterious Bookshop (1979). He has won a Raven, the Ellery Queen Award, two Edgars (for the *Encyclopedia of Mystery and Detection*, 1977, and *The Lineup*, 2010), and lifetime achievement awards from NoirCon and *The Strand Magazine*. He has edited more than 70 anthologies and written extensively about mystery fiction.

T0021472

THE GREAT MISTAKE

MARY ROBERTS RINEHART

Introduction by
OTTO PENZLER

AMERICAN MYSTERY CLASSICS

Penzler Publishers
New York

This is a work of fiction. Names, characters, places, and incidents either are the product of the author's imagination or are used fictitiously. Any resemblance to actual persons, living or dead, businesses, companies, events, or locales is entirely coincidental.

Published in 2023 by Penzler Publishers
58 Warren Street, New York, NY 10007
penzlerpublishers.com

Distributed by W. W. Norton

Copyright © 1940 by Mary Roberts Rinehart, renewed.
Reprinted with the permission of The Mary Roberts Rinehart Literary Trust.
Introduction copyright © 2023 by Otto Penzler.
All rights reserved.

Cover image: Andy Ross
Cover design: Mauricio Diaz

Paperback ISBN 978-1-61316-460-0
Hardcover ISBN 978-1-61316-459-4

Library of Congress Control Number: 2023908398

Printed in the United States of America

9 8 7 6 5 4 3 2 1

THE GREAT
MISTAKE

INTRODUCTION

Mary Roberts Rinehart once described *The Great Mistake* as "a murder story set in the suburbs, involving a bag of toads, a pair of trousers and some missing keys," which is a neat summation, though hardly a complete foreshadowing of what the reader might expect.

Having become a successful author instantly, Rinehart instinctively understood what readers wanted to read: engrossing stories with mystery, romance, humor, and suspense, and she was able to deliver it skillfully and consistently.

A common element in Rinehart's mysteries was the author's penchant for moving the storyline along with foreshadowing. While this is a frequently used device in contemporary literature, Rinehart often employed a method that has become mocked by some, partially because of its simplicity as well as so much overuse that it has been defined as a cliché in her work.

Rinehart's use of this contrivance is now famously credited (or blamed, depending on your point of view) for creating the "Had-I-But-Known" school of fiction. Straightforward detection is less evident in Rinehart's mysteries than in the works of her predecessors, which generally concentrated on the methods of eccentric detectives. Rinehart's stories involve ordinary people entangled in a situation not of their making that could happen to anyone.

The heroines of these books often use poor judgment. Warned never—*never*—to enter the basement under any circumstances, for instance (hyperbolically), they are absolutely certain to be found there within the next few pages, only to be rescued at the very last instant, generally by their lovers. These heroines often have flashes of insight—just a little too late to prevent another murder.

The statement (and its numerous variations) "had I known then what I know now, this could have been avoided," often creeps into her books and has given its name to a school of fiction that has produced innumerable followers.

Few of Rinehart's book deliver the suspenseful foreshadowing as profoundly as *The Great Mistake*. A mere four pages in, Pat, our heroine, notices an outbuilding on the enormous estate of Maud Wainwright, the wealthy widow who has recently employed her. She says, "that awful playhouse of hers, with all it was to mean to us later." From that point on, any mention of the playhouse suggested something sinister enveloping it, and Rinehart didn't disappoint.

A few pages later, Pat sees Mrs. Wainwright, looking lonely "against the panoply of wealth, kind and totally unarmed against the world. Perhaps that's why she made her great mistake. For make it she did, with terrible results." What was the great mistake of this kindly, generous old lady? Readers had to turn the page to learn what it could possibly be.

Compelling stuff, and pretty much unique to Rinehart, until legions, seeing her extraordinary success, tried to emulate it.

During what is often called the Golden Age of mystery fiction, the years between the two World Wars, Rinehart was one of a handful of the bestselling writers in America. Not a bestselling mystery writer—a bestselling *writer*. The list of the top ten bestselling books for each year in the 1920s showed Rinehart on the list five times; only Sinclair Lewis matched that impressive feat. The only mystery titles that outsold her in those years were *Rebecca* by Daphne du Maurier and two titles by S.S. Van Dine, *The Greene Murder Case* and *The Bishop Murder Case*.

In many regards, Mary Roberts Rinehart was the American Agatha Christie, both in terms of popularity and productivity. Like her British counterpart, the prolific Rinehart wrote a large number of bestselling mysteries, short stories, straight novels, an unrevealing autobiography, and stage plays, some of which were hugely successful—*The Mousetrap* for Christie and *The Bat* for Rinehart.

Unlike Christie, however, Rinehart's popularity waned after her death in 1958. The lack of a long-running series character (although Miss Letitia Carberry, known as Tish, appeared in several books, she was not strictly a detective, and Nurse Adams, dubbed "Miss Pinkerton" by the police for her uncanny ability to become embroiled in criminal activities, had few appearances) undoubtedly hurt, but so did changing reading tastes in the United States. While Christie's detectives, notably Hercule Poirot, were reasoning creatures largely lacking in emotions, Rinehart's characters were swept up in the very human responses of romance, curiosity, fear, and tenacity.

Born to a poor family in Pittsburgh, her father committed suicide just as she was graduating from nursing school, where she had met Dr. Stanley Marshall Rinehart, who she married in 1896 at the age of twenty; they had three sons. Because of poor investments, the young nurse and her doctor husband struggled financially so she began to write, selling forty-five stories in the first year (1903). The editor of *Munsey's Magazine* suggested that she write a novel, which he would serialize, and she quickly produced *The Man in Lower Ten*, followed immediately by *The Circular Staircase*, which was published in book form first, in 1908. After her husband died in 1932, Mary Roberts Rinehart, now a fabulously wealthy woman from the sales of her books, moved into a luxurious, eighteen-room Park Avenue apartment where she lived alone for the rest of her life.

A consistent bestseller from that point on, Rinehart's mysteries have a surprisingly violent side to them (though never graphically described), with the initial murder serving as a springboard to subsequent multiple murders. Her tales are unfailingly filled with sentimental love stories and gentle humor, both unusual elements of crime fiction in the early decades of the twentieth century.

Describing some of her books, Rinehart displayed a sly sense of humor while conceding the levels of violence and the body count are not entirely expected from an author known for her romantic, humorous, and heart-warming mystery fiction. Here are some selected titles about which she warned readers:

• *The After House* (1914): "I killed three people with one axe, raising the average number of murders per crime book to a new high level."

• *The Red Lamp* (1925): "A murder is committed every time the sinister red lamp goes out."

• *The Album* (1933): "The answer to four gruesome murders lies in a dusty album for everyone to see."

• *The Wall* (1938): "I commit three shocking murders in a fashionable New England summer colony."

It is not uncommon for Rinehart to introduce elements of

horror into her books. Though they are always rationally explained, she (and her readers) liked that soupçon of terror that lurked without apparent explanation until the denouement. *The Red Lamp* is one example of that whisper of horror and, in her most famous work, *The Bat*, strange events permeate the Long Island manor in which most of the action occurs.

The Circular Staircase, her first book, was adapted for a stage play titled *The Bat* (a sobriquet for a bank robber), which she wrote with Avery Hopkins. The play was then novelized under the same title as the wildly successful drama. Oddly, perhaps wary (or weary) of rewriting her plot yet again, it has been rumored that Rinehart hired Stephen Vincent Benet to write the novelization. *The Bat*, proving to be ubiquitous, was adapted for a 1926 silent movie, then a sound film in 1930 titled *The Bat Whispers*, and yet again in 1959 as *The Bat*, as well as several television adaptations.

Although some of the mores and social niceties of her time have changed, Rinehart's greatest strengths as a writer were her ability to tell a story that compelled the reader to turn the page, and to create universal characters to which all of us can relate. That ability never goes out of style and, as long as people read books, neither will Mary Roberts Rinehart, the universally beloved writer who, for two decades, was the best-paid writer in America.

—OTTO PENZLER
New York, January 2023

CHAPTER ONE

THE FIRST time I ever spoke to Maud Wainwright was in her boudoir at the Cloisters. She was sitting in front of her famous expanding table, the one at which she seated her dinner parties, with a bunch of place cards in her hand and a completely baffled look on her face.

"Come in and sit down, Miss Abbott," she said. "I can't get up. If I move, this wretched table collapses. I've seated this dinner three times already."

I didn't wonder that the table had collapsed. It was drawn out to its full length and there must have been a hundred slots around its border. You know the idea. The table can be made large or small and the cards, already written, are placed upright in the slots. It is a sort of bird's-eye view of the party in advance, supposed to make for harmonious arrangement later. Although there was a general belief that Maud Wainwright merely shuffled the cards and dealt them out, I know she once placed old Joseph Berry next to Mrs. Theodore Earle, who had not spoken to him for years.

She must have moved just then, however, for the table chose that moment to divide in the center and fall again, scattering such cards as had been placed over the white velvet carpet. She leaned back at that and closed her eyes.

"Take it away," she said. "I can't face it again. Get somebody downstairs to fix it, and don't bring it back until it decides it isn't twins."

I saw then that there was an anxious-looking housekeeper in a corner, and a lady's maid hovering about. While I picked up the cards they got the table out of the room, and Mrs. Wainwright sat back with a grunt of relief.

That was my first close view of Maud Wainwright, a big, irregularly handsome woman, probably fifty and not ashamed of it, and clad in an ancient house coat and a pair of bedroom slippers. She had an enormous head of naturally blond hair, and that day she wore it in a long braid down her back. I had not seen a braid of hair since I left boarding school, and hardly then. She saw me looking at it and smiled.

"Don't mind my pigtail," she said. "My dear old John liked my hair, so I have never cut it. Hilda loathes it."

Hilda, I gathered, was the maid.

I found myself liking her at once. She was as plain as an old shoe. Queer how one can hear of people for years, dislike them on principle, and then meet them and fall for them. I fell for Maud Wainwright that day with a crash—braid, bedroom slippers, and all.

She offered me a cigarette and took one herself. Then she looked at me, smiling.

"Well, Miss Abbott, what about this mess I'm in?"

"I don't know," I said cautiously. "Is it a mess?"

"That seems to be the general idea. See here, what's your first name? Or do you mind? It's more friendly, I think."

"I'm generally called Pat."

"Pat," she repeated. "I like it. Short for Patricia, I suppose."

"Yes."

"It's a pretty name. Mine is Maud. You know: 'Come into the garden, Maud.' It's revolting, isn't it?"

I thought, for all her lightness, she was studying me. Not subtly. She was never a subtle woman; but with the semi-direct frankness with which children survey strange people. And I must have been strange to her, God knows, sitting there in that vast house of hers; a fair sample of the unprotected young woman, thrown on the world to sink or swim. When that day I had driven up the hill in my old car and faced the vast mass of the Cloisters, I had very nearly turned back. It had loomed at the end of the drive like a combination of the Capitol at Washington and the new Beverly High School, with a touch of the city courthouse thrown in, and it had frankly scared me.

But I was not frightened now. I think if anything I was amused. She put out her cigarette and sat upright.

"Tell me a little about yourself, Pat. That's only fair. If you stay on, as I hope you will, you will know all about me very soon. Dr. Sterling says you are—well, alone. Have you no family?"

"My father and mother are both dead," I said, my throat tightening.

"Never mind. I'm sorry, my dear. I suppose things weren't too good after they had gone."

"They have been pretty bad," I said frankly. "I have some real estate, mostly unoccupied or mortgaged. Not much else. If you think I can do the work—"

"Of course you can. I only hope you like us here. We'll do our best to make you happy."

Yes, that is what she said. I was to be happy. Everything was to be as cheerful as a morning in May. And it was easy to believe it that day, with the June breeze drifting in through the windows, Maud Wainwright's friendly smile, and the French doors open onto that roof garden of hers, built over a lower wing, bright with early flowers, and with a big mastiff asleep there in the sun. Happy and luxurious, there in the boudoir with its thick white rug, its pale-gray walls and its powder-blue and rose and yellow covered chairs and chaise longue. And outside, partly hidden by the shrubbery, that awful playhouse of hers, with all it was to mean to us later.

She sat up suddenly, as though all details had been arranged and we were now ready for business.

"All right," she said. "What about this dinner of mine, Pat? Is it a mistake, or isn't it?"

Privately I thought it was a mistake. To understand that, or even this story, I must make clear the curious relationship between what we in Beverly called the Hill, and what the Hill called the village. Beverly never thought of itself as a suburb. It was a self-contained unit, with its own club and its own conservative social life. Its residents could—and did—make their money in the city, ten miles away. From the eight-thirty in the morning to the five-thirty at night it claimed them. But Beverly was their spiritual home, its river was their river, its lovely old houses and gardens belonged to them, and so, until twenty years before, had the hill country which rose behind the river valley.

I had lived there all my life. I had learned to paddle a canoe on the river, had ridden to school on a bicycle before I went to boarding school, and in the Beverly Club ballroom I had had my first dancing lessons; Miss Mattie holding up her long, full black taffeta skirt, her neat toes pointing out, and two rows of small boys and girls awkwardly hopping about. "One-two-three-one-two-three." The piano going, the ballroom floor shining, and the future citizens of the village giggling and learning to dance.

Then one day something began to happen to the Hill. Up to that time it had been ours—for picnics, for hiking trips along its green lanes, and for riding our quiet family horses; we children with a groom, who was usually the stableboy, to keep an eye on us, or with Mr. Gentry, the riding master, to teach us to jump. Low brush jumps, and Mr. Gentry erect on his big horse.

"All right, Patricia. Your turn."

A coldness in the pit of my stomach, my small hands moist, and old Charlie or Joe taking the jump as though it was Mount Everest. One day Mr. Gentry's horse threw his head up and broke his nose—Mr. Gentry's, of course—and it looked quite flat and bled dreadfully.

I was seven at the time, and I wept loudly all the way home.

I suppose what happened to the Hill was happening everywhere, only this was our own particular grievance. One day old John C. Wainwright came down from the city in his car, drove up the Hill, picked out a site which concealed the village but let him see the river, and spent the next two years driving his architect crazy by traveling in Europe and shipping home vast crates of stone, marble, mosaics, tiles, and what have you. One of his purchases was an entire stone cloister from an old monastery. The architect threatened suicide, but old J.C. was firm. The plans were changed again, an open court built in the center of the house, and around it was placed the covered walk, pillars, flagstones, and all.

That was how the Cloisters got its name.

He was followed by others, of course. The exodus from the

city had begun. In the next ten years—by the time I was seven-teen—our beloved lanes had become cement roads, the George Washington Spring where all the valley had sent its cars for huge bottles of drinking water had become a clay pipe draining into a sewer, the old Coleman farm was a country club with an eighteen-hole golf course, and in due time a Hunt Club was or-ganized, with a pack of hounds.

There was no feud between the two settlements, of course. Beverly simply went on being Beverly. The Hill remained the Hill. When they met, as they did eventually at the country club, they merely hit and bounced off. Now Maud Wainwright pro-posed to bring them together.

"Why shouldn't I?" she said, eyeing me. "I've lived here eigh-teen years, and I don't know a woman in Beverly by her first name."

I smiled. It was difficult for me to believe that she was not on first-name terms with anybody.

"It took my mother ten years to bring herself to leave cards up here. Then she simply left them and went on."

"But why?" she demanded. "It's idiotic."

"You were city people. Naturally you drew your friends from there."

"And Beverly didn't want us?"

"Beverly had its own life too. It was pretty well self-con-tained. It still is. You have to remember that we seldom saw any of you, especially the women, and it's women who make social contacts. You motored to town and back. The men met, of course; on the trains, or at clubs in the city. It just happened that way," I added. "It's odd, when you think about it. I have lived in Beverly all my life. You've been here eighteen years. And I have seen you exactly twice."

That amused her. She laughed a little, shuffling the place cards in her big, well-shaped hands.

"I see," she said. "The queen was in her counting-house, counting out her money. This awful house! Isn't it silly, Pat? And what the hell am I going to do about this party? Dr. Sterling suggests I get sick and call it off."

"Go ahead with it," I told her impulsively. "Everybody is coming, and everybody is going to like it. You might even have the young crowd in to dance afterward. I can make a list and telephone, if you like."

The idea enchanted her. She liked young people, and in a few minutes I had the best city band on the telephone and we were making a frenzied list. Only the other day I came across the list. Audrey Morgan was on it, and Larry Hamilton, and I found myself back in the car with Audrey the morning last fall when she told me about the revolver. Getting out her black-bordered handkerchief and saying hysterically, "She hated him. She wanted him dead."

I was near committing murder myself that day.

The table came back then—not as twins—and we seated the dinner. It was to be in the court itself, the long table foursquare around the lily pool in the center, with a moonlight spot on the water.

"It will be pretty, I think. I do hope they like it," she said, almost wistfully.

Personally I thought it might be a bit theatrical, but I did not say so. We worked hard, seating the thing. At five o'clock, tea came in and we took time out for it. She talked a little about herself, about her son Tony, whom she obviously adored and whom I had seen on and off for years without meeting him, about her widowhood, and even about John Wainwright.

"He was wonderfully good to me," she said, and sighed.

I was liking her more and more. Evidently she had genuinely grieved for her husband, although my own recollection of him was of a tall bald man with a gray mustache, about as romantic as a toothbrush. She was so essentially simple, for all the grandeur around her. When we went back to work I felt I had known her for years.

Now and then she queried a card. I remember she did that about Lydia's.

"This Mrs. Morgan," she said. "Is she a widow?"

"More or less. Her husband ran away years ago with a girl from his office. It was a terrible scandal at the time. She divorced him, of course."

"How sad. Has she any family?"

"She has a daughter," I said. "She's not out yet, but in a sense she's been out since she was twelve. She's a lovely thing. About eighteen. Her name is Audrey."

"And you don't like her?" she asked shrewdly.

"Not particularly. I'm too fond of her mother, I suppose."

She let it drop then, and we went on with the dinner. At some time while we worked she asked me to make out a card for myself, and after that at least a part of my mind was busy wondering what to wear, and just how a social secretary behaved under such circumstances. At last, however, we had finished. She got up and stretched her fine body, and I remembered thinking that she looked like something out of a Wagnerian opera, big, full-breasted, and with that long, thick braid of golden hair, without a thread of gray in it.

"I'd like to show you the house," she said. "You'll have to know your way around, at least." And she added, "I'm afraid it's a little overwhelming. But my John got some fun out of it, so I haven't changed it."

Five minutes later, still in the house coat but with her braid primed like a coronet around her head, we began our tour of the Cloisters. Overwhelming was certainly the word. We wandered from Louis XIV to the Empire, from fabulous tapestries and paintings to what were certainly indifferent statues, from Savonnerie rugs to billiard and gun rooms, from the console of a pipe organ to a Chinese smoking room, and in one wing to an enormous ballroom with a high Byzantine ceiling, already opened and being aired for the impromptu dance. Much of it was used only on state occasions. In fact, later on I was to discover that Tony and Maud herself occupied only a half dozen or so rooms, although there were twenty-odd servants in the house.

"Tony mostly has his parties in the playhouse," she said. "The young people like it."

But I did not see the playhouse that day. I was to know it well later, to know it and hate the very sight of it. It was twilight before I left, and Maud Wainwright stood on the terrace, watched me get into my ancient car and start it with a clash of worn-out gears, and waved a smiling good night to me. She looked a lonely figure standing there, under the high white pillars, and I find that I always think of her like that; lonely against the panoply of wealth, kind and totally unarmed against the world. Perhaps that was why she made her great mistake. For make it she did, with terrible results.

Someone has said that murder is the great mistake, the one irrevocable error any individual can make. We were to have murder, of course. But behind our crimes there lay that curious helplessness of Maud Wainwright and her inability to see evil in any individual, man or woman.

A day or two before I started this record I went in to see Jim Conway. He had just been re-elected chief of police, and he grinned at me over a desk covered with flowers, including an enormous horseshoe of white carnations from one of the local organizations.

"Sorry if I look like a gangster's funeral," he said. "Is this a visit of congratulation, or is it merely that I've become a habit?"

"I need some help, Jim."

He groaned.

"Not again, Pat!" he said. "Listen, sister, I'm through. I've had plenty. I've had enough to last a lifetime. All I want now is to sit here in peace and maybe look for a stolen chicken or a missing car now and then. And don't look at me like that. I'm adamant, if you know the word."

However, he was mollified as well as highly interested when I told him what I meant to do. He lit a cigarette and sat back in his chair.

"Going to write it, are you?" he said. "Well, it ought to be some story at that. Better start it off with something that will keep them reading, like Evans's trousers. Or how about Haines dodging around mother-naked that night? It isn't often you see a cop without his clothes."

But I could not be lighthearted about it. I got some papers from him that day and made notes as to dates from his records. Then I went out to my car, the same one Maud gave me on my birthday the year before, determined to tell the story as it happened day by day; and to begin it with my first introduction to Maud Wainwright and the Cloisters. And Tony.

CHAPTER TWO

I CANNOT say that my new position was received with any great enthusiasm by the two people I saw that night. For the past six years I had lived with Miss Mattie, whose neat toes were now pointed toward making a handful of boarders comfortable. She was an aristocrat in the old sense of the word, and when I told her she looked horrified.

"I do hope you will reconsider, Patricia. I can't help thinking what your mother would say."

"My mother was rather keen on my eating three meals a day."

"My dear! As though you couldn't live here as long as you cared to. I really do think, Patricia, to be a sort of upper servant in that house—"

"You don't know Mrs. Wainwright," I said gaily, and kissing her lightly went upstairs to my room.

My other talk, with Lydia Morgan, was on the same order. I found her on the small brick terrace at the back of her house. Evidently Audrey was out as usual, for the table set for one was still there, and she was holding her after-dinner coffee cup and gazing at the river at the foot of her garden. She looked up and smiled.

"Hello, Pat," she said. "Come and have some coffee. The river's lovely tonight."

"So are you, darling. Yes, I'll have coffee. I don't care if I stay awake all night."

"What's happened? You look excited."

"So I am," I said lightly.

But when I told her she looked thoughtful.

"I hope it's all right," she said. "I'd rather see you in business, of course."

"I seem to have heard the word. What do you mean, business?"

She laughed a little.

"All right. You win. That place would give me the jitters, but you're younger. I suppose you can laugh it off. What is she paying you?"

"I never asked her," I said, suddenly remembering, and we both giggled like a pair of schoolgirls.

How old was Lydia then? Perhaps thirty-eight to my twenty-five, for I remember when she and Don Morgan moved there, into that house on the river next to our own. I was a youngster at the time, and I fell madly in love with her. She was gay and lovely, and I was furious with jealousy when, a year or so later, Audrey was born.

She was still lovely. She had inherited a modest income, and on it she managed to run her house, dress Audrey beautifully, and always look better herself than any other woman I know. She was slim, with a little gray in her sleek black hair, and with the most exquisite hands I ever saw. Useful hands too. She was never an idle woman.

We talked a little that night, of the Cloisters, of Audrey's dress for the dance, and of what the social secretary should wear on such an occasion, Lydia being in favor of forgetting the job and looking my best. She had seen a full-skirted blue taffeta in town which she thought would suit me. But for long intervals we were silent, Lydia busy with her own thoughts, and I remembering, as I always did there, the days when my mother and father were living, and when I used to see Don—Don Juan to the village—riding out on Sunday mornings on his big horse. Smiling down at me and saying, "Hello, Pat. How's the jumping?"

"I fell off yesterday."

"That's part of the game, sweetheart. Don't let it get you."

I had been eleven when he disappeared. One day he was there, handsome and debonair. The next he was gone, and I was not to talk about him.

"Why not, mother? Is he sick?"

"I can't discuss it, Patricia."

"Will Lydia go too?"

"I hope not."

That had satisfied me. And Lydia had not gone. She had stayed in her house next door, a little less gay but still lovely, with only the touch of gray in her black hair to denote any change in her. As I grew up I realized what had happened, but it had been Lydia, not Don, who had been a part of my daily life. It was Lydia who had cabled to my school in Switzerland when my father died, and met me in New York on my hysterical return.

"It's all right, Pat darling. He didn't know what he was doing. The doctors say—"

But I knew, even then. He had given up his horses the year before and dismissed Weaver, the old butler-houseman who had been with us as long as I could remember. He had managed somehow to send me abroad, but the winter before that must have been one of quiet desperation on his part. I used to meet him with the car in the evenings, and he would alight from the train gray of face and weary.

"Had a bad day, dad?"

"Not too good."

One evening he told me that he had enough insurance to care for us in case anything happened to him. I did not take it very seriously. He had always been there, a small cheerful man, dapper and neat, the background of my life. And six months later they found him dead in a hotel bedroom in New York. He had registered under another name, and it was two or three days before he was identified.

I was remembering this as we sat there that night, a new moon hanging over the hills across the river, Lydia quiet with her hands folded in her lap, and only next door my carefree childhood, and the bench at the foot of the garden where my mother had sat, evening after evening, alone and quiet after Father's death.

She did not survive him long. She managed, after a year or so, to give me a debut of sorts: an afternoon tea, she in black and I in white organdy holding a bunch of roses. Lydia had made the dress, and I still have it. But Mother never really rallied. She went on for a few months after that, looking lost and helpless. Things were pretty bad, however. One day the house went up for sale, and on our last day there she made a sort of pilgrimage from room to room. Then she went out into the garden. Much of it she had worked over with her own hands, and I watched her anxiously from a window.

She seemed all right. She went to the bank of the river and stood there. Then she sat down on the bench where she and Father had so often sat on summer evenings. She was there for a long time, and at last I went back to my packing. When I looked out again Lydia was standing beside her.

I shall never forget Lydia that day. She went quietly to the house and back to the kitchen, where the maids were preparing to leave. Then she came in to me.

"Have you a minute to run over and see Audrey?" she said. "She's not been well, and I've put her to bed."

"I'd better wait for Mother."

"I'll bring her in," she said. "This has been a hard time for her, but she has had a happy life. Always remember that, Pat."

When I came back from next door Lydia had indeed brought her in. She put her arms around me and told me.

"No pain, no anything, Pat," she said. "Such a wonderful way to go. And I think she wanted to be with your father."

I never went back to the house. Lydia took me home with her, and I stayed there during those first desperate weeks. I think she would have kept me indefinitely, but her house was small, and I began to feel that Audrey resented me. She was spoiled and jealous even then, although she was the most lovely child I ever saw. In the end I took a room at Miss Mattie's and faced a world which had no particular use for a girl of nineteen who could play good tennis, indifferent golf, speak fair French, and ride a horse when she had a horse to ride.

It was Lydia who suggested the business course, Lydia who dictated to me at night while I struggled with shorthand and a typewriter. She never let me lose courage.

"Things look pretty dark just now, Pat. I know it. But they have a way of straightening out. I know that. It takes time and courage, and after all, you're young. You'll marry someday."

That was the nearest she ever came to mentioning her own trouble, but sometimes I had seen her watching Audrey as though she was afraid she had inherited some of Don Morgan's instability as well as his charm. He had plenty of that. It was a legend in Beverly that when old Mrs. Anderson's vicious parrot got loose and flew up into a tree, Don Morgan had simply talked to it from below and it came down. Moreover, that it had climbed up his trousers leg and sat on his shoulder, making soft cooing sounds.

But Don had been gone for years by that time, and if I knew Audrey, her lovely little head would always dominate the sturdy pump she called her heart.

In the end I found a position in the city, but a slackening of business promptly killed it. For a while I had a small income from Father's real estate. Then some of it was sold for taxes, and the remainder barely carried itself. As his insurance had gone to pay his debts, I was practically penniless.

I don't like to recall those years, the pinching over lunches in town, the constant problem of clothes, the moving from one office to another. Somehow during that period I managed to pay Miss Mattie and to keep myself clothed after a fashion. And, of course, early in that interval I fell in love.

I can laugh at that now. Bill Sterling was a local boy and our best doctor. He was fourteen years older than I was at nineteen, a big, broad-shouldered man, certainly not handsome; but I took the thing sickeningly hard. I invented excuses to call at his office, and walked past his house at night on the chance of seeing him getting in or out of his car.

The only excuse for recalling that is that Bill plays his own part in this story. As for the love affair, Bill solved the question one day in his own characteristic fashion. He had stuck a thermometer in my mouth, eyed it gravely when he removed it, and then leaned back in his office chair and smiled at me.

"Let's have this out, Pat," he said. "I can't go on sending you bills for nothing. You're as healthy a specimen as I ever saw."

I suppose I changed color, for he leaned over and patted my hand. "It's all right," he said. "We're great friends, aren't we? I like you and you like me. But the next time I put a thermometer in your mouth it had better show something, and holding it against a hot-water bottle is barred!"

It was a year before I could look at him without blushing, but it was good medicine. For a long time now he had been devoted to Lydia. I think they would have married, but Audrey did not like him. It was to have frightful repercussions, that dislike of Audrey's for Bill Sterling.

He came in that night before I left Lydia's. He kissed Lydia matter-of-factly and gave me a bang on the shoulder.

"Well, how did you like Maud?"

"I liked her, Bill. Thanks for telling her about me."

"I told her you were a model of ability, tact, and diplomacy," he said modestly. "Also that you would let her Tony alone, being a spinster at heart. She couldn't wait to get you. How's the party coming along?"

I left soon afterward, but I did not go back at once to Miss Mattie's. I drove slowly up and down the streets, looking at the houses, and wondering about the mental picture some of the occupants had of Maud Wainwright. It was so unlike the truth. But also my mind was on the dinner and dance to come, and I was mentally checking my lists.

I remember that there was a dance at the Beverly Club that night, and as I passed it I saw Audrey Morgan come out on the porch and stand there, looking like a peri at the gate of heaven.

She was not alone for long, of course. It is the fate of the Audreys of this world always to have some male hovering about.

This time it was Larry Hamilton, and I hastily ran over the list again in my mind. Yes, Larry was on it, so I went back to my room and slept wretchedly, my brain seething with a hundred gilt chairs with brocaded seats to come from town, a blue taffeta dress with a full sweeping skirt and not too low in the neck, a manicure and shampoo when and if possible, place cards, flowers, candles, and a stag line for the dance.

My life for the next three days consisted of just those things. Tony Wainwright was away, and did not show up until the afternoon of the dinner itself. By that time I was quietly frantic. When my fountain pen rolled under a leather sofa in what was now my office I crawled after it. Then I simply lay there, exhausted and using language which, as old Weaver used to say, was unfitting for a little lady.

I heard a cool voice behind and above me.

"Such nice legs," it said reprovingly, "and such bad words. Dear, dear!"

I pulled myself out and sat up in a rage.

"Don't worry about my legs," I said furiously. "If you're interested, they ache like the devil."

"I wasn't worrying. Miss Abbott, I believe?"

That was my first real view of Tony Wainwright, a tall, debonair young man with cool gray eyes and an amused smile.

"See here," he said, "you've worked yourself into a fit. Why not come out and get some air? I've sent Maud up to bed. For a woman who has given parties most of her life, she's a wreck. What's the matter?"

I didn't bother to tell him. I simply said I had thought of going somewhere, preferably to Burton, which is our local institution for mental illness. However, I would go outside, although if he mentioned dinner party to me I would probably burst into violent shrieks. After that I washed my face and hands in the lavatory off the office, while he watched the process with interest.

"Had an idea no girl used soap on her face any more," he observed. "Must be the influence of the ads. Rather a nice skin, haven't you?"

"It's one of my great charms," I said, and followed him outside.

That was the first time I had been inside the playhouse, which like everything about the Cloisters turned out to be much larger than I had thought. Built over the side of a small ravine, the roof of the indoor tennis court was not much higher than the rest. But it was much more than a pool and court. There was a long living room, with a balcony over the court so observers could watch the players below, a game room with a bar, a small kitchen, and even two or three bedrooms with baths.

"For rowdy bachelors," Tony said, watching me. "Ideal place for hangovers, isn't it? Bed, breakfast, and a swim. Headache tablets in every room. My contribution."

"It's not what I would call a playhouse."

"Well, what is play, my dear Miss Patricia?"

"I wouldn't know," I told him, and started back to the house.

Most of the return was in silence. I thought him patronizing and deliberately annoying, and he saw that I was irritated.

"Not very keen about me, are you?" he said, smiling down at me. "After I rescue you from under sofas and probably other furniture and take you for a walk. Is that gratitude?"

"You might have brought the dog along too," I said sweetly. "Then you'd have given us both a bit of experience."

CHAPTER THREE

THE DINNER that night was a howling success. Certainly it did what it was meant to do. It healed the breach between the Hill and the village.

I took my first full breath when everyone was seated, with no leftovers; that nightmare of all large parties. I believe, too, that the food was wonderful. Pierre, the chef, had hardly been approachable for two days. Maud—she had asked me to call her that—was radiant. She wore a full ice-blue dress, and with that gold crown of hair dressed high on her head she looked almost young and certainly happy.

I suppose all dinners are alike. Perhaps it was because of my six years of exile from the elegance of living that I found that one so impressive.

What is chiefly important about the party is that, with one or two exceptions, it brought together so many of the people who were to be involved in our tragedy: Bill Sterling and Lydia; Julian Stoddard, who was master of the Hunt Club, and his wife Margery; Dwight Elliott, Maud's attorney; Jim Conway, our most popular Beverly bachelor, who had run for chief of police on a bet and won the election; and even Audrey and Larry Hamilton.

Audrey was exquisite that night, and knew it. She wore a white lace dress over crinoline, and she might have stepped out of *Godey's Lady's Book*. Tony danced with her whenever he could, and I saw Maud watching them. But I was too busy to notice much of anything. There were bridge foursomes to be arranged in the Chinese room and the library, the stag line to be kept in the ballroom and away from too much champagne, and at one time Roger—the mastiff—showed a determination to go outside which could not be denied, and I had to let him out myself.

Only Audrey annoyed me. She was dancing with Tony when she saw me, and she came over and gave me a condescending hand.

"How are you, Pat?" she said coolly. "It's a nice party, isn't it? But I do wish you'd see that they ice the champagne. It's nasty when it's warm."

It was deliberate, of course. Little Audrey putting me in my place. I knew the champagne was not warm.

"Aren't you a trifle young for champagne, Audrey?" I inquired gently. "There's punch in the hall. It's quite mild."

I dare say Tony saw it was time to interfere, for he came forward holding out his hand and grinning.

"Miss Abbott, isn't it?" he said. "I'm Mrs. Wainwright's little boy. Haven't we met before?"

"Possibly. I'm afraid I don't remember. There are so many young men about," I said, and gave him a vague but pleasant smile.

Some time later I found Maud at my elbow. The dancing

crowd had gone down to the playhouse, where a ball supper was being served, and the music had followed them. The sudden quiet was almost startling.

"It really is a success, isn't it, Pat?" she said. "That Morgan child is a lovely creature. If I were a man I'd fall for her myself. Tony seems to like her." She sighed and looked thoughtful. "Do you mind going down to the playhouse? I don't want anybody to decide to take a swim in his dress clothes."

As it turned out, I was just in time. I found one youth from the city who had suddenly considered it a good idea, and was poised on the springboard over the pool, tailcoat and all, when I got there. But I had a puzzling experience myself on the way.

The route to the playhouse is a sort of dogleg. The building lies behind the main house and two hundred yards away in a direct line. To get there one goes straight along a sort of green alley of lawn between trees to a fountain at the end, and then turns to the right around a planting of shrubbery. The playhouse is only a few yards away.

The fountain of white marble was floodlighted that night from the trees above it, and the playhouse was ablaze with lights and shrill with laughter and music. Outside of it a man was standing, peering in.

He was not in evening clothes and at first I thought he was a reporter, or perhaps a cameraman trying to get a picture. As we had guards at the gate to keep out all interlopers, I was surprised, to say the least.

He seemed to be watching something inside; watching intently, his hands on a window sill, his body tense. As I was on the grass he did not hear me until I was fairly close. Then he did a surprising thing. He turned and ran, and for some time I could hear him crashing through the underbrush in the direction of the country club golf course, which adjoins the Cloisters property. I was astonished, but not worried; and as I have said, I had my hands full after that, what with the diving youth and one of the waiters from the city who had crawled into a guest-room bed and was peacefully sleeping, an empty bottle beside him. So I did not tell Maud about our visitor, either then or later. Perhaps I should have. Still, what good would it have done? She would have known no more than I did.

It was the next day that she asked me to give up my room at Miss Mattie's and stay at the Cloisters. She looked as fresh as though she had slept an entire night, although she had gone to bed at six in the morning after an al fresco breakfast to everybody of scrambled eggs and sausages.

"I'd like it," she said. "Tony's in town all day and out a good many evenings, and unless I give a party or go to one I'm alone too much. I used to turn on the organ, but an organ's a melancholy substitute for the human voice."

In the end I agreed, and that day she took me over the estate. For the first time I realized its extent. It was not only the house, with its fifty-odd rooms and its twenty or more servants. There were over a hundred acres of land, with forty men to look after them. There were conservatories and an orchid house, and even a stable where Tony kept his hunters and a saddle horse or two. I met Andy McDonald, the old Scot who was in charge of the grounds, and Gus, the head chauffeur. There seemed to be men everywhere, although Maud said she had cut down both outdoor and indoor staffs. We went back by the west wing, and inside the house she showed me where the key to the playhouse was kept, in the drawer of a table in the hall near the door.

"You can swim there whenever you like, of course," she said, "but lock it when you leave. We used to keep it open until Evans, the watchman, came on duty at night. But we found the caddies from the golf course were slipping in."

Weeks later that key was to become of vital importance, and the playhouse itself a thing of horror. I was to answer innumerable questions about both:

"The key was always in this drawer?"

"Unless the playhouse was in use, yes."

"Then anybody had access to the playhouse?"

"Anybody in the house."

"That would be—?"

"The servants when they cleaned it, and the family, naturally. I sometimes swam there myself. And twice a week one of the outside men drained and cleaned the pool. That's all, except for invited guests."

The house had been restored to order that day when we came back; the caterer's van had taken away the gold and rose damask chairs, the tables were gone from the court, and the ballroom was being closed. Tony appeared for lunch, looking rather the worse for wear, but cheerful.

"Quite a night," he said, kissing his mother. "In fact, quite a night. It's amazing, but I seem to have more brains than I have room for. What do you make of that, Miss Abbott?"

"It must be unusual."

He turned to Maud.

"She doesn't like me," he complained. "And I like to be liked. Do you have to have her around?"

Maud only smiled.

"She's coming to stay with us," she said placidly. "And for

heaven's sake call her Pat and ask her to call you Tony. She is a nice girl and you'll like her."

"That's my trouble," he said. "I like her already, but she snubbed me last night, Maud. I had to go into the powder room and cry it out."

Evidently she was used to his nonsense. She paid no attention to it, save to warn me against it.

"Don't bother about him," she said. "All week he is a hard-working businessman. I don't know what the mills would do without him. Or I," she added.

That was the first thing I noticed, the perfect understanding between mother and son. His use of her first name was purely affectionate; and later on, when she was in trouble, she became "mother" again. And I know now that his nonsense was largely an act, put on partly to put me at ease.

"All right," he said to me as we sat down to lunch. "You're Pat and I'm Tony. You'll probably call me other things at intervals, but Tony is the name. Age thirty, weight one hundred and eighty, bad golf, good tennis, fair to middling on a horse, amiable disposition, and no strawberry marks."

It was a long time since I had heard that sort of carefree banter. The day before, tired and tense, it had annoyed me. Now I accepted it for what it was.

"I am Patricia Abbott," I told him. "Weight one hundred and fifteen, age twenty-five, fair French, poor golf, good tennis, and excellent on a horse."

"No strawberry marks?" he asked anxiously.

"No strawberry marks."

Maud gave me the choice of eight guest suites that afternoon, each with its bath and sitting room. I chose the simplest, with a feeling of being in a dream world where such things as imported soaps, new toothbrushes in cellophane wrappers, towels like satin, and soft luxurious beds were taken for granted.

I told Lydia about it that night when, after packing my trunk, I stopped there on the way back up the Hill. She looked rather uneasy.

"Don't let them spoil you, Pat," she said. "Too much money can be pretty devastating. What about Tony?"

"He's all right," I said evasively.

"Audrey has raved about him all day," she said, and sighed.

CHAPTER FOUR

THAT, AS I have said, was in June of last year. I settled down to a life which began when Nora, one of a half dozen housemaids, brought me my breakfast tray at eight, and might end at night with double solitaire with Maud or a dinner party for thirty.

Little by little I fell into the routine of the establishment. I ceased to jump when at midnight Evans made his first round of the house, his heavy, solid footsteps passing my door, or when I saw his flashlight in the grounds. I think more than anything else those rounds of Evans's impressed on me the responsibility of wealth and possessions. At nine I went to my office and opened the mail, sending up by a footman Maud's personal letters. At ten I went to her boudoir, or sometimes to the adjoining roof garden, and we made plans for the day. She was systematic. She would already have seen Mrs. Partridge, the housekeeper, and she used that time with me for Hilda to brush her hair.

By eleven we were through. She would finish dressing and go out. Sometimes she merely made a circuit of the grounds, going over the gardens with old Andy at her elbow. Sometimes she wandered over to the Stoddard place, which was only a half mile away by a footpath. It was called the Farm, and if she had an intimate friend, it was Margery Stoddard.

It was a curious relationship. Margery was perhaps thirty-five, a rather quiet woman, with two small daughters. She was an attractive woman, with a head of prematurely white hair which was very becoming, and she obviously idolized her husband. But oddly enough she did not ride.

"I'm afraid of horses," she told me once, with her quick, shy smile. "It seems queer, doesn't it, with Julian so interested in the Hunt Club. He's very nice about it, but after watching me fall off for a month or two after we were married he gave it up."

Maud's attitude to her was always that of an elderly sister. I think, too, she realized that Margery was lonely at times, for she took very little part in the life of the Hill. But months later I was to think of them at that time: Maud big, cheerful and self-confident, with her hearty laugh; Margery small, shy and uncertain, and both ignorant of the story which was eventually to tie them so closely together.

I was kept busy during those early weeks. Not only with dinners. There were the people who wandered in late in the afternoons to drink highballs or cocktails on the terrace or—in bad weather—to play indoor tennis in the playhouse. The summer was always the season, both to the Hill and in Beverly. People went away in winter, to Florida, to California, or to Europe. In summer they stayed at home, absorbed in business, in gardens, in golf or tennis.

And last summer was particularly gay. It seemed to me that we entertained constantly. I remember a garden party late in June, with a marquee on the lawn and Audrey dancing with Tony and looking up at him from under a broad hat which set off her beauty like a frame. There was a series of Sunday breakfasts for the riding crowd also, and in July Maud, who liked children, invited all the youngsters from the Hill and village families, and turned over the playhouse to them. She had a Punch and Judy show as well as a conjurer for them, but it was not an unqualified success. The little darlings took to throwing the peas which accompanied their creamed chicken, and at the last minute I had to leap into the pool in my best summer dress and rescue a five-year-old who had tumbled in.

I saw little of Tony during those first two months or so. The mills were working overtime. When I did see him he was either surrounded by people or on the way somewhere. He was always friendly, however. He would greet me with a grin.

"Still crawling under furniture and using bad language?"

"No. I go upstairs and bite the pillows on my bed. It's easier."

He would laugh and go on.

I heard that he was seeing Audrey a good deal, but weeks passed without my seeing even Lydia. Now and then I hurried up to town for clothes—Maud had at last mentioned salary, and it was a good one—but there was very little time.

We were seldom alone, for one thing. It was not unusual for Nora, bringing in my breakfast, to ask me if I could tell Mrs. Partridge, the housekeeper, who had spent the night there. Not only Tony's friends. One of our most frequent visitors was Dwight Elliott, Maud's attorney. He lived alone in town, and on hot evenings he often drove down to cool off, as he put it.

Sometimes I thought he was in love with her. He was a tall man in his fifties, not handsome but with considerable distinction of dress and manner. He was, it turned out, remotely related to her. Indeed, it was from him that I learned that Tony was not John Wainwright's son.

"She ran away and married a worthless fellow when she was

under twenty," he said. "When he died things were pretty bad
for her. She came back here where she was born, with Tony who
was a youngster then; but I couldn't help her. I'd just been admitted to the bar. It was all I could do to pay my office rent."

It had been through him, however, that she met John Wainwright. He was somewhat complacent about it.

"J.C. took to her like a duck to water," he said. "And I will say
she made him happy. She's a wonderful woman, Miss Abbott.
They don't make them like that any more."

I rather liked him. He was only a few years older than Maud,
and sometimes I wondered if she would eventually marry him.
Certainly she depended on him. In any emergency her immediate reaction was to send for him. But he said something that
night which surprised me. There had been a small dinner, and I
was not needed. I was alone on the terrace, with Roger, the dog,
at my feet. He came out, stating that he was dummy, and having
lit a cigarette sat down beside me.

"There's something you can do, Miss Abbott," he said. "I don't
like to speak about it, but I shall have to. Maud Wainwright is
spending too much money."

"This place costs a lot to keep up, Mr. Elliott."

"Well, old J.C.'s fortune was big, but not limitless. I happen
to know that she gave Bessie a large sum, and—"

"Bessie?" I inquired.

But he was called back to the game just then, and I did not
learn who Bessie was. I took for granted that she was a relative,
one of the impecunious Wainwrights perhaps who hung on the
fringes of society in town, and let it go at that. But I asked Maud
the next day if we were not spending a lot, to see her more nearly
impatient than ever before.

"Of course, I spend a lot," she said. "I can't turn the servants off, or the gardeners."

"Nevertheless, we are spending a great deal of money," I said stubbornly. "The butcher's bill last month—"

"Don't tell me," she interrupted. "I suppose I could stop entertaining. I'm tired, and I don't give a hoot about it anyhow. I like to see people happy, that's all. But I've always given a lot to charity. Maybe I'm buying my way into heaven! What am I to do about that?"

"This place is pretty close to heaven."

She shook her head.

"I never wanted this place," she said. "It was John's idea. Nothing was too good for me. But I've got it and what can I do? Sometime you ought to write about the poor rich, left with their servants and houses and charities while the government takes most of their money."

She always had a naïve idea that because I used a typewriter I could write.

"You could let me go," I suggested. "After all, the summer is about over. You'll be going to Palm Beach after Christmas."

But she refused that with a gesture. "That's the last thing I'll do," she said, and getting up came over and put her arm around me. "I've been really happy since you came," she said. "Stick by me, Pat. I need you."

That was on a Monday in August. She went into the city the next day, in her shining limousine, went gaily and cheerfully, as though she had no worries or had forgotten them. She was taking Margery Stoddard with her, leaving her in town to come out with Julian, and Margery had walked over by the path. She had brought her two little girls with her, and their English nurse.

"Julian's having our pool repaired," she said. "May they swim in the playhouse?"

I got the key and they started off. Margery sat down on the terrace and fanned herself, but I thought she looked worried. She glanced around before she spoke.

"Look here, Pat," she said. "Has Evans seen anyone lurking around the place at night?"

"He hasn't said so."

She lowered her voice.

"There was a man at the Farm last night. I couldn't sleep for the heat, and I went outside. He disappeared when he saw me. It wasn't any of our own people. I've asked. It's my children I'm thinking about, Pat. If anything happened to them—"

Then Maud appeared, and I remember waving them off and going back to my office, totally unaware that the first happy phase of my life at the Cloisters was over.

Tony came home early that day. I was busy at my desk when he came in, and for once he seemed to have nothing to do. He sat down on the edge of the desk and picked up a letter for Maud which had just arrived. He scowled at its blue envelope.

"When did this come?" he asked.

"Afternoon mail."

"Has Mother seen it?"

"No. Not yet."

"Then she isn't going to," he said, and put it in his pocket.

I protested, but he was firm.

"See here, my darling," he said, "don't interfere in things that don't concern you. This is a private matter. And another thing, sweetheart. If you tell Maud about it I'll bite off one of your pretty ears. That's final. I mean it."

He went out then, and soon after I heard him leaving in his

car. He always drove fast, but that day I felt that something serious had sent him off as if he had been fired out of a gun.

He was still out when Maud returned. I was in the lower hall sorting over music rolls for the organ when I heard her car drive up. Thomas, one of the two footmen, was at the door, and when I looked up, Gus, her own chauffeur, was helping her out. I caught a glimpse of her face, and for a minute I thought she was dying. She was entirely white, and Gus was holding her by the arm as though she was unable to walk. I rushed out and took her other arm.

"Are you sick?" I asked.

She did not answer, but she shook her head faintly.

"Get me inside," she said feebly. "And call Hilda."

We got her into the hall and then Tony came in from the garage and saw her. He looked dazed.

"What's happened?" he said. "What's wrong, darling?"

He got down on his knees beside her and rubbed those big shapely hands of hers. For some reason men always seem to think that will help. But there was sheer devotion in his upturned face as well as fright, and I liked him better than I had before. Gus had followed us in and Tony turned on him.

"Hit somebody with the car?" he asked sharply.

"No, sir. She was all right up to an hour or so ago. We'd left town and I happened to look back in the mirror. She was kind of slumped in the seat, so I stopped the car and asked if she wanted a doctor. She said no, to bring her home."

All through this Maud sat still; our cheerful laughter-loving Maud, sitting there as though she were alone, not listening, not hearing. Hilda brought some aromatic ammonia and she swallowed it obediently. I took her pulse, to find it weak and thin, but steady. The hall seemed to be full of people by that time:

Reynolds and the footmen, Thomas and Stevens; Hilda, Mrs. Partridge, wringing her hands, and Tony and myself.

I took hold of the situation as best I could, sending Hilda to turn her bed down, Reynolds to the elevator, and Tony to call Bill Sterling. But Maud rallied then. She tried to sit up and straighten her hat.

"I don't want a doctor," she said. "It was the heat. I'm all right."

And then the thing became pure farce, for we got her into the elevator only to have it stick halfway between floors. Luckily there was a seat in it, and I held her there while Tony yelled orders and vituperation at everybody within hearing distance. It was a full hour before the local electrician arrived, an hour when Bill Sterling tried to shout his directions from below and Tony alternately pressed buttons and watched his mother.

When at last we were lowered to the hall again, Maud had recovered somewhat. For the first time she seemed to be aware of us standing around her.

"Good heavens, what a fuss!" she said. "Don't look so worried, Tony." She took off her hat and ran her hand over her hair. "I must be a sight. I think I'll go to bed. Where's Hilda?"

She refused the elevator this time and went slowly up the stairs, Bill on one side, Tony on the other. Halfway up she tried to shake them off. "I can manage all right," she said impatiently. "What I want is a cold compress on my head and to be let alone."

She got them both. She could be stubborn enough when she wanted to, and it was less than fifteen minutes before Bill Sterling, looking ruffled, came down the stairs. Tony was with him, and the three of us stood there, not knowing what to do next. It was Bill who suggested that we call Gus.

He came in, immaculate as always in his pale-fawn uniform with its breeches and shining puttees. There were a half dozen men in the garage, but Gus was Maud's own chauffeur. He had driven her for years, and now he was visibly shaken.

His story, in detail, was puzzling. According to him, Maud and Margery had done some shopping together. They had seemed cheerful, even gay. At five o'clock he had left Margery at Julian's office, and at Maud's order had started for home.

He had driven perhaps a half dozen blocks when she suddenly called to him. The window behind him was open, so she had not used the telephone. He thought now that her voice had been strange.

"What do you mean, strange?" Tony asked.

"Not like her. Kind of strangled."

"Good God, why didn't you look at her? What did she say?"

"She told me to drive to Mr. Elliott's office," said Gus doggedly. "I did so. She was not sick then, but she looked sort of pale."

The rest of the story was not helpful. At the building she got out, but seeing the five o'clock crowd coming out she had glanced at her watch, stood uncertainly on the pavement for a minute or so and then got back in the car and told Gus to take her home.

That was all, until halfway back he had looked in the car mirror and saw her collapsed on the back seat. He had stopped the car and asked if she was sick, but she had waved him to go on.

"You don't know why she decided not to see Mr. Elliott?" Tony asked.

"No, sir. Except that it was getting late. She may have thought he would be gone."

So there we were. We accepted the heat hypothesis because

there was nothing else to do, but I don't believe either Bill or Tony believed it. Something had happened to Maud that day in town, something she did not intend to talk about. It was the beginning of our mystery.

Bill Sterling sent up a nurse that night and another the next morning, it being the unhappy fate of the very rich seldom to be left alone and in peace. There was a procession of icebags, thin soups, and starched uniforms through the house. And for three days Maud lay in that Empire bed of hers, with the peach taffeta curtains hanging from a gilt crown above it; lay very still, accepting what was done for her without comment, sleeping now and then under the barbiturates Bill ordered, slowly improving, and quietly and alone fighting the battle of her life.

CHAPTER FIVE

It was a trying time. Tony, usually rather casual with his mother, was more concerned than I had ever seen him. He hardly left the house for two or three days. Morning and evening he went in and sat beside her for a short time. She would put out her hand and he would hold it, and as if the contact soothed her she often dozed off. She spoke very little, however.

He was bewildered and unhappy. I don't believe he even called Audrey Morgan, which must have annoyed her. Indeed, I think he grew up during that time. There was no attempt at his usual cheerful nonsense. During the few meals we ate together he was silent, almost morose; but as to his mother he fell back on the usual masculine explanation.

"She's done too much all summer," he said one day. "All those crazy parties. Who wanted them anyhow? You?"

I refused to take offense. "They made a lot of work for me," I told him. "No, she wanted them herself. She liked to have people around her. And I don't think they hurt her. After all, I was here to take most of the load."

He looked at me as if he had not seen me for some time, which I think was literally true.

"You look as though you've been having a pretty thin time yourself," he said. "Why don't you take a day or two off and rest? Or get out and play some golf?"

I am afraid my eyes filled, out of sheer self-pity and nerves that day. After all, I have rather understated my case. All summer I had been working at top speed. Not only that. I had been at the beck and call of Maud's friends on the Hill as well as my own in the valley. I had filled in at any number of dinners when a woman dropped out at the last minute; rushing to my room, dressing frantically, and trying to be agreeable for hours on end afterward. Also for the same reason I had lost a good bit of money at bridge, playing for stakes I could not afford.

"You don't mind playing, do you, Miss Abbott? That wretched Jamison woman insists on going home early."

Anyhow, I cried that day, and Tony patted me awkwardly on the back as though I had swallowed something the wrong way. "Now see here," he said, "don't *you* crash on me. It's bad enough with Mother going smash. Somebody has to carry the flag."

It was that same day, I think, that the telephone message came for Maud. The telephone had been ringing steadily, of course, but this was different. It was a man's voice, muffled and rather rough. "I want to speak to Mrs. Wainwright," it said.

"I'm sorry. Mrs. Wainwright is ill."

There was a pause, and I began to think the connection had broken. Then: "Well, tell her—no, don't tell her anything. I'll be seeing her." He hung up then, and I left the phone, feeling rather ruffled.

It was on the fourth day of Maud's illness that she came out of that partial stupor of hers, compounded of drugs and the original shock, whatever had caused it. She fired both nurses, overpaying them extravagantly, had Hilda pin up her hair, and saw me for the first time. I was startled at the change in her.

For one thing she was thinner. The skin on her face and neck seemed loose, and her big, hearty voice had gone. But the real change was in her expression. She looked almost grim against her background of lace pillows.

"Come in, Pat," she said. "I want to talk to you. Close the door and tell Hilda to keep out. Where's Tony?"

"He's got Roger somewhere outside."

She closed her eyes, as if even the effort of talking tired her. I sat down and waited, and at last she put out her hand and I took it. "You're a good girl, Pat," she said. "I've had a lovely summer. I've been happy."

"You're going to have plenty more happy summers."

"I'm not so sure. Not so sure," she repeated. "Everything has to end sometime. Look here, Pat, I want to see Dwight Elliott as soon as I can, and I don't want Tony to know. Can you manage it?"

"When do you want to see him?"

"Tomorrow if possible," she said, almost feverishly. "It's Saturday. I don't suppose Tony will go to town."

I thought for a minute. "He told me I ought to get out. He even recommended some golf. Perhaps he'll condescend to take me on. I'm just bad enough to keep him cheerful."

She nodded. "Fine," she said. "Of course, the servants will have to know—unless we can fix it. Dwight might leave his car in the road and walk to the house. He could use the west door, if you left it open, and I can take care of Hilda up here."

It was too pat. I knew she had already planned it just that way. Probably she saw my face, for she smiled faintly.

"You're a smart girl, Pat," she said. "It's taken me two days to think it out, and you know it, don't you? It's not really serious, but I don't want Tony to know. It would worry him. I want Dwight Elliott to draw a will for me. I ought to have done it long ago."

I heard Tony whistling to Roger from somewhere close to the house, so I promised to call Mr. Elliott as soon as I had a chance and got out quickly. At the door, however, she called me back.

"Get me my jewel case, will you, Pat? My legs are still wobbly."

I got the case from her dressing table and she opened it and took out a small key. It was the large leather case in which she kept the things she used every day. The rest—her emeralds, her long diamond chain, her two pearl ropes, and dozens of other things—were in a wall safe set in the panel of her bedroom and only discoverable if one knew where to find it. No, this is no story of robbery. The jewels were still there when everything was cleared up. But the police always harked back to them.

"How many people knew about that key, Miss Abbott?"

"I haven't any idea. I suppose her maid knew. I did myself. But it was only the key to the panel in the wall. The safe itself had a combination lock."

That, as I have said, was Friday. I managed to get Mr. Elliott on the library telephone and he agreed to come out the next afternoon. He had been calling every day about Maud, but he seemed surprised when I told him why she wanted him.

"A will?" he said. "Does she want to change the old one?"

It was my turn to be astonished. "I don't know," I told him. "She doesn't want Tony to know she's doing it."

"She's not cutting him out, is she?" he inquired dryly.

But when I told him of the elaborate preparations to keep his visit a secret he was silent for a full minute. "I don't understand it," he said at last. "I'll do it, of course, but why all that nonsense? It isn't like her."

I told him she was not allowed visitors, at which he snorted. He agreed finally, however, and I rang off just as Tony sauntered into the room.

Perhaps I should explain here the elaborate telephone arrangement at the Cloisters. There were, of course, house phones everywhere. It was an old-fashioned system, with labeled buttons: *Mrs. Wainwright, Mr. Wainwright, Housekeeper, Blue Guest Suite, Rose Guest Suite, Pantry,* and so on. Also in practically every room of the house there was an outside telephone. These were on the same line, so that one could lift off the receiver almost anywhere and hear Mrs. Partridge ordering the day's supplies, her high thin voice, always plaintive: "That last roast was short weight, Mr. Keeler. I put it on the scale myself. I do think—"

Only the library had its own outside connection. All our private talks took place over it, a fact which was to be important later on.

Tony was more cheerful that day. He came in whistling, accused me of having a lover to whom I had been talking, and proceeded to ring for a highball. Then he eyed me quizzically. "You look as though you'd been doing something you shouldn't."

I tried to look wistful and, if possible, frail. "I suppose I really need exercise. Air and exercise. I thought I might play some golf tomorrow afternoon. I'm not up to tennis."

"Sure. Fine. Go to it."

"I'll see if I can find somebody. If not I'll go around alone."

Perhaps I rather overdid the pathos, for he laughed a little. "That's a sad picture," he said. "All right. I'll take you on. Tomorrow at two-thirty, eh? And you'd better be good."

I was thoughtful as I went back to my office. Why had Maud

thought it necessary to lie to me? She already had a will. Tony must have known it. Certainly Dwight Elliott did. And I myself had no interest in it. So why?

It was too much for me. I played my worst possible golf that next afternoon, while Tony grew more and more cheerful. When at last I topped a ball and saw it roll twenty yards and stop I was ready to bite him. But he did not laugh.

"Something on the little mind, isn't there?" he inquired. "Tell papa and you'll feel better."

"There's nothing on my mind," I said furiously. "This is the way I play golf, and you can take it or leave it alone."

I did better after that, out of sheer fury; but all in all it was a bad afternoon. The only comfort I had—and it was not much— was that Audrey Morgan, looking sulky, was on the club veranda when we went there after the game. Tony was extremely nonchalant.

"What, no tennis?" he asked her, smiling.

"It's too hot for tennis," she said coldly.

Larry Hamilton was with her, but there was not much further conversation. It was evident that she was not far from tears, and I guessed that Tony had broken an engagement with her to play with me. It ended with Tony asking her to the club dinner-dance that night, and I went home rather put back in my place.

I was relieved, however, when we arrived, to find that our ruse had apparently been successful. Reynolds reported a half dozen callers to inquire for our invalid, eight boxes of flowers, and a telegram to Maud which Tony opened and promptly confiscated, scowling as he did so. But evidently Mr. Elliott had entered and gone without the knowledge of the staff, so I went up and took a shower and dressed for dinner.

Though the heavens fell, the ritual of the huge house had to be carried on, and I think it was that night that it—the house—began to depress me. Up to that week either Maud or Tony had dined with me. Usually when alone we used a small breakfast room rather than the enormous ghostly dining room, its walls hung with tapestries and the candles making only small oases of light on the table and here and there on the walls. I ate my dinner alone, but even the breakfast room, gay with its tiled floor, its hothouse fruit and flowers, failed to cheer me. I would gladly have exchanged the elaborate service, with Reynolds directing the footmen from somewhere behind my chair, for Miss Mattie's dining room, with its glaring chandelier overhead and Miss Mattie's Sarah telling me to stir up the gravy so I could get the giblets.

And after dinner it was no better. The lights in the court were out, making it only a black hole, so that the French doors became mirrors reflecting only myself in my thin white dress. The service wing was carefully cut off. I knew there was light and noise there. The staff had its own large servants' hall, with an upright piano and a billiard table. But it seemed miles away that night.

I had a moment of hope when Tony came down the staircase whistling, on the way to Audrey and the club; but I had only a few words with him when, in white dinner clothes, he stopped in the doorway. "What's the matter with Mother?" he asked worriedly. "She looks feverish."

"I haven't seen her. Hilda said she wanted to rest."

"Damn this dance anyhow. I wish you'd have Bill Sterling look at her."

Maud, interviewed through Hilda, definitely declined Bill. I was uneasy myself. But there was nothing I could do. I laid out a game of solitaire, and resigned myself to the company of Roger.

At nine-thirty, in reply to Roger's imperious demand, I let him out for a while. At ten he came back, rubbed against me to express his gratitude, and lay down majestically at my feet. And at eleven, gathering up my flowing skirts to go up to bed, I got the first shock of the many which were to follow. Where Roger had touched me there were bloodstains along the front and hem of my dress.

My first thought was that the dog had been hurt, but when I tried to examine him he merely turned playfully on his back and thrust his big legs into the air, regarding the whole performance as a new sort of game. There was blood on him, though, and fresh blood at that. It was on his paws and his muzzle.

I was still bending over him when Reynolds came in to close up for the night. He started to back out, but I called him.

"Come here," I said. "Look at the blood on this dog."

"He may have found a chicken somewhere, miss," said Reynolds. "Or he may have hurt himself," he added, stooping in his turn. "These cars, the way they go is wicked, miss."

But Roger had not been hurt. We could find no mark whatever on him. Nor did I believe he had found a chicken. What was only too ghastly apparent was that he had been walking in blood.

That was when I thought of Tony. He always drove like a lunatic, and where the drive from the Cloisters enters the main highway was a bad spot. I suppose I panicked at once, as I had done years ago when our house caught fire, and I was found in my nightgown three blocks away and still running. Anyhow, I ran out of the house and down the drive to the gates. Everything was quiet there, however. There was no crashed car, no crushed Tony. And in the end it was Roger who led me to the playhouse.

He started across the grass and I followed him. To my surprise the door was open and the lights were on. Still following the dog I went in, to find the night watchman Evans lying face down beside the pool, unconscious and bleeding from a wound in the back of his head. And minus his trousers.

Weeks later we could still only surmise what had happened to him. He maintained that he had never seen his assailant, who must have followed him in after he unlocked the door.

"I was just standing there by the pool," he said. "I don't know yet why I didn't go into it."

The fact was that he had gone into it. He was soaking wet when I found him. So we had to conclude that somebody unknown had first struck him down and then fished him out. It was not rational, but then most of the things which followed could not be rationalized either. Perhaps most curious of all was the fact of the missing trousers, although Tony refused to consider them significant that night when he came hurrying home. "That's easy," he said. "The fellow switched them for his own after he got wet in the pool. Took off his coat when he jumped in. Didn't have time for his pants."

"But Evans's must have been wet too."

He laughed, although he looked rather crestfallen.

"That's right. Spoil everything," he said. "But what the hell did he want with the old boy's trousers? He looked like a scarecrow most of the time."

There was no answer to that, and soon the ambulance drove in. Tony went to the hospital with the injured man. But we did not tell Maud the real story until later. Perhaps it would have been better if we had. She did not know, of course, but she might have guessed. Or would she?

CHAPTER SIX

ALL IN all it was not a pleasant night. Following some burglaries a year or two earlier the river settlements around Beverly had united to support a local police car with a radio, and a local boy, Graham Brown—naturally called Cracker—was in charge of a small but neat radio outfit above the police station and jail.

I had not thought much of the arrangement, after noticing that the car spent most of the nights in the alley behind Miss Mattie's, where I presume the two officers took turns in sleeping. And I have no doubt that it was there when, having seen Tony and the still unconscious Evans off, I notified the police. Certainly Jim Conway arrived before it did, skidding to a stop on the drive and leaping out without killing his engine. I was waiting for him on the terrace.

"What's happened, Pat?" he said. "You sounded as though you had a murder."

"I don't know what we've got," I told him, and began to shake violently.

He caught me by the arm. "Stop it," he said. "Here, you," he called to Reynolds, hovering in the background, "get some whisky, will you? Now, Pat, who was in that ambulance? I passed it."

"Evan Evans, the night watchman."

"Not dead, was he?"

"No. He'd been hit on the head. He—"

The patrol car arrived then, and he left me to deliver a few choice epithets to the men inside. When he came back I had had the whisky and was feeling stronger.

"All right," he said. "Evans was hit on the head. Where was he? In the grounds?"

"In the playhouse, beside the pool."

But, of course, the patrol car had come in wide open, and Maud had heard it. I saw her on the stairs, her hair in its usual braid and her face livid.

"Tony!" she gasped. "Is he—is he hurt?"

"It's not Tony, Maud," I called. "It's Evans. He's all right. He fell in the playhouse and hurt his head. He's gone to the hospital. It isn't serious."

"What are the police doing here?" she inquired, her color slowly coming back.

"I suppose I got excited. I called them."

She seemed satisfied with that. She went back to her room to call the hospital, and I took the men to the playhouse. Jim was highly interested, especially when I told him about Evans's trousers.

"His trousers?" he said incredulously. "You mean they were gone?"

"They were."

"Carry anything in them?" he asked.

"I wouldn't know, unless it was keys. He had a lot of them, to the house and all the buildings on the place."

"You didn't see them when you found him?"

"I don't remember them."

"How did he carry them?"

"On a chain."

"He might have had the chain fastened to him somewhere. They were pretty important. This house must have a million dollars' worth of loot in it. Did he have a gun?"

"I suppose he did. I never saw it."

"You didn't see it tonight?"

"No. But listen, Jim. There has been someone around. I saw him looking in the playhouse window the night of the party in June, and last Monday Margery Stoddard told me there had been someone lurking around the Farm."

But he was unimpressed.

"Somebody after Stoddard's chickens," he said, and went to the pool, hot on the trail of Evans's gun. It was not there, and they found nothing else of importance in the playhouse that night; only the bloodstains on the tile, and Evans's old soft hat still in the water. Jim said it had probably saved his skull if not his life, and with the aid of a golf club managed to fish it out. But before he went that night he had examined every inch of the place: game room, living room, guest bedrooms, and the tennis court.

He came back to the house before he left. "Nothing there," he said. "But the playhouse is something, isn't it? Never realized before how big it is. Funny what money will do. I'll bet you had more fun out of that two-by-four you used to have in the back yard than the Wainwrights ever get out of this."

I was instantly on the defensive. "They don't use it much, but their friends do."

He gave me a quick look. "Like that, is it?" he said. "Well, I say it's a show-off place, and to hell with it."

Before he left he said he was putting a police officer in Evans's place to guard the house, and that tomorrow he would drain the pool. The gun might still be in it. But it was to be a long time before Evans's gun was found.

I told Maud some of the truth that night before I went to bed. She looked worried, so I did not tell her about the keys and the missing gun. Although she knew now that Evans had been attacked, the news she had had was reassuring. He had a bad concussion but no fracture, and Tony was on the way home. Roger had gone into her room with me, and I was relieved to see that someone had washed off the stains. She asked me to leave the dog in her room when I left, and for the first time I realized that she was uneasy.

I cheered her as best I could.

"Jim Conway says it was only a vagrant looking for a place to sleep," I told her. "Evans probably surprised him and he knocked him out. It couldn't be anything else, Maud. There was nothing to steal there."

"Maybe not," she said. "Tell Tony to see me when he comes back, Pat."

I waited up to tell him. Then I went along to my rooms. Not to bed, however. Looking out, I saw the entire place covered with what looked like gigantic fireflies and realized that Jim was still looking for Evans's trousers and the keys. To do so he had apparently enlisted the entire male staff, including the gardeners, chauffeurs, and stablemen. But it was not until the next day that a caddy at the club, searching in the rough for a lost golf ball, found the trousers in a damp heap between the tenth and eleventh holes. The keys were gone.

By that time Jim Conway had rounded up every vagrant along the railroad for miles in both directions. He said later that he made an astonishing collection of pants in every stage of age and condition. None of them showed any signs of having been in what the press referred to as the Cloisters' million-dollar pool, but in the hospital Evans, slowly recovering consciousness, was able to tell why they were missing.

The keys, he said, had been padlocked to a thin steel chain which ran like a belt around his waist. It ran through the belt straps, and unless there was a knife handy to cut it loose, it could only be taken with the trousers. This was borne out by the fact that when the trousers were found the straps had been neatly cut. So the keys were gone, as well as the revolver Evans had carried in a shoulder holster.

We did not tell Maud that someone unknown now had possession, not only of a gun but of the keys to the Cloisters. But within a day or two all the doors on the lower floor of the house had chains to supplement the locks, and Tony himself made a careful round, night after night to see that they were fastened.

That is the way things stood with us toward the end of August of last year. Maud was slowly improving, sitting sometimes in the evening on that roof garden of hers and gazing at the sunset over the river. But something had gone out of her, her vast zest for life, even her physical vitality. Tony often sat there with her in the evenings. It seemed to me that he was watching her, although he was as casual as ever on the surface.

"How about a shawl, old girl? Night's getting chilly."

To amuse her he brought her the local gossip. The greens committee at the country club was talking about eliminating the steep grade at the tenth hole. Theodore Earle was selling his Florida house. And one night he told her that there was a rumor that Bill Sterling and Lydia were supposed to be marrying that autumn, and that Audrey was raising hell about it.

"She's a spoiled kid," he said. "Somebody ought to turn her

over a knee and spank her." A statement which pleased me extremely.

Maud was only languidly interested.

"I hope they'll be happy," she said, and went back into that unhappy world of her own where none of us could follow her.

How unimportant it all seemed that night, with the river a distant silver strip in the moonlight, and a tug slowly making its way, pushing a crowd of loaded scows ahead of it. Lydia and Bill and Audrey. Cracker Brown and his radio. A bored desk sergeant half asleep at the desk in the station house. The river itself. Even the cemetery halfway down the hill, lovely and quiet and orderly.

Aside from my interest in Lydia, they seemed very remote. But even then the valley and the Hill, having run their parallel courses for years, were gradually approaching each other, and trouble, in the shape of a young woman in a shiny sports car, was on the way from the East.

I remember that Maud roused herself after a long silence.

"I'm glad Lydia Morgan is marrying," she said. "It's a lonely business, a woman alone. And I suppose Audrey will marry before long." She stopped there and looked at Tony, but he only grinned at her.

"She's a good-looking child," he said coolly, "but she's a bit of a brat, Maud. Don't get ideas in your head."

That seemed to relieve her mind. I remember that she asked about Evans that night, and that Tony finally told her all the details. She was startled, but certainly not shocked. Looking back now, I am certain she never suspected the truth. Nevertheless, the fact remained that somebody had intended to break into the house, and that night Tony urged her to let him take her jewels up to town. But she merely shook her head. There was a queer streak of obstinacy in her sometimes. It annoyed him.

"I wish to God you'd show some sense," he said irritably. "What good are they there in that safe? You don't wear them half the time."

"Nobody can get at them. I'm the only one who knows the combination."

"A lot of good that would do, with someone burning matches on the soles of your feet!"

But she was stubborn, and at last he got up in a bad humor and left us.

I think Tony's uneasiness communicated itself to me during that interval. In spite of the guard Jim Conway had installed in the grounds, I was sleeping badly. Also I was feeling lonely. I missed Maud's hearty laugh, her shrewd views of people and affairs, the evenings when Tony was out and we sat and she knitted while I made notes on this and that to be done the next day.

Then, too, as she improved Tony was away most of the time. He had lost a week. Now with a strike at one of the mills I seldom saw him. What time he had he spent with Maud.

Then one day another letter for her in a blue envelope arrived. This time I saved it for him. He took it without comment, but he looked as though I had handed him a bomb.

We saw a good bit of Mr. Elliott during that convalescence of Maud's. He was as distinguished as ever, but I began to feel they were at odds over something or other. I had an idea that he wanted her to marry him, and she was refusing. He looked worried and unhappy when he thought he was unobserved. And I remember that he asked me once if I had any idea what had caused her collapse.

"Has she spoken about it?" he asked. "After all, a strong woman like that—"

"Not to me, Mr. Elliott."

He was disturbed about the attack on Evans too. He had me go over every detail as I knew it, the blood on Roger, how I had found Evans himself, the missing keys and gun.

"I suppose Evans kept pretty regular hours?" he asked.

"I think so. He made rounds of the house every hour, punching a clock. Then two or three times at night he would take a look around the grounds. I don't believe he had any particular time for that."

"Did he always go to the playhouse?"

"I don't know, Mr. Elliott."

The whole thing evidently puzzled him. As Tony once said, outside of Maud's jewels the house could hardly appeal to a burglar unless he brought a moving van along. But there were the jewels, and some attempt might be made to get them. I gathered that Mr. Elliott had tried to get Maud to go away, and that she had refused.

"She is a very self-willed woman," he said, and sighed.

I was alone a good deal at that time. Now and then Margery Stoddard wandered over for a cup of tea. She had seen no more of the intruder at the Farm, but the attack on Evans worried her.

"An old man!" she said. "It was so brutal, Pat. After all, he could not have put up a fight. To knock him out and then half drown him . . . !"

I thought she looked badly, but then I dare say we all did at that time.

I filled in the time as best I could. One day I made a crude chart of the Cloisters, and as the house played its own part in the tragedies to come, it might be well to describe it here. Aside from the open court in the center the plan was simple enough. The entrance hall was two stories high, with a painted ceiling and a balcony across the back. Long windows, above and below, opened onto the court, and from the hall two long corridors, one called the east and the other the west hall, opened from it. The west hall was the one toward the playhouse, and over the end of it were Maud's rooms with their view of the golf course and the river.

Both corridors had doors leading to the grounds outside. The main entrance, of course, was at the front of the building, where there was a long terrace, with a center portico with high white pillars.

Inside, most of the house was pretty appalling. In the main hall the floor and stairs were white marble, which had to be washed each morning. Indeed, one of my earliest recollections of the place was of the stealthy swishing of wet cloths more or less heralding the dawn. And scattered all over were the pictures, statues, bronzes, tapestries, and pipe organ with which old J.C. Wainwright had successfully hidden the probably excellent architecture of the place.

The west wing contained, in order, a formal French drawing room, a long and gloomy picture gallery, a library—the one livable room there—Maud's unused morning room and my office at the end; while across the hall were the double doors leading to the vast white ballroom. The east wing had a horror called a Chinese room, filled with teak, red lacquer, and bronze, the state dining room, Tony's private study, and at the end the cheerful tile-floored breakfast room.

There were other rooms, of course: a small card room, a powder room off the main hall for women, a corresponding retiring room for men, and a room for cutting and arranging flowers. Behind all these and across the court were the service quarters, the pantries, the enormous kitchen, Mrs. Partridge's sitting room, the servants' hall, and so on.

The elevator shaft opened onto the west hall. In fact, it was the west side of the house which, outside of meals, was the one in common use. There outside my office was the door which led to the playhouse and the garage, and just inside was the table where the playhouse key was kept. What coming and going there was by the family was by this hall, and the library was the one room downstairs in customary use.

The servants were housed on the third floor, while—outside of Maud's suite—the second contained the usual bedrooms. Or were they usual? I find on my chart that the end of the east wing on the second floor is left a blank, with a question mark in the center. The space is marked *locked suite*, and I remember having an idea that perhaps old John Wainwright had died there and that Maud had kept it sentimentally inviolate; like that old aunt of my father's, who had kept her husband's room for twenty years as he had left it, including the funeral flowers.

Those locked rooms intrigued me. However, Maud had never mentioned them, and so they remained a mystery during those early months at the Cloisters. I presume they were opened and cleaned at intervals but I never saw this done, and when I learned their real significance it practically changed the world for me.

CHAPTER SEVEN

THOSE LATE August days were pleasant. Maud was better; the heat had passed and the nights were cool. Jim Conway had finally removed the guards from the grounds, but Maud refused a new watchman.

"I'll wait for Evans," she said. "I don't want any strange man wandering around the house at night."

I was busy once more. It was amazing the number of invitations to be answered, notes of thanks to be sent, and letters which had accumulated during Maud's illness. I had called Lydia as soon as I had heard the news, and there was a thrill of happiness in her voice when she replied.

"I suppose I'm being silly," she said. "There's nothing definite really, but I'm frightfully happy. Do come down."

Actually it was the first of September before I saw her, and I noticed at once that there was a change in her. She was sewing in the garden, and I thought she had been crying. I kissed her and told her she was lucky, that I had been crazy about Bill for years. But she still seemed depressed.

"Audrey doesn't like it," she said in a low voice. "She has some silly idea about her father. I suppose it's my fault. I never told her all the truth, and naturally no one else has. She thinks he left me because he couldn't support us any longer. Now she has idealized him. It makes it awfully hard, Pat."

"Then tell her," I said. "It's time she knew. She's not a child."

"It would be a dreadful blow. She's proud, you know. That awful story, Pat. I just can't do it. You can't build up a man to his child for fifteen years and then destroy him. I don't think she'd even believe me."

I was indignant. "If you're going to let Donald Morgan ruin your life all over again I have no patience with you. As for Audrey, she'll have to know sometime. Anyhow, she'll marry soon. Then where will you be?"

I think I convinced her, there on that warm early September morning, with the dahlias and asters in full bloom in her garden, and her face turned toward the river and the hills beyond as if she saw hope and happiness there. She looked very young that day, very young and very lovely.

"I suppose you're right, Pat," she said. "It won't be easy, but I have to think of Bill too."

"You marry Bill Sterling and forget the rest," I advised her, and left her there with a new look of determination on her face.

All seemed to be well with my particular world that day as I turned my old car up the hill. Maud was improving; not her old self, perhaps, but getting about. Evans was on the way to recovery. No one so far had tried to get into the Cloisters, and I was planning some new clothes for the fall. To complete my contentment, Tony dined at home that night, and with me.

Maud had sent down word that she was tired and would have a tray in bed; so he gravely gave me an arm and escorted me down the long hall.

"Just an old-fashioned girl after all," he said, smiling down at me. "Don't ever go modern on me, Pat. I'm fed up with it. You're no more modern than Maud herself."

"No," I said, feeling absurdly happy. "I suppose I'm the sort that brushes its teeth at night and says its prayers, and then drops into wholesome slumber. At least I used to. I haven't slept so well lately."

He gave me a quick look. "See here, Pat, you're intelligent and you're fond of Mother. Have you any idea what's been wrong with Maud?"

"She's worrying. I don't know why."

"She hasn't said anything? You haven't told her about those letters?"

"Certainly not."

Then we were in the breakfast room, with Thomas and Stevens circling around Reynolds like the rings of Saturn, and Tony grinned at me.

"Now you know how a canary bird feels," he said. "How about a little seed, Reynolds?"

"Seed, sir?"

"Never mind," said Tony. "I'm very particular about my seed, Reynolds. Otherwise I can't sing."

"I see, sir," said Reynolds, looking bewildered, and retired to the sideboard.

It was a gay meal, but later in the library Tony was more sober. He told me about the strike at the mill, and about a minority stockholders' meeting, headed by some of J.C.'s relatives.

"They want control," he said. "They'll never get it, but that's what they are after. They never forgave the old man for leaving the business to Mother."

Like so many other things this seemed unimportant at the time. What did matter was that Tony was his old self again, and that we were on friendly terms once more. Not that he had been unfriendly, but since Maud's illness and the attack on Evans I had felt as though I were largely a useful piece of furniture to have about. "Ask Miss Abbott. She'll know." Or, "Are you busy, Pat? Do you mind making a call for me?"

I suppose I was foolish, but I trailed up those marble stairs that night with a song in my heart, and no birdseed about it.

It was the next day that Bessie arrived. Maud was downstairs that afternoon, and we were in the main hall when she drove up in a cream-colored sports car. I had been filling some vases in the flower room and I came in to find Maud staring helplessly out through the open door to the drive.

"Dear God," she said in a half whisper. "It's Bessie."

A young woman was getting out of the car and coming up the steps to the terrace. She was an ash-blonde with a long bob, an innocent face, and a pair of the coldest blue eyes I have ever seen. Maud seemed paralyzed. She didn't even move. And Bessie came up the steps and into the house as if she belonged there. The hall must have been dark after the sunlight outside, for she blinked. Then she saw Maud and gave her a cool little smile.

"Well, Maud," she said. "Here I am."

Maud moved then, although she made no gesture of greeting. "So I see," she said. "Although I don't know exactly why."

"Why not?" said Bessie, and taking off her hat ran her fingers through her hair. "I wrote you and wired you. Don't say I didn't warn you."

It was then that I dropped the vase. An old Dresden one at that, but Maud never noticed.

"I thought we had an agreement," she said coldly. "I paid you to get out and stay out. I paid you a lot, you may remember. That agreement still holds, so far as I am concerned."

But the crash had attracted Bessie's attention to me. She looked at me with interest.

"We can discuss that when we're alone, can't we? Just now I'd like a bath. I've been motoring for two days."

I think Maud saw then that she was helpless. She asked me to ring, and Stevens, the second footman, came and took Bessie's bags out of the car. Bessie was entirely nonchalant. She told Stevens to have her car taken around to the garage. Then she got out a small gold case and lit a cigarette.

"Where's Tony?" she inquired.

"In town. He still works, as you may remember."

"And how!" said Bessie. She glanced around her, giving me a good hard look.

"Do I know you?" she said. "I don't seem to remember you."

"Miss Abbott is staying here," Maud said hastily. "She is my secretary and my friend. I hope you'll remember that."

Bessie raised her eyebrows. "Like that," she said softly. "It must be a nice cozy job, Miss Abbott. Congratulations."

I saw red for a minute, which probably saved me from a retort. But Reynolds had appeared by that time and after a bow to Bessie, who ignored it, was, so to speak, standing by. I have often thought how many scenes are saved by servants, especially upper-class ones. Certainly Reynolds did so that day. Maud became the mistress and hostess at once, although her face remained set.

"Miss Bessie will have her old rooms," she told Reynolds. "Tell Mrs. Partridge to have them opened. And there will be four for dinner. Or are you staying to dinner?" she asked Bessie.

"I wrote you that I meant to stay awhile," said Bessie, raising her eyebrows. "Don't tell me Tony intercepted my letters!"

I had known from Bessie's first mention of letters that they were the ones Tony had taken. Now I began to pick up the flowers from the floor, to hide my face, but neither of them noticed me.

"I see he did," Bessie said, smiling her amused smile. "How like him! Well, tell old Partridge not to have a fit—and, Reynolds, bring me up a Scotch and soda. I'm thirsty!"

I suppose I should have known. It seems impossible that I had not known. I had lived for three months in the house. My relations with Maud Wainwright had been more or less intimate. I would have said, until the day when she came back from the city and took to her bed, that she had no secrets; that she was congenitally unable to keep a secret.

Yet the thing itself was no secret at all. The village knew it as well as the Hill. Both had accepted it. It was no longer even a matter for gossip. My only defense is that for six years I had been busy and largely detached from all social life. I had been too tired at night to do more than go to bed; and, as I have already said, the Hill was an entity in itself which concerned me not at all.

But that day, when I followed Maud out onto the terrace, I had no idea who Bessie was. I found Maud angry rather than stricken; angry with a cold fury that I had never seen before. She looked at me and tried to pull herself together.

"That devil," she said. "It wasn't enough for her to spoil Tony's life. She has to come back and do it all over again. What brought her here? She's got some wickedness in her mind. It sticks out all over her."

"Who is she, Maud?" I asked. "I've never seen her before."

She gave me a look of sheer incredulity. "Who is she?" she repeated. "Do you mean to say you don't know?"

"No."

"Good heavens," she said. "I thought all the world knew it. It wasn't her fault if it didn't. The papers played it up enough, God knows—bell, book, and candle, whatever that means." She looked at me, and I must have been pale, for she sighed. "I thought you knew, Pat. I'm sorry."

Bessie, she said, was Tony's wife.

I cannot remember how much I heard that day or how much of it came later. I was not thinking. It was not that I had fallen in love with Tony, but I must have been on the way without knowing it. Perhaps Maud knew it. As I have said, she was shrewd enough, for all her occasional naïveté.

They were not even divorced. Maud, telling me the story that day, said that Bessie had refused to go to Reno and that, while Tony was suspicious of her, he had no proof. Then, too, he had been pretty badly burned. He had not wanted to marry again. He had simply drifted.

"She played him for a sucker from the start," said Maud, lapsing into the vernacular as she sometimes did. "That was five years ago. It lasted only a year or so, and she never liked it here. We were too provincial, she said. Then she started a flirtation or worse with a man in town, and I paid her half a million dollars to get out and go to Reno. I didn't tell Tony that," she added. "He was pretty badly hurt. So far as he knows, she just left him." She groaned and got up. "I'll have to let him know somehow. It will give him a little time."

I could see that she was badly shaken. She had always gone her way, big, placid, and simple, with an almost childish faith in her fellow men.

"She hasn't been to Reno yet," she said. "I don't think she means to go. And she's nothing, Pat. Just nothing. Tony met her in a bar somewhere in New York. Not that she's much of a drinker. Money is her weakness. Money and men. I think I'll call Dwight," she went on. "I wonder—would you meet Tony at the station and tell him, Pat? He took the train today. He's fond of you. He might take it better that way."

I found that I was trembling, and Maud must have noticed it, for she came over and put a hand on my arm. "When I think of the plans I had—" she said.

I managed to control my voice. "Is he still in love with her, Maud?"

"I don't think he ever was."

She told me a little about Bessie then. Not much. She had been a New York girl, one of that band of young women who hangs on the fringes of society. She had gone to a good school, however, and somehow she had managed to get into the Junior League. Her people were quiet and respectable enough, but Maud suspected that Tony had financed the wedding, from white orchids and St. Bartholomew's to reception at Sherry's.

"I saw some of the bills later," she said wearily.

I drove down to meet the train at half past six that night. Already the days were shorter, and it was almost dusk when it drew in. I saw Tony get out, carrying the evening papers and nodding the casual good nights with which one commuter leaves another. My heart was thudding as he came toward the car and saw me.

"What is it? An anniversary or something?" he inquired, smiling.

"An anniversary?"

"Your meeting me," he explained. "Or have my personal attractions at last melted that hard heart of yours?"

"I was doing some errands. Maud asked me to meet you."

He got in beside me, leaving me to drive. My old car creaked under his weight, and he had trouble disposing of his long legs.

"So that's it," he said. "I might have known you'd never think of it yourself."

We were both silent as we left the village and began to climb the hill. I remember that there was already a feeling of fall in the air, although it was only very early September. My hands were trembling on the wheel and halfway up the hill, where there was a level spot, I pulled the car to the side of the road and stopped there. He seemed surprised.

"Out of gas?"

"No, I'm a little nervous. Tony, I have something to tell you."

He turned in the seat and faced me.

"Mother's not sick again?"

"No, it's not that. It's about you. Maud thought it would be better if I told you before you got home. I don't know how, really. It's not my affair."

"You're not leaving us, are you?"

I shook my head, and I thought he looked relieved. Then I felt his eyes on me, and all at once he stiffened and drew a long breath.

"I suppose it's Bessie," he said.

"Yes. She's at the house."

"I see."

I started the engine after that. He said nothing more, as though he was bracing himself for what was waiting for him. Only as we reached the entrance to the Cloisters he asked me if I minded driving on a bit. I did so, and it was a half hour later when I let him out at the house and drove back to the garage. He had told me little, except that he had tried to head her off. She had both written and wired to Maud, and he had intercepted the letters and the telegram.

"I told her to stay away, but if you knew her you would realize what good that did," he said.

I was glad he had that half hour to get ready. It was all he had. I dropped him at the house, and Bessie's cool voice spoke from a long chair on the terrace.

"Hello, Tony," it drawled. "Been having a ride with the pretty secretary?"

I was boiling as I took my car to the garage and walked back to the house. Neither Bessie nor Tony was in sight, but Maud was coming down the stairs and I took my cue from her. Her face was quiet. Also she had dressed for dinner in long trailing black, and she wore her pearls. Evidently the idea was to be business as usual.

"You'd better hurry, Pat," she said. "Where on earth have you been?"

"We took a little drive."

She nodded, and I knew she understood.

I put on a printed chiffon that evening. It was what Bessie would think a secretary should wear, with short sleeves and a high neck, although it swept the ground. But I might have spared myself the trouble, for Bessie pointedly ignored me. Not that she gave me any particular thought at the time. It was merely her way of putting me in my place. Outside of that we might have been any four well-bred people dining anywhere, from cocktails in the library to the end of Pierre's long and elaborate dinner. Bessie did most of the talking: Paris, London, Vienna. Tony hardly spoke, and I was still the secretary, to be seen and not heard. I was proud of Maud, however. She looked the great lady that night, quiet and regal, with that mass of fair hair piled high and her really beautiful neck and shoulders gleaming in the candlelight. Beside her Bessie, heavily made up and in a full white skirt and red cocktail jacket, looked cheap and common.

We went back to the library for coffee and liqueurs. Bessie was restless, and I knew she was waiting to talk to Tony. But Maud was on guard.

"We might have some bridge," she said briskly, and without waiting ordered a table.

It was a strange game. Nobody was paying any real attention to it. I myself saw Maud revoke twice, without anyone's discovering it. At the end I was in ten dollars, most of it from Bessie, and she paid it ungraciously.

"I've held rotten cards," she said. Then she laughed. "Maybe I'm lucky in love," she added, and looked at Tony.

But Tony had had enough. He slammed out of the house, and we did not see him again.

Maud and I went up to bed early. I saw that the closed suite was opened, which ended one mystery. But I did not sleep much that night. The birds were chirping in a gray dawn before I dozed off. It seemed to me that one phase of my life was over, and another strange unhappy one beginning. I went to sleep wondering whether Maud had seen Bessie in the city the day she had collapsed.

I was wrong, of course. It was not so simple as that, although Bessie was to bring us trouble enough. She lost no time in getting to work, either. At two o'clock in the morning I heard Roger rumbling from where he slept outside my door, and getting up, I opened it cautiously.

The hall lights were on, and Bessie in a tweed coat over pajamas was coming up the stairs.

CHAPTER EIGHT

BESSIE'S ARRIVAL changed everything for all of us. There were no more quiet days, no more still evenings when we watched the sun go down over the river and talked or were silent as we chose. Not that she was always unpleasant or even arrogant, but she had an air at times of amused triumph that seemed to puzzle Maud and drove me practically frantic.

Tony took to staying away as much as possible. Maud was uncertain and unhappy. Even the servants looked somber. The house, always overwhelming, became an actual weight of gloom. And on the third day after her arrival Bessie sent Nora to ask me to go to her sitting room.

I had never been inside that suite of hers, and it made me gasp. I may have failed to do justice to the Cloisters. It was bad in some ways, but it was filled with beautiful things. Bessie's rooms, furnished by her after her marriage, were almost a shocking contrast. They were a mass of glass and chromium and strong colors, and I found myself blinking in the morning sunlight.

She was sitting at a desk with a lot of papers in front of her. She had not dressed, but from the odor of bath salts and powder

I suppose she had already bathed. Without her make-up she was not pretty, and her voice was petulant when she saw me.

"Hello, Miss Abbott," she said. "I wish you'd give me a hand with these. God knows where all the bills come from. I don't."

I had a wild inclination to tell her to go somewhere, but I kept my temper.

"I'll see if Mrs. Wainwright needs me," I said stiffly. "If she doesn't—"

She lit a cigarette and smiled at me. "Listen," she said, "I'll not bother you much. Or long. I wouldn't stay in this mausoleum for a million dollars. But we have to get along together for a while. Why not try?"

She smiled again, more pleasantly, and I came nearer to liking her that morning than I ever did, before or after. She looked younger and simpler, and not too sure of herself.

"I'm perfectly willing," I told her. "Of course, I'll help you. Do you want to pay the bills?"

"Good heavens, no," she said, looking startled. "I want to know how much they amount to. I can't add to save my life."

It took some time. She owed money everywhere, especially in New York, and the total was over twenty thousand dollars. There were millinery and clothes bills, and one or two from jewelers. So far as I could see she had paid nothing for the last two years except for her bare living. Even the car was not paid for, and—she had gone to her dressing table and was making up her face—she threw in the fact that they were threatening to take it away from her.

She talked as she worked over her face. She usually traveled with a maid, but she had had to let her go. It was hell to be poor, wasn't it? But her spirits had risen, as though by merely handing me the bills she had gotten rid of them.

As she had, for a few days later Maud paid them.

"I suppose I'm an idiot, Pat," she said as she gave them to me. "It's the price I pay for peace. But what on earth has she done with the money I gave her? Or Tony's allowance? It's a big one." She sighed.

"I wonder how long she means to stay?" she said fretfully. "Hilda says her trunks have come. I don't think I can bear much more, Pat. I've paid her bills. Why doesn't she go?"

I told her Bessie had said she didn't intend to stay, but it failed to comfort her.

"She's up to something," she said drearily. "She is different this time, Pat. She has some mischief in her mind. She almost frightens me."

I do not believe that in those first four days Bessie and Tony had any private conversation whatever. She had begun to go about, looking up old friends and acquaintances, and one afternoon she asked me about Audrey Morgan.

"What's she like?" she asked. "I hear Tony's been playing around with her."

"She's very young and very lovely."

"Does he want to marry her?"

"I haven't any idea."

She laughed. "He's not going to," she said coolly. "He's not going to marry anybody. I'll see to that."

We managed somehow, although the conservative part of the Hill rather pointedly avoided us. Even Margery Stoddard only came when she knew Bessie was out, and then usually to let the children bathe in our pool, the repairs on their own being still unfinished. Once or twice Julian came with her, a handsome, stockily built man who had married late in life and adored his little girls. Dwight Elliott came, of course. I overheard him one evening urging Tony to get a divorce or force Bessie to get one.

"Don't be a fool," he said. "Suppose both you and your mother by any chance pass out of the picture. She's your legal heir. Do you want control of the Wainwright Company in her hands?"

Tony went to Bessie after that, but she only laughed at him when he put the question to her.

"Divorce you?" she said, raising her eyebrows. "Why? So you can marry the Morgan child, or Pat Abbott? Why should I?"

"I'm not going on with it, Bessie."

"Oh, aren't you!" she said, flaring with anger. "You'd better think it over. You might get an unpleasant surprise."

"What does that mean? If it's a threat—"

"That's all I'm saying," she said, more quietly. "And remember this. You haven't got a thing on me. What's more, since I was thrown out of here three years ago I've written you a dozen letters offering to come back to you, and my lawyer's got copies of them. They're pretty good letters, if I do say it."

He had no belief in the surprise she threatened. He had no belief in her whatever. But his hands were tied. Not only the business. Bill Sterling had said Maud's heart was not too good. It was no time to fight Bessie, and she knew it as well as he did. But the real change in him began at that time. His lightheartedness was gone, his boyish nonsense. He ate almost nothing, he drank more than usual, and he looked tired and depressed. He was restless, too. He would take out his car and be gone for hours.

Only one thing saved us. While the Hill disliked Bessie, she had friends in town. There were long quiet evenings when she simply disappeared, driving to the city and coming back toward morning to sleep most of the day. One of the men had to stay up to let her in, however, and what with her irregular hours and innumerable demands the servants were almost in revolt.

One day she told me she had lost five hundred dollars the night before at bridge.

"I gave a rubber check for it," she said airily. "You might tell Maud about it. She won't like it when it bounces."

She had been at the Cloisters for a week or more before I had a chance to talk to Tony. Then one night, Bessie being in town again, he asked me to go for a walk.

"That is, if you can stand it," he said. "I'm not fit company for man or beast just now."

I went, of course. We walked down to the fountain with its floodlight and then toward the playhouse, with Roger pacing beside us. But Tony was silent and morose. He walked with his head down and his hands in his trousers pockets, until we were out of sight of the house. Then he stopped.

"See here," he said. "I'm sorry as hell. About Bessie I mean. Mother says you didn't know."

"I suppose I heard it at the time. It just didn't register."

He hesitated. "I'll just say this, then we'll let it go for good. Every man makes a mistake now and then. Mine was Bessie. I've paid for it. Maybe she has too. Only don't let her hurt you, my dear. She's rather good at that."

He was more cheerful after that, as though he had gotten something off his mind.

"How's your tennis?" he inquired. "I feel like swatting something tonight. Better than your golf?"

He turned on the lights in the playhouse, found me some tennis shoes in a locker, and we played a couple of sets. He

played like a demon that night, but at the end his face was relaxed, as though he had worked off some deep anger. He grinned
at me when it was over.

"I'll bet you never learned that game of yours at business
school."

"Can't you let me forget my job for a minute?"

"My darling, that's the only thing about you I ever do forget."

To my surprise he put his arms around me, and rested his
head on my shoulder, like a small boy seeking comfort.

"What am I going to do, Pat?" he said thickly. "What am I
going to do?"

That was all. He let me go, and after closing and locking the
playhouse we started back. He was quiet. He spoke only once,
and then it was about his mother.

"She's not like herself," he said. "She's changed. It isn't Bessie.
She was different before that. Don't tell me it was the heat. She's
a salamander, whatever that is. What's wrong, Pat?"

"I don't know," I said honestly. "If it didn't seem impossible I'd
say she was afraid of something."

"She's never been afraid of anything in her life," he said, almost roughly. "Never."

I lay awake for a long time that night. I heard Stevens admit
Bessie at two o'clock, but shortly after that I fell asleep and slept
heavily. As a result I never knew the house had been entered until morning.

I had not even heard Roger give the alarm, or Tony going
downstairs to investigate. He had taken his automatic, but by
that time the intruder was gone. The door at the end of the west
hall was standing wide open, and it looked as though the chain
had not been put up.

Stevens, however, interrogated by Tony, insisted that it had been. "I let Mrs. Wainwright in by that door after she left her car at the garage," he said stiffly. "She stood by while I put the chain up. She was lighting a cigarette. I'm sure she'll bear me out, sir."

But Bessie, awakened at the unreasonable hour of eight in the morning, said she knew nothing about it.

"Why should I?" she said shrilly. "I came in and went to bed, and if you'll let me alone I'm staying there."

Nothing had been taken, but Jim Conway, coming up that day to look about, was inclined to discredit Stevens's story.

"Man was half asleep," he said. "Probably forgot the chain altogether. But it all ties up. Fellow who got Evans's keys has started to use them. Only he didn't know about the dog."

"Anyone who knew Evans had the keys would know about Roger," I told him. "And Roger only barks at strangers."

Jim was unimpressed. "Sure it was a stranger," he said. "Who do you think it was? An old family friend?"

But the police discovered nothing. There were no footprints on the dry ground outside, and the net result was merely an intensified watchfulness on the part of the entire household which made the second invasion—when it occurred—more puzzling than ever. But even aside from that incident I suppose we had all the elements of a domestic tragedy in the making at that time. Certainly no one of us was entirely normal. Tony, after the night by the playhouse, was once again bitter and somber. Maud was strange, almost remote, and Bessie both arrogant and disagreeable. It seems odd, then, to remember that the first indication of real trouble when it finally came did not apparently involve any of us.

It happened a few days later, and it involved, of all people in the world, Lydia Morgan.

That day stands out in my memory for more reasons than

one. First, it was my birthday, and my twenty-sixth at that. I had almost forgotten it until, after Tony had gone to the city, Maud called me on the house telephone and asked me to go out to the drive.

"There's something there for you," she said. "Happy birthday, my dear."

I was in my office at the time. I rushed out, and in front of the house was Gus, grinning, and a brand-new car. I could not believe my eyes.

"But it can't be—" I said. "What does Mrs. Wainwright want me to see?"

"The car, miss," said Gus, looking very pleased with himself. "It's for you. Happy birthday, Miss Pat."

Of course, I did the idiotic thing. I put my hand on a shiny new fender and burst into tears. Gus's grin died.

"It's joy, Gus," I said. "I never hoped to have a car like this. I never—" I kept on crying, and altogether we had rather a moist time of it. Before I went in I drove around a bit. It handled like a fine horse; one touch and it moved. I took it down to the garage, where the men looked it over and rendered a satisfactory verdict; and to the stables, where old James, head groom for years and now with only a stable boy or two to help him, said that it could probably do everything but jump.

On my way back to the house my common sense began to assert itself. Maud had no right to give me a car. She was spending too much money already. But one look at her face when I saw her made any protest difficult.

"Do you like it, Pat?"

"Like it! I'm so excited I could scream. It's wonderful. But do you think—"

She raised a hand. "Listen," she said. "I've had to do a lot of hateful things in my time. Paying Bessie's bills is only one of them. Let me have a little pleasure, Pat. It's about all I have left."

There was no answer to that, of course. She kissed me and told me to take the day off; but when I left her she had already lapsed into that strange new lethargy of hers.

The second thing which happened that day was a telephone call from Lydia. Her voice sounded strained, but she was calm enough. "I want to see you," she said. "Something has happened, and I don't know what to do about it."

"What is it?"

"I'll tell you when I see you," she said, and hung up.

I drove down in the new car as soon as I could. I was anxious, and I was not relieved when I saw Bill Sterling's old car parked in the drive. As I stopped he slammed out of the house, and I called to him.

"Is anyone sick?" I asked.

He looked at me, but I don't think he even saw me. The next moment he was gone and I was left staring after him. I went into the house then, to find Lydia in her living room. She looked shockingly ill, and it was some time before she could even talk. When she did I was horrified.

Don wanted to come back. After fifteen years of desertion and neglect he wanted to come home again.

A day or two ago he had called her from New York, saying that he was hopelessly sick and practically penniless. All he wanted was a place to rest for a short time, he had said. She owed him nothing. He had no right to ask it. But he would like to see Audrey before he died, and he needed sanctuary for a few weeks.

I listened grimly. "Sort of old-home week in the town," I said, thinking of Bessie. "I hope you told him what you thought."

"How could I, with Audrey listening?"

"For heaven's sake, Lydia! What did you tell him?"

She threw out her hands with a helpless gesture. "What could I do?" she said. "I told him I would think it over and wire him. Then Audrey got hysterical and I had to call Bill. It's been dreadful, Pat."

"I don't believe it. It's a trick, Lydia. He's not your husband now. He has no claim on you whatever."

"Except Audrey," she said listlessly. "Of course, Bill thinks I am crazy. Sometimes I think I am. But with Audrey caring so much—"

"Oh, damn Audrey," I interrupted impatiently. "Don't tell me he's coming, Lydia."

She nodded helplessly. He was coming.

I got the story finally. She had wired him to come for a short rest and had sent him the money for his fare. That had been the night before, and she expected him in a day or so.

"I don't care about the talk," she said listlessly. "I don't even mind seeing him, after all these years. I do mind dreadfully about Bill, Pat. That's all over."

I was too indignant that day to say much. I drove slowly back up the hill, still boiling with rage; but even then if anyone had told me that Don Morgan and Maud and Bessie and even what had happened to Evans would be eventually tied up together, I dare say I would have laughed.

CHAPTER NINE

THAT WAS on my birthday, the twelfth of September, and on the fourteenth Donald Morgan came home. Got off the train like a sick man, shook hands with Lydia, and at the house turned on the magic of his charm and took Audrey to his arms.

"My baby," he said. "My little girl."

Yes, he went over big with Audrey. That is a part of the story.

The valley and the Hill alike fairly shook with gossip. There were two camps: the majority party thinking Lydia a spineless idiot; the minority—mostly the young—siding with Audrey. Very little of this reached us. As I have said, since Bessie's arrival both the Hill and the valley had not so much ignored us as stayed away from us.

"As though we had a slight touch of leprosy," was Maud's dry comment.

I imagine much the same thing, only worse, was happening to Lydia. The situation there was too anomalous for comfort. Everyone knew that Bill Sterling had not been in the house since Don entered it, and that Lydia had had to call in a doctor for Don from a neighboring borough. I myself was still smoldering with indignation, and it was two or three days before I called her on the telephone.

"Well, how's the old-home week going?" I said.

"Is that you, Pat? I thought you had deserted me, along with the rest."

"You've put everybody in an impossible position, Lydia. You can't blame them. Do you want to see me?"

"I'd love it," she said simply.

I got there that afternoon, but I was startled at the change in her. She not only looked ill, she looked older, as though all the life had been drained out of her.

"It's nice of you to come, Pat."

"Don't be an idiot. Why wouldn't I come? How is—how is the invalid?"

I thought she looked at me queerly.

"He seems better. Of course, with angina—"

"Who says he has angina?" I could not keep my resentment out of my voice. "I wouldn't believe him on oath."

Then that little fool, Audrey, had to come down the stairs, carrying a tray and with her eyes like stars.

"He ate it all, Mother," she said. "He seemed to like it."

"I'll bet he did," I said savagely. "Ate it and asked for more. Don't look at me like that, Audrey. I give you a week to be good and fed up with it."

She gave me a nasty look and went back to the kitchen. Lydia sighed and changed the subject, asking me rather abruptly about Bessie.

"It's a queer world, Pat," she said helplessly. "Here am I, and as for you—I had hoped Tony would divorce her and marry you."

"Not a chance," I said as lightly as I could. Then a man's voice called Lydia from above, and young as I had been when I last heard it, eleven or thereabouts, I recognized it.

"If that's little Pat Abbott," it said, "bring her up, Lydia."

There was nothing else to do, and then and there I had my first and last view of Don Morgan after his return. How old was he at the time? Over fifty, I imagine, yet he had kept that curly hair of his and his disarming smile. Outside of that he was changed, of course. He looked dissipated as well as sick. There were pouches under his eyes and his well-kept hands had a slight tremor. He was sitting in a chair by a window when I went in.

"Well," he said, "so the little girl has grown into a woman! And a lovely one too. Sit down for a minute, Pat, and talk to a lonely old man." That was purely rhetorical. The Don Morgans of this world may change but they do not grow old.

I sat down, and he lit a cigarette and gave me one. It was then that I noticed the tremor.

"Now tell me all about yourself. Audrey says you are up on the Hill. Like it there?"

"I like Mrs. Wainwright," I said briefly.

"There's a son, isn't there? How about him?"

"I don't see very much of him."

He gave me a quick sharp look, but he made no comment. Instead he talked about himself, and I began to understand the hold he evidently held over Audrey; the easy, beautiful voice, the youthful smile, even the debonair manner in which he announced that he was not long for this world.

"Not that I mind," he said cheerfully. "I've made my mistakes and been damned sorry for them, and Lydia is a saint. But I've lived my life, my dear."

I left him in that gently melancholy mood, sitting by a window facing the river, a box of cigarettes at his elbow and a book on his knees, clad—under an elaborate dressing gown—in heavy blue silk pajamas. Penniless he might have been, but he had certainly brought his wardrobe with him.

I never saw him again.

It was late that afternoon when I got back to the Cloisters, to meet Bessie in the west hall. She had evidently been telephoning, for she had a list in her hand.

"Look here, Pat," she said. "I'm having some people at the playhouse tonight. Tell old Partridge, will you? Sandwiches and so on for twenty, and plenty to drink."

I looked at my wrist watch. "The shops will be closing soon," I told her. "I suppose it can be managed."

"It's got to be managed," she said coolly, and went on up the stairs.

I went down to the village myself to save time. Poor Mrs. Partridge was frantic, and Pierre stiff and sulky in his chef's cap and apron. But we did get food and drink ready before her guests arrived. They were mostly from the city, with a sprinkling of the less desirable from the Hill. None of them came to the house, however, where Maud and I played double solitaire up in her boudoir, and Tony had escaped by the simple device of getting into his car and driving off.

I do not know much about that party. I do know it was extremely noisy, and that late in the evening the menservants were sent back to the house and the windows closed. But if there was nude bathing there, as was rumored later, I did not know anything about it. In fact, it was several days before I knew much about anything.

For that was the night I fell down the elevator shaft.

It was an idiotic performance, from start to finish, although I still grow cold when I think of it. The facts themselves are simple.

Bessie's party was still going on at two o'clock that morning, and it made Roger restless. I was reading in bed when he came whining and scratching at my door. I remembered then that I had not let him out, so I got up, put on a dressing gown and slippers, and went down to the west hall door. The hall itself was dark, but I knew my way perfectly. I let Roger out and stood waiting for him. He was gone for some time, but when I whistled he came back obediently enough. I closed the door and put up the chain. Then I saw that the elevator door was open. The elevator had been under repair again for a day or two, and out of sheer curiosity I stepped in to see if it worked.

Only, of course, the car was not there. I remember falling, the awful feeling of that drop. But I remember something even worse. I did not hit the floor. I fell directly on somebody below, somebody who was either standing or crouching there. I heard a grunt, then the two of us collapsed together and I promptly fainted.

I must have come around rather quickly. I was alone by that time and the door into the basement was open. Also there was cold air from somewhere which helped to revive me. But my ankle was red-hot torture. I reached out for something to help me to my feet, and I distinctly felt a ladder. I did get up partially at least, holding to a rung, but the pain was ghastly. I must have fainted again, for when I came to Roger was whining above at the open door, and the ladder was gone.

That was when I realized what had happened. Someone who had no business to be there had been at the bottom of the shaft when I fell. He might still be there, lurking in the darkness, and ready to attack me if I made a move. The same man who had hurt Evans. The same man who had gotten into the house before. It was horrible.

I did not move. I simply lay there and waited. And nothing happened. Nothing whatever.

When Bessie came in that night I do not know; probably while I was unconscious. When the intruder slipped out I shall never know. It was half past seven in the morning when Stevens, helping to open the house for the day, heard my voice at the bottom of the shaft and brought help. I can still see his astounded face as he peered down the shaft.

"Is somebody there?"

"I'm here, Stevens. I've hurt my ankle," I said feebly. "Get me out, please, and hurry."

There was a great deal of excitement after that. It seemed to me that the entire household rushed down, and I know that an excited kitchenmaid threw a cup of water over me before anyone could stop her. Reynolds kept his head, as usual. He had a chair brought, I was lifted into it, and a small procession carried and escorted me out of the basement and up the main staircase. It must have been quite a sight, for I looked up to see Tony staring down at it from the balcony, his face half covered with shaving lather.

"Good God!" he shouted. "Are you hurt, Pat?"

I gave my best imitation of a cheery smile. "I'm all right. I've hurt my ankle."

"She fell down the elevator shaft, sir," said Reynolds, panting under my weight. "She's been there all night."

"Down the shaft! She couldn't!"

"I'm glad to hear it," I said. "I certainly fell down something."

He stood aside then, and they carried me to my room. Tony

followed, and somehow I was on my bed, with my leg giving me pure hell and everything going about in circles. I could hear Tony shouting orders, to get Dr. Sterling, to get a nurse from the hospital, to bring some whisky. Then what with pain and excitement I passed completely out. I must have gone from that into exhausted sleep, for it was noon when I wakened. My leg was up on a pillow, and Amy Richards, in her uniform, was putting compresses on my ankle. Otherwise I was as I had been, on top of my bed with a blanket over me, and still in my dressing gown.

Amy grinned at me. She was a valley girl and an old friend.

"Well," she said, "for a girl with a foot like this you certainly can sleep. I'll bet you'd have slept through the San Francisco earthquake."

"You'd have slept yourself if you had lain all night where I did," I said peevishly. "How bad is that foot, Amy? I need it."

"You won't need it for some time," she said in her brisk professional manner. "How about some food? You didn't land on your stomach, did you?"

I sat up and looked at my foot. It was something to see, and I lay back and groaned. "I can't stay in bed," I said. "I have too much to do."

She only laughed at me, and I felt better after I had had a bath and a sort of combination breakfast-lunch. Amy was in a state of suppressed excitement through both. I suppose she had been ordered not to talk to me about the night before, but there was plenty without that.

"Maybe you haven't caused a fuss!" she said. "They think a lot of you, Pat. Mrs. Wainwright's been in and out all morning, and your boy friend had the elevator people here and threatened them with jail. I suppose the girl with the hangover is his wife?"

"Yes."

CHAPTER TEN

THAT DAY, like the others that followed, brought nothing exciting. In the afternoon Maud appeared, with Hilda behind her carrying silk blanket and covers and pillow slips. She looked anxious, but she was businesslike and practical.

"The doctor thinks there is no break," she said. "We'll have an X-ray anyhow as soon as you can be moved. How on earth did it happen?"

I told her, but I did not mention the body I had fallen on, or the ladder. But that night I told Tony. He sat beside the bed, and I related the whole story. He was incredulous at first. He said the elevator people had left the elevator up and the power cut off; that the door to it was partly open, but that they had put a heavy hall chair in front of it and a sign to keep out.

"They weren't there last night, Tony."

"You're sure of that?"

"Positive."

He drew a long breath. "Well, thank God you're all right," he said. "See here, Pat, are you absolutely sure you fell on somebody?" he asked. "After all, with a fall like that—"

"It grunted. And it moved. I never heard of a cellar floor doing that."

"And what about this ladder business? Sure of that too?"

"I tried to pull myself up by it. Then I must have fainted again. When I came to it was gone."

He sent for Jim Conway after that. I had to repeat the story to him, and he seemed to find part of it highly diverting.

"Even money we'll find it was one of Bessie's crowd," he said. "The men had been carrying liquor from the cellar down to the playhouse, and they probably left the door open. Some drunk came along and wandered in. How does that sound?"

"It would be a lot funnier if someone wasn't making a habit of breaking into this house," I said crossly.

"Well, after this let Roger attend to his own troubles, especially at night," he told me, and went away.

I know now that both Jim and Tony were deliberately making light of the affair that day. At the time, of course, it merely made me indignant. For one or two things came to light which bore out part of my story. Stevens admitted that the areaway door to the basement under the west wing had been standing open when he found me. There were indications that a car had been driven across the grass inside the gates and parked there behind the shrubbery. And Maud, interrogated by Tony, came out with a curious small incident which was to be more important than it seemed at the time.

Like myself, she had been unable to sleep, and just before I started downstairs with Roger the house telephone rang beside her bed. She had thought it was Bessie, calling from the playhouse, but when she answered it there was no one on the wire.

Bessie sulkily denied using the phone at all. "I had better

things to do," she said. "Why on earth would I call her, day or night?"

I had rather a pleasant day or two after that, what with Maud fussing over me and Tony spending a brotherly hour or so with me before dinner every evening. Also my rooms were full of flowers. The Hill people had sent a lot of them, and so had the valley. Amy said the place looked like a first-class funeral parlor, but was secretly proud.

"Good heavens!" she would say dramatically when Thomas or Stevens brought up more boxes. "I wasn't hired to take care of a greenhouse."

My ankle steadily improved. Once a day Bill Sterling came in to change the bandages. He was determinedly cheerful, but he looked wretched, his ugly attractive face drawn and his eyes showing a lack of sleep. One evening he sent Amy out of the room on an errand and sat back, eyeing me.

"See here, Pat," he said. "What's it all about, anyhow?"

"You know as much as I do, Bill."

"I'm not sure I do. What's Bessie doing here? What happened to Maud Wainwright last month? She'd had a shock of some sort. All that talk about the heat was pure poppycock. And what's the matter with Tony? He looks as though he'd seen a ghost."

Well, he looked that way himself. I had no answers for him, although I did say that when Bessie first came Maud had thought she had come about money. He shook his head.

"These people don't worry about money," he said. "It's something else."

He did not mention Lydia, of course, and Amy was indignant when he left. She has cherished an open passion for him for years. "These people who nurse hopeless love affairs and do nothing about them!" she said. "Why doesn't he kill Don Morgan? It would be easy enough."

"How about yourself? You're crazy about him, but you haven't killed Lydia!"

"That doesn't mean I haven't thought about it," she said darkly. "Turn over and let me rub your back."

Once or twice during that period Bessie wandered in. She would find my door open and see me propped up in bed with Maud's pale rose and blue pillows behind me, and she would stand over me, making perfunctory inquiries about my foot. Her real interest was not in me, however. She questioned me repeatedly about my accident, as if she thought I had not told all the truth. "You must have pushed the chair away," she said. "It was there earlier. I saw it myself."

"I didn't. It wasn't there."

After she had done this more than once I began to wonder if she herself had moved the chair. It was ridiculous, of course. How could she have known that Roger would want to go out in the night? Or for that matter, why would she want to hurt or kill me? She was hard enough, God knows, but I had never thought her deliberately cruel. But she was certainly uneasy. It was as though something had happened to upset her careful calculations, and she was as puzzled as I was. Indeed, on her second visit she put that into words. "Did you really fall on somebody?" she said. "Or did you put that in to make it harder?"

"Why should I? I wasn't trying to make a good story of it."

"You didn't see who it was?" she asked, watching me intently.

"I fainted. That's all I know."

"You weren't in a faint all night."

Amy heard this from my sitting room and came in, with a hard glint in her eyes. For some reason she had hated Bessie from the first moment she came. Now she sent her out and slammed my door viciously behind her.

"I'm going to keep that damned little troublemaker out of here if it's the last thing I do," she sputtered. "What's wrong with her anyhow? What's she snooping around for? I'll bet she's playing some dirty little game of her own."

Which as I look back was a mild term for the sort of game Bessie Wainwright was playing and was to play for some time to come.

I had my bad times. Tony, since the night at the playhouse, had been friendly but remote. He would sit by my bed, talking of inconsequential things or even lapsing into long silences. I wondered if he was drinking, and one night I was sure of it. He fell asleep in his chair, and Amy could hardly rouse him to get him out of it. When she came back I was wiping my eyes. She gave me a sharp look.

"Don't be a sissy," she said. "Let him forget that wife of his now and then. What else do you want him to do? Go and have a good cry?"

He did not do it again, and outside of Bessie's visits my convalescence was undisturbed. Flowers and notes poured in, and on the fourth day, a Friday, an enormous box of roses came from Don Morgan, with a card evidently in his own handwriting: *Do get well soon, my dear, Lydia misses you.*

I was rather touched, but Amy was furious.

"Like him, isn't it?" she said. "Probably called up and ordered them, and Lydia will pay the bill. What a fool she was anyhow, taking him back and nursing him. Nursing him! He'll outlive her for years. His kind go on forever."

She was wrong. Don Morgan did not go on forever. He had even then only a few more hours to live.

It was on Saturday that Maud gave her first dinner since her illness; only a dozen people or so, but it cheered everybody immensely. She looked pleased when she told me about it. "Tony is going to the club," she said. "He hates bridge. I don't know about Bessie. She usually makes her own plans."

And Bessie did. A breathless Amy, gazing out the window that evening, reported them to me.

"Well, can you beat that," she said. "Your boy friend was driving off when little poison ivy ran out and got into his car. All dressed up too. Better get that leg well in a hurry, Pat. She looks as though she's out for blood."

I lay back. There was nothing I could do about Tony, or Bessie either. Downstairs I could picture what was going on; Pierre shouting French at the kitchenmaids, the house gay with lights and flowers, and cars coming and going. I could hear the sharp slap of their doors as Gus closed them, and I was feeling rather sorry for myself when Margery Stoddard came up.

"I have only a minute," she said. "I'm so sorry, Pat. It looks queer downstairs without you."

I raised up on one elbow. "That's a lovely dress," I told her. "But you're thinner, aren't you?"

"Me? I'm always thin. But I've got a rotten headache. I'll slip off early if I can."

Actually she looked feverish. She never used rouge, but that night she had a bright spot of color on each cheek. Amy looked after her when she left.

"If I were to keep count of the worried-looking people I've seen around here since I came," she announced pontifically, "I

wouldn't have enough fingers. What's the matter with everybody?"

That was on Saturday, September the twenty-third of last
year.

So far as I know there had been nothing to indicate that tragedy was in the making. The Hill had turned from golf to hunting, the weather had been dry for weeks so that already the leaves
were falling, and down in the valley Don Morgan had improved,
had even taken to walking around the grounds and to sitting in
the sun on the bench which faced out over the river. Amy said
she had seen him once on the street, looking handsome and well
dressed, but making a great show of being a sick man. "Using a
stick to lean on!" she said. "A gold and malacca one, too. Trust
old Don to have a gold and malacca cane. And Audrey beside
him, holding his elbow. That brat makes me sick."

The first warning I had was when Lydia called me up shortly
before twelve o'clock that night. Amy was asleep by that time in
the next room, but the door was closed.

"Did I waken you, Pat?" Lydia asked.

"No. There was a small dinner here tonight, and some of the
die-hards are just leaving."

"Is Tony there?"

"I don't think he's back. He had dinner at the country club.
What is it, Lydia?"

She lowered her voice. "I'm terribly worried," she said. "I don't
want Audrey to hear me. Pat, Don's not in his room."

"Maybe he couldn't sleep and took a walk."

"I've been out. Anyhow he was in his pajamas. He couldn't go
far like that. Pat, do you think—He's been downhearted the past
few days, and with the river right here—"

"Don't be foolish. He'd never do that. Look here, I think Bill Sterling's still here. He filled in for Margery at bridge after he saw me tonight. Let me send him down."

She refused that. She said she would wait an hour or so before doing anything, and rang off. But I could not sleep. Just about midnight the party below broke up. I could hear the cars drive up and move on, and some time later Maud coming up the stairs. At something after one Bessie came home from the club in the car, and I hobbled to the window to see her coming alone from the garage, and to wonder where Tony was. Then at half past one he wandered in on foot from the direction of the golf course. He was bareheaded and apparently weary. I saw him stop and look up at the house, but as my light was out he did not see me.

At two o'clock Lydia called again. Don had not come back. His clothes were all there, but his overcoat was gone. And she had been to the garage. Her car was missing.

She had already notified Jim Conway. He was there now, and the patrol car was out looking for Don. "Although with all these roads—" she said helplessly. She seemed relieved in one way, however. The car showed that he had not gone to the river, and there was the possibility that he had simply been sleepless and taken a ride.

Nevertheless, I roused Amy, and she went down to spend the rest of the night with Lydia. "Not that I care a damn about Don Morgan," she said, "but I'm sorry for her. It would be a good thing for her if he never showed up again."

I have always been glad that I did that; sent Amy, I mean. For she was there when word came that they had found Donald Morgan's body at daylight on Sunday morning, lying in a ditch beside a road leading back from the far end of the valley into the hills. He had been dead for hours.

CHAPTER ELEVEN

MAUD BROUGHT me the first news, coming in in her nightgown and a negligee, with her long braid down her back. All she knew, however, was the mere fact that he had been discovered.

"I suppose it will be hard on Lydia," she said, helping herself to a second cup of coffee from my tray. "She will blame herself, although I don't see why. If he had heart trouble he might go any time. Of course, she may still have cared for him." She sighed. "The curse God put on women was not the pain of childbearing, Pat. He simply gave them faithful hearts and let them alone."

The only fact we had that morning was that Don had been found dead beside a road. The further details only reached us at noon when Tony came back from the club, where I gathered that a sort of neighborhood court of inquiry had sat during the morning.

The facts were strange enough, however. Poor old Don, so worthless and so gallant, so careful of his appearance too, had been found face down in a ditch, clad only in a pair of blue silk pajamas. To add to the mystery, Lydia's car was nowhere about, and that he had not left it and walked to where he was discovered was evident. He wore only one bedroom slipper, and the other foot showed no signs of having walked any distance at all.

The patrol car had found him at seven o'clock in the morning. They had almost missed him, as the ditch was well overgrown. But one of the men caught a flash of blue, stopped the car and got out. He stepped down into the ditch and parted the weeds. Then he straightened.

"He's here, Nick," he called. "Guess it's all over. The poor devil's dead."

Nick got out, and the two men surveyed the body. They knew better than to touch anything, although one of them lifted an arm. "Dead for hours," he said. "I'll stay here. Better telephone the chief."

There was a desk sergeant on duty, but he had obviously been asleep. He roused when he got the message, however. "Dead? How?" he inquired. "Hit and run?"

"Looks like he had a heart attack," said the officer. "Get the chief, will you?"

He gave the location, and a half hour later Jim Conway drew up with a squealing of brakes. He had brought Bill Sterling with him, and Bill had grabbed his case and filled a hypodermic on the way out. But he needed only a look to tell him that Don was gone again, this time to a far distance.

"Dead," he said. "Looks as though he'd been here all night."

"What killed him? Any idea?"

"He said he had a bad heart," said Bill curtly. "I never examined him. All right if I turn him over?"

Jim nodded. This was not the city with a homicide squad all ready for fingerprint men and photographers; and also there was still no suspicion of foul play. Certainly there was no blood in sight.

"Poor devil," said Nick, helping to roll him over. "Say, Chief, I thought he was wearing an overcoat."

"So Mrs. Morgan said," Jim replied. "Look around and see if it's here. There's a slipper missing too."

But it was neither overcoat nor slipper that made Bill Sterling and Jim, after turning over the body, stare at each other. The pajamas were soaking wet. They had dried somewhat on the back, and any moisture there might have been the heavy dew. Rolled over, there was no question about what had happened. The body had been in the water somewhere. Jim was stunned.

"Looks as though he'd jumped in the river," he said. "Lydia was afraid of that. May have done it and changed his mind."

"And then walked a mile with one slipper gone and had a heart attack!" said Bill gruffly. "Use your head, Jim."

"What do you mean?"

"If he's been drowned he's been murdered. I think he's been murdered anyhow."

That, of course, changed everything. Before he left Beverly, Jim had ordered the ambulance, and it arrived soon after. But he did not let them move the body. He sent word to the coroner's office, and to the village for his camera. He had taken half a dozen pictures before the coroner arrived.

In the meantime the two patrolmen examined the neighborhood. The road was the one which had once led up to the George Washington Spring, but the body was only a short distance from the main highway. At this point the valley widened, and it was a mile or more to the river. The patrolmen found nothing. The weather had been dry, and the road, little more than a lane, showed no tire marks.

But Jim had noticed one thing, although he had kept it to himself. When the body was turned over he saw that a button had been torn from the coat of the pajamas. He did not mention this, but he made an exhaustive search for it, going down on his knees and examining the ditch thoroughly. After that he walked about with his head down, looking, as he said later, for God knew what. "I had to go through the motions," was the way he put it. "I had to find a button, a car, an overcoat, and a slipper; and I had to figure out what a man like Don Morgan was doing back there on that road in his pajamas. You know what he was like, Pat. Used to wear gloves and spats. I'd seen him a thousand times when I was a kid. Yet there he was, as if he had just gotten out of bed."

When the coroner came, however, he found something Jim had missed. Don had been struck on the back of the head. The injury was there, under that heavy hair of his; not enough to kill him, but enough to knock him out. He also found some bruises on the body, old ones, and seemed puzzled about them.

But he was sure that it was murder, although he refused to commit himself until after the autopsy. All this time Bill Sterling was standing by, and with the coroner's dry comment Jim looked at him. It was the first time, he said later, that he realized Don's death would be a happy release to several people. And that one of them was Bill Sterling himself.

"After all, he'd hated Don's guts," he said inelegantly. "He didn't even pretend to be sorry. He looked uneasy, but that's about all."

However that may be, the body having been taken away and the two men driving back to the village, Jim made a stab at the facts.

"I don't suppose Lydia Morgan will grieve a lot," he said. "She did the decent thing, but after all, what was he to her?"

He felt Bill stiffen beside him. "Keep Lydia out of this," Bill said curtly. "It has nothing to do with her."

Jim dropped Bill at the local hospital, where Don's body already lay in the mortuary, ready for the autopsy. After that he had a busy morning. First of all he set out to locate Lydia's car, putting Cracker Brown to work on the police radio in case it had been driven far, and himself telephoning up and down the river boroughs. But he had a strong hunch, as he put it, that the car was not far away.

"It looked like a local job to me," he said. "Somebody who would leave it within walking distance of town, or the Hill. That's what I went on anyhow."

He himself still believed Don had been in the river. He sent the police car into the hills and took the valley himself, investigating every lane and street leading to the water front. Lydia's car was not to be found, however, and at one o'clock he threw the stream overboard, so to speak, and went home to lunch.

The patrol car had been equally unlucky. It was Sunday, and the back roads and lanes were filled with cars, many of them parked for a family picnic. Then at three o'clock with the coroner's verdict that Don had died by drowning before Jim on his desk and Cracker Brown in the radio room self-importantly eating a ham sandwich, Julian Stoddard called the police station.

"One of my men has found an abandoned car in the ravine below my house, Mr. Conway," he said. "I understand you're looking for one."

"I'll be there," said Jim. "If I had a feather I'd fly."

Julian did not think that funny. He was a reserved man, careful of his dignity. "If you will come to my place I will show it to you," he said coldly, and hung up the receiver.

It was Lydia's car. It had been driven along a wood road into a deep ravine behind the Stoddard house, and carefully hidden. The gardener who had found it was still on guard when Jim and Mr. Stoddard reached it. He had a small rifle with him and he claimed to have touched nothing.

"I was looking for the skunks that have been cutting up the lawn," he explained. "Nasty little devils they are. I came down the hill, because I've seen one or two down here. Then I saw the car. I think there's a coat of some sort in it."

The car was not locked and, using a handkerchief, Jim opened the door. Don's overcoat was there, a light-brown one with the name of an English tailor in it. It was still wet, and so was the rug on the floor at the back. There was no sign of the slipper or of the button.

Julian Stoddard stood by, looking formal and detached as usual. Also he looked annoyed.

"I hope this doesn't get into the papers," he said. "I don't want photographers and reporters overrunning my place."

"Afraid it can't be helped, Mr. Stoddard," Jim told him. "I understand they're running a special train from town for them! We'll move the car after it's been gone over for prints. That's the best I can do."

It was on the way back up the hill that something occurred to Jim. "You've got a swimming pool around somewhere, haven't you?"

"I have. Why?"

"I'd like to take a look at it."

"Good God, you don't believe Don Morgan was in my pool!"

"Well, look at it," said Jim reasonably. "You know the story. It's all over the place. Morgan had been in water somewhere.

Then here's his car, or his wife's. Something wet has been in it, and it's not far down this hill to the car."

"It's ridiculous. Why my pool? There are a dozen on the Hill, not counting the one at the club."

He was indignant. He was one of the most important men in the community, and here was this amateur policeman trying to mix him up with a possible murder. Nevertheless, he led Jim to the pool and stood by while he surveyed it. It was clear enough at the shallow end, but at the deep one the bottom was not visible.

"I'll have to ask you not to empty it until we've searched it," Jim said, in his best authoritative manner. "I wouldn't use it either, Mr. Stoddard."

"My little girls have some children coming this afternoon to swim."

"Sorry," said Jim. "They'll have to play tiddly winks or something." And seeing Julian's face: "If necessary I'll put a man on guard. I don't want it disturbed until I've had it examined; and I may have to empty it. You'd better have someone on hand to do it."

He left on that, and half an hour later Julian had the doubtful pleasure of seeing an old Ford drive in, park itself on his handsome driveway, and a man in plain and certainly not handsome attire settle himself on a bench beside the pool and light a pipe.

By four o'clock that afternoon every pool in the district was similarly guarded, including our own in the playhouse. For by that time the result of the autopsy had been made public. Donald Morgan had died by drowning. There was water in his lungs, and his body being found as it was, the presumption was certainly murder.

It was Tony who brought us this last news. Bessie had not appeared, having sent word she was resting, and Maud and I had passed the long hours together in my room. Tony had called us when the body was found; then he joined the group of unofficial searchers who were helping the police to look for Lydia's car. Where he was when he telephoned the verdict that Don had been murdered I do not know.

"Probably knocked out first and then dropped into somebody's pool to drown," he said. "That's Conway's idea, anyhow. Gruesome thought, isn't it?"

He came back soon after that, looking tired. He had had no lunch, and Maud sent for some. I had managed to get downstairs by that time, with the aid of Thomas and Stevens, and we were in the court when he came. I remember how peaceful it was there that day, the water from the fountain dripping softly, Maud concerned for Lydia but otherwise welcoming the peace of Bessie's absence, and Tony eating hungrily while he talked.

I even remember getting up and walking a few steps to show the extent of my recovery. Then Reynolds came in to announce the arrival of a guard to watch our pool, and suddenly the whole tragedy was close to us.

"Our pool!" Maud said. "But the playhouse is always locked. Did you tell him that?"

Reynolds looked uncomfortable. "I'm sorry, madam. I found it unlocked just now. It has been used recently. There are damp towels around. I thought perhaps Mr. Tony had been using it."

Tony glanced up quickly. "Haven't been near it for days, Reynolds."

Maud looked unhappy. "What do you mean by used, Reynolds? Not—the pool."

"I'm afraid it is the pool, madam. There is water on the tiles. The guard is telephoning Mr. Conway from the library."

So there we were, tied up with poor Don's murder in spite of ourselves. I don't think any of us moved for a minute or two. Reynolds was standing by looking important, and filled with that peculiar repressed pleasure with which all servants seem to bring bad news. Then Maud stirred and Tony was on his feet.

"Don't worry, Mother," he said. "It doesn't mean a thing. Maybe Bessie was down there."

But Bessie had not been there. She appeared just then, and Maud told her the whole story. I think none of us were prepared for the way she took it. She turned a sort of greenish-white and dropped into a chair.

"I'm sorry," she said, her lips stiff. "I haven't been well today. It's a shock. Any murder is a shock, isn't it?"

Tony was watching her.

"Did you happen to know him?" he asked her.

"Know him? Of course not. He's been gone for years, hasn't he?" She had recovered somewhat. She picked up her vanity case and examined her face. "What's this about the pool in the play-house?" she inquired.

"There's a chance that he was drowned in it," said Tony dryly.

Maud got up then. "We'd better go there," she said. "It can't be true, but I must see for myself."

They went out by the west door, and on the way Tony looked inside the table drawer. The key to the playhouse was there as usual, and he looked bewildered.

Jim Conway arrived before they had reached the building. He had two men in the car with him, and he was immediately followed by a car which I learned later was filled with reporters.

They trailed close on his heels, but at the fountain he stopped them. They seemed to argue with him, but one of his men remained behind to watch them while he went on. After that they stayed where they were, obviously irritated. Then, I suppose with the usual acceptance of the inevitable, they lit cigarettes and waited.

I was standing in the doorway of the west wing while this was going on, and I was still there perhaps a quarter of an hour later when Maud came slowly back alone across the lawn, looking pale and worried.

"They're going to search the pool," she said. "Jim Conway is looking for something, I don't know what. He's got an officer in it now, diving. That's why I had to leave." She stood still for a moment, looking haggard in the strong afternoon light. "What on earth do you suppose it is, Pat?"

"I wouldn't worry about it. Come in and have a glass of sherry."

She shook her head. "He's going to drain the pool too. He wants a piece of wire screening. I suppose Reynolds can find some. Pat, do you think we may have a lunatic around? When you think of Evans, and now this—"

But she did come in and the sherry picked her up. I went upstairs with her, using the elevator—which now worked perfectly—and from a window in her bedroom both of us saw Reynolds carrying what looked like an entire window screen and a heavy pair of shears across the lawn. He did not come back, nor did the group by the fountain move. They smoked and talked, but always they faced toward the playhouse, as wary as good hounds on a scent. It was almost dark when at last Jim Conway and Tony came into view again. The floodlight was on the fountain and I saw Jim stop there. He was carrying what looked like a bath towel rolled around something, and he stopped to speak to the reporters.

I know now what he told them. He said it briefly and went on: "I'm making no positive statement. It is still too soon for that. All I can say, at this moment, is that from certain evidence discovered, I believe Mr. Donald Morgan came to his death in the pool here."

They crowded around him, expostulating. They wanted to see the pool, to know what he carried, what the evidence was. When it was clear that they could do none of these things, they broke for their car, and Tony came toward the house looking grave and unhappy.

He and Maud had a long conference before dinner that evening. It ended by his sending for Dwight Elliott, and asking him to meet him at once in the police station in the village; for by that time there was no longer any doubt as to where Donald Morgan had died, or how.

Bill Sterling was being interrogated down in Jim Conway's office, and there was a sodden slipper and a large pearl button on the desk in front of him.

CHAPTER TWELVE

IT WAS totally informal, that interrogation. It might have been a talk between two men, acquainted if not actually friends. Jim said further on in the case that he had no idea how far his authority went, and that Bill Sterling did not seem to care.

Bill said at once that he had no alibi.

"I didn't kill him," he said. "I thought he was a dirty scoundrel. For that matter I still think so. He walked out on Lydia years ago. Then when he got sick—and I doubt that sickness of his; his heart was all right at the inquest—he came back. Find out why he came back and you'll know something."

"Perhaps. You needn't emphasize how you felt toward him, Bill. It's understandable, but it might be—well, unfortunate."

"Meaning I may be guilty. Well, I'm no fool, Conway. If I'd meant to do away with him, I know a dozen ways, not only easier but less dangerous. Any medical man does. And certainly I'd have had an alibi, and I haven't."

"You didn't have a quarrel with him?"

"I've never laid eyes on him but once. Then he was taking a walk, with Audrey holding him up. Holding him up! You saw him today. Do you think he was feeble?"

Jim grinned at that. "I suppose you're set on making a case against yourself," he said. "Suppose we do this thing according to Hoyle for a change. Where were you last night, for example?"

"You know that. I went up to see Pat Abbott at the Cloisters. There had been a dinner there, and Mrs. Stoddard left early. I filled her place at bridge, and if you want all the details, I lost exactly eleven dollars."

"When did you leave?"

"Around twelve o'clock."

"Then what?"

"The usual story. I wasn't sleepy, so I drove around a bit."

"Where was that, Bill? Where did you go?"

"Over the hills. It was a nice night. I was on the Beaver Creek Road, where that lane turns off below the Stoddard place, for one thing," he added truculently. "Make something of that if you can."

He had been clear enough so far, angry and aggressive. But after that things did not go so well. Asked if he had seen Lydia's car at any time, he denied it, but with less conviction. Indeed, his whole manner changed. From indignant belligerence he became cautious. Asked about the playhouse at the Cloisters, he said he had been in it only once or twice in his life, to play indoor tennis with Tony. Of course, he had no key to the place. What the hell would he want with such a key? He had his keys with him. There they were. Look them over.

They were still there an hour later when Tony and Dwight Elliott were admitted. The questioning had gone on endlessly.

"Tell me this, Bill. How long would it take a man to drown if he was knocked out first?"

"Not very long, if he couldn't put up a fight. Quite a while if he could. And if you had a pulmotor handy and tried to revive him—"

"Well, nobody tried to revive Morgan," Jim said, and smiled. "See here, Bill, how well did you know Evans, the night watchman at the Cloisters?"

"I've seen him about. I didn't know him at all until he was hurt. I've taken care of him since." Then the import of that question dawned on him. He looked thoughtful. "I see. I knocked out Evans to take his keys. Then I—"

"How did you know Evans's keys were taken, Bill?"

"Tony Wainwright told me, when Pat Abbott fell down the elevator shaft. We looked the place over that morning."

But the mention of keys had drawn Jim's eyes back to the desk. He had picked up Bill's key ring when Tony and Dwight Elliott appeared, and he still held it in his hands.

"We're discussing the keys to your playhouse," he said to Tony. "I suppose you would know one if you saw it?"

"I would. I'm damn sure Bill Sterling never had one, if that's what you mean."

But Bill was staring at the keys as if he had never seen them before. "Look here," he said thickly. "One of those isn't mine. I only carry four. There are five on that ring." He jerked them out of Jim's hands and held them up. "Look," he said. "Two car keys, office door, house door. What's the other one?"

It needed only one look at Tony's face to identify it. It was Evans's key to the playhouse.

They were all stunned, apparently, after Tony's nod of identification. Even Dwight Elliott had nothing to say, although later on he was to protest that Jim had gone beyond his authority that day; that there was nothing against Bill then but his hatred of Don, and no reason for questioning him. Until, of course, the key turned up. And that was purely fortuitous. Would any guilty man in his senses produce that key as Bill had done? No. A thousand times no.

Jim Conway must have looked very grave that late Sunday afternoon, with the September sun shining into his tidy office and those three men confronting him. Certainly he was puzzled.

"I didn't know what the hell to do next," he said to me later. "I couldn't see old Bill as a killer, and a nasty one at that. And why would he throw those keys at me, if he were?"

Bill was the first to speak that day. He put the keys quietly down on the desk.

"Well," he said. "I suppose you'll have to hold me, Jim. You won't want to do it, but there you are."

"Any idea how the key got there?"

"Not the slightest. I leave them in the car pretty generally when I'm making my calls. Half the valley and most of the Hill could have done it."

"You hadn't noticed it at all?"

"Do you suppose I would have left it there if I had? No. I suppose a man takes his keys pretty much for granted, and that's a small one. We might check the time, approximately. I left the car and keys at Tim Murphy's on Friday, to have the carbon cleaned out of the cylinders. Tim might remember how many there were."

They called Tim. He was out in his yard taking a Sunday rest, and it took some time to get him to the phone. When he came he corroborated Bill's story. There had been only four keys on the ring.

"I noticed, because his house keys were there. I had to get the car back before night, in case he needed them."

So at some time, if Bill's story was correct, between Friday evening and that Sunday afternoon, Evans's key to the playhouse at the Cloisters had been placed on Bill's ring. Dwight Elliott, quiet up to that time, had a suggestion to offer.

"This man Morgan," he said. "Was he really a sick man? Was there any way he could have gotten hold of that key?"

"What's the idea?"

"Well, it's rather crude. I'm feeling my way. Could he, for instance, have been the one who knocked out Evans and took his keys?"

"Why on earth should he? He had his faults, but he wasn't a highwayman. Anyhow I don't think he had come back when that occurred. He hadn't, as a matter of fact."

Tony had recovered somewhat. It might have been amusing if it had not been so grave, those three men there with Bill, and all of them jumping at straws to prove his innocence. Anyhow Tony took his turn at it.

"There's a duplicate key, of course," he said. "It's kept in the house."

"Where?"

"In a table drawer in a side hall. The men use it to clear the place in the morning. Then it's brought back. The playhouse is out of sight of the house, behind shrubbery, so it's usually kept locked. Anyone who wants to use it knows where to find it. The key, I mean."

"Where is it now?"

"It's still there. Of course, it could have been put back," said Tony stubbornly. "Everybody knew where it was kept."

But none of them believed that, although Jim took it up at once. "What about your household, Tony? The servants, of course. Anybody there have a grudge against Morgan?"

"He's been gone for fifteen years," said Tony stiffly. "That's a long time to carry what you call a grudge. As for my mother and my wife, they didn't even know him. I imagine that eliminates them."

"I wasn't thinking of them," Jim said shortly. "No woman could have done it anyhow. He was a big man. As Bill Sterling says, he looked like a healthy man. And that body was handled. It was put in the pool and then taken out again. After that it had to be carried or dragged to a car and placed in it. It was a man's job. Maybe two men."

They were silent for some time. Bill had relaxed somewhat, and Jim was filling his pipe.

"You were present at the autopsy, Bill," he said. "What about those marks on the body?"

"One or two old bruises on his back. A bruise on his forehead where he was probably stunned. But there was one odd thing: the scar on his chest."

Jim looked up. "What about it?"

"He always claimed to have been struck by a piece of shrapnel during the war. You've probably seen it, Jim. He used to bathe in the club pool. I don't happen to think it was shrapnel, that's all. It looks to me—and the coroner says so too—as if it was only skin-deep."

"And what would that mean?"

For almost the first time that day Bill Sterling smiled.

"You never knew Don well, did you? You were pretty young when he left. Well, he was a great one for women. Rather more than that; and this looks as if he'd had a girl's name tattooed across his chest at some time or other. Then it became embarrassing, so he had it cut out."

"Must have been a kid when it was done. It's a kid trick."

"Probably. There's a long vertical cut, and a transverse one from it, as if the first letter of the name had a loop to it below the line. It might have been a J. Not many letters have a loop, especially in script." He hesitated. "There's something else too, Jim. Those bruises on his back. How do you think he got them? I've asked Lydia. She doesn't know about them. She says he hasn't fallen since he came home. He spent most of his time in bed or in a chair."

"What do *you* think?"

"I was wondering if he was the man Pat fell on, the night she dropped down the elevator shaft."

"Good Godamighty," said Jim, exasperated. "First he hits Evans and steals his pants and keys as well as his gun. Then he stands in the bottom of an elevator shaft and lets Pat Abbott fall on him. I didn't know much about Morgan, but what the hell would he be doing in the Cloisters? So far as I know he was never there in his life."

He got up. He was tired mentally and physically and showed it. "All right, Bill," he said. "Better go and make your calls. That's all for today."

"You're not holding me?"

"What on?" said Jim Conway, ungrammatically. "Maybe the district attorney will see something I don't. He's off somewhere for a weekend. Just now all I've got on you is that you didn't like Don Morgan and you haven't got an alibi. The key is out. There were two of them, and I don't think you're fool enough to hand that ring to me if you're guilty; or smart enough, if it comes to that." He smiled wryly. "I suppose I'm a hell of a police chief, but what I want just now is my dinner."

Bill seemed rather stunned when he left. Tony came home, as I have said, but Dwight Elliott stopped off at the hospital to see Evans. He was much better; up and down from his bed, his bandage a small one, and his appetite—the nurses reported—enormous. But he had still no light to shed on his attack. He maintained that he did not know who had struck him or who would want his keys.

But he was surly that day. He had heard about the murder, and he said Don's death was no loss to anybody, so far as he could see. Then he intimated that he would like to be alone, leaving Mr. Elliott puzzled and indignant.

"He's not like himself," he reported that night at dinner. "I've known him for years, but he didn't want to talk. I don't suppose he knew Morgan, did he?"

"Don't be ridiculous," Maud told him sharply. "He's old and just now he's feeble. Why would he kill Don Morgan? It's silly."

Curious, since the time was to come when even Evans was under suspicion. But then so was everybody else, including most of us at the Cloisters. In fact, something of that sort began that same night.

We were having coffee and liqueurs when Jim Conway was announced. We were all there: Maud, Bessie, Tony, Dwight Elliott, and myself. Bessie had been quiet through dinner, and I thought still looked pale under her make-up. Maud appeared worried but nothing more. But Tony was tired, and showed it.

"More detective business?" he said when he saw Jim. "Well, come in and have a drink. Whom are you suspecting now?"

"Everybody," said Jim cheerfully. "Morgan died at twelve o'clock or thereabouts last night. Maybe a little earlier. We don't know. Just now I want to talk to Pat Abbott."

"I suppose she hobbled out with that game ankle of hers and pulled off a crime to pass the time!"

"Well, somebody did it," said Jim, still amiable. "Now listen, Pat, you've insisted all along that when you fell down the elevator shaft you fell on somebody. I suppose you're sure of that?"

"I am."

"It wasn't by any chance the dog you hit?"

"Roger was inside by that time. He was whimpering in the hall over my head when I came to. Anyhow it was no dog."

Jim looked around at us, his genial face apologetic. "It's like this," he said. "I'm sorry to bring up anything unpleasant. The fact is, the autopsy today found some bruises on Morgan's back. They were only a few days old. Lydia knows nothing about them. If you fell on him—"

It was then that Bessie dropped her coffee cup. When order was restored Maud was still looking astounded.

"What would he be doing in this house?" she asked. "I never even saw the man."

"I'm not sure he was. All the same, he wasn't a sick man. If he took Lydia's car out last night he could have done it before. He might have had his own reasons for coming here before—well, before last night. You didn't know him, Mrs. Tony, did you?"

Bessie stared back at him. "No," she said. "How could I? And it's indecent, this bringing up one horror after another. I hate this house anyhow. It gives me the jitters. It always did. Now I can't even have a quiet evening. It makes me sick."

She slammed out of the room, leaving us wordless and uncomfortable. It was Maud as usual who took the situation in hand.

"I don't know that I blame her," she said calmly. "I've felt like shrieking my head off all day. I'll send Hilda to see if she is all right. Now, Mr. Conway, what can we do for you?"

What we could do was simple enough on the surface. He

wanted the details of the dinner the night before, the list of guests, when they left, and so on. I have that list before me now. Of the people immediately concerned, most had left shortly before midnight. Bill Sterling had remained a few minutes, talking to Maud on the terrace about her condition. It had been exactly twelve when he left. Everyone had gone in cars except Julian Stoddard, who had said he wanted a walk and would take the footpath home.

As for the rest of us, Tony and Bessie had been at the club, and I had been in my room. Jim looked over his list discontentedly.

"In other words, at least a dozen people were in the vicinity about the time Morgan was killed," he said. "Not counting the servants. Where were the cars the guests came in, Tony?"

"I wasn't here. The chauffeurs usually wait down by the garage."

"They were gone before midnight?"

"All but the doctor's," Maud said. "We talked on the terrace for a few minutes."

"You saw no lights in the playhouse?"

"You couldn't see the playhouse."

He was still interviewing the servants when I went up to bed. They came in, looking scared and virtually tongue-tied, but they had no information to give him. All of them insisted that they had not been near the playhouse, either the night before or at any time recently.

I watched Tony through most of that long interrogation. He drank three highballs that night in rapid succession. Then abruptly he left the room, and when I went upstairs I was surprised to see him coming out of the door to Bessie's sitting room. He looked puzzled and angry. When he saw me limping along he came over and took my arm, and I could feel that he was shaking. He followed me into my room.

"Let me stay a minute, Pat," he said. "I need to get quiet, or I'll go out and kill somebody myself. Do you mind if I talk? I've either got to talk or get drunk. Maybe both."

At first, however, he seemed to have nothing to say. He lit a cigarette and began to pace the floor, his hands in his pockets, his head bent. When he did speak his voice was thick.

"What does Bessie know about all this, Pat?" he said. "She knows something, or suspects something."

"I think she suspects somebody. I wouldn't let it bother me, Tony. It's rather foolish, really. What can she know?"

I put a match to the fire and got him to sit down in a big chair beside it. He leaned his head back and closed his eyes.

"If I didn't know better," he said, "I'd say she suspects me! Good God, the only time I ever saw Morgan I liked the fellow."

He did not stay long, nor had he much more to say. He got up and yawned, as though he was physically exhausted.

"Sorry, Pat," he said. "I didn't mean to bother you. It's not important. Go to bed and get some sleep. You look all in."

But I suppose nobody slept much at the Cloisters that night. Amy called me rather late and I had the impression that someone was listening in on the telephone. The message was unimportant. She said that Lydia was bearing up well, but that Audrey was having what Amy called a fit.

"I stood all I could. Then I doped her to the eyes."

I gathered that Audrey had been dramatizing herself as usual, and that Amy was fed up with her. But aware of that listener I said little.

I had only settled myself in bed again when Bessie came in. I remember the light shining on that ash-blond hair of hers, and on the blue satin house gown she was wearing. But when she sat down and took a cigarette from my box I saw that her face, cleaned for the night, looked colorless and almost old. For the first time I wondered about her age, whether she was older than Tony.

"I'm sorry about tonight," she said. "I suppose I'm tired, and this thing about the pool—" She shivered. "Only a few nights ago we were all swimming there. Who would have believed—" She let that go, and looked thoughtfully at her cigarette.

"What do you make of it, Pat?" she asked.

"Not a thing. Of course, Bill Sterling didn't do it."

"There might be other people who would want him out of the way." She glanced at me. "I rather think there are."

I sat up in bed and stared at her. "You sound as if you knew him. Or knew something about him."

She considered that, her eyes cold and calculating. "I don't think so. Of course, I know a lot of people. I met a man named Morgan years ago in Paris, but it's a common name."

I did not believe her. I felt confident that she had known Don Morgan and known him well, and that she was leaving herself a way out if it was discovered. But she dismissed that with a gesture.

"I thought I'd give you a word of advice," she said smoothly. "Keep out of things that don't concern you; and keep my husband out of your room. It doesn't look well."

She got up and stubbed out her cigarette. "You look very nice lying there," she said. "Very pretty and wholesome. One of the golfing and riding girls, aren't you? But if I were you I wouldn't dream any dreams about Tony Wainwright. I can crush him flat any minute I want to."

CHAPTER THIRTEEN

WE ALMOST lost Maud the next morning. I had been hours in getting to sleep after that visit of Bessie's, and I did not rouse until Nora brought in my breakfast tray and a rather puzzling piece of news. The pool at the Stoddard place, she said, had been emptied during the night, and Julian Stoddard was raving all over the place.

"He's had all the men up, miss," she said. "They deny it, but somebody did it."

I lay back and thought. Nobody outside of the police and the men gathered in Jim Conway's office the day before had known positively where the button and the slipper had been found. True, Jim had taken all the guards away from the other pools, but not until late in the day. But why drain the Stoddard pool at all? The murderer knew he had used our playhouse, and an innocent person would have no object in doing it.

That was to remain a puzzle for a long time. "Every time I thought I was on my way," Jim was to say later, "that damned pool of the Stoddards' got up and hit me in the head."

But I was to have other things to think about that day. So far Maud had taken the affair as might be expected. She was shocked, especially that the murder had taken place where it did. She was sorry for Lydia and had sent her masses of flowers from the conservatory. She had even considered asking Audrey to the Cloisters at least until the funeral was over. But she had never really recovered from her early illness in August. She would start for a walk around the place, only to turn back in ten minutes or so.

"I must be getting old," she would say. "Go on, Pat. I'll rest a little and go back."

And that morning she finally collapsed.

I was still in my room when, about ten o'clock, Hilda came running in looking as though her world had dropped from under her.

"Please hurry, Miss Pat, Mrs. Wainwright has fainted."

I went over as I was, pulling on a dressing gown as I ran but not bothering with slippers. Maud was on the floor of her bathroom, that famous marble room with the sunken tub and the gold-plated fixtures. She lay flat, but she was conscious. She looked up at me from a face as white as chalk.

"Don't tell Tony," she whispered. "Get me out of here first."

She was partially dressed, but she was shivering as if with a chill. I found some aromatic ammonia and gave it to her while Hilda slipped a pillow under her head. But she would not let us call Tony or Bill Sterling until we had gotten her back into her bed. I held her on the side of it while Hilda undressed her and slipped a nightgown over her head. I think she was barely conscious, and once in bed she collapsed entirely.

We got Tony then. He looked desperate and helpless, as any man does in the presence of sickness. He stood looking down at her, his face almost as white as hers.

"What happened?" he asked. "She was all right last night."

"She was all right this morning," said Hilda tearfully. "She ate a good breakfast, and looked over her mail and the papers. Then she took a bath and I dressed her, or partly. I left her to get something I had pressed, and when I came back she was on the bathroom floor. I thought she was dead."

She burst into tears, and it was some time before she could answer our questions. No, she was certain the telephone had not rung, nor had Mrs. Wainwright had any bad news. The mail was there on the desk in the boudoir. There had been only four letters and after glancing at them Maud had told her to give them to me. "Invitations and bills," she had said. "Give them to Miss Pat, Hilda."

Tony looked at her suddenly.

"Has my wife been in, Hilda?"

"I don't think so. I don't think she's awake yet."

All this time we were waiting for Bill. Tony alternated from bed to window, Hilda moaned under her breath, and I stood by Maud's bed, feeling helpless. Once she opened her eyes, and I saw she wanted to say something. I stooped over the bed.

"Get Dwight," she said in a whisper. "Dwight," and slid off again into a stupor.

It was a bad day. Bill Sterling, looking as though he had been up all night, came up with an oxygen tank and mask which had to answer until the oxygen tent arrived from the hospital. He gave her a hypodermic at once. After that there was nothing to do but wait. Tony, deprived of cigarettes because the oxygen was inflammable, paced the floor. I dressed and came back. Amy Richards arrived and threw out Hilda, who was still hysterical. A heart specialist from the city drove up in a hurry, had a conference with Bill, and asked Tony if she had had a shock or been under a long strain. Tony said dryly that there had been some strain; his wife was staying in the house. The heart specialist nodded gravely, and later ate a hearty lunch.

That is all I remember of the morning. By afternoon Maud was better. Except for her lips, the blue look had gone, but she was still under the influence of morphia. She lay in a semistupor under the cellophane curtains of the oxygen tent, and it was evening and I was relieving Amy for her dinner when she opened her eyes and looked at me.

"What's this thing?" she whispered, indicating the tent. "And who's that man, Pat?"

I did not wonder. Her big bed had been moved out into the room to allow space for the large cylinders behind it; and as she spoke a strange man tiptoed into the room, to inspect the pressure and to pack ice into a tank to cool the oxygen.

"I wouldn't talk," I told her. "You fainted this morning. Bill Sterling thought you needed oxygen. That's all."

She seemed satisfied. She did not mention Dwight Elliott again, although he was in the house at the time. She closed her eyes, and this time she seemed to sleep normally. Nevertheless, we had had an anxious day. Bill slept in the house that first night, and two other nurses came to relieve Amy. I remember wandering around the house, feeling lost and forgotten, and it was a subdued Bessie who found me on the terrace long after dark.

She was quiet. In fact, I thought at the time that Maud's illness had been a real shock to her.

"What do the doctors say?" she asked. "Is she going to die?"

It was blunt but characteristic. Nobody ever accused Bessie of any particular delicacy.

"She's a little better," I said, "and she's a strong woman. That's all I know."

"All these nurses around, they scare the life out of me," she observed, and lapsed into silence. It must have been late when Tony found us there and openly accused her of causing his mother's collapse. It was not a nice scene. Both of them ignored me, and I think there was pure murder in Tony that night. But one thing I remember.

"You hated her," he said. "You've always hated us both. It wouldn't mean a thing to you if she died."

She gave him a sort of twisted smile.

"Believe it or not," she said, "that's the last thing I wanted. If I were you," she added, "I would be inventing an alibi for myself for Saturday night. You were pretty late getting back. Suppose I tell the police that?"

"Tell and be damned," he said furiously, and went back into the house.

They had held the inquest that day, Monday; of course, none of us had been present. Maud's condition had been too critical. But it was impossible to ignore what had happened. Early in the morning Jim Conway roped off the playhouse, and hour after hour I could see an officer in uniform patrolling it. Tony had ordered the chain put up across the entrance to the drive, but it did not prevent people from leaving their cars on the road and swarming in over the wall and through the shrubbery. It at least kept the house quiet, although there were times when the grounds looked almost like a garden party.

There were still reporters. They took pictures of everybody, and there was a graphic one in the papers that evening of Thomas carrying a lunch tray to the guard. Also one of the oxygen tanks being carried into the house, with the caption *Millionairess Succumbs to Shock*.

All in all it was pretty sickening, but Maud was at least holding her own. That was all that mattered to us then.

What I learned of the inquest I acquired largely from the papers; that the borough hall was jammed with "socialites," and that the testimony was filled with drama. I suppose it was, although the early portion brought out nothing new: the finding of the body, the approximate hour of death, the discovery of water in the lungs, and so on. There was much interest when the slipper and button were produced, and Jim told of finding them in the playhouse pool. But the real excitement came later. An undergardener at the Stoddards', put on the stand, stated that he had seen what he thought was Lydia's car going up the lane to where it was found, and that it had been followed part of the way by a second automobile.

That was at one o'clock in the morning. It being Saturday night he had gone to the movies in the village and then played some pool. At half past twelve he had started up the hill, using the main highway to where the Beaver Creek Road branched off. He had followed the Beaver Creek Road a hundred yards or so, and from there he had turned into the lane leading to the ravine where Lydia's car had been found. He had used the lane, he explained, because he did not want to be seen going home so late. It was at the entrance to the lane that he had seen the Morgan car.

"Did you recognize it?"

"Not at the time. I ducked into the brush. But nobody uses that road. It doesn't go anywhere. When they found the car up the lane next day I was pretty sure it was the one."

"The car passed you?"

"Yes. It went right up the lane."

"Can you tell us the time?"

"One o'clock exactly. I looked at my watch. It never varies a minute, one way or the other."

"Did you see who was driving this car?"

"No, sir."

"Did you see it again?"

"No, sir. Where it was found was beyond my place."

"Now about this second car. Tell the jury about it."

"Well, I got a better look at it. It came along about two minutes later. It looked to me as if it might have been chasing the first one and lost it. It stopped at the entrance to the lane, and then backed and turned. There was a man in it. I couldn't see who it was."

"Did you recognize the car?"

The witness hesitated, turning his hat around in his hands.

"I can't be sure. I thought at the time it was Dr. Sterling's."

That made a sensation, and Bill looked almost rigid when he was called again. But his story was straightforward enough. It was twelve o'clock when he left the Cloisters. He had some late coffee and he was not sleepy. He drove around for an hour or two. He frequently did that at night, as his housekeeper could testify.

The coroner was a dry little man, and he merely nodded. He had a map of the district before him and glanced at it.

"In the course of that drive did you reach this lane off the Beaver Creek Road?"

"I did. I turned there and went back."

"Now, Doctor, a previous witness has stated that you were apparently following another car. Is that a fact?"

"It is. I saw what looked like the Morgan car on the highway. It was late for Mrs. Morgan or her daughter to be out, especially in view of what has been happening; the attack on Evans, and certain other things. I turned around and followed it, but it was going very fast. I lost it entirely where the Beaver Creek Road branches off the main highway."

"There is a fork there?"

"Yes."

"Why did you choose the Beaver Creek Road?"

He reddened somewhat. "Because I knew it was a favorite drive of Mrs. Morgan's."

"Did you see either Mrs. Morgan or her daughter in the car?"

"No. I saw nobody."

"What time was this, Doctor?"

"One o'clock. I looked at my watch when I turned back."

There was a profound silence when he left the stand. Everybody there knew he had loathed Don and loved Lydia. Now he had been placed near the scene of what the press called the murder car, and they were bewildered. Bill Sterling, in whom they had believed—as people will about their doctors—almost as they believed in God, Bill Sterling was virtually being accused of murder.

Everything was anticlimax after that: Jim's testimony as to finding the car, the floor covering in the rear still damp and the overcoat wet. There were no prints. Either the car had been carefully wiped or whoever left it had worn gloves. There was no evidence that the body had been in it when it was hidden, the general idea being that the body had been left where it was found and then the car driven to the lane.

"In other words," said the coroner, "whoever hid the car left it on foot?"

"It looks like it. The ground was too dry for footprints."

The slipper and the pajama-coat button were produced, while the crowd craned its necks to see them.

"You found these in the pool on the Wainwright estate?"

"I did. The slipper was recovered by one of my men. The button was found after the pool was emptied."

The coroner looked at his notes. "One more question," he said. "How was the body taken out of the pool?"

"That's pure guesswork," said Jim. "Whoever did it might have taken off his clothes and gone in after it. Personally I think that's what he did. There were a number of damp towels lying around."

That was practically all. At the end they had a pretty clear picture—up to a point—of what had happened to Don Morgan. For some reason he had taken Lydia's car out the night of his death. At some place not as yet known he had met his murderer. He had been knocked out and drowned in the playhouse pool, his body disposed of, and Lydia's car driven into the hills and left.

There was no mention of the key found in Bill's possession, perhaps at the suggestion of the police. All they wanted that day was a verdict of murder; and, of course, they got it. It was six o'clock that Monday evening when it came in. There was not a man on the jury who believed Bill Sterling had done it, and the verdict was that Donald Morgan had been murdered by some person or persons unknown.

CHAPTER FOURTEEN

THEY BURIED Don Morgan the next day from St. Mark's. Maud was a little better that morning. Not well. It would be a long time before she was herself again. Her lips were still blue and looked swollen, but she was at least fully conscious. Shortly after Amy came on—all three nurses were on eight-hour shifts—she asked for me. I went in, to find her under that miserable tent, her voice little more than a whisper.

"Send some flowers to the church," she said. "When is the funeral?"

"This morning. Would you like orchids? McDonald has some lovely ones."

But she shook her head. "Not orchids," she said. "Anything else, but not orchids."

I was a little surprised. The Cloisters orchids are famous. But Andy McDonald and I managed to do our best with the time and the flowers we had, and I myself took them to the church.

It was crowded that morning. It looked as though the whole district had come to see Don off on that last far journey. And both Hill and valley had rallied to Lydia's support. Old Mr. Berry and Theodore Earle from the valley, Julian Stoddard and Tony from the Hill, were among the pallbearers. Audrey was not present, nor could I see Bill Sterling, but Lydia came alone, in dark clothes and with her head high. Then they carried in the casket, and the service began.

I thought there was a slight stir when Dr. Leland, reading the lesson, came to the line: "Behold, I shew you a mystery." But his quiet voice went on: death was swallowed up in victory, the mortal become immortal. There was hope and another life. Many were in tears when it was over, but Lydia's face was quiet.

They buried Don in the lovely Beverly cemetery where my father and mother lay; did it decently and with decorum. Then they went away, back to their houses and their comfortable lives. It was over. They had done the right thing. The amenities had been observed. Now, thank God, they could forget about him.

Probably they thought, if they thought about it at all—those first families of both the valley and the Hill—that everything was over. Bill Sterling was still free, and Don dead and buried. I know that I myself felt a sense of relief that day as Gus drove me home in Maud's limousine; as though a page had been turned and the new one was fresh and clean. The hills, I remember, were beautiful as I drove back, the trees a tapestry of gold and red and green, and at a turn of the road I could see the river, a shining band of silver, remote and yet near. I had always loved the river.

Bessie was on the terrace when I came back. She looked sulky, but she gave me a cold smile.

"Been doing your Christian duty, I suppose," she said. "Better stay out here awhile. The police are inside."

"The police? What do they want?"

She pretended to yawn, but it was only a pretense. "How do I know? Reynolds says they are in the basement."

Jim had left word for me to go down, and I found a half dozen men there, most of them strange. For now both the city and the county had stepped in: the county because now we had a murder, and the city because Jim had asked for help. The commissioner of police was there, the district attorney, a self-important individual whom I detested on sight, and two or three men from the homicide squad in town. One of them was a tall redheaded individual with a drawl. His name was Hopper, as we were all to have plenty of occasion to remember. They were standing at the bottom of the elevator shaft and Jim introduced them.

"We want you to re-enact that accident of yours, Pat," he said. "You don't mind, do you?"

"Not at all," I said brightly. "Whom am I to fall on?"

But they were not amused. Hopper stooped over and asked me if I thought that was the way I had struck the unknown below as I fell. I rather thought it was, although all I could say was that I fell on something alive which grunted and gave way beneath me. They had brought a ladder too, from somewhere outside. I showed them how I had found it in the dark and tried to pull myself up by it; but I had no idea which side of the shaft it was on. All in all I was not a great success. Hopper plainly considered me an idiot, if not a liar. He stood there, eyeing me with distaste.

"I don't get it," he said. "One night this fellow comes and is chased away by the dog. A few nights later he comes again, dog or no dog. The first time he apparently didn't know about the dog at all or he knew him well enough to think he could keep him quiet. The second night he simply took a chance on him. Provided," he added, eyeing me, "this young lady is telling all she knows."

I was furious. "Maybe I didn't fall down that shaft at all," I said. "If you doubt it you can look at my ankle."

"Thanks," he said dryly. "I already have. It's a very nice one. Do you usually get up at night to let the dog out, Miss Abbott?"

"When he seems to think it necessary."

"You were not afraid? There had been someone in the house a few nights before, but you went downstairs in the dark just the same."

"It wasn't entirely in the dark. The main hall was lighted."

"So? Why?"

"Mrs. Wainwright—Mrs. Anthony Wainwright—was having a party at the playhouse that night."

He hadn't known about the party. He asked at once for a list of the guests, but as it had been an impromptu affair I referred him to Bessie. The last I saw of him—that day at least—he was sitting on the terrace with her, with a glass of Coca-Cola beside him and a pad on his knee.

"Now about this party, Mrs. Wainwright. Did you miss anyone from the playhouse at any time?"

"How could I? They were in and out all evening."

"Was your husband there?"

"Tony?" She shrugged. "No. If you knew us better, you would know that my husband is seldom where I am."

"Do you know where he was?"

"I doubt if he was in the elevator shaft, if that's what you mean. He was as far from me as he could get, but that's rather stretching a point, isn't it?"

He finally got the list of her guests from her, and I believe the younger crowd had a bad day or two. One thing he did learn, however. Larry Hamilton had left the party early, at midnight or thereabouts, and as he went out a car had turned into the drive. He had thought it was the Morgans'.

I imagine Mr. Hopper pricked up his ears at that.

"You're not certain?"

"I didn't stop to look. I was kind of—well, I'd had one or two drinks and I'd quarreled with a girl. I wasn't paying much attention."

"Who was driving it? A man or a woman?"

Larry didn't know. All he was certain of was the time, and that was only approximate. Nevertheless, both Hopper and Jim Conway agreed on one probability: that Don Morgan, on the night of Bessie's party, had for some reason tried to get into the Cloisters, and that by pure chance I had fallen on him.

Hopper had his own explanation. "The fellow was hard up, we know that," he said. "And everybody knows about that jewelry of Mrs. Wainwright's. She's supposed to leave it lying about, isn't she?"

Jim shook his head. "Morgan wasn't a burglar. And remember this: whoever got into the house had Evans's keys. Apparently Morgan wasn't even in the neighborhood then."

I had a long talk with Dwight Elliott on the terrace that night. He had been staying at the Cloisters ever since Maud's message to him, but so far he had not seen her. He looked his full age that evening. I felt sorry for him, dapper in his dinner clothes, his long nervous fingers playing with his brandy glass.

"She didn't say why she wanted me?"

"No. Just to get you."

"Nothing had happened to upset her? No letters or anything?"

"She'd read her mail and the papers. Hilda said she was perfectly normal when she left her."

I left him sitting there. I don't think he even noticed that I had gone.

The next morning we had the astounding news about the

cemetery. It was Nora, the housemaid who looked after my rooms and me, who told me about it. She looked horrified as she put down my breakfast tray.

"That man's been around again, miss," she said.

"What man?" I asked drowsily.

"The one who killed Mr. Morgan. He's been in the cemetery."

"And a good place for him," I said. "I hope he stays there." Then the full import of what she had said dawned on me. I sat up in bed.

"What about the cemetery? Was somebody hurt there?"

"No, but it's all knocked about," she said with unction. "Tombstones turned over and flower beds trampled. They say it's a sight."

Half an hour later I was there. Jim Conway and two of the local policemen had already arrived, as well as Dr. Leland, the rector of St. Mark's. There were others, of course; people like myself, anxious and angry, or merely stupefied. For vandals, or a vandal, had certainly been there. Several small headstones had been pried off their bases and lay on the ground, urns had been overturned and broken and the windows in a large stone vault had been broken. My own graves were untouched, but the useless vindictive destruction was sickening.

Jim saw me and came over. "I'm glad your lot is all right, Pat," he said. "I knew you'd be worried. It's crazy, isn't it?"

"It's malicious and horrible."

"It's irrational anyhow. What good did it do? You can figure that someone with a grouch against the cemetery people might have done it, but these fellows have been here for years. Old Hodge, the superintendent, has had to be put to bed."

I could not talk about it. The cemetery had always been our pride. It lay on a ridge halfway up the hill, and my earliest mem-

ories of it were of a handful of Civil War veterans being taken
there in cars on the Fourth of July, and escorted by the local post
of the American Legion. There would be speeches, and a brass
band would drown out the efforts of Mrs. Dawes, our local so-
prano, to reach the high notes of the national anthem.

It was distinctly a valley affair, the cemetery, and as such the
village cherished it. It was beautifully kept, and naturally sacred
to me since both my father and mother lay there.

No one had told Maud, of course, but Bessie had already
heard the news when I got back. She seemed to find it highly diverting. "Somebody sure had himself a time," she said. "I'm going
down to look at it."

Which I believe she did at once.

Maud was slightly better the next day. The gloom percepti-
bly lifted in the house, the servants were more cheerful, even my
ankle was improved. So in the evening I had Gus bring around
my car and drove down to see Lydia. I took Roger with me. He
loved to ride, looking huge and important on the seat beside me,
and also there are long empty stretches of road on the way down
to the valley; and I remembered Jim Conway's final words the
day before in the cemetery.

"Just be careful, Pat," he said. "No roaming around the house
and grounds at night, and no driving after dark. We only have
two guesses on this thing. One is that we have a pretty shrewd
killer at large. The other is a lunatic. Maybe we have both."

"You're serious about a lunatic, are you?"

"Look around you," he reminded me grimly. "And if you can
make sense out of Don Morgan's being drowned up there in your
pool, with the river at his back door, you're smarter than I am."

I found Lydia alone on the bench by the river. The sun had
set a long time before, but there was still some light. She was

sitting without moving, her hands in her lap and her eyes on the water. I thought she was disappointed when she saw who it was.

"Oh, it's you, Pat," she said. "Come and sit down. Audrey's in bed and I'm alone. She's taken this thing hard, poor child."

I sat down and lit a cigarette. There was a boat going by, its searchlight swinging from side to side of the stream, and it struck us both for a minute. She looked, I saw, pale and exhausted. She tried to be casual, however. She asked for Maud and told me to thank her for the flowers. There had been a good many. She would write the notes later. Just now she couldn't.

"I wish you wouldn't worry so, Lydia," I said. "After all, you did what no other woman I know would have done. You took him back and cared for him."

"I let him down too. Audrey thinks so. But how could I know he was able to get about? Pat, what was his idea? He wasn't sick. He wasn't even penniless. Why did he come back? If he'd stayed away he would still be alive."

"Not necessarily. There's a story about that, isn't there? Whichever road a man chooses leads to the same end."

She was not listening. She turned to me suddenly. "Pat, could it have been that girl he ran away with? He left her, you know. Abandoned her somewhere abroad."

All at once I remembered Bessie. Bessie who had vaguely known a man named Morgan in Paris. Bessie who had been at the club the night of the murder, Bessie with her cold blue eyes and her baby stare. But Jim Conway had said no woman could have done it; at least, not alone. Besides, how old was Bessie? She claimed to be twenty-eight, although I thought she was older. Still, fifteen years ago—

Lydia was still talking. It did her good, I think. She went back over the whole story. Don's telephone message to her and his arrival. He had seemed discouraged and feeble when, after dark that night, she had met him at the train and brought him back.

"He seemed hardly able to get into the car," she said. "But I don't believe it now, Pat. I think he was acting."

However that might be, Audrey had made a great fuss over him, and between them they got him upstairs to the guest room, where the bed was already turned down, and Audrey had put new magazines beside the reading lamp. She herself had unpacked his bags, and had been surprised to find how good his clothes were: a dinner suit, a blue serge, and the suit he had worn for the journey. He had said a friend in New York gave him an outfit, but it wasn't true. The suits had been made in London and his name was in the pockets.

"He had overlooked that," she said, "but I began to be doubtful that night. It was too late, of course. He was there and Audrey was excited and happy. I had to go on."

The first time she really wondered about his illness was a day or two later. A bottle of Scotch was missing from downstairs and she thought he had taken it. She said nothing but after that she watched him.

"He wasn't really weak," she said in that new flat voice of hers. "And, of course, if he was actually sick he oughtn't to have had whisky."

It had resulted in his never being left alone. She or Audrey was always about. Not in his room necessarily. Just somewhere at hand. She thought it annoyed him. He would try to get them away together, but she was increasingly suspicious. He had come back for some purpose of his own, but she couldn't imagine what it was.

"After more than fifteen years!" she said. "He didn't care for me. He was charming, of course; grateful too. But I began to worry. I knew there was something wrong."

She couldn't tell Bill. He never came near her. She couldn't tell anybody. But she slept with her door open, and one night she found Don halfway down the stairs in his pajamas. She had thought then he wanted liquor. Now she wasn't so sure. One thing was certain: he had not telephoned anybody. There was only one phone and it was in the hall downstairs. Of course, Audrey might have mailed his letters, but she never knew him to write any.

"I began to wonder if it was that woman again," she said, "or another one. But you saw him, Pat. You know how agreeable he could be. He seemed so pleased about everything. He even asked to see Bill. He said he would be gone soon, and I ought to marry again. But Bill wouldn't put a foot in the house."

Nobody had come to see Don except myself. It had been as though the three of them had suddenly been cut off from the world about them. "Like living on an island," Lydia put it.

Nevertheless, he must have communicated with somebody. On the day he was killed there had been a telephone message for him. As it happened Audrey had been out and she had gone into the garden. When she came into the lower hall he was there, hanging up the receiver.

"You were out, my dear," he said, "so I managed to get down."

"Who was it?"

"Wrong number," he told her, and she had helped him up the stairs again.

But she had been suspicious. She had begun to wonder if he had not had the car out at night. She had found the gas low once or twice, and that day he looked secretive. It was an old familiar look to her.

"I made up my mind he wouldn't go out that night," she said. "I was willing to care for him, but not to connive at anything."

So she had sent his clothing to the cleaners.

"All of it," she said drearily. "Everything except his overcoat. So you see what happened. He had made an appointment with someone, and his clothes were gone. It must have been pretty bad. But he went anyhow. I—"

Her voice trailed off, and we sat for some minutes in silence. When she spoke her voice was husky.

"I didn't love him, Pat. He had made me too unhappy for that. But I'm tragically sorry for him. He liked to live. He liked good food and drink and clothes. He liked this view too."

I asked her if she had heard him take the car out. She shook her head.

"No. I never dreamed he would go out. How could he? Anyhow, the garage is on the other side of the house. He knew the car would be there, of course. Larry Hamilton had taken Audrey to the country club that night." She drew a long breath. "I'm frightened, Pat. Bill is so queer, and that story about his following the car—Pat, if I thought he did it I'd jump in the river."

"Bill is saving you from more talk," I told her. "As for his doing it, you ought to know him better. What about this woman Don ran away with, Lydia? Who was she?"

"I don't really know. It's a long time ago. She was in his office, a stenographer. He didn't stay with her long. He couldn't stick to any woman. Anyhow, so far as I know she'd been a nice girl, decent and all that." The subject seemed distasteful to her, so she dropped it. "Pat, do you think Don was here before he came back?"

"What makes you think that?"

"I don't know," she said vaguely. "That playhouse at the Cloisters hadn't been built when he went away, yet he seemed to know about it."

We talked until late that night. She was shocked but grieving. Most of all she was worrying about Bill Sterling. He had a motive. Who else had? Not that she believed he was guilty, of course, but she was afraid of the police, especially of Hopper, who had been questioning her. He didn't know Bill as Jim Conway did. But she had had an angle on that drowning of Don's which I had not thought of. She did not believe he had been meant to go into the swimming pool.

"It only made it harder," she had said. "There was sure to be an autopsy and they would know he had been drowned. There were so many other ways to kill him. If he was to be drowned, why not put him in the river? Pat, why on earth would Don go to the playhouse anyhow? Was it to meet somebody?"

"He might have been unconscious when he was taken there, Lydia."

"I don't believe it. He went there for some purpose of his own. And it was to hide that purpose that he was taken away later and thrown where he was found."

Before I left we went upstairs to Don's room. It was much as he had left it: the chintz-covered chair by the window with the cigarette box on a little taboret beside it, the old maple three-quarter bed with its narrow posts and ruffled Swiss curtains, his silver brushes on the maple lowboy, his cigarettes on the table beside his chair.

"I don't suppose there is anything here," she said dully. "I've searched every inch of it. So have the police."

But she was wrong. In the closet were the suits she had mentioned, and also a coat, a brown one with almost invisible red stripes in it.

"What's the coat?" I said. "You didn't mention it."

"I forgot it. The trousers were worn out, he said. He never wore it."

I took it out and looked at it. No doubt it had already been examined, and certainly the pockets were empty. Like the others it had been made in England, and the Bond Street tailor's name was in the pocket. But there was something else there, something the police had probably thought was a number written in by the tailor himself.

It was not. Inked in carefully on the label was a series of numbers, and I knew them at once.

They were the license numbers of Maud's limousine.

I did not tell Lydia. Fortunately she was not looking at me. She was gazing helplessly around the room.

"I've just remembered, Pat," she said. "Where are the keys? He had a lot of them, on a long steel chain. Do you suppose he took them with him?"

I felt suddenly cold.

"Did you tell the police that?" I asked.

"No. Is it important?"

"It might be," I said carefully. "It looks as though they might have been Evans's keys, Lydia. They were taken the night he was hurt."

"Evans? The watchman at the Cloisters? Do you know what you are saying, Pat?"

"I'm afraid I do."

CHAPTER FIFTEEN

IT HAD become a habit with me to lie awake, and I had a lot to think over before I tried to sleep that night. Without any proof to speak of I was certain that Don Morgan had been in the neighborhood long before his official arrival. Perhaps even as early as June, and that I had seen him—possibly watching Audrey—through the windows of the playhouse. The rest was not so clear, however. His attack on Evans, the keys, and his two attempts to get into the Cloisters. And that final rendezvous of his with someone at the playhouse, and its ending.

It had been a rendezvous. I was certain Lydia was right. Someone had telephoned him that day and made the appointment. Then again there was the matter of Maud's license number. Why had he kept it? Was Bessie mixed up in this, after all, and had he seen her in Maud's car? Then I remembered something that seemed to eliminate Bessie. The evening papers had stated that a clerk in the motor vehicle license bureau, seeing Don's picture in the paper on Monday, had recognized him as a man who, some weeks before, had inquired as to the ownership of a certain car.

"It damned near knocked me down," the man had said. "I had the lights too. I'll get that bastard's license if it's the last thing I do."

The clerk had turned it over to someone else and did not remember the number. But he said the man looked as though he had had a narrow escape. He was pale and his hands shook as he lit a cigarette.

It was possible, of course. It might even account for Maud's collapse. If Gus had almost struck someone with the heavy car she would never tell on him. But the next morning when I spoke to Gus he flatly denied anything of the sort.

"You can ask Mrs. Wainwright, if you don't believe me," he said stiffly. "I never touched anybody that day, or came near it."

That was on Thursday. Don had been murdered on Saturday night, and the case was apparently at a standstill. Hopper and the other detectives from the city were pretty well disgruntled. They had what looked like a well-planned murder, but outside of where it took place there was nothing.

"Not even a motive, outside of Bill Sterling," Jim Conway said that day, sitting on the terrace while Roger tried to climb into his lap. "No prints, no cigarettes with lipstick on them, no weapons, no bullets for their ballistics department, no anything. If I wasn't sitting on their necks with a few odds and ends they'd claim Morgan had a heart attack and got drowned in a puddle."

Which, as I know now, was certainly not giving the redhead-ed Hopper his due.

As a matter of fact, he was quietly digging away at the case. One day he saw the young doctor Lydia had called in for Don when Bill Sterling refused to see him. His name was Craven, and he proved a vague sort of witness.

"You considered he was a sick man?"

"Well, he thought so. You can't see angina, of course," he added defensively.

He had been giving him small doses of digitalis daily, "just in case." Otherwise he had recommended rest and a careful diet. "I thought he was under some sort of nervous strain," he said. "I asked him if he was worrying, and he denied it. 'Except that I can't stay here,' he said. 'Mrs. Morgan has been kind to me when I needed help, but it can't go on, of course.'"

"He didn't strike you as being afraid? You didn't get the idea he thought his life was in danger?"

"Not at all."

So there they were. They had only one suspect, and that was Bill. He had motive and opportunity, and only the sworn statement of Julian Stoddard's undergardener about the two cars kept them from arresting him at once. Even they couldn't prove that he had hidden the murder car where it was found, and two minutes later have shown up in his own.

Nevertheless, they did their best to build a case against him, tried to break down the gardener, combed Bill's car, searched his clothes and his house, examined and cross-examined him.

"Did you know Donald Morgan before he came back?"

"No. I was in medical college when they moved here from the East. When he left I was an intern in a New York hospital."

"But your home was here? Your family lived here?"

"Yes. My father and mother both died while I was in college."

"You spent your summer holidays here, didn't you? You'd have seen Morgan then."

"I worked my way through college. I had no holidays. I never saw any of the Morgans until I came here to practice, and he had gone by that time."

They shifted then, to the key to the playhouse and the attack on Evans. How well had he known Evans? Did he know that he carried keys to the Cloisters? He merely said that he had not thought about it. He supposed a watchman would do so. As to the key found on his key ring, he had no idea how it got there. But they kept after him, like dogs after a bone. Where was he when Evans was attacked? He showed them the small book he carried, his evening office hours until eight or after, a call or two, and a visit to Lydia until eleven that night.

They were still not satisfied. The two crimes had both taken place at the Cloisters pool, therefore they were connected. But whoever had knocked Evans into the water had not wanted him to drown, whereas in Don's case they had.

"How many suits of clothes do you own?" Hopper asked him abruptly.

He looked surprised. "Clothes? I don't know. Enough. Not too many."

"Who looks after them, Doctor?"

"My housekeeper, Mrs. Watkins."

"She sends them out to be cleaned and pressed, I suppose."

"Yes."

"Any gone out lately?"

"She would know. I don't."

"Haven't had your watch repaired recently, have you?"

For some reason that annoyed him. "No," he said shortly. "I suppose you mean I shoved Evans into the pool and then jumped in after him. Well, I've been taking pulses with this watch ever since, and if there's water in it, it must have been built for a diver. As to my clothes, ask Mrs. Watkins." He smiled rather grimly. "I have no secrets from her. She put diapers on me when I was a baby, and if you think I could smuggle a suit of wet clothes into my house or lose it somewhere in the bushes, you don't know her."

But as to the night of Don's death they had him, more or less. "Certainly I followed the car," he said impatiently. "Why not? I thought Mrs. Morgan or Audrey was in it. I never got a close look. It was on the way up the hill when I saw it. I had to turn and follow it. By that time it was well ahead, and I lost it at the Beaver Creek Road."

"What about Morgan's return? It upset some plans of yours, didn't it?"

"It did."

"You resented that, naturally?"

"I did. He had no claim on his former wife. I thought her taking him into the house was a piece of sentimental nonsense."

They could not shake him. Why should he kill Donald Morgan? Lydia had divorced him. There was no question of a remarriage.

After that they went back to the night of the murder. The autopsy had placed it between four and five hours after Don's last meal, or not later than midnight. Bill had left the Cloisters at midnight.

"So did a dozen other people," he said. "What the hell's that got to do with it? I wasn't sleepy. I just drove around."

It was, I think, on Thursday night that in desperation Hopper and Jim Conway tried a reconstruction of the crime. Leaving the Cloisters at midnight—when Bill Sterling had left—they drove out to the main road. Here they parked their car, and walked back to the playhouse, staying out of sight of the house as they figured the murderer would have done. They made it in ten minutes.

Once inside the playhouse they staged a brief quarrel. Jim as the murderer knocked Hopper out, and Hopper lay in the empty pool, with a stopwatch in his hand, and realistically drowned. The problem was to get him out, however. Jim stripped to his shorts and jumped in, but there was no water in the pool to help him. It was some time before a cursing Hopper lay on the tiles and, allowing for the lack of water, they clocked the whole performance at another ten minutes and let it go at that.

They had only an hour, and they had already used a third of it.

But the worst was to come. Not only had Jim to pretend to dry himself and get into his clothes. He had to carry or drag Hopper to the car. But Hopper weighed a hundred and sixty-five, which was Don's weight, and the playhouse was almost three hundred yards from where they believed Don had left Lydia's car. Jim sweated and Hopper was limp and disagreeable. "For God's sake, keep clear of the bushes. You almost put my eye out."

But the dressing and the hauling had used up another twenty minutes, and taking off Hopper's overcoat and covering him with it in the rear of the car had taken a couple more. Hopper's watch showed a total of forty-two minutes before they were ready to start to where the body had been found in the ditch. Jim drove like a lunatic, but it required ten minutes to reach that back road.

He grinned as he dumped Hopper out of the car.

"Eight minutes to go," he said cheerfully. "And if anybody made it back to that lane below Stoddard's in eight minutes he had wings."

It began to look as though the crime had been committed before midnight, which let Bill out. Hopper was surly.

"There's a catch in it somewhere," he said. "You cheated on the dressing end, for one thing. Do you suppose the fellow waited to tie his tie?"

Back at Jim's office that night they checked their lists again. The women at the party, they agreed, were out. Of the men most of them had not, even in the old days, had more than a bowing acquaintance with Don. Dwight Elliott had said, "Never saw the fellow in my life. What's all this about?" Julian Stoddard had known Don slightly years before. He had not seen him since he came back. Theodore Earle, almost seventy, had merely smiled and said their suspicions were a compliment, and the other two had never even heard of him.

It was two in the morning when Hopper looked up from his list. "What about Tony Wainwright?" he said. "He's got no alibi for that night. What time did *he* get home?"

"Don't be a damned fool," said Jim. "He was a kid when Morgan left."

Hopper yawned again. "Morgan had a mighty pretty daughter. He might have objected to her playing around with a married man."

CHAPTER SIXTEEN

IT WAS precisely a week after our murder when Evans disappeared from the Beverly hospital. He had been better, so much so that he had been given his own clothes and a certain amount of freedom. That is, he would wander out now and then and talk to the nurses or to the convalescents; an old man in a shabby suit and carpet slippers, and still with a small scrap of dressing on his head.

His escape—if that was what it was—had been easy. Tony had put him in a private room on the ground floor, and it was not six feet to the path below. Nevertheless, the situation had its unusual points.

He had taken his pipe and tobacco pouch, but none of his clothing except what he wore. Some underwear had been sent there as he improved, as well as his razor and so on. It was all still in his room.

It was one o'clock in the morning when Tony got the message. The bedroom telephone bells were shut off so that they could not ring during the night, but one of the nurses, below on an errand, heard the one in the library ringing. She came up and told Tony, and as his room was not far from mine I heard her knocking at his door. It took some time to waken him, and the noise roused me also.

"The hospital is calling, Mr. Wainwright. Evans isn't there," she said, when he finally replied.

"What do you mean, isn't there?"

"He's gone. Disappeared."

"Gone! Where could he go? All right. I'll be down in a minute."

I did not hear him on the telephone, but I was at the top of the stairs when he came up, yawning and only half awake.

"What about Evans?" I asked. "Is anything wrong?"

"Nothing much, I imagine. Old boy's probably gone out to take a walk. He's used to being up at night."

I found myself shivering a little. Somehow I did not think he had merely taken a walk. "I hope that's all," I said weakly.

"Of course, that's all. See here, Pat, don't look like that. You are all eyes." He put a hand on my shoulder. "Go back to bed, girl. We didn't bring you here to wear you down."

He stooped and kissed me lightly; and, of course, Bessie, having heard the noise, chose that moment to open her door at the end of the wing. She did not speak for a moment. She stared at us, and I dare say we looked like a couple of bad children. Then she smiled unpleasantly. "I hate to spoil anything, Tony," she said coldly, "but what's all the fuss about?"

"Only old Evans out for a night walk. But the hospital is worried."

I thought she looked startled. Certainly she was puzzled, as though she could not fit this piece into some mental jigsaw of her own. But she merely shrugged.

"Well, sorry to have butted in," she said coolly, and closed her door, leaving both of us feeling rather ridiculous. Tony recovered first. He grinned down at me.

"You shouldn't have looked like a scared little girl," he said. "My fault anyhow. Excuse it, please."

He must have dressed in a hurry, for soon I heard his car going out at its usual reckless speed. It was four in the morning when he came back. He tapped lightly at my door and I opened it.

"Evans hasn't come back," he said. "Don't let Mother know. And don't get any ideas in your head. He went of his own free will, by his window. But I'm off to see Conway. No use letting the poor old boy go wandering around alone at night. He can't go far. He had only a dollar or two in his pockets."

Later I heard about his part in the search that night. He had clung to the theory that Evans had gone for a night stroll, and he had combed the surrounding estates and woods for him. Since his boyhood he and Evans had had a signal, a whistle of their own. When Tony was out late and did not want Maud to know, he would use it; for Evans carried his revolver at night, and was a bit on the handy side with it. Tony had, I gathered, gone whistling through the night, without result.

By morning the situation began to look sinister. There was no question but that the old man had left voluntarily. His window was open and his pajamas neatly folded on a chair. But he had been in bed. The night nurse reported him sound asleep at half past ten.

"What it looks like," said Tony, eating a hasty breakfast and looking harassed and weary, "is that he got some sort of message that took him out. Not by telephone. He wasn't called. But his window was up. Someone might have spoken to him from the path below."

"But who?" I asked. "Who on earth would want to take him away or—hurt him?"

"We don't know he's hurt. As to who took him away, he might have had his own reasons for leaving. The police had been talking to him, and he may have known something he shouldn't have known. He might have been scared."

There was no sign of him by noon. We had kept the news from Maud, but Bessie, having learned he was still missing, immediately went into what Amy Richards, reporting to me, called a tailspin.

"She's packing up to leave," she said cheerfully. "Thank God for His mercies. I've never seen her breakfast tray pass without being tempted to put something in her coffee."

The police, local and city, did all the usual things that day: sent out radio descriptions of Evans, notified the Missing Persons Bureau, and got his fingerprints from his room at the hospital. But Bessie did not get away, after all. It was the saturnine Hopper who stopped that, sitting in the library and referring now and then to a small black book he carried.

"We're still investigating a murder," he told her. "It took place here, at the Cloisters. I am not insinuating that you know anything about it. But I am going to ask you a question. Why did you leave the country club that night? And walk in this direction? Don't tell me you didn't. I know you did."

She went pale, but she was defiant. "I deny it absolutely," she said.

"That's very foolish of you," he observed calmly. "We have your footprints here and there, and—"

"Rot! All women's evening slippers are the same."

"And we have a small bunch of artificial flowers that you lost out of your hair that night," he went on. "That was when you ducked under the shrubbery down near the stables here. Do you remember? Now, Mrs. Wainwright, I want to know just where you went that night, and why."

She was still defiant. "If it's any of your business, I was meeting somebody."

"Was that somebody Don Morgan?"

She broke then. It wasn't Don Morgan. She hadn't seen him for years. She wasn't sure she had ever seen him. As for killing him, why would she do such a thing? And even if she had, could she have gotten him out of that pool and into a car? "Go on up and look at the dress I wore," she said. "See if it was wet."

"I have already seen it," he replied.

That stopped her. At least she didn't say anything further about going away. But as to whom she had met that night she was stubbornly silent.

"It has nothing to do with this," she snapped. "God knows I haven't much life of my own here, but I have some. And what I have is my own affair."

He let that go. He was imperturbable. He reached into a pocket and brought out a photograph of Don, taken before he went away. "This the fellow you knew in Paris?"

She took it gingerly. "It looks like him. I wouldn't swear to it."

"I suppose you see why you can't run out on us," he observed, still placid. "We'll make it easy for you, but I advise you to stick around. Does your husband know you met this man that night?"

"I haven't said it was a man. No, in any case."

"You're sure of that, are you?"

"Good God," she said, and laughed. "Can you see me meeting Don Morgan that night, and Tony protecting my honor by killing him?"

"He might have been protecting his own honor," said Hopper.

She stubbed out her cigarette and sat still for a moment. I have wondered since if she was not tempted that day. She could have told the story, even her own part in it, and then gone away. She must have thought of that, sitting there in her English tweeds and English-made walking shoes, confronted by that tall, gaunt nemesis. But evidently she decided against it. She looked at him and then got up.

"All right," she said. "You win. I'll stay."

CHAPTER SEVENTEEN

THAT WAS the afternoon after Evans had disappeared. The house had been pretty well demoralized even before that, with Mrs. Partridge going about like a scared rabbit, some of the maids threatening to leave, and none of them willing to go out of the house at night, even to the movies. As Sunday passed with no news of the old man, even Reynolds' impassive face began to look moody. As for the two footmen, they were obviously in a state of jitters.

Tony was out all that day, and on Monday they started a search of the hills. Evans had been gone for thirty-six hours by that time, and there was still no trace of him whatever. Things were being reported, however, that gave his disappearance a sinister look. For one thing, the hospital reported that he had not been the same since the murder.

"The nurses say he was greatly changed," the superintendent said. "He had been cheerful up to that time. After he heard the news he was morose. He stayed in his room, and he ate little or nothing."

It was over Evans that Hopper and the city crowd almost split with Jim Conway; the city detectives being inclined to believe he had merely wandered off, and Jim was taking a more sinister view of the disappearance.

"Somebody might have wanted him out of the way," he maintained. "He couldn't go far in a pair of hospital carpet slippers. Then, too, he'd been accustomed to sleeping in the daytime and being up at night. It's only a mile or so from the hospital to the Cloisters. Suppose he'd been out of that window and near the playhouse the night of the murder. He might have seen something."

He stuck to that. While the state police and the others were searching the hill country he went to Evans's room that day and went over it carefully.

"If he'd gone by himself, he might have picked up at least a pair of shoes there," he said. "It was worth looking into, anyhow."

Evans had lived for years in Andy McDonald's cottage on the Cloisters grounds. He had a room on the lower floor there, and Jessie, Andy's wife, offered no objection to the search. The room revealed nothing, however. It was neat and, except for what she had sent to the hospital, much as he had left it. There was writing paper and envelopes in a drawer and a pen and bottle of ink around. But the pen was old and rusty.

"He didn't write letters," she said. "I don't know as he ever got any, either. He didn't seem to have any people."

His closet was equally unrevealing. There were two pairs of shoes on the floor, which Jessie said were all he owned. The old trousers he had worn the night he was hurt were still, she thought, down at the police station, but the coat was there, crumpled after its wetting in the pool. She had brought it back from the hospital and hung it up, along with the empty shoulder holster for his gun.

"Did he ever speak to you about his gun?" Jim asked. "When you saw him in the hospital?"

"No, sir. He didn't mention it."

"Did he talk about the attack? Had he any idea who did it?"

"He talked about it a lot. He was rather pleased with the attention he was getting. You know what I mean, Mr. Conway. Here was Mrs. Wainwright sending him flowers and things to eat, and everybody looking after him. Then I suppose it was a nice change for him, to be able to sleep at night. He's been here for years, and he's never been off duty until now. Except once. Then he was gone for several days. That was a funny thing. He never explained where he'd been. Not to us, anyhow."

"He just walked out, eh?"

"Well, I don't know. He walked out, all right, but when he came back I thought maybe he'd had bad news. If he had, he never spoke about it. Only one thing I did notice. Now and then he used to get a letter from somebody. He's never had one since."

It was early October by that time. The trees were already turning, making the hillsides a soft blending of red and yellow and brown. The hunting season was on, meeting at the Stoddards'. It was bad hunting country, but rides had been cut, and there were some native foxes, as well as others which had been imported. In the valley the summer season was definitely ended. The city bachelors who had used the Beverly Hotel as summer quarters had gone back to town, the horse show was over, and both Hill and village had been prepared for a rest before Palm Beach or Jekyll Island or Nassau.

Into this peace, however, had come Don's murder and the disappearance of Evans. True, life went on. The gardeners were getting ready for winter, wheeling about mulch or manure, digging up Maud's annual garden, and still nursing along their dahlias, asters, and chrysanthemums. The golf links were filled, especially on Saturday and Sunday. The river boats were pushing huge scows laden with coal for the coming cold weather, and one day a couple of police boats appeared, and systematically set about dragging the river bed.

Maud was still in ignorance of Evans's disappearance, but I was allowed to see her for a few minutes each day. It was early in the week that she asked about Evans.

"How is he getting on? We might send him some fruit, Pat."

She must have seen something in my face. She tried to lift herself up in bed. "Not Evans, Pat!" she said. "Don't tell me anything has happened to Evans."

I had to tell her. I made it as easy as I could, but she looked so strange that I called Amy. That afternoon she sent for Dwight Elliott, and he was shut in her room for a long time.

Whatever happened during the talk, he looked badly shaken when he came out. Amy, going in to tell him that the time was up, said she found him standing over Maud, his face red with indignation.

"You can't do it," he was saying. "Think of what it entails. At least I implore you to wait until you are yourself again."

"I've had plenty of time to think it over, Dwight."

Then he saw Amy and pulled himself together.

I do not remember much of that week. Evans had not been found. Wearing a pair of hospital slippers and carrying his pipe, he had vanished as completely as if, Amy said, he had been rubbed out with an eraser. There were still guards at night in the Cloisters grounds, and a man at the gates all day. Tony looked exhausted. Bessie had taken to spending most of her time in her room, with the door locked. And one day Hodge at the ceme-

tery, crawling into a clump of shrubbery, found a pick which he
believed had been used to cause the damage and took it down to
the station house.

Stamped on the handle was the *C* with which all the Cloisters tools were marked. Jim took it up to Andy, who recognized
it at once.

"I've missed it," he said. "And where would you be finding it,
Mr. Conway?"

"In the cemetery," said Jim grimly, and took it away.

It was toward the end of the week that I had a visitor.

I was in my office, checking the house bills, when I saw Larry
Hamilton outside in the grounds. Roger was making a fuss over
him, leaping up to put his big paws on his shoulders. My desk
faced the open window, and Larry saw me and came toward me.

"Hello," he said. "Any chance to talk to you? I sneaked in, but
somebody's likely to put me out any minute."

"I think the door's open into the hall here. Come on in."

As usual I welcomed any interruption to my work. He came
in, and I gave him a cigarette and took one myself. He was a
good-looking boy, perhaps twenty-five but seeming younger. I
know that I felt like his mother that day, for he was evidently
unhappy and certainly nervous.

"All right," I said briskly. "I don't suppose you sneaked in here
just because you can't keep away from me. Let's have it, Larry."

He looked as if he wanted to bolt, but he only got up and
walking to the window, stood looking out of it.

"I don't know what to do," he said jerkily. "Maybe I shouldn't
have come here at all, but I've been scared stiff. It's about Audrey
and Tony Wainwright."

I confess to a feeling of shock. That had seemed to be over, if
it had ever really existed. Now here it was again.

"I suppose you know I'm crazy about her," he said, his voice shaking. "I have been ever since we were kids. And I'm afraid I've started something. It's all over the place anyhow."

"What's all over the place?"

It did not seem so important as he told it, although it was disagreeable enough. Briefly, one of the first things Don Morgan had done when he came home was to forbid Audrey to go about with Tony.

"He had heard Tony was married, and Audrey says he threw a fit. He sent for Tony, and I guess there was a row. You know Tony. He gets pretty mad. Well, Audrey told about it. You know how she is. She talks first and thinks later. But the rest is my fault."

"What rest?" I asked impatiently.

"About Mr. Morgan and Bessie Wainwright."

"Mr. Morgan and Bessie Wainwright? What on earth do you mean, Larry?"

"I saw them out together one night," he said doggedly. "It was pretty late, but I saw him, and it looked like Bessie's car."

I was stunned. "Have you told anybody?"

"Well, that's the trouble," he admitted. "I was pretty sore; him pretending to be sick, with Audrey carrying his meals to him and everything. Then he rides around at night with a woman. I told some fellows at the club, and now everybody knows it. There's a lot of talk. You see"—he stopped, then floundered on— "Tony wasn't at the dance all the time, the night Mr. Morgan was killed. Neither was Bessie. She was seen coming this way about eleven o'clock, and Tony was following her. At least that's the story."

It was a long speech for him. He got out a handkerchief and mopped his hands, as though they were sweating.

"But it's preposterous," I said, my mouth dry with fright. "It's got to be stopped, this talk, Larry."

He gave me a twisted smile. "Try it and see," he said, and picking up his hat went out the way he had come in.

I knew then what Hopper had meant about Tony defending his own honor. Tony, perhaps learning that Bessie had a rendezvous with Don at the playhouse, following her when she left the club, and in one of his quick rages killing him. I went cold all over.

Tony was in a vicious temper when he came home that night. Evidently part of the story had reached him.

"See here," he said. "Have you heard that I had a row with Don Morgan?"

"Something of the sort."

He gave a bark of bitter laughter. "So my friends and neighbors are after me!" he said. "Of all the damnable absurdities—Listen, my dear, you're entitled to know about it. There was no quarrel. As a matter of fact, the old boy behaved pretty handsomely. I'd dropped around to leave some fruit I'd promised Lydia, and he sent for me. He looked embarrassed, but he was clear enough. Audrey was young. He didn't want her falling for a man who had a wife already. When I told him I had no intentions, honorable or otherwise, he grinned. That's all there was to it. But I suppose Audrey was outside the door."

I did not tell him the rest of Larry's story. He looked all in, and after dinner he went down to see Jim Conway. But I did take it up with Bessie that night. It was too serious to ignore.

She was in her sitting room lying on a chaise longue with a movie magazine in her hand. She got up to unlock the door and admit me, then went back. But when I told her she leaped to her feet.

"That's a dirty lie," she said. "I never did such a thing. Do you think I've lost my mind?"

She was angry as well as frightened, but I did not believe she was lying. I left shortly after, and I heard her locking her door behind me. Whatever she was afraid of was in the house itself, apparently.

Roger found the garter the next day. It was an ordinary man's garter, comparatively new but showing exposure to the weather. I had taken him for a walk, and he came out of the shrubbery with it in his mouth. He played with it for a while, throwing it with a toss of his head, then pouncing on it.

When I rescued it it was rather the worse for wear, and as it was of an ordinary make it was not much of a clue. But Jim Conway, inspecting it when I showed it to him, looked worried. "We may have to cut some time off that hour of Bill Sterling's," he said. "It looks as though the killer, whoever he was, didn't wait to dress."

The house was quiet that week, with Maud shut away in those big rooms of hers, with Tony alternating between business and the search for Evans, and even Pierre, limited now to nurses' trays and food largely uneaten by the rest of us, sulking in his kitchen. Down on the river the dragging for Evans's body was going on, without success, and search in the hills had been abandoned.

One day James, the head groom, asked me if I cared to ride one of the horses, and I asked Tony about it that night. To my surprise he refused. "They haven't been out for weeks," he said. "I wouldn't trust you on them, Pat. I don't want anything to happen to you."

"I've ridden all my life."

"I know. Nice tame horses. These are different."

I was indignant. I'd shown hunters at the valley horse show off and on for years, so the next day I took out Prince. James smiled grimly when I mounted.

"Take him easy at first, miss. You'll do all right. I've seen you ride."

I did all right, despite an inclination of Prince's to regard a twittering squirrel as a deadly menace and the bit as something to be shifted, if possible. It was a hard ride, but it was good to be in breeches and boots again. I was almost cheerful when, coming back from the stables that day, I found Bessie in the hall.

She eyed me. "Always the outdoor girl!" she said. "Well, I hate horses like the devil, but it might be better than this."

"Better than what?"

"Better than this mausoleum. Someday I'm going to give that redheaded grass-Hopper a shock and beat it for New York." She watched me as I lit a cigarette. "You'd like that, wouldn't you?" she said. "You and Tony both. I rather spoil the little affair, don't I?"

She turned then to a mirror and began to go over her make-up. But not before I had seen something she did not expect me to see. Her bag was open on the table, and inside it was a small pearl-handled revolver.

CHAPTER EIGHTEEN

It was that night, the eighth of October, that Bill Sterling was arrested.

It happened soon after he had made his evening call on Maud at the Cloisters. I saw him in the lower hall that night, and I thought he looked better. After all, the disappearance of Evans must have relieved him, for he had been operating in the hospital when Evans vanished, and after that he had taken one of the interns out on a country call. They got back at three in the morning, and had coffee and scrambled eggs in one of the floor kitchens before Bill drove home.

He greeted me cheerfully. "Hello, Pat," he said. "How's everything here?"

"We're doing as well as could be expected. I hear the village has picked on Tony for the criminal."

"Don't let that bother you. The police haven't. They still have an eye on me."

And Hopper chose that very night to search his house and offices again. I suppose he had a warrant, or maybe at some time Bill had told him to go ahead. Whichever way it was, he was there. Mrs. Watkins was indignant.

"You've been here once and I've just got the place straight after the mess you made of it. What in time do you want now?"

"Only a little look-see," said Hopper. "You just stand aside, lady, and keep on standing aside."

She went back to her kitchen, banging the door; and the first thing Hopper found was Evans's gun. It had not even been hidden. It had been slid into the drawer of the desk in Bill's consulting room, and it was covered with his fingerprints.

They found him at Lydia's. Rather, Jim found him. He watched the prints being examined and compared with Bill's. Then he shot like a bat out of hell, as he said, to the Morgan place. He found them together on the bench near the river. They were sitting there quietly; two people who had loved each other for years, and now were contented merely to be together. They were not even holding hands. Just at peace with each other and with the world.

"I hated like the devil to break it up," Jim said. "But what was I to do? I'd left Hopper trying to locate him, and I wanted to get there first. I suppose Bill knew what had happened the minute he saw me, for he got up and kissed her. 'I'll be back or call you later,' he said. Then he came along."

Jim didn't take him to the station house at once. They drove around for half an hour or so, Jim doing most of the talking.

"Look here, Bill, you know I'll do all I can. When did you get that gun?"

"You won't believe me, but I don't know."

"You must have seen it, Bill. You couldn't miss it. Maybe you picked it up the night Evans was hurt."

"Meaning I hurt him? No."

"I didn't mean that. Don't be a jackass. After all, he had it on him that night. You might have taken it from him after they took him to the hospital."

"Thanks, Jim. Who would believe that? Where have I had it since? The house was searched before. You know and Hopper and his crowd know it wasn't there then."

Jim was resentful as well as indignant. "Why in hell did you leave it there to be found? It was a fool thing to do."

"What was I—" He checked himself. "Damn it all, Jim, I keep forgetting you're a policeman yourself. Let it go at that. They'd searched the house once. I didn't think they'd be back. Anyhow, what has the gun got to do with it? Nobody's been shot."

"You'll have to answer that yourself," said Jim laconically.

They took him in to the city that night. They treated him well enough, I believe. He sat in the district attorney's office, smoking and answering the barrage of questions they threw at him. Stewart, the district attorney, did most of the talking; and Jim Conway, telling me about the interrogation later, said he hammered at Bill like a pile driver.

"Now, Doctor, why did Donald Morgan go to the Wainwrights' playhouse the night he was killed?"

"Good God, how do I know?"

"Did you have an appointment to meet him there?"

"I had no appointment with him at all, at any time."

"But you telephoned the Morgan house that afternoon?"

"I had not telephoned it since Morgan came back."

"You telephoned it that day, Doctor. You called and made an appointment to meet Morgan that night."

"That's a lie. I never spoke to him, over the phone or otherwise."

They shifted then. The police commissioner took over the inquiry. "Now see here, Doctor," he said blandly, "we're not trying to bully you. We only want the facts. About this playhouse. How well did you know it?"

"Fairly well. I've been in it several times."

"You didn't think it would be a good place for a quiet talk?"

"Why the hell should I? I could have talked to Morgan anywhere, anytime."

But the one thing they had which could not be denied was Evans's revolver. It lay on Stewart's desk, and he picked it up and looked at it.

"Let's get back to Evans, Doctor. When he was knocked out, his keys were taken, including one to the playhouse. That key was used to open the door of the playhouse the night Morgan was killed, and later found on your key ring. But Evans's gun was taken too. It's important to know where you were that night."

Bill looked up. "How do you know that key was used? There were a dozen people in the house that night. Any one of them could have taken the one from the table in the west wing, slipped out and used it, and then put it back again."

"Oh!" said Stewart. "So you know about the key at the Cloisters too. That's interesting."

But they were not through with Evans.

"On the night the watchman was attacked, where were you?"

"I have already testified to that. I made some calls. The rest of the time I spent with Mrs. Morgan."

"You had expected to marry her?"

"I still do."

There was more about Evans. It was obvious that they believed Bill had been behind his escape—if it was that—from the hospital.

"He recognized you when you struck him, and so you had to—let's say—get him away. That's it, isn't it?"

"Good God!" he shouted. "I'd done my best to save him, sewed up his head, saw him every day. Now you claim I killed him. Ask the hospital. Ask Tony Wainwright. Ask him if he thinks I did away with Evans. He knows better, if this gathering of prize damned fools doesn't."

Stewart kept his temper. He was still suave. He handled the gun gently. "All right, Doctor. Now this is Evans's gun. It has been identified. We also have the serial number on his license to carry it. You know where it was found. Can you account for its being in your desk?"

"I saw it there last night for the first time."

"If you didn't put it there, who did?"

He hesitated. Then he smiled. "I suppose I could say I'd been framed. That's the usual thing, isn't it?"

"Do you claim you were framed?"

"I don't know how it got there," he said stubbornly. "There are always people in and out of my offices. Almost anybody might have done it."

They picked up the gun and handed it to him. "Just look it over, Doctor. Your fingerprints are on it."

"What did you expect? I told you I had picked it up when I saw it there. What are you trying to prove anyhow? If I had taken it from Evans, don't you suppose I'd have done away with it long ago?"

"We're saying that you did just that. You buried it. There's earth in the barrel. Now why did you bury it, if you were innocent? And why did you recover it again?"

He sat very still. Perhaps he had some inkling of the truth then, but he had been tired after a busy day when he was taken, and his exhaustion by that time was acute. He merely made a gesture with his hands and smiled faintly.

"Sorry," he said. "I can't answer that. All I can say is that I didn't bury it."

It was almost morning by that time. Tony, learning of his arrest, had tried to barge in, but they had kept him out. He had spent most of the night pacing up and down the hall, but when Bill had been put in a cell at police headquarters in the City Hall, he and Jim went to a hotel for such sleep as they could get.

They left a weary crowd behind them. But they were sure they had their case, those men in the district attorney's office that night. Stewart sat back after they had gone and yawned.

"Tighter than a drum," he said. "Plenty of motive, a key to the scene of the crime, and the attack on Evans to get that key. Where the hell do you think he's had that gun buried?"

"How about the cemetery?" said Hopper, grinning. "He's probably buried a lot of mistakes there."

They laughed. Their eyes were red with smoke and lack of sleep; all of them were on the point of exhaustion. But they laughed. The law was served, and they had done their job. There were two grand juries in session, and it would be a matter of days only before they obtained an indictment. Stewart got up and buttoned his vest and the waistband of his trousers. He was a portly man.

"All over but the shouting, boys," he said genially, and went down to his car and home to bed.

I knew nothing of that the next morning, nor of the long interrogation which followed it. It is typical, too, of life in a house like the Cloisters that I did not even know that Tony had not been home that night; that he had gotten a call from Jim after he came in the night before and had gone out again at once.

As a matter of fact, I had troubles of my own that morning. One of the difficulties in writing this story is of putting myself on paper. Events happened all around me, but I myself feel rather like a ghost, moving unseen and unreal through them. Yet like poor old Shylock I had dimensions, senses, affections, and passions. I felt pretty sick that day. For one thing, Amy reported that Bessie had tried to slip into Maud's room while she was out of it on an errand.

"She'd asked to see her, and I'd told her she was asleep. What does she want in there anyhow? This isn't the first time she's tried it."

The other was a growing fear that Tony might have been somehow involved in Don's murder. I was confident that Bessie knew something. Her uneasiness, the fact that she locked herself in her room, the revolver in her bag, pointed to it; even her attempts to see Maud, and her statement to me that she could crush Tony any time she wanted. I could even go back on the morning Maud had fallen in the bathroom. Hilda out of the room, Maud partially dressed, and Tony coming in.

"Listen, Mother, I've got to tell you something. I can't go on like this. I—"

I had no one to talk to that morning. Bessie was out somewhere. Maud was out of the question. And when I tried to talk to Hilda she shied like a frightened horse. I suppose Bill's arrest had reached the servants' hall, although no one had told me.

"How long were you out of the room, Hilda, when Mrs. Wainwright fainted? The day she took sick?"

"Not more than ten minutes, miss."

"Did Mr. Tony see her that morning?"

"I wouldn't know," she said stiffly. "It's not likely with her not dressed, miss."

"Or Miss Bessie?"

"I don't think she was up."

But Hilda looked uneasy, and she escaped as soon as she could.

To escape, myself, I took Prince out before lunch and rode through the hills. Roger went along, and what with his companionship, the soft rustle of Prince's feet among the fallen leaves, and the exercise I began to feel better.

As it happened, I met Julian Stoddard on the trail that day. He looked sober, but he unbent enough to speak as we passed.

"Glorious weather, isn't it?"

"Wonderful," I said.

As Prince chose that moment to shy at a pheasant and nearly knock my head off against the limb of a tree, this was the extent of our conversation. But I was to remember it later, his fine figure, his big horse, his general air of pride and well-being. He stood by until Prince discovered that the bird's intentions were pacific.

"All right?" he called.

I waved back at him. "Nothing but a broken neck," I said, and went on.

It was on my way home that morning that I saw Margery Stoddard and Bessie. They were together on the path between the Stoddard place and ours, and they were so deep in conversation that they never heard Prince as he approached. Bessie was sitting on a log smoking a cigarette, and Margery was standing in front of her, looking down at her.

"I've done all I can," she said angrily. "If you let Bill Sterling go to the chair I'll tell everything I know. Everything."

Bessie laughed. "I don't think you'll do that. Better think it over."

Then Prince rounded the underbrush and Bessie threw away her cigarette and got up. "Here's Pat," she said. "Well, I've had my exercise. I'll wander back home."

I walked Prince back to let him cool off, and Bessie kept close to his heels. I had a faint hope that he would haul off and kick her, but he did not. And it was Bessie who told me about Bill's arrest. I could not believe it. Not until I had telephoned Mrs. Watkins was I convinced. Then riding clothes and all I took my car and drove down to see Lydia.

Lydia was seeing nobody. The maid who answered the door said she had eaten no breakfast, and that her door had been locked since the night before. She had not even seen Miss Audrey. No, Miss Audrey was not there. She had gone to the cemetery, she thought.

I still had no idea what it was all about. I turned up the hill toward the cemetery, and it was on the road there that I saw Audrey, still dressed in deep mourning and on foot. Neither she nor Lydia had used the car since Don's death, and she was limping along on high heels, carrying a rather wilted bunch of dahlias from their garden.

I stopped and picked her up, but she had little to say. For the first time I felt sorry for her. She looked young and hot in her black, and her eyes were swollen as if she had been crying. She put her flowers on the seat and got in.

"Thanks a lot, Pat," she said. "My feet were about gone."

She got out a handkerchief and dabbed carefully at her face. I had meant to ask her about Bill's arrest, but the moment was not propitious.

"Why don't you get away, both of you?" I asked. "You certainly look as though you could stand a change."

"Mother won't go, and I don't care where I am."

"Well, get out the car and use it then," I said impatiently. "After all, you'll have to use it sometime. You can't go wandering around on foot forever."

She shivered. "I never want to see it again. It—it's horrible."

"Listen, Audrey," I said. "You hadn't seen your father since you were a small child. I know it is sad and all that, but you can't let it spoil your life. You're still young, and perhaps if you knew all the facts you would accept the thing better."

"What facts?"

"Why don't you ask your mother? I don't think she has been entirely frank with you. After all, he went off and left you both, and I don't imagine it has been easy for her."

"She hated him. She wanted him dead," she said with sudden violence. "I've seen her face when she thought she was alone. She looked murderous."

"Audrey," I said sharply, "don't talk like that. It's wrong and it's dangerous. What are you trying to do? Make trouble? You know she would never hurt anybody, or even think about it."

"No?" she said. "Then why was she burying a revolver in the garden?" Her voice rose. "I saw her, I tell you. I'd always believed in her. She was all I had for years on end. And she never had a gun. Never."

I stopped the car. I did not know why Bill Sterling had been arrested, but I did know of the search for Evans's missing gun. Certainly it would not do for a hysterical girl to go about accusing Lydia of hiding such a weapon. I suppose there was fear as well as anger in my voice, for she drew away from me like a scared puppy.

"When was all this?"

"The night before last."

I turned on her furiously. "Are you deliberately trying to

involve your mother in a murder?" I demanded. "She's been damned good to you for years. You were a spoiled little brat, but she tried to make you into something. I thought maybe she had. But first you spread a story that Tony Wainwright and your father had quarreled, and now it's this. How many people have you told? It's too much to hope you've kept your mouth shut."

"I haven't talked about it," she said sulkily. "I haven't seen anybody but Larry, and he was having a fit about something. But Mother knows I saw her. I told her."

I sat still, trying to think. The gun was important, I knew. Whoever had knocked Evans out had taken one; and knowing my valley as I do, I did not believe there were many such weapons knocking around loose. I tried to think, with Audrey sniffling beside me. Lydia had not mentioned a gun to me, although she had been frank enough about everything else. Now Audrey had found her burying one. I never doubted that for once she was telling the truth.

She stopped sniffling and wiped her eyes. "I'm all right now, Pat," she said, in a little-girl voice. "I'm sorry. I don't think Mother killed him. I never did, really. She was just hiding it for Bill Sterling."

I had my hand on the starter, but I took it off. "Now what do you mean by that?"

She looked startled. "I wish you wouldn't jump at me," she said fretfully. "I just thought, with the police watching Bill, maybe he wanted to get rid of it."

"See here, Audrey, I want to hear this whole story. Where is it now? Is it still buried?"

She looked at me defiantly. "No," she said. "I dug it up yesterday and I took it back to Bill Sterling's office and left it in his desk."

CHAPTER NINETEEN

I PUT her out of the car then and there, and ten minutes later I was at the station house. The desk sergeant was eating an apple, and Cracker Brown had left his radio and was looking important over a ham sandwich. I had known them both all my life, but I must have looked pretty wild just then.

"Anything wrong?" said the sergeant. "Excuse the apple. I didn't have time for breakfast. We're pretty busy here just now."

"Where's the chief?"

"He's up in the city. He's been there since last night."

My heart sank like a stone. "What's happened?" I said. "Have they arrested anybody?"

The sergeant grinned, "I couldn't say, miss."

I was turning away when Cracker Brown spoke. "Don't be a sap, Sam," he said. "It's all over the place already." He turned to me. "Take it easy, Pat. They took Bill Sterling up to the city last night, and nobody's come back yet."

"You mean they've arrested him?"

"I don't know. Held as a material witness or something. They got something new on him yesterday. I don't know what it was."

But I knew, of course. They had found the gun.

There were other things, too, that I did not know. For instance, that Hopper had already been in Beverly early that morning. He had had three hours' sleep, breakfast, and a shave, and he went at once to Bill Sterling's house. Like most valley houses it sat in its own grounds; that is, there was perhaps half an acre to the property. It was an old place, and when Bill took it he had added a small one-story wing with three rooms which were his offices. There was a narrow cement walk to this wing, with a sign at the entrance and shrubbery on both sides, and when Mrs. Watkins first spied Hopper he was on his knees there, looking at a recently dug hole in the ground.

She descended on him with a fury.

"Where's the doctor?" she demanded. "If you idiots are keeping him you can come in and answer the telephone. It's driving me crazy. And what are you doing there?"

"Looking at a hole," said Hopper cheerfully. "Just curious, that's all."

"If you look hard enough you'll find a bone in it," she said. "The dog's been working there for the last hour."

She stooped and triumphantly produced the bone, and Hopper got up, looking sheepish.

"Sure you didn't put it there yourself?" he said.

"When I feel like burying something—and I do at this minute—I won't do it in the front yard."

All this, of course, I learned later. That morning I simply stood in the station house and wondered what to do next. What I finally did do was to go to Lydia. I did not ask to see her. I simply marched up the stairs and into her room, to find her standing by a window. She had not bothered to dress. She had thrown a kimono over her nightgown, and she looked as if she had not slept all night.

"Are they holding him, Pat?"

"He's still in town; I don't know." Then I plunged. "Lydia, where's that gun of Don's that you buried?"

"What gun?" she said, almost in a whisper.

"You know better than I do. Do you know that Audrey took it yesterday and left it in Bill Sterling's desk?"

"Audrey!" she caught at a chair. "Not Audrey, Pat. Why would she do that to me?"

I told her, not mincing words: Audrey's story, the almost certainty that the police had found the gun, and Bill's arrest as a result. She seemed hardly able at first to realize what it meant.

"These children," she said. "They know so well what is right and what is wrong. They have no mercy, Pat."

Then the full impact of what I had said about Bill reached her, and I thought she was going to faint.

It was some time before I got the story from her. Even then it was not particularly helpful. Don had had the gun. She had not known it until after he was killed, when she found it under his mattress. The police had not been there yet, and she had no reason to hide it. Why would she? Nobody had been shot. But she was afraid of firearms, so she had taken it and put it in the top of her closet, in a hatbox.

Then, little by little, the Evans story was brought out. Evans's revolver was missing, and she began to wonder if this one was his. Of course, so far as she knew, Don had not been in Beverly when Evans was attacked, but he might have been. It didn't sound rational, but it might have been that way.

She began to worry about it. One of the maids might find it, or Audrey. A night or two earlier she had buried it in the garden among the delphiniums, and Audrey saw her doing it.

"I thought she had gone out," she said drearily. "Why would

she do a thing like that? Putting it in Bill's desk! She can't think Bill killed Don. She can't."

"She does," I said grimly. "She isn't sure about you, but she's pretty sure about Bill."

That shocked her into speech. She tried to defend Audrey. "You don't understand, Pat. She was crazy about Don; on the defensive every minute about him, and—oh, well, what does it matter now? She wanted me to take him back. She wouldn't even speak to Bill."

"Did she think it was Bill's gun?"

"She said so. I suppose it's understandable. I was hiding it, and she knew I never owned one. Don't be too hard on her, Pat. I suppose she thinks she is avenging her father's death."

Audrey came in soon after that, but I did not look at her. I was at the telephone in the hall, having located Jim Conway in town, and Lydia was hastily dressing upstairs. Audrey sneaked past me just as Jim replied.

"It's Pat, Jim," I said. "Hold everything, will you? I'm bringing Lydia and Audrey Morgan in as soon as I can get there. I have some news for you. It ought to help."

"Good girl," he said. "Hurry, will you? They're moving pretty fast here."

I hung up and faced Audrey. She was pale and sullen.

"I'm not going to town," she said.

"Oh, yes, you are," I said. "You're going to town all right, and you're going to tell the dirty little trick you pulled. You can have your choice of going with me or of being taken there by the police. So far as I'm concerned you can roll a hoop all the way. But you're going."

She went, of course. I think she knew that I was ready to take her by main force if necessary. She sulked all the way in, but she was frightened too. I began to feel sorry for her, but when she snubbed Lydia by refusing to speak to her at all I was cold with fury.

Everybody who followed our murders knows what happened that day in the district attorney's office. They could not break Lydia's story. She had found the gun, put it away, and forgotten about it. Then when Evans disappeared and she heard about his revolver, she had decided to hide it.

No, she had no idea how her husband had happened to have it. He had had it, that was all. She had not told Dr. Sterling about it. He had never seen it until he found it in his desk. Certainly she had buried it in her garden. If there was dirt in it they could prove that, couldn't they? There must be ways to identify the kind of earth. She had used Irish moss on her borders. That could be recognized, couldn't it, if it was there?

It was not conclusive, but there was obvious honesty in her face and manner; and Audrey, brought in after Lydia, gave her own story with such obvious prejudice against Bill that she was equally convincing. No, she had never known her father to have a gun. All she knew was that she had seen Lydia burying it. "And she would do anything to protect Bill Sterling." Protect him from what? Why did she associate the revolver with the doctor? Did she knew it belonged to Evans? Had she examined it?

Her lovely face was set with hatred. She had loved her father and she believed Bill had killed him. In the end it became clear that her motive in putting the revolver in Bill's desk was merely that she thought it belonged to him. Then she burst into hysterical crying, and they let her go.

There was a conference after that. The district attorney lit a cigar and sat back in his chair. "We can get an indictment," he said. "We've still got that key on the doctor's ring, and his car in the Beaver Creek Road that night. There's no doubt that he detested Morgan and wanted him out of the way. But we've a long way to go before we've got a case."

Jim Conway was in on that conference. They hadn't wanted him, but he was there. Now he grinned at Stewart.

"You never did have a case," he said. "How in heck could Bill Sterling have been just behind the murder car? He's not twins." He got up and jammed his hat on his head.

"It's no dice, gentlemen," he said. "No dice whatever." And banged the door as he went out.

They released Bill Sterling the next day. But they put a man to watch him, and out of that Bill got the first fun he had had in weeks. The detective only went to bed when Bill did, and every now and then Bill would call him up at the hotel in the middle of the night.

"All right, brother," he would say cheerfully. "Get your clothes on and I'll be around to pick you up. Baby case in the country."

"Go on and have your baby. I need some sleep."

"Not on your life. I'll be there in ten minutes."

The relief was tremendous. It was wonderful to have Bill, big and quiet, coming in to see Maud once more. And Tony was himself again. One Saturday morning I found a sheet of paper in my office typewriter:

> Mr. Anthony Wainwright requests the pleasure of Miss ABbott'S company—two damns here. This machine's crzay—on horseback at the stalbes at three o8clock this afternoon. R. S. V. P.

I went. I remember that Tony rode hatless, and how the wind stirred his hair. I remember the tang of autumn in the air, and the sharp click of the horses' hoofs as we cantered along the trail. And most of all I remembered stopping at the top of a hill, and Tony suddenly serious.

"Why can't life be like this, Pat?" he said. "Work and play, and a girl like you to come home to?"

I controlled my voice. "It could be," I said steadily. "One mistake needn't ruin everything."

He sat still, looking out over the hills. Then he leaned over in his saddle and touched my hand.

"Some day, my darling," he said quietly.

The case was not over, of course. It was, in a way, only beginning. But except for the police boats still on the river, things had largely settled down. True, Hopper was to be seen now and then, and the little detective in Bill's car began to be a familiar figure. When Bill was seeing Maud the man would wander about the place.

One day I saw him with an orchid in his buttonhole, and only hoped he would escape before Andy discovered it.

But aside from these reminders, everything was fairly quiet. Even the reporters had abandoned us, although there was still a corporal's guard of them, indignant that the Beverly Hotel had no liquor license. They hung mostly around the station house, getting Coca-Cola at the drugstore when nothing else was to be had. Now and then in the grounds I would be disconcerted to hear the click of a camera, and see a face grinning at me from the shrubbery.

"Atta girl! Thanks a lot."

It would disappear, and incredibly soon after I would see a hideous distortion of myself in the papers.

Maud was allowed to sit up by that time. She was very thin, for her, and her color was not good. One day she asked me if I thought Evans could have murdered Don.

"Evans? How could he? He was in the hospital."

She was not convinced. Old men got queer sometimes. There were the long winter months when for years he had been alone in the house, with her in the South and Tony at his club. It must have been pretty dreary, she thought.

But the subject seemed to distress her. She had definitely changed since her illness. What suspicions she had, sitting there alone in her chair, I do not know. Physically she was better. Two of the nurses had gone and only Amy remained. But she had lost her old decision. I would see Mrs. Partridge, the day's menus in her hand, stand there for a long time before Maud so much as realized she was there. But she was always gay with Tony. He would push her wheel chair out to her upstairs garden when it was warm enough, and sit there with her.

"You look like a debutante, with that new figure of yours," he would say, smiling at her.

She would laugh, showing her strong white teeth.

"Debutante!" she would scoff. "Just because after thirty years I can see my ribs again. Get along with you."

But with Amy and me she did not bother to act. She would sit for hours, gazing out over the dying autumn garden, her big hands folded in her lap, her expression remote. Amy's chatter passed over her head entirely.

"What did you say, Miss Richards?"

"I was just talking to myself," Amy would say. "Time for your eggnog. I'll go and get it."

It was on one such occasion that Maud gave me the combination to her safe. We had been talking about Don's murder. She could not understand why our playhouse had been used, although she said she could perhaps understand the murder itself.

"If he had behaved badly to some woman," she said. "But this girl he ran away with—He married her, didn't he? And it seems strange, his being dressed as he was. Or not dressed. If he had meant to meet somebody—"

"He had no other clothes," I told her. And then and there I gave her a picture of poor old Don in that house in the valley; the two women, Audrey and Lydia, exercising their constant espionage over him, the one through suspicion and the other through belated affection. Even the telephone in an open hall downstairs, and on the night he was killed the fact that his clothing had been sent away by Lydia.

She listened intently, as though she were attempting to reconcile what I said with some secret inner knowledge of her own. Once she asked me if Tony was still seeing Audrey. She seemed relieved when I said I thought not. Of course, she knew the revolver story by that time, as indeed did everybody.

"I'm glad," she said. "The girl sounds neurotic." And Amy coming in just then, she dutifully drank her eggnog and changed the subject.

That is how matters stood with us during those early days in last October. Don had been dead for two weeks. Evans was still missing. Bill Sterling was at liberty but going about, as he said, like a large comet with a tail, the tail being the detective. And as the leaves fell the playhouse, locked and deserted, became more and more visible from the house. There was no escaping it, from the west wing at least.

Now and then I saw Hopper prowling about, and Bessie was

still with us, locking herself in her rooms, talking now and then of Palm Beach or Nassau but making no move to go.

"That tart," Amy would say. "Just keep her away from me, or some day I'll knock that nose of hers so flat she'll have to smell with her ears."

Then one day something happened to Bessie, and we knew our troubles were not yet over.

She had been buying clothes lavishly, and that day she went to the city to be fitted. She drove her own car, but at seven o'clock that night she had not come back. Gus came up from the garage to tell me about it.

"She doesn't like being out after dark," he said. "I wondered if I'd better go and look for her. She may have had trouble. She's a fast driver."

He avoided my eyes. Both of us knew that Bessie had been drinking considerably during the past few weeks, and I thought rapidly. Tony was not back from town, and I did not want to worry Maud.

"I'll go with you, Gus," I said. "Wait until I get a coat."

He brought the station wagon around, and five minutes later we were on the road to the city. It was almost deserted, the people who preferred it to the railroad having already passed. At that, we almost missed her. Gus's eyes were good, however. Suddenly he stopped and backed up. There was a car about fifty feet off the road, jammed against a tree.

We got out and ran to it. It was not a pretty sight. Bessie was bent over the wheel unconscious, and the car was a total wreck. Together Gus and I got her into the station wagon, and I held her as best I could on the way back. She was partially conscious some time before we reached the Cloisters. She opened her eyes and looked up at me.

"Somebody shot me," she said, and closed her eyes again.

I got Gus's flashlight and looked her over. There was no blood on her that I could see. She'd given her forehead a terrific bump against the windshield, and she moaned that it hurt her to breathe. She refused to be taken to the hospital, however. We took her back to the Cloisters and called the men to carry her in. Not until then did I see she was still clutching her small revolver.

CHAPTER TWENTY

It was Amy who told me her condition that night, an Amy reluctantly pressed into service but once more the nurse. Bessie had a slight concussion and several broken ribs, "and I guess that will hold her for a while." But she was frankly incredulous as to Bessie's insistence that somebody had shot at her.

"I don't believe her," she said. "She's smashed her car and she'll want a new one. Not," she added judicially, "that plenty of people wouldn't like to shoot her. I couldn't be trusted with a gun myself."

Tony did not get home until nine o'clock that night. Reynolds told him at once, and he found me in the library.

"What's this about Bessie? Is it serious?"

"I don't think so. She's got some broken ribs. Bill Sterling says there's some concussion too. Not much."

"Does Mother know?" he asked.

"I've told her. Tony, she says somebody shot at her."

"Nonsense! Who would do a thing like that?"

Jim Conway came in soon afterward. I thought he looked pretty grim. He accepted Tony's offer of a highball, but he did not relax. He fairly bristled with suspicion, and I dare say finding us together did not help matters.

"I've been looking over your wife's car," he said. "It looks as though somebody tried to kill her tonight, Tony."

"Kill her? Are you serious?"

"As serious as three bullet holes in the rear tire of her car and one in the body."

"Good God," said Tony, and got up. "Where is the car? I want to look it over."

But Jim did not move. "I suppose you can account for your own movements tonight?"

"I didn't shoot at my wife, if that's what you mean," said Tony savagely.

His account that evening, however, was not entirely satisfactory. I could see that on Jim's face. Tony had left his office at five as usual. He had gone back later to do some long-distance telephoning. At seven-thirty he had gone to his club for dinner, and left for home about half past eight.

"Where were you at seven?" Jim asked.

"Still in my office."

"Anybody prove that?"

"I was alone. The man in the elevator may remember taking me down. He wouldn't know the time, probably."

Jim got up. "I'm sorry, Tony. It's a hell of a mess. You see, the clock on the instrument board stopped at seven. You carry a gun, don't you?"

"Not always. It's usually in my room. It's there now."

But it was not there. The two men went upstairs together, to come down a few minutes later. I heard them going out, and it was midnight before Tony came back. He was not alone. Both

Jim and the detective Hopper were with him, and shortly after that Dwight Elliott drove up.

It was Amy who kept me informed, an Amy now happily relieved of Bessie by another nurse and enjoying herself hugely. But it was days before I learned what had taken place that night in Tony's study: the four men with drinks at their elbows, Tony's set face, Hopper's shrewd one, and Mr. Elliott's watchful. At first it was genial enough. When Bill Sterling, making his final call on Bessie, was brought in, Hopper greeted him with a grin.

"How about letting that fellow of mine get some sleep, Doctor? He's threatening to resign."

"It won't hurt him to learn how a hard-working medical man earns his living."

They let him go, after he described Bessie's injuries. They were not serious, but she was suffering from shock; some concussion too.

After that the quartette settled down to business. Jim lit his pipe and Hopper took a small sip of his highball.

"Tell us about tonight, Mr. Wainwright," he said pleasantly. "We're particularly interested in the time between five and seven-thirty o'clock. Did you spend all that time in your office?"

"Not all of it. No. But I finally left there at half past six."

"And after that?"

"I went to the public library."

Even Hopper looked surprised. "The library?" he inquired. "Do you care to explain that?"

"No," said Tony flatly. "Or the telephone either. I suppose you can check the calls, if you want."

"Were you seen at the library?"

"It was pretty crowded. I don't know."

Hopper sat looking at him. "I suppose you realize, if that's the case, that you have no real alibi from six-thirty to the time you got to your club. I'm afraid you'll have to be more explicit."

"I've told you all I'm going to," said Tony stubbornly. "I didn't shoot at my wife, if that's what you mean. I didn't even have my gun with me."

They were off after the gun then. When had he seen it last? Where was his license to carry it? He produced the card, and Hopper made a record of the serial number.

"You kept it loaded?"

"I did."

"How long since you've seen it?"

"I don't know. I've kept it in my room since we had the two attempts to get into the house. That's some time ago. I haven't noticed it lately, but that doesn't mean anything. I wasn't looking for it."

"Who would take it?" said Hopper. "It was kept in your room. How many people had access to it?"

He went on. Mrs. Wainwright—Mrs. Anthony Wainwright—had been nervous recently, he understood. She had insisted on locking her doors. Wasn't that unusual, in her husband's home? "She is here, surrounded by—well, let's say a loving family." He smiled sardonically. "But the lady is terrified. Have you any explanation of that, Mr. Wainwright?"

"I have never pretended to explain my wife," said Tony gruffly.

They did not arrest him, of course. The meeting—if it could be called that—broke up at half past two, and Dwight Elliott spent the rest of the night there. But in the hall before he left Hopper turned to Tony.

"Just what is your theory about this man Evans?" he asked, almost gently. "Think he knew something?"

"About what?" said Tony aggressively.

"That's what I'd like to know."

"See here, if you think I dragged Evans out of the hospital and did away with him—"

"Nobody dragged him," said Hopper, still gently. "I imagine he went willingly, with somebody he knew. And trusted," he added, watching the smoke from his cigar.

"And then what? I suppose I hit him on the head and carted him off! I did a good job, didn't I, since nobody's been able to find him."

"That doesn't necessarily follow," said Hopper, and followed Jim out to his car.

The morning papers had the story of the attack on Bessie. It had taken place at a sharp curve, and when her rear tires blew out she had lost control of the car. There were even photographs of the car itself, with a wrecking crew working over it and Jim standing by. Maud was badly upset by the whole affair. When she learned that Dwight Elliott was in the house she sent for him.

They had a long talk, and he came out looking less like his dapper self than usual. He stopped me in the hall and asked me to search the house that day for Tony's gun.

"It's important," he said. "I needn't say how important, Miss Abbott."

Bessie was better that morning, although in a vile humor. She maintained that someone had tried to murder her, that she knew who it was, and that the police did not have to go to look. All in all it was a mad day. I searched the house from the trunk room on the third floor to the basement. There was no gun. And late in the afternoon—as usual in my desperate moments—I went down to see Lydia. Of all people in the world Miss Mattie was there, in the black taffeta which looked like the one she used to wear at dancing school, and sitting with her neat toes neatly pointed out.

"I was telling Lydia," she said, "I don't know whether to go to the police or not. You see, I think I saw the man who shot at Mrs. Wainwright last night."

"Saw him!" I gasped.

She fluttered. "I certainly saw somebody. I was driving out from town. I'd been in to look for a gift for you, my dear." She looked at Lydia. "I was coming out slowly. You know I'm a nervous driver. And about where the accident happened I saw a man standing by a parked car."

"What sort of man? What sort of car?"

"Well, now, I really can't say. It was dark, you know. It was just before you get to that curve." She shuddered. "I almost stopped and asked him if he needed help. Just think, if I had!"

"I don't think he would have hurt you, Miss Mattie," I said. "Whoever it was was after Bessie Wainwright, not you."

"I see," she said in a gentle voice. "Poor Tony Wainwright! But then I believe she was always rather fast."

I looked after her as she got into her car.

"You see how it is," I said bitterly. "They all believe it was Tony. Even the police."

"The truth has a habit of coming out, Pat," Lydia said quietly.

Some boats were dragging the river for Evans that day. Not the police. They had ceased operations some time before. Tony, however, had offered a reward for Evans's body, dead or alive, with the result that half a dozen small craft were at work. I could see them from where I sat. They made me shiver, but Audrey and her young crowd seemed to be enjoying it. They had established a sort of headquarters down by the water, and I could hear them that day from where I sat.

"Look! They've got something!"

"They have for a fact. Who's got the field glasses? Well, for Pete's sake, it's only a log!"

Lydia saw my face. "They're young, Pat," she said. "Death is still only a word to them."

She looked better. She said she and Bill hoped to be married before long, and she talked a little about her plans. But once she looked out at the river, and then at me.

"Pat, do you think Evans could be doing all this? He may still be alive. He could be hiding near by, you know. Back somewhere in the hills, perhaps."

"Why would he shoot at Bessie?"

"I don't know, unless—What do you know about Bessie, Pat? Really know, I mean. Who is she? Who was she? Why did Don go out at night with her? He did, you know, at least once. Larry Hamilton saw them. I've wondered—how old do you think she is?"

"She's older than she says she is. I don't know how much."

"The girl who ran away with Don was only eighteen, Pat. She'd be about thirty-three now. I never saw her, but—it's possible, Pat, isn't it? Why did Don come back? Why is Bessie here now? Suppose she'd feathered her nest by marrying Tony Wainwright, and Don comes back and threatens to spill the beans. She'd do almost anything to get rid of him, wouldn't she?"

"It would have taken a lot of nerve, Lydia. Suppose somebody recognized her?"

"She has plenty of nerve, hasn't she?"

"You mean—"

"Somebody killed Don."

"She couldn't have done all of it alone, Lydia."

"No. Not alone," she said composedly.

I knew what she meant. If Bessie had killed Don, Tony might have helped her to get rid of the body. Not to save her. Not for her sake, but for his mother's. I lit a cigarette, and tried to think back, as well as I could. I knew very little, really. Only of his marriage, as Maud had told it to me: that Bessie had had perfectly respectable parents at her wedding, that she had gone to a good school, and that she belonged to the Junior League. Still, a clever girl could have managed that, have borrowed parents for the occasion and invented the rest.

"You see, I wouldn't recognize her," Lydia said. "You know how it is in a business office. I never even knew her name until they were gone. She was just another girl to me."

"What was her name?"

"She called herself Marguerite Weston. I imagine the Marguerite at least was a slight touch of—well, of imagination." She stirred. "See here, Pat, we might find out about it. Or rather you might. I can't very well, an account of Bill."

"How can I? After fifteen years?"

"There might be something in the newspaper files. I think they have them at the library here. Maybe even a photograph, although I never saw any."

I agreed to think about it, and that day, with Audrey's crowd screaming on the river bank and the boats moving slowly along, she told me something of herself and Don.

"I was only eighteen when I met him," she said, "but you know what he was. When he was younger he was any girl's dream. I met him in Paris. He had a good position there, in the export office of one of the big American companies. Then, too, he'd been born here in the city. His family was all dead, but it was a sort of bond between us."

She had been in France with an aunt, and the aunt had objected. "She thought he wanted my money. I had a good bit then. Besides, she thought he was too old for me. But—a girl of that age—" She sighed.

Anyhow, she had married him in London. Patou had made her dress, and Don had sent white orchids for her bouquet. She had been frightfully happy. But when business began to contract the foreign office was given up. Don was sent back to New York and then to his home city. He hadn't wanted to return, but she was enchanted. They bought the house at Beverly, with her money, and Don commuted.

But he was gay. He liked going about. Then Audrey was born, and nothing was the same after that. "I was tied to the house and he wasn't. He adored her, but—"

She looked down at her finger, where she had once worn a wedding ring.

"He was never faithful," she said. "I knew that even then, but he would come home and be so remorseful that I forgave him. Perhaps if I had been harder to him—"

Her voice trailed off. She was busy with her own unhappy thoughts, and I was seeing Don riding out on his big horse on Sunday mornings. "Hello, Pat. How's the jumping?"

"I fell off yesterday."

"That's the game, sweetheart. Don't let it get you."

The crowd on the river bank was still noisy when I left.

"Two bits they've got him!"

"Gimme the glasses, somebody. You lose, Larry. It looks like an old tire."

CHAPTER TWENTY-ONE

TONY DID not come home that night at all, but I had plenty to think of. If Bessie had been Marguerite Weston, where did that leave him? Suppose the police learned it? It would give them a motive for the attack on Bessie, perhaps even for Don's murder.

I slept badly, and early the next morning I went down to the public library on Main Street. Old Dan Reeves, who has been in charge there since my Elsie Dinsmore days, looked surprised when I asked for files of old city newspapers. At one o'clock I emerged, black with dust but no further along than I had been before. Fifteen years before there had been no scandal sheet in the city, and there was no mention of Donald Morgan's elopement or of Marguerite Weston. Only a year or so later a brief announcement from Reno of Lydia's divorce.

I called her and told her. She accepted it quietly.

"I suppose it was a foolish idea, anyhow," she said. "Let's forget it, Pat."

That was the situation by the middle of October of last year. The Cloisters had been entered twice, Don Morgan had been murdered in the playhouse. Evans had disappeared, and Bessie had been shot at and barely escaped with her life. To the people who knew something of the inside story there were a dozen possible explanations, but the general public was bewildered. It is not surprising that the theory of a lunatic at large began to grow.

I think Maud herself inclined to that opinion.

"There might have been a reason for Mr. Morgan's death," she said, looking white and tired. "A good many people seem to have had reason to want him out of the way. But Evans, and now Bessie—"

I would have sworn that the effect on her was one of pure bewilderment. She would sit for hours, her big hands folded in her lap, her eyes fixed on nothing. Once a day she made a slow pilgrimage to Bessie's bedroom, where Bessie lay resentful among her pillows. I think Maud dreaded those visits. Amy said her pulse would be more rapid after them. And Bessie would be uncompromisingly rude. I went with her one morning. Bessie was up, lying on a chaise longue, with the usual movie magazine in her hand.

The nurse had to unlock the door to admit us, and Maud made a protest. "My dear, do you think it is necessary to keep your door locked all the time? After all, we are responsible for you."

Bessie looked at her coldly. "I'm not trusting anybody around this place," she said.

"I'm afraid I don't understand that, Bessie."

"I think you do. If you don't, ask Tony."

"Tony? Surely you don't believe—"

"Listen," said Bessie. "Tony's got plenty of reason to want me out of the way. Who else gives a damn?"

"What reason, Bessie?"

She looked at me. "I can see one," she said. "The other—better let it go at that. I'm not talking, unless I have to."

It was not pretty, nor was Bessie just then. I can find excuses for her now. She was genuinely terrified and for the time at least helpless. She had walked into a trap, and she could see no way out. As for Maud, I do not believe until then she had even considered that Tony might be involved in the shooting.

Later on, however, she sent for Dwight Elliott, and asked me to be present at the interview.

"I want to be sure he tells me the truth. All the truth," she said. "I don't want him trying to save my feelings."

But Mr. Elliott showed no indication of trying to save her feelings. He tried to evade her at first. Of course, nobody believed Tony had shot at Bessie. But she was too shrewd for him. In the end she learned about the missing gun, and Tony's lack of an alibi.

"One trouble," he said, sitting thin and distinguished beside her bed, "is that Tony changed his usual procedure that night. Normally if he's not coming home for dinner he plays squash at the club. That day he didn't. He went back to his office for an hour. After that he went to the public library."

"The public library, Dwight? I don't believe it."

"That's what he did. He tells me he wanted some files of old newspapers. The clerk at the desk was busy. I've seen him. He says someone asked about the files that night, but there was a crowd around him. He can't identify Tony. I'm sorry, my dear. I'd do anything to save you this, but you insisted."

It was some time before she spoke. "I see," she said in a low voice. "And the office. Why did he go back there?"

"The police have discovered that, I'm afraid. He went back to use the long-distance telephone, and they've traced the call. Tony refuses to explain, but they know about it. He talked to a firm of private detectives in New York."

She sat bolt upright at that. "Private detectives, Dwight! Dear God, what are we to do?"

They sent me out of the room then. Mr. Elliott had not wanted me at all, and he was glad to get rid of me. It was a full hour before he came out, to take his car and start back to town. And Amy, going into Maud's room, found her crying wildly.

Tony never knew of that visit. He was putting up a good front during that week or so. And Maud, after that outburst of hers, was doing the same, although I thought she watched him.

"You're not worrying about anything, Tony?"

"Certainly I'm worried."

"Can't you tell me about it?"

He would grin at me. "It's that strawberry mark. I hate to seem indelicate, but I'm sure Pat's holding out on me."

He brought her foolish little gifts, a small poker dice machine in the shape of a cash register, toys that wound up.

Maud would laugh, and for a time the shadow would fall away. Alone with me, however, Tony looked tired and depressed. His gun had not been found, although the grounds as well as the countryside had been combed. They had even drained the fountain near the playhouse, and a man with a ladder had examined its upper basin. There was no sign yet of Evans. The boats had ceased dragging the river, but the hunt was still on. And Bessie was up and about; she was keeping a nurse by her side, although I think her suspicions of Tony had weakened.

Some time during her convalescence he had had a long talk with her. Amy swears that she had her little pearl-handled revolver under a cushion while it was going on. However that may be, I believe he told her that her whole attitude was absurd as well as dangerous.

"Why should I shoot you?" he said. "Or shoot at you? It's

nonsense. And I'm not a complete idiot. If I wanted to do that to anybody you can be damned sure I'd have an alibi."

She was less defiant after that. Not friendly. She was never that to any of us. She still locked her doors. But I think now she was floundering like the rest of us. All she had been able to tell the police was that she had been on her way home, traveling fast, that she had heard three or four shots, and that her car had suddenly gone out of control.

Unlike Miss Mattie, she had not seen anybody; and Miss Mattie, questioned by Jim, was completely vague.

"It was just a man, standing by a car," she said.

We were having a breathing space at least, those October days. Maud was stronger, Bessie was planning to go away, the local excitement was dying down, and the weather was fine. I rode a great deal, generally hatless, with Prince's feet rustling among the leaves on the trail and Roger loving the long upgrades where horse and dog could gallop. One day Nan Osgood called up from the village to say the dramatic club was going to give *Lady Windermere's Fan*, and would I help them out.

"I'll be the fan," I said cheerfully. "Otherwise I'm afraid it's out, Nan. I'm having a little time now, but it won't last."

Nor did it. It was, I think, the next day that Maud sent for me. She was alone except for Hilda, Amy being off for a nap, and she sent Hilda away without ceremony. I had brought my notebook and pencil, but she waved them aside.

"I want to talk to you," she said. "There are some arrangements I ought to make. I'm better. I'll probably live to be a horrible old woman. But just in case—"

What she wanted to tell me was about the contents of her wall safe. Not only her jewels. A good many of them were in the bank anyhow. She kept only what she usually wore. They were all listed, and Tony would have to pay a huge inheritance tax on both lots. But there was an envelope in the safe. If anything happened to her, she wanted me to get it "before the appraisers step in, or whatever they are."

"Get it and give it to Tony," she said. "Don't let anybody else touch it. There are some papers in it, and a letter for him. I don't want it read by anybody else. I wish you'd open the safe now. And lock the door first."

She read off the combination after I had opened the panel, and asked me to make a note of it. Then I opened the safe and gave her the envelope, a large brown manila one. She sat for some time with it in her hands. Then she drew a long breath and gave it back to me.

"For Tony," she said. "He will understand."

After that she decided to look over her jewels, and I laid out on a table beside her the cases containing those extravagant ornaments of hers. She checked them and I made a list, but she handled them indifferently, with a strange remote look on her face. I suppose they were worth half a million dollars as they lay there.

She was tired after that. She lay back in her chair with her eyes closed, and I realized more than ever how greatly she had changed. Her big hearty laugh had gone, her zest, even the sheen from her lovely hair.

"I feel old, Pat," she said. "Old and tired. I had hoped to see my grandchildren, but I suppose I never will. If only you and Tony—"

Amy came back then. I had closed the safe and the panel by that time, and unlocked the door; but she looked suspicious.

"What's the conspiracy?" she demanded. "You two look as

though you had been plotting something. Out you go, Pat. If you want to stir up trouble, go to Mrs. Tony. She likes it."

Things were still moving, of course, although inside the house we knew nothing about them. It was about that time, for example, that Jim Conway searched Evans's room again. The fact that the police had interrogated Tony and were searching for his gun had reached Jessie McDonald. She was resentful, and at first she refused to admit him.

"I'll thank you not to be bothering me," she said, fixing him with cold Scottish eyes. "I'm house-cleaning for the winter. But I'll say this: if the police would keep their nebs out of this, honest folk might sleep at night."

"Honest folk don't have to be afraid of the police, Mrs. McDonald," he told her amiably.

He had not expected much. Certainly he had not expected what he found. Evans's carpet had been lifted and was hanging in the yard, and under the bed he discovered a loose board. Over Jessie's indignant protests he pried it up, to reveal that it was a cache of sorts. When at last he got up he held a small savings bankbook in his hand. It looked unimportant at first. He eyed it glumly. Then he opened it, and his eyes almost popped out of his head.

It showed that over a period of ten years or more Evans, in addition to his normal savings, had deposited at regular intervals a total of some eighteen thousand dollars.

"You see what it looked like, Pat," he said later. "He'd put by a hundred and fifty dollars a month for all that time. He got eighty dollars a month and his room, and it cost him about forty to live. Where did he get the rest?"

He showed the book to Jessie, who seemed bewildered, and

later he called the bank in town. Yes, Evans had made the deposits. Always in cash. No, there had been no withdrawals. The money was still there.

Thus Evans came back into the story, and Jim, sitting back in his office chair, tried to fit him into it. It looked like blackmail, but blackmail of whom?

He went back over his notes: Don's murder, Bill's arrest, the attempt on Bessie's life.

"Bessie was out," he said. "She'd only been married to Tony five or six years. Lydia was out. She had just enough to live on. Anyhow, I couldn't see her paying blackmail to anybody. Same with Mrs. Wainwright. She could have paid it, but she wouldn't be likely to have kept him around the house in that case. Even Tony was only twenty when it began. So what?"

He telephoned Hopper what he had found, and Hopper came down at once.

"It has to be somebody around here," was his opinion. "He got it in cash, and it never came through the mail that way. Anyhow, the McDonalds say he had no letters for years."

Together they made a list, including everybody in any way connected with the crime. At the end Jim sat back and grunted. "Let's go back to Morgan's death," he said. "That's the key, Hopper. Suppose that girl he eloped with is back again. Suppose she's all settled down, married, and so on. Then Don comes back and threatens her. Maybe he wants a spot of cash. She kills him, and Evans sees it."

Hopper grinned. "Meaning Bessie Wainwright?" he said. "She only married Tony six years ago. That lets her out."

Jim threw the bankbook on the table in disgust. "All right," he said. "It's a lunatic. Or I'm one. I'm headed for Burton right now, if you ask me."

"If it's a lunatic he certainly knows his way about," was Hopper's dry comment.

Nevertheless, both men were now agreed that two things were probable: that Evans had been receiving blackmail money from someone, and that as a result he was dead.

"It may have nothing to do with Morgan's murder," said Hopper laconically.

Jim disagreed. "When we get to the bottom of this," he said, "we'll find that Don Morgan, the attack on Bessie Wainwright, Evans's disappearance, maybe even the cemetery, are all tied up together. This district hasn't had a crime for as long as I can remember. These are law-abiding people. Then it breaks out with a rash of mysteries. You can have all sorts of symptoms, with only one disease," he added, and grinned.

Hopper went back to town, to renew the search for Evans or Evans's body. The next day the police boats were back on the river, and an intensified search of the countryside began once more. But Jim sat in his office, going through the routine of his job, and for long intervals staring at the walls.

In the end he sent for me. It was late in the afternoon, and he gave me a cigarette and lit it before he began. "I want you to help me, Pat," he said. "I seem to remember you worked in town for a while. You know about offices and so on."

"I do," I said with some bitterness. "I've been thrown out of some of the best."

"Still and all," he argued, "you'd know your way about; where the stenographers and so on eat, what they do, how to get to them."

"Get to them? How?"

"Get them to talking. Not the young ones. The old girls. The ones who have been in one position for, say, fifteen years. There's one like that in what used to be Morgan's firm, only her mouth is sewed up so tight I'll bet she's a nose-breather."

Then it came out. He wanted some information about the Weston girl. "You've got to get this," he said. "When Morgan came back he interfered with Lydia and Bill Sterling. All right, you needn't look like that. I don't think either of them killed him. But he was killed. It was no accident. It was thought out, planned. He had to be gotten rid of. Why? Because somebody hated him or else was endangered by him."

"Endangered? Whom could Don Morgan hurt? He'd been away too long."

He shrugged. "Maybe. Maybe not. You know how he left. Everybody does. He ran away with a girl, didn't he? All right. Let's suppose she's married since. Settled down anyhow, become respectable, made a place for herself in the world. Wouldn't she want to hold onto it?"

"I still don't see why he would be a danger to her."

"He might have tried to get money from her. Or maybe her husband didn't know anything about that past of hers. How old would she be, at a guess? Thirty-five?"

"About thirty-three, I think. Not sure. She was very young when it happened, according to Lydia."

"Well, what I want you to do is to get at this old girl. Find out what the Weston woman looked like. Where she lived. Maybe there's a photograph of her around somewhere. If there is I want it. How about it?"

I got up angrily. "You believe it was Bessie, don't you? And that Tony helped her get rid of the body? All I can say is that I think—"

"Listen, Pat," he urged. "Be reasonable. Suppose she meets Morgan, has a fit of temper, and knocks him into the pool. She can't get him out, so he drowns. We know Tony was out that night, and not all the time at the club either. Maybe she finds him and tells him. It's a hell of a mess, and there's his mother to think of. What can he do? He gets the body as far from the Cloisters as he can, and as he's never known Morgan nobody suspects him. He had plenty of time, remember. He admits he didn't get back until half past one that morning."

But I refused. Let somebody else do their dirty work. I couldn't spy on the people who employed me. I remember Jim's arguing, even following me to the door when I left.

"Think it over," he said. "If Tony's mixed up in this he probably couldn't help it. If he isn't, why not try to clear him before that bunch of weasels from the district attorney's office begin to chew him up? And by the way," he added, "in case you change your mind, the old girl's name is Connor. Miss Connor. A virgin and proud of it."

I spent a sleepless night. It fitted together too well, that story of Jim's. It might even explain Evans. Suppose Evans had slipped out of the hospital that night? Where would he be more likely to wander than back to the Cloisters? He might have seen Tony. He might even have helped him. But he would never involve him. Rather than do that he would run away. It was even possible, I thought unhappily, that Tony himself had helped him to escape.

CHAPTER TWENTY-TWO

So I come at last to our real tragedy. Not immediately. There were still some peaceful days, with Amy gone and Maud downstairs every afternoon for tea. Tony made it a point to be there at those times, but he saw the change in her, as I did.

One day, when the sun was bright, she decided to go out into the grounds. I got her a coat, and accompanied by Andy McDonald she made a slow round of the property, the orchid houses, the hothouses, and so on. When she had finished she sat down on a bench and looked up at the old man. She was very fond of him.

"You've been here a long time, Andy," she said. "If I ever have to give up this place I hope you can stay on."

"Give it up, ma'am?"

"It's pretty big for me alone, and nobody lives forever."

"You'll outlive me by years," said Andy stanchly. "As for giving up the place, you'd never be happy elsewhere."

"No," she said, and was silent for some time. When she spoke again it was about Evans. "What about him?" she asked. "You knew him well. Did he have any enemies?"

"Well, yes and no," said Andy cautiously. "He was not what

you'd call a well-liked man. On the other hand, he kept to him-self, as you might say. He was never one for talking."

She got up then, looking almost even into the old Scotsman's eyes. "You think he is dead, don't you?"

"Where there's a corpse there's a body. There's no body yet."

"Still, there's the river, Andy."

"Aye, there's always the river, ma'am," said Andy and lapsed into silence.

We were besieged with visitors as she improved. Most of them I saw, but now and then she would make an exception. One day she said she would like to see Lydia, and Lydia came that afternoon. It was a pleasant little visit, with Maud pouring tea by the fireplace while I passed scones and cakes. Only once, while Lydia said something to me, I saw Maud's eyes on her, thoughtful and almost sad.

When Lydia rose to go Maud took her hand and held it. "Let the past go, my dear," she said. "It's the future that counts. I hope you will be very happy."

"I am very happy now," said Lydia.

I have wondered since why she sent for Lydia that day. Was she still uncertain? Or had she already made that plan of hers? I remember Lydia's stopping me in the hall outside and holding my arm. "She's frightfully worried, isn't she, poor dear? What's it about? Tony?"

"She's been very sick, Lydia."

"Well, maybe that's it," she said. "But if you ask me—"

Then we were in the main hall, with Reynolds holding her coat, Thomas the door, and Stevens outside at her car.

"Heavens, what state you live in, Pat," she said. "I don't be-lieve I could bear it."

We saw a good bit of Margery Stoddard as Maud improved.

I think she was lonely, what with Julian either at the office or out with the hounds. She had never gone about much socially. But she was worried about the general situation, although she said nothing to Maud.

She found me alone one day and told me she had sent the children to Julian's people for a visit. "I miss them dreadfully," she said, "but Julian thought it safer. After all, if there is a homicidal maniac around I don't want them here."

She never mentioned Bessie or the quarrel I had overheard on the path; but sometimes I saw her watching me, as though she wondered what I made of it. When they met, which was seldom, they were coldly civil. But more than once I saw her follow Bessie with her eyes, and was puzzled by what I saw in them.

One day Maud told her that she might give up the Cloisters. We were in the court, for there was a brisk wind blowing, and Maud, I remember, was knitting. She threw her bomb quietly. "It's too big, and anyhow the day of such houses is over. It would make a good orphanage, wouldn't it? All the room for children to run in, and this court for the sick ones to get the sun."

Margery looked incredulous. "You can't mean it," she said. "You're not serious, are you?"

"Of course I'm serious."

"But Tony! He loves it, Maud."

"Tony will understand," she said gravely, and changed the subject.

She had made her decision by that time, although we did not know it. How could we? But all those weeks upstairs she had been thinking about it. Now she was ready.

Not at once. She gave herself a few days first. She needed her strength. Also she had plans to make. Outwardly she was perfectly normal. She even had some people in to tea that week;

a tea which was mostly cocktails, but which brought her old friends around her. She was at her best that day, handsome, smiling, even gay. Dwight Elliott stayed mostly at her elbow, and I wondered again if she would ever marry him.

At her request I poured. Bessie was not in sight, and even Tony seemed his old debonair self. There had been death and mystery, but it seemed far away with that crowd of complacent men and women.

Then Bessie appeared. I saw Tony's face tighten and Margery Stoddard's laugh die on her lips. Bessie, however, was unconcerned. She made her way to the tea table and stood over me. "Thanks a lot, Pat," she said. "I'll take over now. Sorry I'm late."

I got up, and she took my place. It was a mistake, of course. They did not like her, that hard-riding, straight-thinking crowd. They moved away from the tea table, and soon after the party broke up.

It did not seem important at the time, that small bit of self-assertion and its result. But it was. In a way it precipitated our tragedy, perhaps even caused it. For two days later Bessie herself had a party. She was planning to go away, to the relief of everyone in the house, and this she said was her good-by.

She had about thirty people, mostly young and all noisy. The trouble started when she called Reynolds and told him a dozen of them were staying for dinner.

He ventured to expostulate. "I'm sorry, madam, I don't think there is sufficient food in the house."

"Well, you'll have to get it. I've asked them."

Pierre, notified in his kitchen, stubbornly refused to do anything about it, and Tony flung out of the house in a rage and went down to the Beverly Hotel, the country club dining room being closed. Had it not been for Maud I am sure he would have thrown them all out; but we were trying to keep everything quiet on her account. And poor old Partridge, wringing her hands, came to me almost in tears. "The shops are closed, Miss Pat," she said. "What am I to do?"

"What about the servants' dinner?"

"They had it in the middle of the day. They had their supper at five-thirty, as usual."

It was dark and very cold, but late as it was I took Gus and the station wagon and drove down to the village. The shops were closed, but I routed the butcher and the grocer from their homes, and before eight I walked into Pierre's kitchen, followed by Gus laden with parcels. Pierre was standing with his arms folded, his cap over his forehead and his eyes glaring, while the kitchen maids were cowering in a corner. He did not move when I entered.

"I'm sorry, Pierre," I said. "I've done the best I could."

"I cook no food for the drunken crowd," he said implacably. "Me, Pierre, I am employed by Mrs. Wainwright. Not by that woman."

"Then get out of the way," I said, as angry as he. "I can cook, and I will. I'll not have Mrs. Wainwright worried with this, and you ought to be ashamed of yourself."

I rolled up my sleeves and began opening the parcels. Then—whether my mention of Maud or the sight of English mutton chops did it I do not know—he turned suddenly on the shivering women in the corner.

"Come out of there and get busy," he said. "I'll have no good food spoiled while I'm in charge of this kitchen. Get out of my way, Miss Pat. You and your cooking!"

Maud ate her dinner upstairs that night, and I ate with her. She had been using the telephone when I went in, and she looked pale but composed. She ate very little. I remember that even in that vast house the noise from downstairs reached us, but she made no comment. Only once did she seem to notice it, and that was indirectly. She leaned over and touched my hand. "I wonder if you will ever know what a comfort you have been to me, Pat. I hope and pray that some day Tony and you will marry. He's so frightfully in love with you, my dear."

Hilda put her to bed after dinner. As I have said, Amy had gone for good, after warning me to be careful of what she called "that little hell-cat," and shedding a few tears over the jeweled wrist watch which was Maud's farewell gift. Maud had asked me to wait until she was settled, and when she called me she was alone, sitting up in her bed.

"I've sent Hilda off," she said. "I want you to do something, Pat. Get me the list you made the other day of the stuff in the safe. I want to look it over."

I got it and she sat there looking it over. It was all recorded: the two pearl ropes, the emeralds, a half dozen diamond bracelets, and the big square-cut engagement ring she seldom wore. In addition there were brooches, earrings, clips, and a long diamond chain. It looked like the riches of the Indies to me, but she eyed it with dissatisfaction, trying to remember the cost of each piece and even to estimate its resale value.

"It's not a great deal," she said. "Still, with care, it might be enough. It's something, anyhow."

I was puzzled. Although I kept only her private checkbook, I could not imagine any necessity for selling her jewels. She did not explain, however. She kept the list, lying back among her pillows and looking tired but content.

"I feel happier than I have for a long time," she said. "Good night, my dear, and sleep well."

They were the last words she ever spoke to me.

Bessie's party was going strong when I went back to my room at ten o'clock. I undressed and got into bed, still puzzled. Then I thought I had hit on the solution; that she was buying Bessie off once more, paying what she had once called her price for peace.

It made me furious. Only a day or two before I had handed Bessie a bill for two thousand dollars for clothes and she had merely laughed at me.

"What am I to do with it?"

"Do with it? Give it to Tony. I'm still married to him."

She looked amused when she saw my face. "Give it to him, with my love," she added. "It's chicken feed to him, and to hell with it."

Now Maud was buying her off again. I am afraid I saw red that night, with the noise below, the incessant movement of the men carrying drinks, and the occasional bursts of laughter. For whatever Tony had, he had earned it. Long before that he had told me about it.

Old J.C., he said, had put him to work as soon as he left college. "He put me in the mill," he told me. "All he told me was to buy some overalls and to spit on anything before I sat down on it. I forgot one day, and I burned more than the seat of my pants. But when I left, at the end of three years, I had calluses an inch thick on my hands, and I knew the business, from start to finish."

He had liked the mill. He had even carried a lunchbox. He got to know the men, and liked them too.

"The old man had done his best by them, according to his lights; did away with the company store, built bathrooms for them and laundries for their wives. He didn't understand it, but they didn't want benevolence. They get a share of the profits now. It's not much, but it helps."

I fell asleep finally. As Bessie's party had commenced at five it was over by eleven. The house was suddenly quiet, and about that time Tony came back and came up to bed. I was dozing off when I heard Roger moving uneasily in the hall. Then he settled down again, and so did I.

It was still dark when I awakened. I had the feeling that someone was in the room. I remember sitting up in bed and saying, "Who is it? Is anything wrong?"

No one answered, and I turned on my reading light and looked over the room. It was empty. So was my sitting room, but when I glanced into the hall Roger was not there. That made me uneasy. Downstairs all seemed quiet, but it was unusual for the big dog to leave my door. I wondered if he had been let out and not brought in again.

My clock said half past three when I put on my house coat and went downstairs. Roger was in the west hall, lying close to the door and whimpering, and I saw at once that the chain was off. When I tried the door it was unlocked.

I was still not alarmed. I opened the door to let the dog out, and stood waiting for him. If I thought at all, it was that the tired servants had overlooked the door, or that some of Bessie's party had opened it. Even when I saw the light in the playhouse I was only annoyed. My first idea was that some of Bessie's party had stayed on, to sleep in the guest rooms there. But the light was in the living room, and it looked more like firelight than anything else.

That worried me. The fire there, when it was used, was always put out before the place was locked for the night. And Roger had not come back. I whistled for him, but he did not appear.

It was a black cold night outside. There had been a light rain earlier. Later it had turned to snow. It had stopped, but there was a thin powdering of it on the ground. I could see Roger's footprints, heading toward the playhouse, and at last I decided to follow him. I was still not uneasy. Someone had lit a fire and left it, and I cursed Bessie and all her works as I felt my way toward it.

I got there safely enough, and I felt for the doorknob. But I could not find it. The door was standing open, and from somewhere inside Roger suddenly gave a long, heartbreaking wail.

It practically shattered me. My first impulse was to run wildly back to the house. Everything was quiet, however, although from somewhere there came the sound of running water. Then, my eyes accustomed to the dark, I found that the fire from the living room sent a faint glow into the hall. Roger was standing there, looking at me. I remember scolding him, although my voice was shaky. "Keep quiet," I said. "You're a damned nuisance, and I'm fed up with you."

My hair fairly rose as he raised his head and howled again. Then I took a good strong grip on myself and decided to look about the place. Everything seemed orderly, but it was evident that someone had been using the living room. There was a chair drawn up to the fire, and a new package of cigarettes on a table had been opened. One had been smoked, I thought by a man, since Bessie and her women friends were always plastered with lipstick.

Roger had not followed me. I said a few words about Bessie and her parties, and began looking for a pail of some sort to put out the fire.

That was how I found Maud. I went to the swimming pool, and she was there. Not in the pool itself. She was lying on the tiles close to the edge; so close that one arm hung over the edge. A small handkerchief lay beside her. I remember that, and that I stooped over and touched her. I remember too, running to the door and screaming. When I came to I was lying alone on a bed in one of the guest rooms, and Maud was dead. She had been dead for hours.

CHAPTER TWENTY-THREE

I MUST have been out for some time, for when I staggered back to the pool Tony was there, on his knees beside her, and Jim and the men from the patrol car were standing by. Outside I could see Reynolds and the footmen, as well as Gus and the other men who slept on the place. One of the officers was holding them back.

"Stay out now," he said. "You can't do any good here."

Gus was crying. His face was impassive, but tears were rolling down his cheeks.

"We can carry her back to the house," he said.

"All in due time, boys. All in due time," said the officer. "They'll not be moving her yet."

Jim saw me then and asked me if I could get Tony away. "He's taking it hard," he said. "Get him to bed. I'll have Sterling see him later."

I was shaking violently, but I managed to speak. "What happened to her, Jim? Was it her heart?"

"Maybe, maybe not. We'll know about that later."

It took some time to get Tony away from her. He stood up, looking wild and desperate, but he refused to go.

"I can't leave her," he said. "Not here. Why leave her here, on those tiles? They're cold as ice."

"That doesn't matter now, Tony," Jim said soothingly. "We'll bring her up soon."

"It was her heart, wasn't it?"

"Sure. Sure it was her heart."

He looked about him, dazed. "But why here?" he said. "Why here? What was she doing here?"

I spoke up then. "I think she saw what I did, Tony. Somebody had lit a fire here in the living room, and she came down to put it out. You know how afraid she was of fire. I don't think she suffered at all."

"Suffered!" he said. "Oh, my God!"

Nevertheless, he went with me. Someone had turned on the floodlight. He held tight to my arm, and I knew he was crying, the long dry sobs of a man facing more than he can endure. He never spoke at all until we reached the door. Then he turned and looked back. "Leaving her there!" he said thickly. "Leaving her on that floor, Pat. I can't do it."

He tried to turn back, but somehow I got him into the library. He stumbled like a drunken man, and I told Reynolds, who had followed us, to get some hot coffee and brandy. Tony sat down, his face colorless. "Sorry, Pat," he said. "Just stick by me. I still can't believe it. It was her heart, wasn't it?"

"It must have been. Just remember this, Tony. It must have been quick and easy. She didn't have any pain."

And all at once I was back at Lydia's years earlier, and Lydia was saying something like that to me. "No pain, no anything, Pat. Such a wonderful way to go." Now I repeated that. "No pain, no anything, Tony. Such a wonderful way to go."

It is strange to remember that, to realize that neither one of us knew then how she had died. If we noticed the blood—there was not much—perhaps we laid it to her fall; and there was that heavy hair of hers, loose from its pins and spread on the tiling. I doubt if even Jim saw it at first. When he did, his first thought was that she had fallen and cut her head. Then he lifted her hair, and what he saw made him stiffen.

He did not say anything. There was I, still unconscious by the door, and Tony was on his knees beside her, trying to call her back to life. He let the hair fall again. But he glanced into the pool, and there was the revolver, as if it had fallen from her dead hand. That was when he barred everybody but Tony and the two patrolmen from the place.

Back in the house, aside from my grief I was having troubles of my own. Bessie, wakened by the coming and going of cars, had heard the news and for some reason gone into shrieking hysterics. After Maud's body had been laid in her big bed and Tony was shut in his room, Nora asked me to see her.

It must have been seven o'clock in the morning by that time, a cold gray October day. I was still in a house coat, still stunned. But the sight of Bessie roused me. She was fully dressed, and a packed suitcase lay on her bed.

"I'm going," she said feverishly. "Don't try to stop me. I'm getting out."

"You can't do that. Not now," I told her. "Anyhow, why should you go?"

"Why? Because I don't want to be the next. That's why enough, isn't it?"

"Listen to me, Bessie," I said. "She died of a heart attack. She wasn't killed."

She stopped trying to close her suitcase and looked at me. "You're sure of that?"

"It looks like it. You see, you left a fire going in the playhouse, and she must have seen it from her window. She got the key and went down, and—"

She stared. Then she laughed horribly, hysterically. "So I left a fire in the playhouse!" she cried. "You fool, do you think I'd go near that place? I haven't been there for weeks."

I met Jim in the lower hall after I left her, and told him. He listened carefully.

"I see," he said. "Well, she's not leaving. Nobody's leaving, Pat. Either Maud Wainwright killed herself or somebody staged a suicide for her. Keep that to yourself, will you?"

"She didn't commit suicide, Jim."

"Well, that's for us to find out. Go to bed, Pat. You can't help now."

Weeks later he was to tell me about that early morning, when he found Reynolds on guard over Maud's body, and Thomas and Stevens preparing to carry me to a bed. He had had a little time to himself before the patrol car came. He did not touch anything, but he took a careful survey. Maud, as I have said, was lying at the edge of the pool, a small handkerchief beside her, and her right arm over the edge of the pool itself. She was fully dressed, even to her coat, and she looked quiet peaceful.

Then Tony came, and Jim found that awful hole in her head. "I couldn't say anything," he said. "Not with that poor devil rubbing her hands and trying to bring her back to life. But she'd been shot, and a shot meant a gun. That's when I found it, in the water in the pool."

It was a suicide to him at first. But the water in the pool made him wonder. It had been running in faster than it ran out, and there was already a foot or two there when he arrived.

"Look at it yourself, Pat," he said. "Either you fill a pool, in which case you close the outlet, or you leave it alone. Not only that. Every pool around had been drained for the winter. Then why the water? What did it mean? Did she want to be sure that if the shot didn't kill her she would fall in there and drown? She didn't fall in. So what? Anyhow, why dress and go to all that trouble to kill herself? She had a lot of sleeping dope in her room. That would have been a simple, easy way out. Why didn't she take it?"

Not, he said, that he thought it all out at the time. He wasn't doing a hell of a lot of thinking just then. He left Tony alone with his mother and went over the playhouse. He was surprised to find the fire in the living room. It was still smoldering, and he thought it had either been lit or had fresh wood put on it not many hours before. Not only that. There was a fresh package of cigarettes there. One had been smoked, and there was a chair drawn up by the fire.

"She didn't have to go to the playhouse to sit by a fire. It looked to me as though she had expected to meet somebody there. Somebody she didn't want in the house, but somebody she wanted to make comfortable."

He had only a minute or two. He sent Thomas to turn on the floodlight on the fountain so the others could find the way. Then he went outside and examined the ground. He could see a vague outline of Maud's footprints and mine in the thin snow, although the men running from the house had almost obliterated them. But there was another set, leading from the direction of the entrance to the grounds and back again. They were little more than vague depressions, but they looked small to him. He had no tape measure with him, but he found one print still fairly clear and marked its length with a pencil on his handkerchief.

"Looked like a woman's to me," he said. "Here and there I

found what looked like the mark of a high heel. I wasn't sure, of course. All I was sure of was that somebody had come in the gate that night and gone away again. It didn't look right, somehow. I thought of Bessie Wainwright, but the direction was wrong. Anyhow, she could see Bessie any day. Why the playhouse?"

He said nothing to anybody. When the patrolmen came he shut off the water, but left the gun where it lay in the pool. He had gotten rid of Tony and me soon after, and Bill Sterling was there. Of course, all Bill could say was that she was gone, which he knew already. Bill got up from his examination and looked down at her. "I don't get it," he said. "Why would she do it, Jim? She had everything."

"That's what I'm thinking," said Jim. "That is, if she did do it."

The coroner arrived at daylight, with Hopper not far behind him. But the coroner considered it suicide.

"Not all the autopsies in the world can change the picture," he said with a thin smile.

Hopper was inclined to agree with him, even when the automatic, retrieved from the pool, showed only smudged fingerprints. "Water would take care of that," he said, "especially if it was running."

"Who the hell turned on the water?" Jim demanded.

"How do you know one of the gardeners didn't do it? To keep the pipe from freezing?"

"Why would she kill herself?"

"Maybe she knew Tony was mixed up in Morgan's death, and couldn't take it."

"Listen," said Jim stubbornly. "You didn't know her. She could take anything."

It was after Jim showed him the living room that Hopper sent for the homicide squad from town. He was still unconvinced. Only, as Jim said, it looked queer even to him that anybody would light a fire and smoke a cigarette in comfort, and then walk to a cold swimming pool to shoot herself.

It was a little late by that time. Men had been tramping in and out, even Maud herself had been taken to the house. But at that the result was unexpected. The prints on the gun were of no use to them. Maud's own prints were on the chair and table by the fire. But the door to the outside was still standing open, as it had been, and there were no prints on it whatever.

The two men looked at each other.

"She had no gloves," Jim said. "So how did she get in? Through a window? Pat Abbott found the door standing open, but Mrs. Wainwright had to open it; unlock it and open it. Don't tell me she did all that and then wiped that knob clean."

They went back over the place together. Jim had already dug the bullet out of the plaster in the wall, and the gun lay on a table. Hopper took it up and examined it. Then he looked at a memorandum in a notebook. "Tony Wainwright's gun," he said, looking at Jim. "Suppose she's had it all along?"

"Maybe. If she killed herself."

"Or if Tony did it."

"Look here," Jim said angrily, "if you think Tony shot his mother you're off your head. He was crazy about her. If you'd been here tonight when he saw her you'd know better."

"Then who killed her, and why?"

"The same guy who killed Morgan," said Jim, and Hopper laughed softly.

There was not much more that early morning. The coroner placed the hour of Maud's death between eleven and twelve the night before, although it might have been somewhat later. The open door and the cold night might have brought on rigor mortis earlier. The footprints Jim had seen in the snow had disappeared with the snow itself by daylight. But inquiry revealed that the snow, such as it was, had ceased by midnight.

Naturally none of us at the Cloisters knew this at the time. I did not go to bed at all. Tony was in his study by that time, with Bill Sterling trying to give him something to quiet him, and Tony refusing. By daylight Mr. Elliott appeared, and finally the two police officers joined the group.

It was Hopper who told Tony his mother had been shot. He refused at first to believe it.

"Shot?" he said. "I don't believe it. Who would shoot her?"

"I'm sorry, Mr. Wainwright. Do you know any reason why she would have done it herself?"

He stared at them with reddened eyes. "Mother kill herself!" he said. "Never." Then the import of what had been said dawned on him. He got up, his face dead-white. "If she was shot she was murdered," he said, "and before God I'll kill whoever did it."

The men had breakfast before they dispersed. Reynolds managed to get Tony to drink some coffee and finally to go up to his room, but he was still profoundly shocked. The telephone began to ring early, and at last in desperation I settled myself in the library and stayed there.

We were virtually in a state of siege that morning. Jim threw what amounted to a cordon of men around the playhouse and the Cloisters itself. The big entrance gates were closed, and men stationed there. I have thought since that in the presence of great tragedy there is almost no time for grief. Certainly there was no time for thought, so far as I was concerned. Only Maud, still lying in her big bed, was at peace that day.

It must have been eleven o'clock when Dwight Elliott came into the library. He was quiet enough, but he looked profoundly shaken. He sat down and passed a hand wearily over his face. "I would like to ask you some questions," he said at last. "When you searched the house for Tony's automatic did you search Mrs. Wainwright's rooms?"

"No. I never thought of it."

"She might have had it then?"

"Why would she take it, Mr. Elliott? She had been worried about something. She had even suggested leaving this place. But I had a long talk with her last night. She certainly had no idea of killing herself."

"Nevertheless, Miss Abbott, I'm afraid that is just what she did. She had no enemies. Who would gain by her death?" He looked at me. "What was the nature of this talk last night? Was it confidential?"

And then I remembered. Maud and the safe. Maud and the manila envelope, for Tony in case anything happened to her. I sat still, seeing her as she had gone over the list of her jewels only the night before. Sitting up in bed while I ran over it, commenting on this and that: her engagement ring, the pearls John had given her on her wedding day. Under that surface veneer of his he must have loved her passionately, that cold elderly man who provided bathrooms and laundries for his workmen because he must, and gave lavish jewels to the woman he adored.

"Not confidential particularly. She went over a list I had made of her jewels."

"Her jewels? Did she say why?"

"I thought she meant to sell them."

He got up suddenly. "In that case I'd better examine her safe," he said. "If she took them with her last night it would account for a great deal."

I went with him. Upstairs Tony's door was closed, as was Bessie's. But there was an officer on guard in front of Maud's rooms, and he refused to let us in. "You'll have to ask the chief," he said. "Sorry, I've had orders."

It took some time to find Jim. When he was finally located he was in the grounds, trying to find some trace of the woman's footprints he had seen the night before. But they were gone. All he had was the mark he had made on his handkerchief, and he was still looking puzzled when he came upstairs. He admitted us, however, standing by to see that we disturbed nothing.

Maud was still lying on her bed. She had not been undressed, but a blue silk cover had been put over her. The windows were wide open and the room very cold. It was that coldness, I think, which was horrifying. My hands were so unsteady that I was afraid I could not open the safe.

But neither the panel nor the door to the safe was locked. The panel was closed and behind it the safe was standing open. There had been no robbery. The jewels were all there, in their cases as I had left them. Only the list we had made and the envelope intended for Tony were missing.

CHAPTER TWENTY-FOUR

It was noon when Stewart, the district attorney, descended on us. Here was a big case, the sort to make him if he handled it right. Don Morgan's death had been merely another murder, sensational largely because it had taken place on the Wainwright property. But now Maud Wainwright herself was dead. Suicide or murder, it was big news. His car that day was followed by three or four others of various vintages, containing reporters and photographers. I saw him myself, posing at the playhouse door, a half dozen cameramen around him, with Hopper out of range and looking more sardonic than ever.

The papers had the picture the next day. Evidently both Hopper and Jim were willing to give him enough rope to hang himself, for the caption read: *District Attorney Says Mrs. Wainwright Suicide*. All in all the procession looked rather like a Cook's tour, with Stewart in the lead showing various points of interest. "The body was here, boys. You can see where it's outlined with chalk. The gun was there, in the pool. Very sad case. Very sad indeed. Shows that money isn't everything, doesn't it?"

Jim managed to keep the reporters out of the house itself.

But Stewart was in his element, sitting in the library with Tony, Dwight Elliott, Jim, Hopper, and when he sent for me, myself. "How did you happen to go to the playhouse last night? This morning, rather?"

I told him as well as I could, the sudden waking, missing Roger, and all that followed. He listened, his small shrewd eyes fixed on me.

"When you started for this playhouse did you have a key?"

"I never thought of it."

"You were there to put out a fire, and you had no key?"

"I didn't start with that idea."

But he was plainly suspicious of me. He looked around the room, as though asking for their admiration. Nobody moved.

"You had no idea that the playhouse door would be already open when you got there?"

And at last I saw red. "Oh, what's the use of all this?" I said desperately. "Somebody murdered Mrs. Wainwright here last night. If you'll stop asking fool questions and posing around here, we might find out who did it."

He never forgave me for that. He kept on pounding questions at me, however. What about the safe? Had I known the combination? Had I left it open the night before? Why had Mrs. Wainwright wanted the jewels listed and where was the list? Tony listened in somber silence. Hopper smoked steadily. Mr. Elliott examined his fingernails and tapped on a table. But there was no stopping Stewart. He brought in Hilda and the other servants, one after the other. Had they noticed a change in Mrs. Wainwright lately? Had she been depressed, low in her mind? Was there a chance she had hidden Tony's gun somewhere, for her own purposes?

Tony broke it up finally. "Tell him about the list and the missing envelope, Pat," he said, "and let's get the hell out of here. I've had all I can stand."

I did, explaining as best I could; but he had his answer even to that. "I see," he said. "Of course, that explains the fire she lit in the playhouse. She burned them there. It's obvious."

He left at last, convinced that Maud had killed herself. He had a highball before he went, and he delivered a short oration to the newspaperman outside before he left.

"Sorry, boys, there's nothing to it. She'd been sick. Bad heart. Probably took the easy way out. Of course," he hedged, "something may develop later. Just now it looks like suicide. You can quote me on that."

It was all pretty dreadful, the common little man on the terrace looking pompous, the cameras working, and the grief and silence in the house behind him. Yet in his own way he was right. The surface picture did look like suicide, and even Tony's faith was shaken. When it was over he found me in my office, my head on the desk, and he looked agonized.

"Why would she have done it, Pat?" he said. "She was happy. I never knew a happier woman. She was gay and brave, at least until this last sickness of hers. But even then, why not some word to me? We were so close. You would think—"

He choked at that. He put his arms around me and I felt him trembling.

"Perhaps she thought she was incurably ill, Tony," I said. "She wouldn't have faced that easily."

"She would have faced anything," he said stubbornly, and let me go.

The inquest was held the next morning. Because I had found

her I had to be present, but little was developed that I did not already know. The medical testimony showed that the shot had been fired from right to left, and that the bullet had passed entirely through the skull. The hair on the right side revealed that the gun had been held close to the head, and death had been instantaneous.

I was called to testify about finding the body, and there was a curious stillness when the coroner asked me if I had not been the one who also found Evans in the same place. I replied that I had, but that I had neither struck him on the head nor removed his trousers. It was silly, but I was sick and angry over it all.

The police evidence after that was rather perfunctory. It consisted largely in identifying the gun in the pool as the weapon used, and in showing the bullet and its markings, along with the ballistics report on it. Jim's own report was limited to his being called after we found her, the position of the body, and so on. Nothing was brought out about the missing list and envelope, and indeed the only incident of any importance that day was Tony's obstinate refusal to believe that his mother had killed herself. The papers carried the story that night; *Refuses to Believe Mother Suicide—Son Says Mother Murdered*. I hid them so Tony would not see them.

He identified the gun, however. The coroner read him the serial numbers, and he corroborated them from his permit card. The coroner nodded.

"Now, Mr. Wainwright, where did you keep this weapon?"

"In my car, up to the last few months. After we had the trouble about Evans, I took it to my bedroom. It was kept in a table drawer beside my bed."

"When did you see it last?"

"I don't remember. Perhaps two weeks ago. I'm not sure."

"You didn't miss it from the drawer?"

"I seldom use the drawer. No."

"Who had access to your room?"

He stirred restlessly. "Anybody," he said. "There are forty people in and about the place. Maybe two dozen in the house."

"I'm sorry to bring this up. Your mother would know it was there, wouldn't she?"

"I don't think she knew I had it. She was afraid of firearms."

"But she could have seen it there?"

"Yes."

"Other people, callers in the house, for instance, did not go upstairs, I gather."

"No. There were rooms below for men and women."

"Who had access to your room, outside of the servants? Who were staying in the house when this happened?"

"My wife and my mother's secretary, Miss Abbott."

Bessie not being present, all eyes turned to me. I knew everybody there, from the tradesmen on the jury to the people who crowded the room: Bill Sterling, Lydia, Julian and Margery Stoddard, a hundred or more who had seen me grow up from pigtails and a bicycle until now. Most of the eyes were friendly, but some were not. I know now that I was not above suspicion myself that day. Although I did not know it, gossip had been busy about Tony and me. If Maud Wainwright had objected, if we had quarreled—

Nevertheless, when the verdict came it was more or less inevitable. Maud, the cheerful and hearty woman before her illness, the brave and kindly one since, had killed herself. I wanted to stand up and deny it. So, I know, did Tony. There was nothing to do, however. When it was over I pushed past the crowd and out into the cold air. When I saw myself in the mirror of my car I was white to the lips.

Jim Conway came to see me that afternoon. I found him in the library, pacing up and down, his hands in his pockets and his eyes grave. He gave me a thin smile.

"Well, we got our verdict," he said.

"And it's a lie," I said angrily. "You know she didn't do it."

"All right. Who did? Use your head, Pat. Who wanted her out of the way? Not you. You lose a good job. Anyhow, I know you liked her. Bessie? I understand she doesn't get anything by the will. She was better off with her mother-in-law alive than dead. Besides, she's scared out of her skin. Tony? He gets the money and the business, but he's out, for any number of reasons. Then who?"

It was some time before he pulled a handkerchief from his pocket, showing me a pencil mark on it. He closed the door before he did it.

"Some woman," he said, "walked in the gate that night and went to the playhouse. She walked in, but from the look of the snow I'd say she ran out. That's approximately the size of her foot."

"A woman! You think a woman killed her?"

"I haven't said that. I've said a woman was there. She went to the door of the playhouse and she left it in a hurry. That's a small size, isn't it?"

It was. Compared with my own it was almost an inch shorter. He saw what I was thinking, but he shook his head.

"It wasn't Bessie," he said. "If Maud Wainwright wanted to

talk to her she would have done it right here. She didn't. The way it looks now, she went to the playhouse to meet somebody; probably a woman. She took Tony's gun with her. Maybe she got it after Bessie was shot, or let's say Hilda got it for her. She hid it anyway. Now she's going out at night to meet somebody she doesn't trust. She carries it with her, and there's a quarrel. The other woman gets the gun and—"

I put my hands to my ears. "Don't, Jim," I said. "I can't bear it."

"Got to face it, Pat," he said. "Either that or she killed herself. Only two guesses, and you don't think it was suicide."

"I don't know," I said confusedly. "I can't even think, Jim. She had been different lately. Only an hour or two before this happened we'd listed her jewels. I thought she meant to sell them. She'd talked of giving up this place too. You can ask Margery Stoddard about it. She knows."

"She was pretty intimate with Mrs. Stoddard, wasn't she?"

"She liked her. She wasn't intimate with anybody."

"Any reason for them to quarrel?"

"Good heavens, no."

He resumed his restless pacing of the floor. He was sure all these things tied together, beginning with Don's murder.

"Leave out Evans," he said, "and think about it. Morgan is killed, here in the playhouse. Maybe Bessie sees something that night, and later on there's an attempt to kill her too. Then come to Mrs. Wainwright. She's all right after Don's murder, but a day or so after it something happens to her. She learns something, and she has a heart attack. If we knew what she learned and how she learned it, maybe we'd know why she died; but first we have to find out why Don Morgan was killed. That's the key to the whole thing."

He continued. He had been on Don's trail ever since his murder. He knew that he had come to America in the spring. He had come back first-class on a good boat, and if he was a sick man nobody on the ship had guessed it. He had made friends on that trip, and one of them gave him a position when he returned. With the exception of a few days in June he had worked until the first of August. Then all at once he had thrown up his job and left town.

"He didn't get here until the middle of September," he said. "I'd give a lot to know what he was doing in that six weeks, outside of trying to get into this house. If he did," he added. "We're still guessing about that."

He looked at his notebook. "See here, Pat, what about this envelope that's missing? Any idea what was in it?"

"It was for Tony. That's all I know."

"If she burned it there may be something in the fireplace. Let's go, shall we?"

It was not easy to get out of the house unobserved. Cars were coming and going, cards were being left, the panoply and dignity of death was all about us. We made it during a brief lull. Jim produced a key to the playhouse and we went inside.

It was cold and damp. I could not even look in at the swimming pool. We went on to the living room and Jim dropped on his knees on the hearth. He sifted carefully through the wood ashes with his fingers, but there was nothing there. I sat down then. My knees were too weak to hold me. I was in the chair that had been drawn before the fireplace, and I tried to light a cigarette. My hands shook so that I dropped the match, and it fell between the cushion and the side of the chair. It was when I felt about for it that I discovered a paper.

CHAPTER TWENTY-FIVE

THE FUNERAL took place the next day. Dwight Elliott had spent the night there, and made the arrangements. The services were held at the Cloisters, but Maud lay quiet upstairs in her room, with Tony sitting beside her, until they were over.

To everybody's surprise, some of the Wainwrights from town came. There were a half dozen of them, including wives, but I do not think Tony ever knew they were there. After the services there was the long drive to the cemetery in the city, with Bessie in the car with me, nervous and smoking steadily.

So far as I remember she said little. Once she shivered. "So this is what it's all about," she said. "You live a while and then you die." She flung her cigarette out a window. "Like that," she said.

It was a strange drive, with Maud ahead, her hearty laugh stilled forever; going to lie beside John Wainwright in the big mausoleum at Fairview. The long cortege winding through the hills, a bright autumn sun, and then the gathering around the tomb, with flowers everywhere and Dr. Leland being handed some earth by the undertaker to sprinkle over the casket. "Thou knowest, Lord, the secrets of our hearts; shut not Thy merciful ears to our prayer." And Tony standing there bareheaded, not listening, only looking. As if he still could not believe it, as if the solid earth had dropped from under his feet.

I felt faint toward the end, and someone caught my arm and steadied me; but not until it was over did I see who it was. It was the detective, Hopper.

That was on Sunday, and on Monday afternoon Dwight Elliott brought a young lawyer from town to read the will, explaining that as he participated to a small extent he had not drawn it himself.

The will had been drawn four years ago, and it was what might have been expected. There was a considerable sum left to charity, there were bequests to all the servants based on length of service, there was twenty thousand dollars left to "my friend and relative, Dwight Elliott, in token of his long friendship to me," and there was a codicil, recently added, leaving me five thousand dollars and a diamond bracelet I had always admired.

There was only one mention of Bessie. She was left one dollar, with the statement that she had been already "amply provided for." The residue went to Tony without reservation.

I had not cried since Maud's death. The shock had been too great, but I shed tears that night over the bequest to me. Hilda, herself red-eyed and stricken, found me weeping when she came into my room after I had gone to bed.

She stood, neat in her black dress and black silk apron, just inside my door. "What am I to do with her things, Miss Pat?" she inquired.

"I don't know, Hilda. I suppose they'll have to be appraised. Better leave them out until we know. Hilda, tell me about that night. Was she all right when you left her?"

"She was in bed. She looked all right, except I thought she

was excited. I asked her if she wanted her sleeping tablet, but she said not yet. She'd take it later. But she put out the light before I could straighten her bed. I think maybe she was partly dressed already. She didn't seem to want me to go near her."

"Did you notice anything different about the room?"

"Well," she said slowly, "there was a big brown envelope on the table beside her. It was open. I thought she'd just put it down. I haven't seen it since."

That was the picture we had by the evening of the fourth day after Maud's death. She had gone to the playhouse, perhaps carrying Tony's revolver. She had taken with her the envelope from the safe and her list of jewels. And she had met someone there, possibly a woman. What had happened after that was anybody's guess, as Jim put it.

Then on Tuesday, the thirty-first of October, something happened which upset every theory the police had developed. That was when a hysterical Hilda brought me a letter for Tony, addressed in Maud's big square hand. Bessie was there at the time, resentful at being left out of the will and threatening to make trouble.

"I know more than he thinks I know," she said darkly. "If he has any idea that he can play me for a sucker he'd better think again."

Then Hilda came in, a hysterical Hilda, wiping her eyes and holding out the letter. "She left it for him," she sobbed. "His name's on it. Oh, my God, Miss Pat, why ever did she do it?"

Bessie stood there, staring at the letter. Whatever she knew, she had not expected that. She even tried to take it from Hilda, but I reached out quietly and got it.

"I'll take care of it. It's for Tony," I said. "If you like, you can call him and tell him it's here."

"Tell him yourself," she said furiously, and went out of the room.

I think that letter almost broke Tony's heart. They had been airing and cleaning Maud's room, and Hilda had found it underneath her mattress. The envelope was addressed in her big sprawling hand, *To my beloved son*, and inside was the letter.

Tony darling—When you find this I will be gone. Try to understand, my dear, and do what you think best. I have loved you so much. So terribly, Tony. Some day when you have a child of your own you will realize what that means. Try to forgive me for what I have done, and don't forget me, darling. God bless you and make you happy. Mother.

I was not with him when he read it. He took it up to his room, and for hours he stayed there. When at last he came downstairs he had it in his hand.

"Read it," he said thickly. "See what you make of it."

I read it, with a lump in my throat. Then I reread it.

"I don't quite understand it," I said.

"Neither do I. What am I to understand? That she killed herself? I don't believe it."

"Unless she was afraid of something," I said.

"She was never afraid. Not in all her life."

It was that night that somebody apparently got into the house again. We knew nothing about it until morning. Then Hilda reported that Maud's room had been opened and searched. "Her clothes are every which way," she said. "The drawers too. I don't know what to make of it, miss."

Nor did I, or Tony when he heard of it. The jewels had been taken from the safe and placed in a safe-deposit box in town, and Reynolds reported that the house had been closed as usual the night before, including the basement doors. Remembering those previous attempts of Bessie's to get into Maud's rooms, I suspected her. But I could not prove it, nor could I think of any reason for her doing it. The envelope was gone, if that was what she was after, and the rooms themselves had already been searched by the police.

Jim Conway surveyed the havoc grimly the next morning. "I'm going to put a guard inside the house," he told Tony that day. "There's some funny business going on, and I don't like it. I've got a fellow named O'Brien. Not much on manners but hell on trouble. You can trust him."

O'Brien came that evening. He was a cocky young fellow who immediately announced that he would like a supper and a thermos of coffee left out for him at night. Also he produced an automatic which he handled with extreme casualness. "You folks'll be all right when I'm around," he said cheerfully. "Only you'd better have the help let me know when they're out late. I'm apt to shoot first and ask questions afterward."

I was not greatly impressed. He wore a cap and crepe-soled shoes, and my own feeling was that he looked more like a first-class burglar than anything else. But he was to prove his mettle later on. Poor O'Brien! He lay in the hospital for months that winter, with a bullet through his chest.

"Just leave it to me," he said, the first night after he had looked over the house. "I'm partial to ham sandwiches, if you get what I mean; but not too damn partial. You might tell Frenchie that."

Nevertheless, I slept better after that for knowing he was on guard.

Otherwise things went on much as usual for a week or so. Bessie was still at the Cloisters. I think she was putting pressure on Tony for a larger allowance, now that he was Maud's heir; but she had what Jim later called an ace in the hole which she still had not used. Probably she was not sure of him or of what his reaction would be. And Tony was in town most of the time, for Maud's death, throwing control of the business into his hands, was being furiously resented by the Wainwright crowd.

I was clearing up odds and ends of my work, preparatory to leaving. I knew it would have to come. Bessie would go, and I could not stay there without her. That phase of my life was over.

I carried on as best I could. The house was quiet. People called, left cards, drove away again. Mrs. Partridge collapsed and was ordered to bed for a day or two. The horses stood unridden in the stables. Pierre cooked in his customary fashion, but without his heart in his work, and at night O'Brien, looking vastly important, paraded through the house.

I had rather expected that Margery Stoddard would come over to see me. She was nearer my age than Maud's, and we had become friendly. But she was laid up for a few days. Bill Sterling, after seeing Mrs. Partridge one day, reported that it was nothing serious. "Nerves," he said. "Misses the children but won't bring them back. That's one advantage of being poor. Kidnapping's out."

He was cheerful that day, although he said he still had the little detective to carry around and was thinking of adopting him. "He'll be a pretty fair doctor when I'm through with him," he said, grinning. "Had to help me cut off a leg back in the hills the other day. Didn't faint until it was over. Says he's going into a sanitarium when this case is over."

But the case, as Bill called it, was not over. Evans was still missing. Even Hopper admitted that Maud's farewell letter to Tony could be read two ways, and there was that search of her rooms to worry us all. Then one day, after O'Brien had been in the house for a night or two, Jim Conway telephoned me. "Better come down," he said. "I want to talk to you. Something's turned up that I don't like."

He was sitting at his desk as usual when I got there, and he had a couple of photographs in his hands. "Afraid it's bad news, Pat," he said. "It's got me anyhow. Ever see one of these?"

He handed me one of the pictures, but it meant nothing to me: a highly magnified cylinder with long vertical scratches on it. I shook my head.

"Picture of a bullet," he said. "Pictures of two bullets, as you see. The hell of it is, they've both been fired from that gun of Tony's. One's the test shot, the other's the one we dug out of Bessie's car. It doesn't look so good, does it?"

"Are you saying that Tony shot at her?"

"I'm saying that Tony's gun fired the bullets. That's as far as I go."

It was not, however, as far as the district attorney's office and the city detectives went. Through a haze I heard Jim putting the case as they saw it: that Tony now had the Wainwright money and the Wainwright business, that he hated Bessie and wanted her out of the way, and that he had probably killed Don Morgan too.

I roused at that. "Killed Don?" I said. "Why would he? What was Don to him?"

"They've got something there, Pat." He leaned back in his chair. "They've been looking Don up in Paris. He and Bessie had been pretty intimate there a couple of years ago, according to the police dossier. If Tony knew that—"

"He wouldn't care, Jim. He didn't give a tinker's dam what she did."

"That's what you and I think," he said, and lapsed into gloomy silence. When he spoke again he sounded more hopeful. "There's one crime they'll never prove against him, because he didn't do it. That's his mother's death. And I'm banking on just one thing. There was a woman in the playhouse the night Maud Wainwright died. I don't believe it was Bessie. Then who was it?"

He had a list of names in front of him. They consisted of practically all the women Maud knew, but one by one as we talked he drew a pencil through them. All except Lydia's. He sat for some time looking at it.

"Funny," he said. "She's the one person who would have wanted Don out of the way, outside of Bill Sterling. Ever thought it might be Lydia, Pat?"

"And Maud too, Jim?"

"All right. Have it your own way." He ran his pencil through Lydia's name. "I suppose when we're all through we'll find that old Mrs. Earle simply went out on a killing spree and Theodore helped her out."

One thing he clung to. We had only one criminal. Don's murder and Maud's were connected, although he didn't know how. Personally he wanted to go back to Don's murder and start from there. "There's one name not on this list," he said. "That's the Weston girl's. Maybe she's gone down in the world. She may be a maid around here somewhere. Or maybe she's gone up. In that case she might be anybody. But I've got a hunch that when we find her we'll have something."

It came down to that in the end. What he wanted me to do was to find the Connor woman in town and get her to talk. "Although I'm warning you she's a hard nut to crack," he said.

"Some of the newspaper boys have been after her, and she's pretty leery. But she was in that office when the Weston girl was there. You can bet she remembers her."

It was the chance to save Tony that made me finally agree, and that night I told him that I had some business in the city the next day. He offered to drive me in, but I said I would take a later train. He nodded, and he stood—we were in the upper hall— and looked down at me with stark misery in his eyes. "How long is Bessie going to stay?" he asked.

"She hasn't said."

"I wish to God she'd go," he said heavily. "I can't stand it much longer, Pat."

"I'll have to go too, Tony. You know that."

"Not yet, Pat. Give me a little time, darling."

I suppose he knew about the bullets by that time, but he did not mention them. As I look back I can see how each of us was trying to help the other, and what a stupid mess we made of it. He must have known that he was close to arrest for the attack on Bessie, if nothing worse. But he smiled down at me as he said good night. "We're fighting it out, Pat," he said. "I can stand it, if you'll stand by."

I went in to town the next morning. The old train was familiar—the dusty smell of the plush seats, the river cold and slate gray under the November sky, the untidy tenements as we neared the city. Just so had I traveled for six years, until the day in June when I had walked into Maud Wainwright's boudoir at the Cloisters and found her there, big and smiling.

The conductor recognized me as he took my ticket.

"Like old times, seeing you," he said. "Understand you've been having a lot of trouble."

I looked up at him, his kind old eyes, his shabby uniform. I had known him since my childhood, and I am afraid my chin quivered, for he leaned over and patted my shoulder. "Just forget about it," he said. "After all, they're not your folks, Miss Pat. It's money that brings trouble. It always has and it always will."

CHAPTER TWENTY-SIX

I saw Bessie that morning in town, on my way to find the Connor woman. She had stopped her car near the building where Mr. Elliott had his offices and was getting out. There was nothing youthful about her face then. It looked hard and determined. She wore a short silver fox jacket I had never seen before, and she walked purposefully on those high heels of hers to the building and went in.

Later we were to know some, if not all, of what happened there in Dwight Elliott's office that day: Mr. Elliott alert and watchful behind his desk, and Bessie leaning forward and speaking steadily in a low voice. Finishing triumphantly too, and then leaving back and powdering her nose.

"That's the story, Mr. Elliott."

"I suppose you know what it means?"

"I have a pretty good idea."

"You can't prove it, you know."

"I'm leaving that to the police, if I have to go to them."

"I wouldn't try any threats if I were you, Bessie. How many people know about this?"

"Don't tell me Tony doesn't. He tried to kill me, didn't he? He was afraid I would talk. But I haven't. Not yet anyhow."

She got up and he rose also, towering over her, his voice shaking. "Let's finish this, once and for all," he said angrily. "You've been here before with this cock-and-bull story about Maud Wainwright. You can't prove it, but what is that to you? Shall I tell you what happened? You told her this story of yours. You probably threatened to go to the police with it. And to get you money to keep quiet she was ready to sell her jewels."

"It's a lie. I never told her."

"She listed them, and the night of her death she met you at the playhouse."

"Never. I wouldn't go there on a bet."

"I think you did. Remember this. Her death was a distinct advantage to you. Tony had a salary before. Now he has a fortune. And what you want me to do is collect blackmail from him to keep you quiet."

She gasped. "If anybody thinks I killed her they're crazy," she said, her lips stiff.

"The official verdict is still suicide," he said. "But she met a woman at the playhouse that night, and she carried the list of her jewels with her. Maud Wainwright never killed herself. That woman killed her."

She was completely routed. She picked up her handbag and went out. She left her car standing where it was, although she took a suitcase out of it. After that she hailed a taxicab and went to the railroad station. There she bought a ticket for New York, and disappeared entirely.

I had no idea this was happening, of course. My work that day was to establish contact with the Connor woman, and I had no idea how to go about it. It turned out to be simple enough, however. I merely went to the offices which had once been Don Morgan's and, standing outside, waited for the lunch exodus. Ostensibly I was making up my face, but I watched some twenty-odd girls come out before my quarry appeared.

There was no mistaking her or her type. I knew them well, those older, anxious women who kept strictly to themselves, away from the gossip, the surreptitious manicures, and even the shampoos in the rest rooms. They are divided between a conviction that the business could not get along without them and a terror that it will; and Miss Connor was true to type.

She did not even lunch with the others. I followed her when she walked stolidly around a corner and entered a small teashop. There she took a table to herself and ordered coffee and doughnuts, chewing them deliberately when they came, with teeth obviously not her own. I let the coffee get in its work before I moved over to her table.

"I'm sorry to bother you," I said. "But I think I saw you in the Atlantic Company's office the other day."

She eyed me. I had purposely worn the shabbiest things I had, but she was suspicious, as Jim had prophesied.

"Newspaperwoman?" she asked curtly.

"No, I wish I were. I'm looking for a job."

I told her where I had been, and her suspicion slowly died. She spent ten minutes telling me that I'd better bleach my hair and make up my face, and at the end I picked up my cue.

"I don't bother with bosses," I said shortly. "There's no luck in it. Look at what's-her-name who ran away with this Morgan man who was murdered not long ago. She got a raw deal if I ever heard of one."

I was afraid I had been too abrupt, but as our local tabloid had already featured that story she merely shrugged.

"That's what I mean," she said savagely. "She was a blonde, and look what it got her! I knew her," she added, and then shut up like a clam, as though she had said too much. I did not dare to push the subject, and I was still eating the slice of lemon meringue pie which had been a staple among the girls when I was working when she got up abruptly and left. She hesitated before she went, however. Then she left a dime beside her plate, and the waitress later viewed it with amazement.

"So the old sourpuss loosened up," she said.

"I imagine every dime counts."

"It counts with me too," she observed and slipped it into her pocket.

There seemed to be nothing more I could do that day, so I went home. Bessie had not come back, and one of the housemaids reported that she had taken a suitcase with her. But Bessie had always lived her own life at the Cloisters, and if I thought about it at all it was that she meant to spend the night in town.

It was still early, so I called up Lydia. After all, Miss Connor's statement that the Weston girl had been a blonde was at least interesting. But when Audrey answered the telephone her voice was sharp. "Sorry," she said. "You can't talk to Mother. She's not well."

"It isn't serious, is it?"

"She's not seeing anyone. Anyhow, she's asleep now. I can't bother her." She hung up the receiver, leaving me with a wild desire to smack her lovely face.

After that I called Jim Conway and told him of the day's results. He seemed satisfied. "Atta girl," he said. "You'll have her eating out of your hand in a day or two."

"Eating a piece out of it, I expect. She has a pretty good set of uppers and lowers."

I was restless that day. My desk was piled high with work. The cards of thanks for flowers and so on had come in. There were notes to write, even the house to look after. When Bill Sterling came in late in the afternoon to see Mrs. Partridge I waylaid him in the hall.

"What's the matter with Lydia?" I asked.

He seemed tired. He put his black bag on a chair and stood looking down at me.

"I wish I knew," he said candidly. "Maybe it's reaction. She's been through a lot. Maybe it's something else. I wish you'd talk to her, Pat."

"Audrey says she won't see anybody."

"Oh, damn Audrey," he said, and picked up his bag again.

He was not greatly concerned, however. I saw him out to his car where the little detective sat at the wheel. Bill laughed at my expression when I saw him. "Makes a pretty good chauffeur," he said. "He's learning some surgery too."

The little man grinned sheepishly.

I drove down to Miss Mattie's late that afternoon. She was pleased when I told her that I would be coming back soon.

"I never did like your being up there," she said in her thin high voice. "The idea of calling a house the Cloisters! It's almost sacrilegious."

It was all familiar and friendly. Even the odor of soap when Sarah offered me a moist red hand was vaguely comforting, and when I went up to my old room I had a feeling of coming home. It was not large, the room, but I had furnished it with some of the things from our old house before it was sold. It looked cheerful and peaceful, and I remember sitting down in what had been Mother's favorite chair, and trying to reorient myself.

All at once violence and sudden death seemed far away. A

boat whistled on the river, there was the slow rumble of a freight train sliding down the grade, and all about me were the familiar streets and houses of the valley.

This was where I belonged. The five-fifteen coming in, men spilling out of it, the evening papers under their arms, car doors slamming, and somewhere lighted windows and a welcome. "Is that you, John?"

"Sure. How's everything?"

I belonged there in Beverly. I wanted peace and orderly living. Not money. Not grandeur. Not the Hill. Not even love.

I put my head down on the bed and cried my eyes out.

The next few days kept me busy. Bessie had not come back. Tony was busy too, not only with the mills but with the preliminaries of settling his mother's estate. At night I worked over my desk. The days I spent on Miss Connor.

We were almost friendly by the end of the week. Each day I managed to lunch with her, and each day her suspicion of me lessened. Once or twice I noticed a small dark man near us, but it never occurred to me that my movements had any interest to the police. Then, on the last day, Miss Connor came through.

That was on Friday. I had met her for the three preceding days as if by accident, and it had become accepted that I sit at her table. She was no longer suspicious of me, but she was still on guard. That day, however, she was more at her ease. The long week was behind her, and Saturday and Sunday lay ahead. She became quite human and she herself brought up the subject of Marguerite Weston.

"We lived in the same boarding house," she told me. "I'm still living there, for that matter. She wasn't exactly pretty, but she had what it takes. I tried to warn her about Mr. Morgan, but she was off her head about him. So were half the girls in the office, but I saw through him from the first. He was the kind of man who'd have an affair with some woman and then carry home a dozen roses to his wife. He never fooled me."

"I was a kid then," I said. "Of course, lately I've heard a lot about it. I always thought she was beautiful."

Miss Connor snorted. "I've got a snapshot of her. I'll bring it in sometime."

But I was getting too close to let her go. On the way out of the teashop I mentioned that I was looking for a room, not too expensive, and after a brief hesitation she said there was an empty room where she lived. I was feeling pretty shoddy by that time, but she asked me to go and see it. Something in her face touched me, and I realized that she was lonely. Anyhow, I went with her after work, and the inconspicuous little man went too, although I did not know it.

I have always been unhappy about that day; my own hypocrisy and what it did to her. Months later I got her a better position, as a sort of mute apology. But she never knew it. I saw her only once after that, and when I did she cut me dead.

The vacant room when I saw it made me shudder. After the Cloisters or even Miss Mattie's it was dreadful, and Miss Connor's statement that the Weston girl had lived in it made that escape of hers more understandable. There was a sagging bed, a chest of drawers with a mirror, a table beside the bed, and two chairs, one a rocker. The window opened on a court, and I stood there looking out. Marguerite must have stood there often, at first listlessly and then with a growing hope. A new life, a man who loved her. Europe. Paris. That small room could hardly have contained her happiness.

When I turned, Miss Connor eyed me. "You look tired," she said. "Come to my room and I'll give you a cup of tea. It's hard work, looking for a job."

I felt guiltier than ever, for when we went to her room—not much larger than Marguerite's had been—she not only put a tea-kettle on a small electric stove in the bathroom. She hurried out to a grocery store.

"If you don't mind my leaving you," she said rather breathlessly. "You just sit down and rest yourself. I won't be long."

I was ready to give up when she came back, her arms full of parcels. But she would not let me go.

"Don't be foolish," she said. "I'll just boil you a couple of eggs. They're filling and they keep up the strength. You can rest on my bed until they're ready."

I could not do that. I was hideously ashamed of the whole performance. I sat in a chair while she took the lamp off the table and spread a clean towel over it. "It's a long time since I had company," she said. "Marguerite used to come in now and then. Once on Sunday morning I cooked her a kipper. Dear me, how long ago that seems."

It was a long time, a decade and a half of loneliness. No wonder she cherished her memories of that bit of romance whose edge she had touched so long ago.

"I remember seeing her off," she said. "I said she wasn't exactly pretty, but she was that day. I was crying because I knew it was all wrong, but she put her arms around me and told me not to worry. She'd be married as soon as Morgan's wife got a divorce, and she'd write me often. She never did, of course. What was there to write about?"

"You've never seen her since?"

"Never, or heard from her. I've lain in that bed often and

wondered what became of her. She wasn't the kind to make her own way."

Any belief that Bessie had been the Weston girl died at that. If ever a woman was able to manage her life it was Bessie Wainwright.

I managed the two eggs, tea, bread and butter. I even got down the chocolate wafers which I knew had been sheer extravagance, and at the end Miss Connor sat back and eyed me complacently. "Nothing like good food to give you courage," she said.

It was some time before I brought her back to Marguerite and the snapshot, and she was an even longer time before she located it. When she did she carried it to the lamp—it was dark by then—and studied it.

"It's not very good," she observed. "I had one of those dollar cameras, and she had a new dress. I took it here, in the back yard."

Then at last she gave it to me, and I took one look and felt the room whirling around me. I put out a hand to steady myself and Miss Connor caught me. "Here!" she said. "Maybe you ate too fast. Lie down a minute."

"It's nothing," I managed to say. "Maybe I'm tired. I'll sit down for a minute or two."

The room settled down then. I saw her pick up the picture and put it away, and I managed to light a cigarette. I even offered her one, but she refused. "It's expensive," she said, "and I'm too old to start. How are you now? Better?"

I got away somehow. I never noticed the little man across the street. It never occurred to me that Hopper would also be on the trail of the Weston girl, and was watching Miss Connor. All I was certain of was that I had solved the mystery, solved it dreadfully, heartbreakingly: Don's murder, what Bessie knew, the attempt on her life, even her flight—if it had been a flight. I even thought I knew the woman who had met Maud in the playhouse the night she died.

I was shaking as if I had a chill when I got out of the train. Gus noticed it. His face was full of concern as he tucked the rug around me. "Better go to bed when you get back, miss," he said. "You look kind of shot. I'll close the windows. Air's cold tonight."

I lay back in the seat, my mind going in circles. Margery Stoddard and her children, coming to swim in the playhouse pool. Margery and Maud, telling her she might have to leave the Cloisters, and Margery's affectionate eyes on her. But there was something else, also. There was Margery on the path, defiant and angry and Bessie unmoved, smoking and listening to her.

For there was no question about it. The photograph Miss Connor had shown me had been of Margery Stoddard. A younger Margery, of course, but the attractive irregular features were hers, the familiar smile. In the picture her hair was blond and blowing about her face, and bearing the two little girls had thickened her figure somewhat. But Marguerite Weston was Margery Stoddard, and I did not know what to do.

CHAPTER TWENTY-SEVEN

I TRIED to get control of myself on the way up the hill. I succeeded fairly well, but I was greeted as I entered the house by a wild-eyed Tony who looked at me as if I had done him a personal injury. "Where the hell have you been?" he demanded. "I've called up every place but the city morgue."

"I'm sorry. I had business in town."

"Business! At seven o'clock on a Friday afternoon! Better think up something better than that, Pat." Then he saw my face. "I'm sorry, darling. I've been nearly crazy. You'd ordered the car for three o'clock, and I thought you'd met with an accident."

I suppose I should have told him. Still, what could he have done? And he had worries enough just then. Bessie had been gone for five days, no word had come from her, and Dwight Elliott had apparently told the police something, for they were trying to locate her.

"I'm only tired," I said, trying to smile. "I'll feel better when I've had a hot bath and dressed."

He let it go at that. He said afterward that he had not believed me, that I looked a million years old and the complete hag that night. But I got through dinner somehow; only the two of us now to eat there, the silver shining, the candles and flowers, the three men never leaving us alone, and Tony watching me, suspecting I did not know what. It was in the library later that I told him I was going back to Miss Mattie's on Monday.

"I'll come up every day until everything is cleared up," I said. "After that you won't need me."

"I'll always need you, Pat. You know that. But one thing's sure, and it's final. I won't have you driving after dark. It's not safe."

"Why not? I've done it right along."

"Read this," he said, and handed me the evening paper. "Most of it's the usual rubbish, but maybe the fellow's right at that."

It was rather an unnerving thing to find, sitting there in the very center of what the writer designated as the reign of terror. As I kept it I give it here verbatim:

> The disappearance of a witness in the Morgan murder case draws attention once more to the strange sequence of events which have taken place in the once peaceful river town of Beverly. Two people have been killed, one murdered and one by her own hand, and two other persons have disappeared, the watchman Evans, who had previously been murderously attacked, and the wife of Mr. Anthony Wainwright. A quiet search for her has been instituted by the police, so far without result.
>
> We publish today a letter from a resident of Beverly, stating that a reign of terror now exists there, and suggesting that an inmate of the State Mental Hospital, located at Burton, some six miles away, may have escaped and be responsible. Inquiry at the institution reveals that no such escape has taken place. Nevertheless this correspondent's demand for additional police protection is apparently justified.

I may say here that the net result of that editorial was one officer from the city, who spent most of his time playing pinochle with the sergeant at the station house. That night, however, it made me shudder.

"Do you believe in this lunatic, Tony?"

"I don't know what to believe."

I went upstairs early, leaving him alone. He did not try to keep me. I know now that he thought I was up to something that night, although he had no idea what it was. "It stuck out all over you," he told me elegantly a few hours later. But I knew well enough what I had to do. I had to see Margery Stoddard, see her and warn her. Not for a minute did I believe that she had ever killed anybody, and if Julian had done it I could even see a sort of elementary justice in it.

It was ten o'clock when I telephoned her. With Tony still in the library I had to call her from my room, which meant that anyone lifting a receiver could hear me. But I was obliged to take the chance and I was as noncommittal as possible.

"I want to see you," I said. "Tonight if I can. Are you alone? Just say yes or no."

"No."

"Can you slip out by the pool and meet me? Say in half an hour."

"Not very well. I'm sorry, Pat."

"In an hour?"

"I don't know."

"Listen, Margery," I said. "It's important. I can't tell you how important. You must do it."

There was a short silence. Then: "I'll try," she said in a different and strained voice. "I haven't been going out much, but if you want me—at five tomorrow? All right. Thanks."

By which I judged that Julian was in the room with her.

It was a quarter to eleven when I heard Tony come upstairs and go into his room, and Reynolds closing the house for the night. It seemed to take him a long time, but at last I managed to get to the lower floor. Even at that I had forgotten O'Brien, and I only escaped him by ducking into a coat closet in the west hall. I was pretty well shattered by that time, but I dare say the closet saved my life that night. A white coat of mine from the summer was still hanging there, and I put it on.

Luckily for me, Roger had taken to making rounds with O'Brien at night. He sniffed a moment at the closet and then went on. Yet I did not get away without further difficulty.

The garage was still open, with no one about; but when I started my motor Gus suddenly appeared, his square honest face looking concerned.

"If you're going out I'd better go with you, miss," he said. "Mr. Wainwright wouldn't like your going alone."

"I have an errand, Gus. I won't be long."

"I haven't got anything else to do," he said stubbornly. "Mr. Tony's given orders—"

"Mr. Wainwright doesn't give me orders, outside of my work," I said sharply, and started the car.

I was shaking again as I went down the drive. I had no idea how to tell Margery what I knew. I must have been frightened too, after that warning of Tony's. I remember the huge dark hulk of the house, and the long unlighted drive, curving among its dead trees, with every clump of evergreens a possible ambush. But when I reached it the highway was cheerful, with cars coming and going, and by the time I got to the Stoddard place I was calm enough.

I left the car in the drive inside the gate and walked to the pool. Margery was not there, and I waited for some time on a cold marble bench before she appeared.

"What is it, Pat?" she said. "You sounded so strange over the telephone."

"I think perhaps you know," I said, as gently as I could. "I've seen Miss Connor."

"Miss Connor?" she repeated. Then I heard her gasp. She sat down suddenly and was still for some time, not speaking, hardly breathing. When she did speak it was in a half whisper.

"Old Connor!" she said. "I'd forgotten all about her. What am I to do, Pat? What am I to do?"

"I don't think she'll talk, Margery."

"She talked to you."

"Not the way you think. She hasn't the remotest idea who you are. But she remembers Marguerite Weston. She seems to have been fond of you."

She was relieved. "Dear old Connor," she said. "She was good to me. She tried to hold me back, but I was young and headstrong. And you know what Don was. I'm not ashamed, Pat. He did marry me, you know. I divorced him later, after he left me."

I can still see her, sitting there by the pool, smoking one of my cigarettes and going back over the past as if it relieved her to talk about it. It was the usual story. For a while she had been happy. Then one day Don went away and did not come back. That was in Paris. He had had some money but had spent it lavishly. When he disappeared she was frantic. She spoke no French, and she had the equivalent of twenty dollars in her purse and a hotel bill to pay. Finally she got work as a stenographer with the American Express Company, and one day Julian Stoddard came in. She had worked in his office once for a short time, and he recognized her.

"I told him the story, and he was very kind," she said. "He advanced me money to pay the hotel and get back to New York, and later on he got me a position there. I saw him pretty often, and—well, you know the rest."

There was more to it, of course. She had been afraid to come back. But Beverly was ten miles from the city, and for years she had only rarely gone to town. She had changed too. Her hair had turned white, for one thing. She began to feel safe again. And then Don Morgan had come back. It had been pretty desperate, both for Julian and for herself.

"We didn't know what to do," she said. "I was almost frantic. But when we learned that he was not staying long. He was sick too. It all seemed safe enough."

They had talked it over. At first Julian had wanted to take her away, but one of the little girls was not well. And everything had been all right apparently. Don was shut away in the village, and she stayed at the Farm and did not leave the Hill. Then came the awful time when Bessie came over one night with a topcoat over her pajamas and told her she knew her story.

"I was stunned," she said. "She knew it all. She'd known Don in Paris, and he had told her. I couldn't go to Julian. I didn't dare to. I paid her all I could, but it never was enough. She was always coming back for more. That day you saw us on the footpath was only one time. There were plenty of others."

I thought of something. "Did you ever tell Maud, Margery?"

"No. How could I?"

She went on. When they had found Don's body, and it was said he had been drowned in somebody's pool, she almost lost her mind. "They were searching all the pools for clues," she said drearily. "And I didn't know, Pat. I wasn't sure. I know now that Julian didn't do it. But there was that awful car, left in our ravine, and Julian hadn't come home straight from Maud's party. Then I heard Jim Conway was going to search the pool. He was looking for a clue of some sort. He even put a guard over it. He sat here on this bench all afternoon. It was dreadful."

So she had done the best she could. When the guard was called off she was puzzled. "I came out that night and emptied the pool," she said. "I couldn't wait. I had to know. And there was nothing in it. Nothing at all."

That had been only an impulse, however, induced by sheer panic. When she thought it over she knew Julian had had nothing to do with Don's death. "It wasn't only that he wouldn't do a thing like that, Pat. He had no reason to. I had never told him about Bessie. So far as he was concerned we weren't threatened at all."

I believed her. I believed her too when she denied that she had gone to the playhouse the night of Maud's death. The very thought of the playhouse was abhorrent to her. She said with a shudder that she had not been inside the place since Don's death, and that she hated even to look at it. "That's the truth, Pat," she said, laying a cold hand on mine. "You must believe me. If Maud had sent for me I might have gone. She never did."

We separated after that, she to go back to the house and Julian, I to go to my car. I did not know what to do, except to forget Miss Connor. I did not believe Julian had killed Don, and Margery's secret was safe with me.

I do not remember being struck. All I recall is hearing someone close behind me, and half turned to see who it was. It was all I was to remember for two full days.

CHAPTER TWENTY-EIGHT

THEY ARRESTED Julian Stoddard on Sunday and took him to the city. I knew nothing about it. There was a complete gap between the time when I watched Margery Stoddard start for her house at eleven-thirty on a Friday night, and the hour when I opened my eyes on Sunday evening, to feel something cold and damp on my head and to see Amy Richards in cap and uniform standing by my bed.

"What's the matter?" I asked. "Am I sick?"

"You've got a bare chance to live, if you'll leave that ice bag where it belongs. You've been throwing it out for the last forty-eight hours."

"I don't want it," I said fretfully, and threw it out again.

I must have slept after that. When I wakened, Amy was dozing in a chair, and I lay still and tried to think. I couldn't remember anything at first. I might have been a newborn baby, with no past whatever. There was no Don Morgan, no Tony or Maud or Margery Stoddard. Only Amy, dozing by the fire with her mouth slightly open. When my mind did begin to operate, it was in pictures, without any chronology.

Ever since that time I have read about people who, after

a blow like mine, immediately go on fighting or talking of whatever they had been doing. I don't believe it. It was actually Monday before I made any sense. Not so much sense even then. I had been walking down the drive at the Farm and somebody had been behind me. That was as far as I got until Monday, some time in the afternoon, when I roused again to see Jim Conway in the room, and Bill Sterling carefully replacing the ice bag.

"I wish you'd take that damned thing away," I said fretfully.

Bill grinned. "She's all right, Jim," he said. "I guess you can talk to her."

That was when my mind clicked, and I knew I could not talk to Jim. "My head aches. I wish you'd let me alone," I said peevishly.

But Jim had no idea of letting me alone. He came over and stood by the bed. "I won't bother you," he said. "All I want to know is how you got that bump on your head."

I closed my eyes. "I must have fallen. I don't remember."

"Fallen? Are you saying you *fell* into that pool?"

"What pool?" I said incredulously. "I wasn't in any pool at all."

He grinned. "All right," he said. "What were you doing at the Stoddards' in the middle of the night? You know that, all right."

I closed my eyes again. "I was taking a ride," I said feebly. "I turned in there, on the chance somebody was still up. That's all, and I wish you'd go away."

But Jim did not move. He stood staring down at me coldly. "You're a rotten liar, Pat. You made an appointment with Margery Stoddard. Reynolds heard you doing it. You drove there and left your car in the drive, and you saw Mrs. Stoddard. Don't deny it. She admits it herself. Then what? She says the last she saw of you, you were on your way to the car. That true?"

I tried to nod, which made me realize that my neck was out of service for the time at least.

"I wouldn't excite her," Bill warned. But Jim stood solidly by the bed, regarding me with unfriendly eyes.

"I'm beginning to wonder about you, Pat," he said. "If you think you are helping anybody, you're wrong. They've got Julian Stoddard. It's too late to do anything."

I was horrified. I remember moaning that I had caused Julian's arrest, although I didn't know how; and finally I told him the whole story: the snapshot of Margery, my appointment with her, her admission of the facts, and my feeling on the drive that somebody was behind me. He listened soberly.

"Sure it wasn't Stoddard who tried to finish you off?" he asked.

"He would never do that to me."

"A man will do a good bit to escape the chair," he said dryly. "You knew about Margery. Nobody else did. Even the Connor woman, according to you, didn't know she had married Stoddard."

"He didn't know I was there."

"How can you tell? There's a lot of evergreen stuff around the pool. He could have followed his wife and heard everything you said. It looks bad, Pat. They know what happened to you. That's why they grabbed him."

"I don't know myself what happened to me."

He told me then. Gus had been worried about me, and when I did not come back he had started out in the station wagon to find me. He went down first to the village, but by twelve o'clock he was back on the Hill. My car was still gone, so he called Reynolds at the main house and asked if he knew where I had gone. "To the Stoddards'," said Reynolds. "I heard her make the appointment."

Gus began to feel foolish. He thought of putting up the station wagon and letting things ride. But there was Tony's order not to let me out alone at night. In the end he drove over to the Farm, to find my car parked inside the drive and the Stoddard house dark.

"It didn't look right to him," Jim said. "He got out and looked around the place. It was pretty dark, and if you hadn't had that white coat on he'd have missed you. But there you were, thrown into the empty pool, and he thought you were dead."

I gathered that there had been considerable excitement when I was brought back. Bill Sterling was afraid of a skull fracture, and Tony had roused a surgeon in town and made him come down. He had wanted to take me to the hospital for an X-ray, but Tony opposed it. "If there's anything to be done," he said, "it will be done here. I want her where she can be watched. She isn't going to follow Evans."

I had no fracture. It was a concussion, although I groaned when I learned that they had shaved a small place on the back of my head and put in four stitches. They had given me hypodermics to keep me quiet, and part of the time I'd been asleep.

"You were a pretty tired girl," said Jim, getting up. "You might as well take a rest now. There is nothing any of us can do for Stoddard. They think they've got him cold."

It looked as though they had. It was the little inconspicuous man, of course, who had done it. When I left Miss Connor, he had simply walked in and showed his badge to the landlady. "Woman here named Connor," he said. "Like to see her."

"Good gracious, she'll drop dead. The police!"

"Just want to talk to her. Nothing wrong."

He found her washing up after our tea and singing softly to herself. The little man stepped in and slammed the door in the landlady's face. "No trouble, Miss Connor," he said. "Just a little talk. You used to know a girl named Marguerite Weston, didn't you?"

She dried her hands, staring at him. "What about her?" she said. "She's not—dead?"

"Not so far as I know," he said cheerfully. "Want a description of her, that's all. She's come into a bit of money, and we'd like to locate her."

"Really!" she said. "How nice for her. I've got a snapshot of her, but it was taken fifteen years ago. Still, it might help."

The little man's face was impassive when she produced it. "I'd like to take it along with me," he said. "Hope you don't mind. You'll get it back all right."

He put it carefully in his wallet, and Miss Connor was beaming as she let him out the front door. The landlady was waiting, all ears, but Miss Connor did not explain.

"Just a friend of mine who has inherited some money," she said, and went smiling happily up the stairs to her room.

The police had spent Saturday making certain investigations, including the attack on me. Then on Sunday afternoon they had sent for Julian Stoddard. District Attorney Stewart was sitting behind his desk with that small snapshot of Margery before him. He picked it up.

"You recognize this picture, Mr. Stoddard?"

Julian took it. He must have known what it meant, but his hand was steady. "I do," he said. "It is my wife."

Nobody in the room moved. There were half a dozen men there: the police commissioner, the head of the homicide squad,

Hopper, and two or three others. Only Stewart stared at Julian with his little pig's eyes. "She was Marguerite Weston?"

"Yes. I married her after she divorced Donald Morgan."

"You knew she had married him and been deserted by him?"

"I did."

Stewart leaned back. "I see," he said. "So this return of his wasn't particularly pleasant for you. Especially since you'd buried your wife's former identity. Is that it?"

"Her former identity was her business, and mine."

"Oh, come, come, Mr. Stoddard! It was more than that. You or your wife had been paying money to keep it quiet, hadn't you?"

It had been a shrewd question. Even Hopper, who had suggested it, was not too sure. But Julian himself looked up indignantly. "I have paid blackmail to nobody," he said stiffly.

"I suggest that someone has, Mr. Stoddard. Perhaps your wife."

They left it at that, although at a word from Hopper one of the men slipped out. Even then I doubt if Julian had fully realized his position. He must have done so with the next question. "Did you see Morgan after he came back?"

"Never."

"Did your wife see him?"

"No."

"Are you positive of that?"

"Absolutely."

Then his iron control broke. He got up. "I don't know what all this is about. I didn't kill him, if that's what you mean, Stewart. Why should I wait a dozen years and then do a thing like that? He wasn't here to stay. He was going away. The last thing I wanted was to blow things wide open, and his murder was sure to do that."

The district attorney sat back, looking complacent.

"Sit down, Mr. Stoddard," he said affably. "I'll soon tell you what it is about. Suppose we go back to the night Morgan was murdered. What time did you leave the Cloisters?"

"About midnight."

"On foot?"

"On foot. It is only half a mile by the path to my place."

"What time did you get back to your house?"

"I'm not sure. I had some things to think over. I walked about for a while."

"Anybody see you, on the way or when you got home?"

"I'm afraid not."

"What about your wife?"

"She was asleep."

"Felt pretty safe, eh?" said Stewart. "No scandal, no anything. Then it blew up. I see."

"Nothing blew up, as you call it," said Julian, again stiff and dignified.

They did not believe him, of course. They went back over that night. He could have telephoned Morgan, making an appointment to meet him at the playhouse. Morgan had had a call, according to his wife. He could have met him there and—

"That's ridiculous. Why would I meet him there? With a hundred other places about?"

But Stewart kept on relentlessly. "Just why did your wife go home early that night, Mr. Stoddard? Was it by pre-arrangement with you?"

That infuriated him. He flushed and clenched his hands. "Another statement like that, Stewart," he said, "and I'll knock your teeth down your lying throat."

Stewart, well surrounded by his cohorts, merely smiled. "All right," he said. "I lay my cards on the table, Stoddard. We believe that you killed Donald Morgan that night, that you took the car he came in and placed the body where it was found, that you then drove this car to the ravine back of your house, and had only to climb the hill to be at home again."

Stoddard went pale, but he was still fighting. "I'm not a damned fool," he said. "If I had done it, would I have left that car where it was found?"

Hopper had been looking over his notes. "You drew three thousand dollars in cash out of the bank last week. Do you care to say why you did that?"

"No. It was a private affair of my own."

"Did you, last Friday night, see Patricia Abbott when she met your wife? Beside your swimming pool?"

"I had no idea my wife had met anybody that night until she told me about it later."

He was getting tired. Tired and confused. He sat there, trying to see where all this was leading; but the barrage of questions kept on. There was no time to think.

Then they sprang their trump card.

"Listen, Stoddard," said the district attorney. "Better come clean. We've got you, and you know it. You didn't go straight home the night Morgan was killed. We know when you got home, and how. We know you'd been seeing Evans at the hospital, and were outside his window the night he disappeared. And we have a pretty good idea you tried to kill Miss Abbott at the Farm, the night she told your wife what she knew. Better talk, Stoddard. We've got it anyhow."

Stoddard turned his tired eyes on the room. There was no

CHAPTER TWENTY-NINE

THEY HAD their case. Tony, hurrying to confer with Dwight Elliott, was appalled when Hopper told it to them. All day Saturday and on Sunday morning they had worked over the case from this new angle, interrogating the employees at the Farm, even the nurses at the hospital.

The first they broke was Julian's alibi for the night Don was murdered. It was broken by the wife of the undergardener, Joe Smith, the one who had seen Lydia's car driven into the lane.

She was reticent, however. She held a baby in her arms and eyed them coldly. "I don't know anything. And it's time to feed this child. Haven't we made trouble enough? If Joe had kept his mouth shut, you wouldn't be here this minute."

"Suppose that baby of yours grew and somebody killed him? Would you want to protect the killer?"

"Mr. Stoddard's no killer," she said indignantly, and then saw what she had done. She looked frightened, but in due time and by threatening to take her to the city, away from her child, she gave in.

On the night Don was killed she was waiting up for her husband. He was later than usual, and she meant to give him a "piece of her mind." It was a warm night. She sat on the dark porch of her cottage, which was not far from the edge of the ravine, and a few minutes after one o'clock she saw Julian Stoddard pass by. He had come from the direction of the ravine, and he was walking slowly, as though he was tired.

"Didn't you think that was unusual?"

"Why should I? He'd been out to dinner. He was often late, and he liked to walk."

"Did he see you?"

"I don't think so."

There were some discrepancies. For instance, she maintained that she could hear Julian on the path before she heard a car stop in the ravine. As to the car itself, she had thought it was someone bringing Joe home. But it was some time before Joe appeared.

Equally damaging was the unwilling statement of Julian's valet. Pressed hard, and told of the Smith woman's story, he admitted that Julian's dinner clothes were in bad condition the next morning. "No worse than if he'd taken a walk in the dark," he said belligerently. "He often did that. There was a bit of dirt and damp on the trousers."

"How about his shoes?"

"They were a bit dirty too," he admitted sullenly. "What's the idea anyway? If you think he had anything to do with the trouble at the Cloisters, you don't know Mr. Stoddard."

They tried to see me, but I was out for the count. Margery, too, was in bed, having heard of the attack on me and making God knows what of it. Nevertheless, they made progress that day. They even succeeded in tying Evans's disappearance to Julian. He had visited Evans a number of times in the hospital, and on the night of his arrest, with the news all over town, a probationer came forward. Not to the police. She walked timidly into the office of the superintendent of the training school. She was frightened but determined.

"I suppose I'll be thrown out for this," she said. "I'm sorry. I've liked it here. I'd hoped I could stay on, but—"

She cried a little then, but she told her story bravely enough. She had been out the night Evans vanished. Not very late, but after hours. There was a way to get in, if you knew it. The X-ray department, being closed all day, was usually open for airing at night, and it was possible to get in by a window.

She had noticed a car parked on the highway when she came in. It surprised her, because there was plenty of room at the hospital itself. She did not recognize the car, but as she started around the side of the building she saw a man standing under Evans's window. No, she did not see Evans himself. She had turned back and gone to the X-ray wing by the other side of the building. But she had seen Mr. Stoddard often, and she thought now he had been the man.

That came in on Sunday night. The district attorney was still in his office, and Hopper was with him. Stewart rubbed his hands. "That about finishes it," he said. "No mistake this time, Hopper. We'll get an indictment next week."

But Hopper was skeptical. "Almost too good," he said. "With a lot left over too."

Stewart was annoyed. "What's the matter with you?" he demanded. "Fellow's guilty as hell. What's left over?"

"Quite a lot," drawled Hopper. "Who killed Maud Wainwright, and why? Who shot at Bessie Wainwright's car? Who tore up the Beverly Cemetery? If Stoddard kidnapped Evans, where is he? And why?"

"Probably dead and buried."

But Hopper smiled. "Ever try to bury a body, Mr. District

Attorney? It isn't so easy. First you've got to get your body. Then you need tools. After that you need time, if you're to make a good job of it. And if Evans is buried somebody made a damned good job of it. Not so much time either. The sun rose before six o'clock that morning,"

"We're not trying Stoddard for Evans's murder," Stewart said sourly. "If you don't like this case—"

"Oh, I like it." Hopper got up and stretched. "I like it fine. Why did Tony Wainwright, the day somebody shot at his wife, call a firm of private dicks in New York? Why did he go to the public library the same evening? When did he learn his wife was blackmailing the Stoddard woman? Who took his gun out of his room? Why was Mrs. Wainwright going to sell her jewelry? Why was—"

"Get out of here," Stewart shouted. "I'll end up by thinking you did the thing yourself."

"Thanks," said Hopper, picking up his hat. "Whoever did it had brains, Stewart. Brains and to spare."

According to Jim later, Hopper still believed that Julian's arrest was premature. They knew Bessie had been collecting blackmail from Margery. In despair Margery herself had admitted it. In fact, she admitted even more. She practically cleared Bessie of complicity in Don's murder.

"On that night," she said, sitting white and still in her chintz-covered living room at the Farm, "I had promised to have some money for her. She left the club, and I met her on the footpath. She wanted a thousand dollars that time, and I had had to sell a bracelet to get it."

But with Bessie out, Hopper still had Tony in mind. He outlined his case against him the day after Julian's arrest. He had driven to Beverly, and he and Jim had a private sitting of their own.

"What about Wainwright?" he asked. "His wife had been intimate with Morgan in Paris. He had a row with Morgan when he came back, and we have only his own word it was about the daughter. Later his wife takes a drive at night with Morgan. Maybe he didn't like her much, but he wouldn't stand for that."

He pointed out, too, that Tony had no alibi for the night of Don's murder. "Maybe it's just a fool idea," he said. "But look at the facts. He took his wife in his car to the club that night. They probably quarreled about something. At any rate she came back without him. He returned at one-thirty that morning. Says he was walking around on the golf course. Fine lot of pedestrians you have around here, Conway."

"I see," Jim said grimly. "He didn't give a damn for his wife, but he killed her lover. And what about his mother? Maybe you have that fixed up too!"

He had. He pointed out that Maud when he—Hopper—had seen her on the day after the murder had been shocked but that was all. She was still all right on Monday morning. Then without any warning, as if somebody had hit her on the head with a hammer, she had a heart attack that almost killed her.

"Suppose Tony told her that morning?" he said. "His rooms are near hers. He says, 'Sorry, Mother, but I've been a bad boy. I killed Cock Robin.' He goes out, and she drops as if she'd been pole-axed. Something happened to her that day. You can bet your bottom dollar on that."

"So she committed suicide!" said Jim. "We go to the devil of a lot of trouble to prove she was murdered. Now it's suicide."

"I haven't said it was suicide," said Hopper, and took his tall gangling body back to town.

I escaped some of the excitement following Julian's arrest, although Amy said the town was hissing like a tea-kettle. Nobody who knew him believed him guilty. Margery's identity was still being kept secret and there seemed to be no motive whatever for Julian to have killed Don Morgan. The Hunt Club held an indignation meeting and sent a delegation to the district attorney's office. It returned chastened. Stewart had spread his fat hands on the desk and glowered at them.

"Stoddard had a motive, gentlemen," he said. "When I'm good and ready it will be told. Now I advise you to go back to your horses and chase your little foxes or rabbits or what it is you chase. I'm busy."

Beyond the bare announcement of Julian's detention nothing was known. Enterprising reporters managed to get pictures of the buildings at the Farm, including the famous kennel, modeled on one near Middleburg, Virginia. The fact that they included a cook room where the food for the hounds was prepared, a feeding room, washing and dipping rooms, and an exercise court as well as hospital and quarters for the kennelmen, made good copy. I think, times being what they are, that account of what was called the Dog Palace did more to prejudice general opinion throughout the country than any other one thing.

The whole business was incredible to me, but I could not take it too seriously. It was a mistake. Even knowing what I did, I could not see Julian actually standing in the dock. I was in bed for a week, with everybody smothering me with kindness. Andy picked his best flowers from the conservatory to fill my rooms, Tony brought me books, and one day a small aquarium from the five-and-ten-cent store arrived from Jim Conway. It contained four goldfish and a card reading: *Something fishy about all this.* Even Pierre came up in the mornings to see what I would like and—to Amy's annoyance—chattered to me in French. "You need the flesh, mademoiselle. It is to me no credit that you grow in four or five months so thin. I could blow you away. Poof and you go."

"Tell that Frenchman to stop blowing garlic into the room and get out," Amy said one day. "What's he saying anyhow?"

"He is telling me I am beautiful and he loves me."

"Like master, like man!" said Amy. "The fat fool!"

Had it not been for Julian and Margery I could have been happy that week. It was a long time since I had been so cared for. But by the time I was able to sit up the case was before the grand jury. The State being the plaintiff, the twenty-three men of the grand jury listened to Stewart and a few witnesses, and indicted Julian without hesitation. Tony, looking rather sick, brought me the news that night.

"We've got Brander Jones to defend him," he said. "Elliott's purely a corporation lawyer. Stoddard never did it, Pat."

"No," I said drearily, "but I've helped to send him to the chair. I'll never forgive myself."

I remember Tony that day, standing by the window staring out. Winter had come at last. The trees were bare, and the playhouse was in full view. He spoke without turning. "Who would want to kill Mother, Pat?" he said. "She never did a wrong thing in her life."

"Maybe there is a crazy man around, Tony."

"How would he get hold of my gun?"

"She may have taken it with her that night. After what had happened at the playhouse—"

"She met someone there," he said dully. "She went there to meet someone, and he killed her."

He came over to where I was sitting, bolstered by pillows, in a chair by the fire and looked down at me.

"See here, Pat," he said. "About Bessie. Will you try to find out how much she got from Margery? I can't have my wife collecting blackmail; and she's still my wife."

I asked him then if he knew where she was, but he seemed utterly indifferent. "She'll turn up," he said. "She always has. I suppose she always will. But not always, Pat. I've learned some things. Bessie is out. I want you to know that."

It was on Tuesday, the eleventh day after I had been hurt, that little Audrey—as Jim always called her—stepped into the picture again.

I had not seen Lydia alone since the time Audrey and her young crowd had made a sort of perpetual picnic out of the search for Evans's body. There had been Maud's death, and after that the days in town tracking Miss Connor. But one day Bill Sterling, examining the scar on my head, opened up about her.

"There's something wrong with her," he said, looking worried. "Of course, none of us are normal just now. But she stays in her room a lot. As soon as you're able I wish you'd see her. She's been a tower of strength for years. Now she's changed. She's not the same even with me."

Amy, cleaning up after him, was out of the room for a few minutes, so we had time to talk. He said it was not Don's murder. She had been shocked, of course, but she was not grieving for him. If he didn't know better, he would say it was something to do with Maud's death.

"She's been different ever since it happened," he said, his pleasant unhandsome face looking anxious. "But she barely knew her. Why would that change her?"

"No," I said, "she didn't know Maud well enough really to grieve for her, Bill. But then that's true of the whole business, isn't it? Don Morgan comes back after fifteen years and is killed. People hardly remembered him. Evans was a solitary who lived at night and slept all day, so he disappears. Bessie comes to make a visit and goes away without notice. And poor Maud Wainwright, who hadn't an enemy in the world, is murdered."

He looked at me. "So you think that too, do you?"

"I'm sure of it. So is Tony. So is Jim Conway. So are the servants in the house. If you want to know anything in a place like this, talk to the staff."

"What do they say?"

"They're divided between Bessie and Evans, with the odds on Bessie," I said bitterly. "They don't like her."

"If that's all they have—"

"They have a little more," I admitted. "They think she put that letter of Maud's to Tony where it was found, for one thing."

"I don't get it, Pat."

"Listen," I said. "Any letter meant to be read after a death can sound like a suicide letter. Suppose she wanted to kill herself. Why steal Tony's gun? Why go to the playhouse to do it? Why turn on the water in the pool? I don't even think she knew how. And why hide a suicide note, if it was one, unless somebody needed to gain some time?"

"I suppose that means it was somebody in the house who did it?"

"Exactly. That's why the betting is on Bessie."

CHAPTER THIRTY

IT WAS that same day that Audrey stepped back into the picture. Bill had gone, and Amy had an errand in the village. I heard her driving out in her old car, with the clash of gears that almost brought tears to Gus's eyes; and half an hour later Reynolds announced that Audrey wanted to see me. I had no time to refuse, for she was directly behind him, looking both defiant and terrified.

"I'm sorry, Pat," she said in a thin voice. "But Larry made me come."

I was not too pleasant. "What have you been doing now?" I asked resignedly. "Come in and sit down anyhow. Better let me send for a glass of sherry. You look all in."

"I am. I don't want anything to drink."

She surprised me by beginning to cry; but I had had enough of tears, including my own, to last me a lifetime. I told her rather stiffly to pull herself together, and at last she wiped her eyes. "I didn't want to say anything, Pat. Only Larry says if I don't he'll have to tell Jim Conway. He thinks maybe you can explain it."

"Explain what, Audrey?"

"You'll have to promise first. If you tell the police, I'll jump in

the river." Her mouth set in sulky stubbornness, and figurative-
ly I threw up my hands. I agreed not to go to Jim, but her first
words made my heart fairly leap into my throat.

"It's about Mother," she said, tears threatening again. "You
see, she was at the playhouse here when Mrs. Wainwright was
killed."

I looked at her. She was a nuisance and dangerous. She had
almost convicted Bill Sterling of murder. She was totally unscru-
pulous about getting her own way. But that day she looked as
though a hand had passed over her face and wiped away all the
life and all the beauty.

"I don't believe it," I said. "What have you got against your
mother, to say a thing like that? What would she be doing there?"

That sent her off once more, but at last I got her story. She
and Larry had been to dinner and the theater in town the night
of Maud's death. They drove back, passing the entrance to our
drive at something before midnight, and as they passed, or just
before it, a car turned in. Larry had insisted that it was Lydia's,
and she had said it was silly. They wrangled about it part way
down to the valley. Then Larry had said he would prove it, and
turned back.

When they were almost there the car came out of the drive,
going very fast, but their lights caught it full as it made the turn.
It was Lydia's car, and Lydia was in it.

"She looked dreadful," Audrey said, still in a thin, strained
voice. "She never saw us. I don't think she even knew a car was
there."

They had not gone home at once. They knew nothing then of
Maud's death, but they were two children facing something they
could not understand. Lydia and Maud had been almost strangers until that summer, and not intimate since. Larry had thought

she might have gone to see Tony, and accused Audrey of playing Tony against him. They had quarreled and he left her at home and drove away in a bad temper.

The next morning changed everything, of course. Lydia was in bed, and sent word she wanted to sleep off a headache. Shortly after breakfast Larry brought the news of Maud's death, and the two of them went out to stare at a cold river in a cold autumn wind, and to wonder what to do. Larry was all for going to Lydia and telling her what they knew, but Audrey was afraid.

"Afraid of what?" I said. "You don't think your mother shot Mrs. Wainwright, do you?"

"Somebody shot her," she said, her chin quivering. "She never did it herself, and Mother was there."

"Now listen, Audrey," I said. "Let's show some sense. In the first place why would your mother do such a thing? She had no reason on earth. In the second place, how would she get Tony's gun? She's never been upstairs in this house in her life. You've brooded over this until you're not rational."

"I know all that," she said. "Larry and I have been over it for days. He thinks she saw somebody do it. But why was she there at all? In the middle of the night, too."

She had not talked to her mother. In fact, she had hardly seen her. Most of the time Lydia was shut away in her room, and Audrey didn't think she had even told Bill Sterling. He seemed worried about her, but he was just the same as usual. Then at last she came to what Larry and she wanted. They wanted me to tell Lydia she had been seen, but not by whom.

"I've made her enough trouble," said this new and chastened Audrey. "But she trusts you, Pat. She'll tell you if she tells anybody."

"She probably won't see me."

"I'll get you in. She doesn't lock her door. She just keeps it closed." Her eyes filled again with tears. "She doesn't eat. I don't think she even sleeps, Pat."

My head was whirling, but then and there I made up my mind what to do. I had to see Lydia, and with Amy gone I had the only chance I might have for another week or so.

"Have you got a car?" I asked.

"Yes. Larry brought me up."

"Then help me into some clothes. I'm still wobbly."

I cannot say she was very useful. Between us, however, I managed to dress and to escape the servants, and shortly after I was on the way down the hill in Larry Hamilton's car, sitting crowded between them.

I soon found that Larry showed more judgment than Audrey. He did not suspect Lydia.

"What I think," he said, driving with the one-handed casualness which sets my teeth on edge, "is that she saw something. She may have looked through a window and seen Mrs. Wainwright kill herself; or more likely she saw someone else there. What we can't make out is why she was there herself, at that hour. When we left she was reading a book and going to bed early. Bill Sterling was out on a case."

Fifteen minutes later I pushed open the door to Lydia's room and walked in. She was not in bed. She was partially dressed, and was looking out toward the river. When she turned and saw me she had to catch a chair to steady herself.

"Pat!" she said. "You scared me."

I took one look at her and put her into a chair. Then I kissed her, and she drew a long breath.

"I thought it was the police," she said, and closed her eyes.

I gave her a little time to recover, talking of other things. Her color came back, but she was still a wreck of her former self. Her eyes were sunk in her head, and the life had gone out of them. Also I saw she was suspicious of me. She dodged every attempt to bring in the Cloisters, and at last I simply sat forward and said, "Why don't you tell me all about it, Lydia?"

I had expected more evasion, but it did not come. Instead she made a small gesture of surrender.

"I'll have to tell somebody. If I'm arrested it will finish Audrey. And poor Bill—"

"You'll not be arrested, Lydia. It need never come out at all. You were there that night. I happen to know it. Do you want to tell me why?"

"You won't believe it."

"I don't see why not, Lydia. I've believed you for a good many years."

"All right. I was there because she sent for me."

"Sent for you!"

"That's what she did. At first I was to go to the house. Then, about seven o'clock that night, she called again. She said Bessie was having some people to dinner, and did I object to going to the playhouse instead."

She hadn't wanted to go there. She couldn't bear to think of the place. She asked Maud to come down to her house instead. But Maud said what she had to say was private. If she went someone would have to take her, and she didn't want it talked about.

"I hate to ask you," Maud said, "but I assure you it is important. It won't be bad, Mrs. Morgan. I'll light a fire in the living room. We can be alone, and nobody needs to know anything about it."

The time, to her surprise, was to be eleven-thirty, and Lydia had demurred somewhat. But Maud had been firm. She could get rid of the maid by that time, and the matter was extremely confidential.

"She said something about Audrey," Lydia said. "I thought she must mean Tony and Audrey, although that was over months ago. But it all seemed strange enough. Then I began to worry about Bill. Perhaps she knew something that would bring him back into Don's murder or connect him with Evans. You know how it is. You build up all sorts of things."

Anyhow, she had agreed.

Audrey and Larry had gone to town, and at eleven o'clock she went out to get the car. But it had a flat tire, and she was no good at that sort of thing. She telephoned to the garage and the night man came around and fixed it. There was a nail in it. When she finally left it was almost twelve o'clock. She drove up as fast as she could, parked the car inside the gates, and walked past the fountain to the playhouse.

She was surprised not to find it lighted; surprised and uneasy. But there was firelight coming through the living room windows, so she went in.

The door was unlocked, and the fire lit the long hall with the pool opening off it. She went there, to find the room empty but a brisk fire going. By that time she was very nervous, however. She managed to discover a switch and turned the light on. It made her feel better. But there was no sign of Maud, so she walked down the hall and glanced into the swimming pool.

Maud was lying there, dead.

"At least I suppose she was dead," she said drearily. "She was warm but she had no pulse at all, and she wasn't breathing. I was too paralyzed to run at first. I remember lifting her hair and seeing that dreadful wound, and I think I was out of my mind for a minute or two. I ran out to the telephone—the one to the house—and took it off the hook. Then I realized what a hole I was in. Don had been killed there, and if I was found with that body I had nobody to prove she had asked me there."

She lost her head entirely then. All she had touched, aside from the body, was the telephone, the knob on the door, and the light switch. She turned out the light. Then she wiped all three with her handkerchief. She was shaking so that she could scarcely walk. She did not dare even to close the door.

She ran back to her car and got home safe, but she did not go to bed. She walked the floor all night. Suppose Maud had not been dead, and she could have saved her? Suppose those tracks of hers in the snow were seen? Who would believe her? And there was water running into the pool. Why that, with winter close at hand? Then, toward morning that was, she remembered that she had worn a fur scarf, and she could not locate it. It was not in her room or in the hall below. She prepared for the worst. But before dawn she thought of the car, and she found it there on the floor by the driving seat. She almost fainted with relief.

"Did you see the gun?" I asked.

"No. I didn't even know she had been shot. I thought she had been killed by a blow, and that someone meant to throw her into the pool. Like Don."

Telling the story had done her good. She trembled, especially when it came to the scarf, but her color was better.

"So that's it, Pat," she said. "It isn't any use going to Jim Conway with it. What could he do? I saw nobody. She was dead when I got there, and Bill says she died at once. I didn't even hear a shot. And"—she tried to smile—"I didn't kill her. The only gun I have ever handled in my life is the one I found in

Don's room, and you remember what happened to that. But how did you know?"

She was suddenly excited again. She half rose out of her chair as the import of this struck her.

"Somebody we both can trust saw your car going in that night," I said. "But you needn't worry. It won't be told."

But she knew the truth at once. "Larry and Audrey!" she said. "The poor children! What am I to do, Pat? What am I to do?"

"Call them in and tell them what you've told me. They're waiting downstairs now. Of course, they don't suspect you but they're worried a lot. Better do it, Lydia."

And to the three of us and Bill Sterling, whom I managed to locate, she repeated that story of hers that day. Repeated it with Bill holding her hand and Audrey on the floor at her knee. She gave it in even more detail than before: Maud's urgent voice, the spot of blood on her hand when she got home, the wiping it off, the drying and cleaning of her shoes.

It was Larry who at the end said the unexpected thing. "What was wrong with your tire that night?"

She looked surprised. "There was a nail in it. Why?"

"Well, look," he said, his young face excited. "Suppose somebody wanted you to be late that night or not get there at all. What's simpler than to blow out a tire?"

"I don't think anybody knew I was to meet her there."

"That's where you and I differ," he said loftily. "Somebody did know, and that somebody found her there waiting for you and shot her. That's easy."

We held a consultation of sorts after that. Bill and I believed Jim Conway should be told, but not the city detectives. Jim knew Lydia and would believe her. Audrey wanted it kept a secret.

"What good does it do to tell it? She doesn't know who did it."
And Larry wanted to form an informal partnership with Bill,
the two of them to solve the mystery and send the murderer to
what he called the hot squat.

In the end it was decided to tell Jim, and we finished with tea
and toasted English muffins, as though by shoving our troubles
onto Jim's broad shoulders we had more or less done away with
them.

It is not surprising that his first reaction to our story was one
of pure indignation. "The whole lot of you ought to be jailed," he
said. "All through this case people have been holding out on the
police. Why didn't you tell that story at the inquest, Lydia? We'd
have had a different verdict."

"She's told it now," said Bill belligerently.

"And so what? Where am I to go from here? What you've
done is to hand me another murder case, with the trail weeks
old. It was murder. She didn't ask you to the playhouse so she
could kill herself."

He reached the point finally when he could ask some questions. For one thing he wanted to know if Lydia had seen the
missing envelope. She had not. He asked if she had heard a shot,
and again the answer was no. His real interest, though, was in
the tire and Larry's statement about it. But when he learned that
the garage doors were always unlocked through the day and often through the night also, he was, as Larry said, fit to be tied.
One thing he insisted on, however.

"Tony Wainwright has to know this," he said. "Did he take
the train or motor in, Pat?"

"The train. He usually comes down on the five-thirty. He'll
be home by now."

Jim called him. There was a long and I gathered acrimonious

discussion over the telephone, Tony furious at my having left the Cloisters, Jim calm as usual.

"She'll live through it," he said, "and tell Amy to stop shouting. I can hear her here . . . Certainly I didn't steal her. She came by herself." He glanced back at me. "Looks fine, too . . . Oh, shut up, Tony, and get down here."

He hung up, looking amused. "Maybe they don't like you up there, Pat, but there's a hell of a rumpus going on. Better let me see Tony first. He sounds as though he's ready to commit mayhem."

It was a sober Tony who drove me home an hour later. He was divided between rage at me and bewilderment at Lydia's story. But halfway up the hill he stopped the car at the side of the road and put his arms around me.

"I'm so frightfully in love with you, darling," he said. "Maybe this isn't the time or the place, but when I found you gone today—Pat, you will marry me some day, when I'm free, won't you?"

"I can't think of anything that will stop me, Tony."

We did not say much the rest of the way. His face was quieter than I had seen it for a long time, as though at last he had reached peace and contentment. Poor Tony, when I think of that day my heart could break for him. There was no warning, no threat that more trouble was coming. But I shall always remember how he looked when he helped me up the terrace steps and into the hall.

Bessie, dressed for dinner, was standing there.

CHAPTER THIRTY-ONE

I DO not want to go into that return of hers, her amused "Hello," the faces of the footmen at the door and of Reynolds hovering in the background. Tony let go of me abruptly and I almost fell.

"What brought you back?" he said, ignoring the men.

"Why not? This is my home, isn't it?"

"Who brought you? The police?"

She smiled that cool amused smile of hers. "If it interests you, I came of my own free will."

She looked different that day. Her long bob was gone, and her hair was pinned in curls on top of her head. But the difference was deeper than that. She was not so tense. She lit a cigarette and smiled again.

"So it was Julian Stoddard all the time!" she said, those hard blue eyes of hers on Tony. "The great Julian, with his airs and his pride. Well, at least that settles it."

"Nothing is settled," he said grimly. "Except that some things you won't like are going to be aired in court."

"I don't know what you're talking about."

But she did know. Her smile died, her easy assurance left her.

When Tony gave me over to an Amy who obviously wanted to shake me, she was still standing poised in the hall, as if on the edge of flight again.

She did not get away. Jim Conway, coming up that night, warned her against it. "You're a witness, and a pretty important one," he told her. "No matter what you did or how you did it, you told Margery Stoddard you knew who she was. The State's case is that to avoid exposure after that Stoddard killed Don Morgan."

"Why didn't he kill me?" she asked shrewdly. "Why poor old Don, who never hurt anybody?"

"I'm giving you the State's case, not mine," he told her. "They'll want you, so don't try any tricks. Those fellows in town don't play games."

There was a meeting at the Cloisters that night, after Bessie had gone sullenly to her room. Dwight Elliott motored out and soon after Amy saw lights in the playhouse. We were on speaking terms again, after a bad hour or two, and she was almost bursting with curiosity.

"What are they doing?" she said, peering out the window. "That's Jim Conway. It looks like your Tony too. Say, listen, Pat. Unless I've gone crazy, that's Lydia Morgan's car. It is. It's Lydia. Now what on earth is she doing there?"

I could not tell her. I did not know myself, although I thought they were probably reconstructing the night Lydia had found Maud. They were, of course. They had her make her entrance, walk to the living room, turn back and find the body. Then, to test whether or not Maud herself had turned on the water, they asked her to try it. She is a strong woman, but she could not do it. The control was a small wheel in a closet, and Dwight Elliott pointed out that only someone well acquainted with the place could find it.

"I suppose Stoddard wouldn't have known where it was?" he asked.

"Not a chance," Tony said.

They did find something that night. Jim had marked with chalk the location of the gun on the floor of the empty pool, and now he got down and examined it with a glass. The pool was painted blue, and inside the chalk mark the paint was broken. "I don't know about such things," he said, "but on a guess I'd say the gun went in while the pool was dry." He looked up at Lydia. "How much water was in it when you saw it?"

"I don't know. I heard it, but I didn't look at it."

Tony was quiet, watching them gravely as they worked. It was Jim's theory, and Dwight Elliott agreed, that after Maud had been shot an attempt had probably been made to put her finger-prints on the gun. But, as Jim said, such prints are not reliable. It is hard to simulate the desperate grip of a suicide on the weapon he uses.

"What he did—I say he, although it may have been a wom-an—was to drop the gun, and then turn the water on. The gun was close to where the water came in, so the current would more or less wash it. It was a fool idea at that, but I imagine he or she went kind of haywire about that time."

Then they held a conference in the living room. It was cold and Tony lit the fire. None of them doubted that Maud had been murdered, but they did not get much further than that. Lyd-ia herself, looking white and tired, had no idea why Maud had wanted to see her, except that she had said it was important.

"She said nothing about her jewels?"

"Nothing at all."

It came down in the end to one of two things: either Maud had had an earlier appointment or somebody knew she meant to meet Lydia and was determined to prevent it. The nail in the tire had not kept her from coming, but it had at least delayed her. The garage was not locked. Anybody could have had access to it.

"Did she say anyone else was to be present?" Jim asked.

"No. I understood she wanted to see me alone."

"How about the telephone? Most of the phones up there are on the same line. Could she have been overheard in the house?"

"I suppose so. Her second message was about seven o'clock in the evening. That was when she changed the time to eleven-thirty."

They made a note then of the people in the house at seven o'clock. There were the servants, but no list was made of them. At seven o'clock, too, Bessie's cocktail party was in full blast. It was a heterogeneous crowd. Even Reynolds, called to assist, knew only one or two of them. The ones who had stayed for dinner had left fairly early, at eleven, and so far as he knew none of them were habitués of the house. Outside of them there were only Bessie, who had gone up to bed as soon as the party was over, and myself.

It was a dead end. When Bill Sterling came for Lydia they gave it up. "We haven't helped Stoddard much," Jim said, getting into his overcoat. "They've got their case. If we prove a second murder they'll only hang it on him. They'll claim Margery had told Mrs. Wainwright, so he had to—well, get her out of the way. He knew this place too. His kids swam here last summer. We'd better keep this under our hats for a while anyhow."

But already he was on the track of something. He did not tell them, but on leaving he went back to his office and taking from his wallet a small clipping from a newspaper, perhaps an inch by two inches in size, sat studying it for some time.

"I'd begun to get a glimmer," he said later. "Not much. No idea as to who had committed the murders, but a bit of the story. And a damned queer story it was."

Nevertheless, he came up to see Bessie the next day. "What did you do the night Mrs. Wainwright died?" he asked, with no preamble.

"What night was it?" she inquired insolently. "I'm bad at dates."

"Now listen, Mrs. Wainwright," he said, "don't put on any act with me. You know what night it was. Go on from there. You gave a cocktail party and a dinner. The dinner was over and people left before eleven. What did you do after that?"

"I went to bed. Alone, if that interests you."

"That's all?"

"That's enough, isn't it?"

But he kept at her, quietly, persistently. She had expected to profit by Maud's will, hadn't she? She had been disappointed when she found she got nothing? Still, when you thought about it, she was not bad off. Tony got it all, and she was still his wife. She listened. Then she began to laugh, loud and rather dreadful laughter.

"So I killed her!" she said. "God, that's funny."

She went from that into straight hysterics. He called Amy and Hilda, but he had to go away without seeing her again. One thing was settled before he left, however. She was on no account to be allowed to leave Beverly. He told Tony that. She was not only a witness at the Stoddard trial. He had an idea she knew a lot of things she had not disclosed.

"What sort of things?" said Tony, red-eyed and weary.

"If I knew that I'd know all the answers," said Jim, and went away to study again the small scrap of paper he carried in his wallet.

They took Bessie to town the next day. She was an unwilling witness, sitting in the district attorney's office in her silver fox coat and a small black hat, and smoking steadily. Yes, she had told Margery Stoddard she knew who she was. No, she had not blackmailed her. That was a dirty word, and she wouldn't stand for it. What had been the effect on Mrs. Stoddard of these revelations? Well, she hadn't liked it, of course. Who would?

"Had she told her husband what you knew?"

"How do I know?"

"You were afraid of him, weren't you?"

"Afraid? Why?"

"Just what were you afraid of, if it was not of Julian Stoddard?" said the district attorney, leaning over his desk and staring at her. "Someone shot at you one night. Who was that? And why live behind locked doors?" He kept his eyes on her. "You see, we know a good bit. We even know you carry a small revolver—or did. Are you carrying it now?"

"No," she said sullenly.

The district attorney glanced around the room triumphantly.

"Not since Stoddard's arrest, eh? I see. That's a nice point."

They were not entirely satisfied when they let her go. They tried to have her admit that she had been near the playhouse the night of Don's murder, but she said flatly she was not.

"If you want to know, I met Mrs. Stoddard that night," she told them, glaring at Hopper. "You and the flower I dropped out of my hair! Ask Margery Stoddard where I was."

"Another little financial transaction?" Hopper drawled.

"That's strictly my affair," she flared.

She admitted that she had known Don in Paris, and that he had told her who Margery was. But she denied absolutely that there had been any collusion between them. "I didn't even know he was coming back to America," she said.

She flounced out when it was over, after being warned not to leave the vicinity. She must have felt relieved, rather than anything else. She had told them enough, but not too much. If she gave Julian a thought, it was probably that few men of his sort go to the chair, and let it go at that.

But she was wrong. The district attorney had set out to send him to the chair, and he meant to do it. Already he was preparing his opening speech for the trial; walking up and down the floor of his office and dictating to a patient stenographer:

"The State will show, ladies and gentlemen of the jury, that this defendant had both motive and opportunity for the crime by which an unfortunate man lost his life. We intend to go into that motive, and to show it was for a cheap and tawdry reason that the crime was committed.

"Here is a man proud of his position in the world. When he found it threatened, it is the contention of the State—and we expect to prove it—that he took desperate means to preserve it and to hide his secret.

"We shall prove not only his hatred of the dead man, but we shall show that, on the night in question, he played bridge—yes, ladies and gentlemen, he played bridge!—until midnight or thereabouts. And that then, dressed in dinner clothes, he started home from this gay party, on foot. Other guests drove cars, but he walked home.

"His house is half a mile away or less. A ten-minute walk at the most. But he did not arrive at that house until after one o'clock in the morning. When he did it was from the ravine where the murder car had been left. He has no alibi for that hour. He says he was walking about. I have his statement here. 'I had some things to think over. I walked about for a while.' Is that the testimony of an innocent man?

"There will be a question of the time element in this case placed before you. It may be argued that the time was not sufficient for all that was done. But we shall prove to you that this defendant had more than one hour. Owing to the lapse of time it was not possible to state exactly the hour of this dastardly murder. But we shall show that it was possible for this defendant to have left the bridge table on some excuse or other, go to the scene of the crime, commit it and return. In fact, we shall show that he did leave the bridge table, to be absent for some minutes. And this crime, ladies and gentlemen, did not require more than a moment. A man feeble from illness, knocked unconscious and then thrown into a pool to drown—how long did that require?

"We shall show that when at last he did return to his home, his clothing was in a deplorable condition. We shall place on the stand his manservant—yes, it required a valet to take care of him and his appearance—to show that his shoes were muddy the next morning, and the cuffs of his evening trousers were damp and soiled. And we shall show something else.

"There was a threat of exposure hanging over him. One other person knew that story. Who can say what danger that person was in? This witness will be called. It will be shown that until this defendant's arrest—for she is a woman—she lived in terror of her life, her doors locked, and that at least one attempt was made on her life."

He went on, building his case not so much on the facts as on an appeal to the emotions of the jury. Here, he said in effect, is a rich man, proud and aloof. Too good for you and me, ladies and gentlemen. He is master of the Hunt Club. I suppose none of us here knows what that means, except for pictures. It's a pretty expensive thing, a Hunt Club. While children are going hungry the hounds have to be fed. They even have kennelmen to look after them and a veterinary to keep them well. Horses too, and stables, and grooms.

This is your defendant. He has a valet. He has a country estate. But he has a secret. He has married a woman not only with a past, but a woman of lowly birth. How far would he go to conceal these two disastrous facts? Would he go all the way? Who can doubt it? Would he do more? Would he do away with inimical witnesses? Why not? One possible witness in this case has already disappeared, and another has been attacked and placed in serious danger of her life. They would produce this witness in due time, and she would state—

Only, of course, it was not to work out that way. Bessie Wainwright never took the stand.

CHAPTER THIRTY-TWO

I MOVED down to Miss Mattie's a day or two later. Amy had gone, and Bessie made it impossible for me to stay at the Cloisters. She came into my room the night Amy left, came in without knocking, and told me in so many words I'd better get out. She stood there smiling, and said that.

"If Tony wants an affair let him have one," she said. "I'm not a jealous woman. But it won't go on under this roof."

I think if I had had a hatchet in my hand I would have killed her then and there. I managed to control myself, however. "Do you have to judge every woman by yourself?" I said coldly. "There is no affair, and you know it."

"That's your story, and you can stick to it until hell freezes over, as far as I'm concerned. All I'm saying is that you are through. Washed up, Miss Pat Abbott."

She stood just inside the doorway, wearing a dark velvet house coat—how well I remember it!—and if ever I saw a devil in a woman I saw it then.

"Another thing," she said. "I'm not divorcing Tony, and he's not divorcing me. He won't even try, Pat Abbott. Wait and see!"

"I'm not interested," I said, and she laughed and went out.

I don't know whether she told Tony or not. I know I never did. The whole thing was too degrading. But I dare say he knew as well as I did that things could not go on as they were.

"Stay on for a few days anyhow," he said, looking wretched when I told him I was going. "Sleep at Miss Mattie's if you like, but—well, finish up here if you can bear it. You needn't see Bessie. I'll attend to that. And she'll be gone before long," he added grimly. "I'll attend to that too."

I thought it over that night, sleeping at Miss Mattie's for the first time in almost seven months. Whatever club Bessie held over his head, he certainly did not know it then.

I slept better than I had for a long time. It was as though I had passed through a reign of terror and it was over. The great quiet house, with O'Brien making his rounds after dark, a flashlight in his hand and his automatic in a holster on his belt, had been a constant reminder of what had happened. Yet I missed O'Brien. His passages with Pierre had been one of my few amusements. He would stand by the huge refrigerator, eyeing its contents.

"Yes, Frenchie! How about that cold lobster?"

"It is for lunch tomorrow. Salad."

"I'll bet you've got some Scotch in you, and I don't mean liquor."

He had a quick reach. Once I saw Pierre chase him into the dining room, O'Brien holding to a whole roasted chicken while Pierre brandished a knife. "I cut off your ears," Pierre was yelling. "I cut out that stomach of yours. You are all stomach. Never have I seen one like you. *C'est terrible!*"

Nevertheless, they were good friends. On the night when O'Brien was shot it was Pierre who went with him to the hospital. Pierre, too, who saw as he recovered that he had the squabs, the sweetbreads, and so on, bought with French thrift out of the Cloisters house money but cooked by himself.

"Guess what I bring today."

"I'll bet it's canned salmon. Why don't you loosen up, you old buzzard?"

And Pierre, grinning proudly, would open his box.

"It is breast of guinea hen, my boy."

"Those birds that need oiling? What are you doing? Playing a joke on me?"

Yes, I missed even O'Brien, lying in my familiar bed that night. But I was more calm than I had been since Bessie's attack on me. For one thing, Miss Mattie's pleasure at having me back had soothed me. While I unpacked she gave me the small talk of the town. Audrey and Larry Hamilton were supposed to be engaged. The Theodore Earles had taken a house at Miami for the rest of the winter. Old Joe Berry had gone to Arizona. All harmless, all part of an ordered suburban life.

Yet even as I lay there one of the most curious incidents of the whole series was taking place. It concerned, of all people, the Theodore Earles themselves, and at first it apparently had no bearing on our mystery.

It was not without humor, at that.

It was Saturday. The Earles had gone to the late movies, and at eleven o'clock were on their way home. They live slightly above the village, and their drive turns off the highway leading up the hill. As they turned in their lights suddenly fell on something, and Mrs. Earle screamed.

"There's a naked man in the drive," she shrieked.

Theodore Earle, who is nearsighted and had been watching the gate, stopped the car and looked ahead.

"I don't see anybody."

"He went into the shrubbery."

"I don't believe you saw anything of the sort," he said. "Why would anybody go around naked on a night like this?"

But Mrs. Earle was positive. They drove on to the house, and Theodore and the butler got a flashlight and started out on foot. They had been looking for five minutes or so when somebody called Theodore by name from a clump of evergreens.

"Mr. Earle."

"Yes. Who is it?"

"It's me, sir. Haines. I'd be thankful for a blanket or something. I'm near frozen."

They saw him then. It was one of the motorcycle policemen who patrol the river road, and he was as bare as the minute he was born. Theodore was furious.

"What the devil are you doing here without your clothes?"

"I've been robbed, sir. I'm sorry."

The butler ran to the house and brought out a blanket. Also he brought some brandy, and before long they were able to smuggle him into the house. A fire and the brandy—and the blanket—restored him somewhat, and he told his story. He had been following a car that was exceeding the speed limit. It had turned up the hill road and he followed it. But he lost it a mile or so beyond the Earles' and was on his way down to the river road again when he was crowded off the road by a car behind him.

"I'd passed it," he said, "and was slowing up for the curve. Maybe he thought I was after him. He stepped on the gas and made straight for me. I tried to turn off, but he struck my rear wheel and sent me flying."

That was all he remembered, until he came to. He had been

dragged a few yards off the road into a field, and his clothing was gone. "Not a stitch left," he said, and blushed under his tan.

"There I was, sir," he said. "I didn't know what to do. I've been dodging about for the last hour, hoping maybe some man would come along on foot and I could hail him. But the only one I saw yelled and ran. I'll bet he's running still."

He had not noticed the car particularly, save that it did not look like one belonging to the Hill. It was small and shabby, and not going very fast. A man drove it. He had an impression that he was middle-aged or elderly.

Mr. Earle called Jim Conway, and—Haines now dressed in some of the butler's clothes—they went back along the road. They found the motorcycle, badly damaged, not far from the Earle property. Of Haines's uniform and automatic there was no sign, but they did locate his underwear, thrown away somewhere down the road toward the village.

Jim eyed it. "What the fellow wanted," he said, "was the uniform. He stripped Haines all the way to keep him from raising the alarm."

"Maybe he thought I was going to pick him up," said Haines, "and he wanted time to make a getaway."

They went back to the Earles'. Haines's wife had sent some clothing by the patrol car, and while he dressed Jim went to the telephone. First he called the borough building and had Cracker Brown send out an alarm, vague as it had to be. "Old sedan, possibly Dodge or Chevrolet. Look for dented fenders or other evidence of collision. Driver probably middle-aged or elderly. May be wearing motorcycle officer's uniform and carrying regulation police automatic. Watch out. This man may be dangerous."

After that he sent Haines home and Theodore Earle to bed. Then—it was one o'clock in the morning by that time—he got into his own car and drove to the Cloisters. He did not go to the house. He went around back to the McDonald cottage and rang the bell. It took some time to rouse them. When Andy finally appeared he was indignant.

"What's wrong now, Mr. Conway?" he said. "I work hard and I need my sleep."

Jim looked around. The cottage was dark and quiet. He stepped inside.

"Been in all evening, McDonald?"

"I have that."

"Had a visitor?"

"A visitor? No. Who would be coming?"

"Got a car, haven't you?"

"Yes. What about it?"

"I'd like to see it," said Jim. "Where is it?"

"In the shed. It's not been out for a day or two. What about it?"

"I just want to look at it."

Andy went, grumbling audibly, to put on some clothes, and Jim went back to Evans's room, turned on the light and examined it. There was nothing suspicious there. It remained as Jessie McDonald's house cleaning had left it, cold and obviously unused. He glanced into the closet, but it was as he had seen it before, with Evans's few clothes still hanging there and his shoes on the floor. He began to feel foolish.

Andy led the way some distance from the cottage to what he called the shed. It was not locked. He threw open the doors, to expose an old Chevrolet, and Jim got his flashlight and examined it. There was no heat in the place, and the radiator was cold under his hand. But he looked up to see Andy pointing at the front of the car.

"Some dirty thief has had it out," Andy said, going very Scottish in his excitement. "Gi' a look to that, sor. It was no there yesterday."

There was no doubt in Jim's mind that night. He had found the car which had struck Haines. The front fender on the right was badly crumpled. He watched Andy, but his indignation was apparently the rightful wrath of a good Scot who was suffered a damage. He left him there and taking his flashlight examined the ground around. A road led to the shed from the garage and stables, but there was another, a dirt lane, leading down the side of the hill. Anyone could have pushed the car out, got in, and releasing the brakes have rolled down the slope before letting in the gears. In that case neither Andy nor Jessie would have heard the sound. As for the return—

"You didn't hear it, going out or coming in?"

"When would that be?" asked Andy cautiously.

"Tonight. Between ten-thirty and, say, twelve o'clock."

"We go to bed early. At nine or thereabouts. Don't you think if I'd heard the dirty rascal I'd have been out and after him?"

He went through the cottage after that. Jessie was up, in an old flannel kimono and a speechless state of wrath. There was no uniform to be found, nor anything whatever suspicious; and the two stoutly maintained that Evans had not been back since his disappearance.

"I'd gone on a hunch so far," Jim said later. "Haines's description of the old car and an elderly man rang a bell for me. I'd seen Evans once or twice driving the McDonald car, and I took a chance."

Both Andy and Jessie, however, when told the story about Haines, angrily repudiated any theory that it might have been Evans. "He was no murdering fool," Andy said. "Nor a thief either. He was welcome to my car, and he knew it. It was never Evans, sir."

Jim was completely in a fog by that time. He saw Tony's light on in the main house, and called him from the cottage. Together the two men went over the car again. Apparently the wheel had been wiped. They could find no fingerprints on it.

Tony looked up after examining the broken fender. "There's one thing sure about this, Conway," he said, smiling wryly. "Stoddard didn't do it."

"No," Jim agreed. "But who the hell did?"

By evening of the next day the papers had the story. Of course, a policeman without his clothes was manna to the press in a dull season. They seized on it, showing photographs of an embarrassed, unhappy young man, with various captions: *Maniac Loose Again—Officer Found Nude*—and one alliterative one entitled *Cop's Clothes Confiscated*. Curious young men with wads of paper in their pockets wandered around the Hill again, picking up this and that, and it made a rather imposing total. They picked up Bessie's accident and the bullet holes in her car. They revived the attack on Evans and the missing trousers. They republished shots of the cemetery, and one youth even managed to get into my office and to inquire if it was true that I had been struck with a hatchet and thrown into the Stoddard pool.

The district attorney in a rage sent for Hopper. "What's all this newspaper stuff about?" he demanded.

"Why don't you read it? It makes good reading. Maybe some of it's true."

"A lunatic! Have you lost your mind? What do you mean,

true? What's a cop losing his clothes got to do with this case? Or somebody with a grudge knocking over tombstones in a cemetery?"

"Well," drawled Hopper, lighting a cigarette, "I'd say it's something like this. Maybe somebody's crazy, maybe not. It's just possible it's a nice little game."

"What sort of game? Are you being funny?"

"Hell, no," said Hopper. "It might be a coverup for Stoddard. He's in jail and these things go on happening. What's the answer? There's a murderous lunatic at large, so Stoddard can't be guilty. Either that, or the killer's still around. Maybe he figures that if Stoddard is acquitted we'll go hunting for somebody with a mania for stealing pants."

"It's lousy."

"Maybe," said Hopper, and got up. "Of course, there's another possibility."

"What's that?" asked Stewart suspiciously.

"He may be getting ready for something that hasn't happened yet," said Hopper, and slouched out of the office, leaving the district attorney staring after him.

CHAPTER THIRTY-THREE

LIFE WENT on for me somehow during the next few days. I took Miss Mattie to the Dramatic Club's performance of *Lady Windermere's Fan*. I saw Lydia now and then. The weather had settled into the usual gray despondency of late autumn, with the smoke from the mills coming down the valley and mixing at night with fog. In the morning I drove up the hill to the Cloisters, but the place was getting badly on my nerves.

I was completely isolated. I have no idea what Bessie did with her time. I never saw her. My lunch was served in the office, and except for Roger—and Mrs. Partridge's complaints about Bessie's attempts to run the house—I was alone most of the time.

Now and then there would be a note from Tony on my desk, brief and noncommittal. He would get home late, having had dinner in town, and be gone before I arrived there in the morning.

Luckily I had plenty to do. One afternoon Mr. Elliott came down early, and together we went over such of Maud's papers as we could find. They were very few. She had always destroyed letters after she answered them. But he seemed puzzled that day.

"She had no private file?" he asked.

"None at all."

"Well, you might look around," he said. "Let me know if you find anything. And I wouldn't talk about it, Miss Abbott. Tony knows I'm here, but probably what I'm looking for was in the envelope which has disappeared."

I continued the search the next day when I listed Maud's personal possessions for the appraisers. Hilda helped me, and in a small inside pocket of the coat Maud had worn the night of her death I found a slip of paper. It was not much. Written on it in Maud's big hand was Lydia's telephone number, but under it was a firm name I did not recognize.

"Summers and Brodhead," I read. "Who are they, Hilda?"

"Mrs. Wainwright's jewelers," said Hilda tearfully. "They did her repair work, and made over things sometimes."

"Had she said she needed anything done?"

"Not that I remember, miss."

It seemed unimportant. I kept the slip, however, and we went on. It was heartbreaking business at best: the gold and tortoise-shell toilet articles; the beautiful furs, including a sable coat; the luxurious negligees and house coats. There were dozens of evening gowns too, rows of slippers to match, and even a book of sketches, each dress shown in color, with the accessories and jewels to go with it. Some of the jewels I had never seen. They were kept in the bank in town and only brought out for special occasions. But the name of Summers and Brodhead stuck in my mind, and at four that afternoon I called them up, explaining who I was.

"Did Mrs. Wainwright call you up the day before she died, or just before that?" I asked.

There was some hesitation at the other end of the wire.

"Who do you say you are?"

"Her secretary, Miss Abbott."

He opened up then, relatively at least. He turned out to be Mr. Brodhead, and said he had known my mother well years ago. That established, we got back to the matter in hand. He lowered his voice. "Well, she did call, Miss Abbott," he said. "It was a confidential matter, but I have wondered since if I should say something about it. Not that it could have any bearing on her—on what happened to her. But as I said to Mr. Summers, after all if she was in need of money perhaps we should tell it."

"You can tell me. I won't talk unless it's important. Then I shall only tell her son."

That relieved him, although his voice was still conspiratorial. "I gathered that she wanted to sell her jewels, Miss Abbott."

"Sell them? All of them?"

"Everything she had."

I waited for Tony that night and told him. His face was a study. "Why? Why on earth sell her jewels? She had plenty of money." Then I saw suspicion in his eyes. "Bessie!" he said. "Bessie, of course. She was going to buy her off again. Pat, there are times when I'm hardly answerable for what I do."

I knew I could not stay much longer. My desk was almost cleared, but he asked me that day to stick it out for a while. He was taking steps about the divorce. He had asked Bessie to go to a hotel in town, had even engaged rooms for her. But she was stubbornly insisting on staying at the Cloisters.

"God knows why," he said. "But since she does—keep her away from Mother's things, will you? Hilda says she's been trying to get at them."

After that Maud's rooms were locked, and I kept the keys.

So far as I could see the police were doing nothing. It was as though with Julian's arrest they had abandoned the case. I was wrong, of course. Hopper was still—or again—hunting for Evans, and down in his office Jim Conway had a drawer in his desk which now and then he opened. He would lay its contents out in front of him and study them.

He gave me the list only the other day.

(*a*) The slipper and button found in the playhouse pool.

(*b*) A rough drawing of the scar on Don Morgan's chest.

(*c*) The man's garter Roger had found in the grounds, and which I had given him.

(*d*) The photographs of the bullets from Tony's gun.

(*e*) The scrap of blue paint from the floor of the playhouse pool.

(*f*) The list of Maud's jewels, left in the chair by the fire the night she died.

(*g*) The prints on Maud's safe, photographed after it was found open, and consisting only of Maud's and mine.

(*h*) The scrap of newspaper, added from his wallet.

(*i*) The label of a London tailor, cut from that coat of Don's, with the number of Maud's car inked in.

"It was all there," he said. "I'd moved them around, like playing checkers, and I'd always get the same result. I was guessing part of it. Take the garter. It looked to me as though whoever got Don out of the pool hadn't waited to dress. That cut a bit off the time. Take the scar. I was guessing there too, but I was pretty sure I was right. But who the hell did it? That stopped me."

It was a gloomy interval, and then one day it turned abruptly to sadness. Roger was poisoned.

I find it hard to write about. He had been my steady companion for months, especially since Maud's death. He had slept outside my door at night, lay in the office when I was busy, and loped along the bridle path when I took Prince for a run in the brisk air.

There was no reason then to think that it was deliberate. I had taken him for his favorite walk, the footpath to the Farm. He had been in high spirits, but on the way back he began to lag. Before I got him home he collapsed entirely, and I ran to the stables for help. But he died before he could get any aid. When Tony came home he found me on my knees in the stable, bending over that big inert body. He looked sick, but he stooped down quietly and kissed the back of my neck.

"Listen, darling," he said. "He had a happy life, and now he's probably in some comfortable dog heaven of his own. Better come back to the house."

I went, still sick at heart and Bessie or no Bessie he kept his arm around me. It was not until night that the veterinary reported the poison, and Tony came down to Miss Mattie's and told me.

"Strychnine in a ball of meat," he said. "Some farmer probably, after the hounds. Most of them loathe the hunt."

But I don't think he believed that. I know I did not.

I grieved over Roger for days. Otherwise things went on somehow. Lydia was at last really preparing for her marriage. In town Julian's lawyers were working on his defense, with Tony and Dwight Elliott sitting in now at the conferences. Maud had been gone for over a month, and the verdict of suicide still stood. I went to town one day and bought myself a fur coat, out of sheer misery.

Then, early in December, I had a visit from Jim Conway. He came into my office, opened a window, sat down, filled his pipe and lit it, and proceeded to pull out an automatic and put it on my desk in front of me. I eyed it warily.

"Ever use one of these things?"

"Never."

"Well, you're going to learn right now." I looked up at him, but he was serious. "No fooling, sister," he said. "I don't care much about your going about alone, especially after dark. I don't want to find you some night in a ditch, freezing without your clothes. Come on outside. I've got a place picked for your first lesson."

It was not very light out of doors, but I had my first lesson in pistol shooting that late afternoon. The place he had chosen was the small ravine beside the playhouse, and I can't claim to have made any records. I did learn, however, not to shut my eyes when I squeezed the trigger, and Jim squeezed my arm in brotherly fashion when it was over.

"Good girl," he said. "I'm leaving it with you. Carry it in your car, will you? Not in a pocket, either. Keep it on the seat beside you."

"I can't see why I need it, Jim."

"You may know something you don't know you know," he said cryptically.

But he had not finished with me. He went back with me to the house that day. There was a fire in the library, and I ordered him a highball while he warmed his hands. He said nothing until, with his drink beside him, he had lit a cigarette. His first question surprised me.

"See here, Pat, did it ever occur to you that Maud Wainwright knew Don Morgan?"

"I don't think she did," I said. "He went away two or three

years after the Wainwrights moved to the Hill, and the valley didn't know the Hill people much at that time. Not intimately. I know she didn't know Lydia. She asked me about her."

"Ever occur to you that he came to the playhouse to see Mrs. Wainwright the night he was killed?"

"In pajamas? Why would he?"

"Well," he said reasonably, "if that's all he had, and had to see her—All right. Let's go back to Evans, and the night you found him in the playhouse. He's knocked out and somebody takes his keys. Why?"

"I suppose," I said, "anybody might want the keys to this house. It has a million dollars' worth of stuff in it."

"You know better than that. So do I. Whoever wanted those keys wasn't out for burglary. If Morgan got them, as seems pretty certain, what did he want them for?" He looked at me over his cigarette. "Who answers the telephone here?"

"I do, or Reynolds. Whoever's around."

"Easy to get Mrs. Wainwright on it?"

"She never used it if she could help it. People gave their names or their businesses. Usually I took the messages to her, and she'd tell me what to do about them."

"I see," he said thoughtfully. "If Morgan wanted to talk to her on the phone he hadn't a chance, had he?"

"I don't think he tried. Jim, what's all this about? Why would he want to talk to her? About Bessie?"

"Maybe Bessie. Maybe not. But he got into this house twice. Why? Suppose he tries to get in touch with Maud Wainwright, and he can't do it. Maybe he hangs around the place, but at first she's sick, and later on she's never alone. Bessie's here. You're here. People are coming and going. If he rings the doorbell he has to state his business, and the one thing on earth he doesn't want to state is his business. That could happen, couldn't it?"

"Why couldn't he state his business?"

"It might have been pretty private," he said grimly. "So private that it killed him."

The one thing he was certain of was that when Donald Morgan slipped out of his house that night of his death it was to see one of two women, Bessie or Maud. He himself believed it had been Maud.

"But she never went there," I said. "She was giving a dinner. Remember that."

"Nevertheless," he said. "I think he went there to meet her. He drove up in his wife's car. He had the key to the playhouse and he probably waited inside. Now I want you to think back, Pat. How did she seem that night? Like herself?"

"I think so," I said slowly. "I had that ankle, you know. She came in to see me before she went downstairs. I liked her dress and she seemed pleased."

He asked a lot of questions that day. What about Evans? Was he in the old family retainer class? In other words, was he devoted soul and body to the family, especially Maud? I had to smile at that. "I didn't know him well. If he had any strong emotions he certainly hid them."

"Not the sort to go around saving the Wainwright honor or what not? Not a loving old soul, in other words. All right, go on."

I told him all I knew; that Maud's attitude toward Evans had been casual as well as indulgent, certainly not affectionate. She had been as puzzled as any of us over the attack on him. Outside of sending him things to the hospital, fruit and flowers mostly, she had merely inquired about him. He nodded when I had finished.

"All right. Keep this talk to yourself, will you?" He got up and threw his cigarette into the fire. "Don't forget the gun, either. Don't laugh. I'm damned serious."

I did as he told me. Driving back and forth after that it lay on the seat of the car beside me. I picked Amy up one night and she saw it.

"Listen," she said. "Put that thing away, will you? I don't get much chance to sit down, but when I do I don't want a bullet hole in the part of me I sit on."

She rather depressed me that night, reminding me that everything went in threes.

"What do you mean, threes?" I said peevishly. "It's silly."

"Not a bit of it. Watch your step, my girl. Two deaths mean another. Watch and see. I hear you've got a guard up at the Cloisters."

"We've got a deputy Jim sent up. Name's O'Brien."

"That little shrimp," said Amy with disgust. "A lot of help he'll be. We took out his appendix once. I'll bet it was the only gut he ever had."

But she was wrong about O'Brien. He was doing his best the awful night when I shot him in the chest, and he almost died of it.

CHAPTER THIRTY-FOUR

I SUPPOSE that fall and winter in Beverly had been much as usual. Debutantes came out, looking young and innocent, and slipping outside now and then for a cigarette. There were the usual benefits for charity, the usual bridge parties and dinners, and naturally more than the usual gossip. I was asked out a good bit, but I did not care to go. Sooner or later the talk would turn to the Hill, and I could not face it.

Nor could I face much more of the Cloisters. When I had time I read the *Help Wanted* ads in the papers. Nobody seemed to require anyone of my peculiar qualifications: "Fair French, poor golf, good tennis, excellent on a horse, and no strawberry marks." But in one business office at that time there was a small scene which—when I heard of it from Margery later—caused me acute unhappiness. Following Julian's arrest the newspapers had published both his picture and Margery's. Miss Connor was in the office at the time, and somebody showed it to her.

She took one look at the one of Margery, then sat down at her desk and began to cry, long dreadful sobbing that brought the entire force around her, helpless. "That girl!" she said slowly. "That snake in the grass! And I gave her tea!"

I can write that now, but among the by-products of our crimes last year I must count Eliza Connor and the wreckage of her last faith in her fellow man. As I have said, I have tried to pay for that treachery of mine. I managed indirectly to get her a better position, and now and then I have sent her things, anonymously; once a small portable radio for that lonely room of hers, and again a small tea set and tray. That last probably betrayed me, but at my request Margery never told her who I was, so she could not send them back.

I didn't know that then. My own life had become a dreary round of going up the Hill, working, avoiding Bessie, and going down to Miss Mattie's at night. Then one day I saw that the Beverly shops had burst into a scarlet, green, and white rash which could only mean Christmas. The florist's window was decked out with small white-feathered trees, and at St. Mark's the waits were rehearsing carols, ready to stop on Christmas Eve wherever a lighted candle in a window beckoned to them.

I felt sick and lonely. Mother had always lit bayberry candles for them, and I could see them standing, men and women, outside in the snow, singing, their earnest faces lifted in the night. We always had cocoa and cake for them. Mother did not believe in liquor on such occasions.

There was no Christmas spirit at the Cloisters. One day Mrs. Partridge asked me if she might order a small tree for the servants' hall—she never asked Bessie for anything—and I told her to go ahead. "It won't be like the old days," she said mournfully. "With the ballroom all lit up, and the tree and presents. I expect the children will miss it."

"What children, Partridge?"

"The poor children. They used to come in buses from all

over, and Mrs. Wainwright would have presents for them, and a Punch and Judy. Or a conjurer. They liked him best, I think."

It turned out that she had Maud's list in her sitting room, and that night I left a note for Tony: *What about children's Christmas party this year? P.A.*

There was an answer for me in the morning. Reynolds passing it to me with the air of a conspirator: *Go ahead. The sky's the limit. She would want it. Tony.*

I sat back and considered. What was I to do about Bessie? So far we had exchanged formal greetings when we met, but I had not spoken a dozen words to her since the night she had ordered me out of the house. But a Christmas party, even for the poor, was unthinkable without at least telling her about it.

That day I asked Reynolds to notify her, and to ask if she had any suggestions. To my surprise she came to the office. She closed the door behind her and stood there, looking uncertain. "So we're going to have a party," she said. "Well, thank God for something, anyhow."

She had changed. Much of her prettiness had gone. She looked almost untidy as she stood there. The curls on top of her head had not been set, and she wore no make-up. I had an idea that she had been steadily drinking since her return, but she was sober now. For the first time I wondered if she had been drinking the night she sent me away.

I explained as best I could. Then I gave the list to her, and she looked it over. "I'll do the buying if you like," she said. "It will give me something to do. But when I think of a hundred and fifty smelly kids all together—"

"They won't be smelly. It's a real party to them."

She took the list and got up. The momentary excitement

was over, and I thought she looked half sick. For the first time I felt sorry for her. She gave me no chance to say anything, however. She moved toward the door and stopped. "Some day I'll tell you a story, Pat Abbott," she said. "It will change your ideas about a lot of things, including Tony Wainwright. But don't start guessing. It isn't safe to guess around here." She grinned. "That's the first disinterested advice I've given in years. Better take it."

She never told me the story, of course. Like Maud weeks before, she must have been tempted to come clean that day, have been divided between malice and cupidity. But, being Bessie, cupidity won. She was still hoping to pull her own chestnuts out of the fire, still hoping for a big settlement with Tony, and after it a divorce and freedom.

I was very busy the next few days. I began to feel more normal. The household brightened too. The ballroom was being opened and cleaned. Bessie went to town every day to buy gifts for the children. I sat over the telephone, and by night was glad to get back to Miss Mattie's, to eat a peaceful dinner with her, and go to the movies or to bed. When he could Tony came there to see me, but Miss Mattie's ideas of chaperonage were very stiff. "He's still a married man, my dear. I must ask you to leave the living room door open."

I have often wondered if any courtship was ever carried on with as little love-making as Tony's and mine. But he was more like himself too. The first shock of his mother's death had passed. He would come in, big and brisk from the cold air outside, hand Miss Mattie a huge box of candy, and then standing off would survey me critically.

"Well how's the S.B. tonight?"

"S.B.? It doesn't sound nice, Tony."

"That's because you have a low mind, Miss Abbott. S.B. stands for string bean, and that's what you look like."

He seldom mentioned Bessie. One night he did, however. He was sitting by the cannel coal fire in Miss Mattie's Victorian living room while I was curled up on the hearthrug.

"Were you very much in love with her, Tony?" I asked. "When you married her?"

"I was crazy about her. It lasted three months. Let's forget it, darling. It's over."

But I did not see him often. He was frightfully busy. When he came home at night it was with a briefcase of papers, and often with Dwight Elliott or now and then a mill superintendent. I gathered, too, that the Wainwrights, heading the minority stockholders, were still making trouble. One night he even went to sleep in the chair by the fire. I saw then that he was close to exhaustion. There is something helpless in a man asleep, and I suppose all women with a scrap of maternal instinct yearn over them at such times. Certainly I did my bit of yearning that night, doing it with might and main until Miss Mattie, hearing a suspicious silence, appeared in the doorway and roused him.

The interval of normality did not last long. I had dined with Lydia one night and stayed rather late. Maud's death was still a mystery. Julian in his cell was awaiting trial, the search for Evans or his body was continuing, on the theory of the prosecution that he had seen Don murdered and—dead or alive— might help their case. We talked until almost midnight, when Bill Sterling took me home, and I was taking off my dinner dress when the telephone rang. It was Bessie, and she sounded unlike herself.

"I've got an attack of jitters," she said. "Don't ask me why. I'm plain scared. That's all there is to it."

"Has anything happened?"

"Not yet. Would you mind coming up? I know it's silly, but I'm alone here. Tony's staying in town, and O'Brien says he saw somebody in the grounds."

I told her I would come. It was a cold night, and it took some time to start the car. It was long after twelve when I started, with Jim's automatic on the seat beside me and a chilly sort of apprehension making goose pimples all over me. When I turned in at the drive I picked up the gun, but I reached the house undisturbed. O'Brien let me in, grinning.

"Nothing to worry about, miss," he said. "Maybe some of the help slipping out, that's all. But I told Mrs. Wainwright and she's having a fit all over the place."

I found her cowering by a dying fire in the library. She had a highball beside her, but her hands shook so she could scarcely lift it. "I suppose I'm all kinds of a damned fool," she said, "but I was about to have an attack of the yelling heebie jeebies."

She refused to be left alone, and the three of us made a careful circuit of the house, including the basements. We found everything locked, however, and at last I induced her to go to bed. I heard her bolt herself in and then, with O'Brien on guard, went to my old room and undressed.

I was tired, but I could not sleep. For one thing, it was strange to be back in those familiar quarters, where I had been at once so happy and so wretched. I lay there thinking over the past six months: the talk at Lydia's that night, of Don's murder, Julian's arrest, and that strange appointment of Maud's with Lydia the night she was killed. Lydia saying vaguely, "She said something about Audrey." Why Audrey? Where was Audrey in all this mystery?

It was then I thought I heard the elevator. The shaft was near my room, and it seemed to me the car was moving. It never made any real sound. In the activity of daylight it seemed entirely noiseless. But I was uneasy. I got up and went out into the hall. O'Brien, as Bessie had insisted, was sitting on the stairs, the remnants of his supper tray beside him, and his revolver in his hand.

"I thought I heard the elevator," I whispered.

He grinned. "Got you too, has it?" he said. "Kinda spooky at night, isn't it? Good thing I got no nerves."

Reassured, I went back to bed. But not to sleep. I had hardly gotten back to bed when I heard a movement of some sort overhead. It worried me. The servants' rooms were mostly over the east wing, and over my own I knew was the trunk room, a huge place filled with trunks and with shelves around it for suitcases and small luggage. And the sound itself was strange. It was like the stealthy movement of a trunk sliding along the floor. Or inching across it, for the movement was infinitely slow. I listened for some time. The sound would come, stop, and start again; but at last it was undeniable, and I called to O'Brien. He was not in sight. On my second shout, however, he appeared in the lower hall, evidently amused.

"Got 'em again?" he inquired.

"Don't be such a fool," I said hysterically. "There's someone in the trunk room upstairs. I can hear him plainly."

He was still highly diverted. "Maybe some of the help packing to get out, miss. I don't know as I blame them."

But then I heard another sound. The elevator was on its way

down. I yelled at O'Brien and headed for the lower floor, but the car did not stop there. It moved steadily down to the basement. The light in it was not turned on, and there was something horrible about that almost silent passage. O'Brien, who had followed me, looked stunned with surprise.

"Jeez!" he said. "It's moving!"

I was beyond fear by that time. I unbolted the door to the wine cellar and shot down the stairs. But I was just too late. There was nobody there.

But someone had been there. The door to the outside, which had been closed, locked, and with the chain up when we examined it earlier, was now standing open. O'Brien ran out through it and, hearing a car start down the drive, fired a shot after it. It got away, however. All he saw of it was the red tail-light. He came back, looking sheepish. "The son of a gun," he said. "He was inside all the time."

It was his idea, and I believe now it was correct, that the chain to the basement door had been left off either by design or by accident, and that the intruder had been already in the house when we made our search. Perhaps hiding in the elevator.

When at last I went upstairs, having locked the basement door and put the chain on it, I found Bessie in the hall. She looked a dead-white, and was holding to the gallery rail to support herself. She could barely speak.

"The shooting!" she said. "What was it?"

She was in no condition to be told the facts. I said O'Brien thought he had seen the intruder in the grounds again, and let it go at that. She went back to bed, locking her door behind her as usual, but I do not think she believed me. She gave me a long hard look before she shut me out.

There was nothing to be seen in the trunk room, in that welter of trunks and bags. O'Brien and I searched it carefully that night. We found one thing, however, which Reynolds the next day claimed not to have seen before. This was a box of trunk keys. There must have been a hundred of them, of every conceivable size and shape.

"No, miss," he said. "It doesn't belong here. All keys are tagged and hung in this case on the wall. You can see for yourself."

CHAPTER THIRTY-FIVE

I TRIED to get Jim Conway that night, but his mother has a habit of muffling the telephone bell when she thinks he needs sleep. It was the next morning, therefore, that I told him in his office in the village. I remember he looked fresh and rested, and that I was furious at him. "I hope you slept well last night," I said, with some bitterness.

"Sure I did. I needed it."

"No matter what happens you have to have your sleep! Is that it?"

He sat upright. "All right," he said resignedly, "I suppose Mother muffled the bell again. Let's have it, Pat. What did happen? And where?"

"At the Cloisters. Somebody got in."

"How do you know?"

"I was there."

It was his turn to be furious. He'd warned me. He had even given me a gun to protect myself. And then in the middle of the night like a little fool I had gone back there. He was in the midst of washing his hands of me when he remembered what I had said.

"Somebody got in! With O'Brien there, and the place locked up like a bank! I don't believe it."

He believed me when I told him, however, although he snorted with disgust when I spoke about the box of keys.

"So you handled it, and O'Brien and Reynolds pawed it too! I ought to fire O'Brien for that. The only chance for fingerprints in the whole goddam case, and you gum the works!"

He quieted down after that. He sat for a time, looking through me rather than at me. "Tell me this," he said. "I'm no woman, thank God. But don't women save things? Sentimental things, I mean. Baby clothes and old love letters, stuff like that?"

I grinned at him. "I still have a note you wrote me in school years ago, Jim."

"Holding it for blackmail, eh?"

"You told me my slip was showing."

"Always was a soft kid," he said. "Look, Pat, Mrs. Wainwright have any such things among what you found? Tony's first diaper or old J.C.'s love letters. They'd be something, wouldn't they!"

"There was nothing, Jim."

"You didn't try the trunk room?"

"No. Hilda said there was nothing there."

There was something there. Bessie was in town shopping when Jim came up to the Cloisters that afternoon. I admitted him by the west wing door, and to evade the servants we took the elevator to the third floor. The room was as we had left it the night before, keys and all, and our first experiments were pretty hopeless. Then at last Jim located in a corner a small, shabby trunk, and finally managed to find a key to open it.

I shall never forget that trunk. It was heartbreaking, in a way. There was Maud's white satin wedding dress and veil. She must have been very young and slender when it was made, for there were small lace ruffles to pad out the bust. Even Jim handled it gently, and I myself could have wept over it. There were Tony's baby clothes, and a quaint book with a record of his weight at birth, and later on an imprint of his foot drawn in ink. There was a lock of his hair too, fine and blond, with a slight curl to it.

I took it to a window to look at it and when I came back Jim was closing and locking the trunk. He looked up at me.

"Sorry, Pat," he said. "A policeman has to do a lot of snooping, and I'm damned if I like it. Don't tell Tony I've been in that trunk, will you?"

"I don't think he knows it's here."

He was more sober that day than I had ever seen him, and I know now that he went down to his office, closed his door, and did a number of things. He took out and studied some letters he had taken from the trunk while my back was turned. He went back over the list of clues he had made a few days before, and he got out some old borough documents and looked them over. After that he made one telephone call and wrote out a cable and some telegrams, telephoning them to the city to avoid a local leak. Then he sat back and went over what he had learned.

"It was in the bag by that time," he said later. "At least I had the story. Probably if you'd thought about it you'd have had it too. It was pretty obvious. But look where I was! I had a motive—and a good one—for everybody from Tony Wainwright and Bessie to Margery Stoddard, Julian, Bill, and Lydia. And to add to the mess Bill Sterling and Lydia were about to get married. Maybe that wasn't something!"

He sent the key box to the city that day. I believe they got excellent fingerprints of O'Brien, Reynolds, and myself, but that was all. A man came down that same afternoon to go over the trunk room itself, with the same result, only more so. He found everybody's prints, from those of the head housemaid to a nondescript thing which turned out to be one of poor old Roger's paws. As the servants had already been fingerprinted, he let them alone. But Bessie, confronted by the detective, defied him at first.

"I refuse, absolutely," she said. "I'm not going to have my hands ruined with that stuff. Take it away. You know what you can do with it."

"Plenty of prints around your room, madam," said the detective impassively. "You'll find this easier."

She succumbed at last, rolling her fingers on the ink pad and then on a sheet of paper.

"What's it for?" she asked. "I suppose I've committed wholesale murder around here!"

"That's for you to say," said the detective, and went away.

Jim spent the afternoon in his office. It was too early for a cable, but he hoped for replies to his telegrams. That was when he made what he called his suspect list. I have it now, written in his small, legible hand.

(1) Julian Stoddard. Motive and opportunity, although time element still uncertain. More likely to have done away with Bessie Wainwright. Morgan making no trouble, but Bessie collecting blackmail. Why kill Maud Wainwright?

(2) Evans. No apparent motive either murder, but possibly still alive. In which case used Andy McDonald's car to attack Haines. Strong for his age. Knew house. Could probably have gotten to trunk room by way of basement if chain not up. Duplicate keys? If so, what did he want in trunk room? Related to Maud Wainwright? In that case, would he have killed her? Again, where is he?

(3) Bessie Wainwright. Reason to kill Morgan if he threatened to expose story. Could not have done it without help. Could have killed Maud Wainwright, especially if she was afraid Maud Wainwright intended to blow things wide open. Not in trunk room last night.

(4) Maud Wainwright. Could have killed Morgan and then herself. Strong woman. Was Morgan's appointment with her at playhouse night of death? In that case Tony helped her dispose of body?

(5) Bill Sterling. Strong motive. (See letters from trunk.) Time element uncertain, but had key to playhouse. Also no time to leave Lydia's car and get his own when seen in Beaver Creek Road.

(6) Tony Wainwright. Improbable, if he knew story. Otherwise had plenty of time. But if he did not know facts had no motive.

(7) Margery Stoddard. Might have killed Morgan, with Julian later disposing of body. Not in trunk room last night. Nurse says sleepless night but not out of room.

He must have thought for a while, for then he wrote:

(8) Audrey Morgan. May have known the facts. Pretty anxious to pin something on somebody. Against it, crazy about father. Also not strong enough unless Hamilton boy helped her. Did Morgan tell her? Pretty young, but might have been desperate.

He was still working with the list when Hopper called up from town. "Got a line on Evans," he said. "At least it looks like it. I'm coming down."

"How'd you do it?"

"Groceries," said Hopper. "That's what a man can do without everything but."

They ate dinner that night at the Beverly Hotel. Jim told what he had found in the trunk room and gave him some of the letters to read. Hopper was duly impressed.

"Good work," he said. "Doesn't help much, however. New angle, of course."

"Rather helps Stoddard, don't you think?"

"Not with Stewart on the case it won't," said Hopper, eating canned-blueberry pie.

No, he hadn't got Evans. But he had found where he had been hiding out. Through groceries, as he had said.

"If he was alive he had to eat," he said. "We canvassed every grocery store and butcher shop in the county. He'd been in a deserted house across the river. Had a bicycle, and went in to a little town called Coventry twice a week for food." He finished his pie and produced a wooden toothpick for the seeds. "Might interest you to know the place belonged to Stoddard."

"Good God! What does that mean?"

"Stewart thinks it means a hell of a lot. According to him, Evans was out of the hospital the night Morgan was killed. He saw something, and Stoddard bribed him to get out. That was the three thousand dollars he drew and wouldn't account for. Remember?"

"Where is he now?"

"Well, we've lost him for a while," said Hopper. "We'll get him. He still has to eat. But he sure got out in a hurry. We found the bicycle ten miles down the river at Coventry. He could have taken a boat across to the railroad. There's one missing. Or he could have gone down quite a ways before he landed. Folks at the grocery store said he didn't talk. He'd come in, load up, and get away. But he bought the newspapers. They had orders to save them for him until he came."

It was Hopper's idea that something had scared Evans off. Not anything in the newspapers. He had been over them. Maybe he thought he had been recognized. Maybe something happened. Anyhow, he had not been seen for some time. But Jim was thinking.

"See here," he said. "What about Haines?"

"Haines?"

"Well, figure it for yourself. Evans gets suspicious you're after him. He can't buy any more at the store you speak of, walks up the hill, and gets Andy McDonald's car. With that he can go to any of the valley towns where he isn't known and stock up. He knows he's wanted. He's read the papers. He gets away all right. Then Haines passes him and slows up, and he thinks they've caught him. He not only makes for Haines. He takes his clothes, so he can put the car back and make a getaway before he's reported."

"Pretty late, wasn't it? Shops open at that hour of the night?"

"Some of the mill towns do most of their buying Saturday night."

Hopper threw away his toothpick. "All right," he said, "it looks as though it checks. We may even find out that Evans was the lunatic the papers have been talking about. But he's not crazy. Don't get that into your head. He's as sane as I am."

"Then what's it all about?"

"The district attorney thinks, and so does the commissioner, that when they get Evans they'll send Stoddard to the chair. He's what they're praying for."

Bessie stayed in bed most of that day. I don't think my story of the night before had deceived her much, for when she came downstairs she looked ghastly. We worked together all afternoon, unwrapping the gifts which had arrived and tying them up again in white paper and red ribbons. She made neat efficient parcels, and she relaxed somewhat as she worked.

She had her plans all made. She had a man in New York who was in love with her, and she would take a cash settlement from Tony and get out as soon as the trial was over.

"Only it will have to be a big one," she said. "I'm not selling out cheap."

What she wanted was a million dollars! "I'll get it too," she said, tying a red bow with a snap. "He'll come over, or else."

We worked until late. In a burst of amity she asked me to stay for dinner, and as Tony was not expected and she seemed lonely, I stayed. The meal was almost over when Tony appeared. He was in a cold rage. He sent the men out of the room and sat looking at Bessie, across the table.

"I've been doing some investigating," he said. "When you married me you had no people. God knows where you got the ones I saw, or what your life had been before I met you. As for the rest—Why did you do it, Bessie? Why couldn't you have been straight even then? I wanted to marry you. I wasn't looking for background. I was looking for ordinary decency."

Bessie was white under her make-up. But she was still cool. "I should think it would be obvious, Tony," she said, with her ironic smile.

"You never cared for me, did you? Even then?"

"You were all right. I've known men I liked better."

"And plenty of them," he said, his voice rising. "So you came here and raised hell. You used us all. You used my mother for your own dirty purposes. You used me. You even used Margery Stoddard. That was straight blackmail, and you know it."

She had recovered somewhat, however. "She paid me a little," she said flippantly. "Why shouldn't she? I'd made some bad investments and I had a lot of bills. She had plenty."

"I see. She had plenty," he said. "That explains everything, doesn't it? It must have been a nice little racket while it lasted. Only it's over now. It's over and you're through. Get that and get it right. You're through."

He got up abruptly, overturning his chair and banging the door as he left the room. It must have sounded like a battle from the pantry. Certainly that was how it was reported the next day, when the police interrogated Reynolds.

"You say they quarreled?"

"It sounded that way. Mr. Tony seemed excited."

"Hear anything he said?"

"He said it was over. He said Mrs. Wainwright was through. That's all I remember."

"He left her there? In the dining room?"

"Yes, sir. He upset his chair getting up. When I heard the door slam I went in."

"Mrs. Wainwright was still there?"

"Yes. She was lighting a cigarette."

CHAPTER THIRTY-SIX

THEY FOUND Bessie dead early the next morning. Andy Mc-Donald, on his way to town in his car, saw something gaily colored just outside the door to the west wing. He got out to investigate, and it was Bessie, still in the flame-colored dinner dress she had worn the night before. She was lying on her face, and her small pearl-handled revolver lay near her. Apparently she had not had time to use it. He bent over her, to see that the back of her head was bloody and crushed.

But he was a canny Scot. He rang the front doorbell, and told Reynolds to get the police. After that he stood guard. He allowed nobody to come near the body, nor did he touch it himself. "Keep back," he called when the servants began to run out. "Keep back, or I'll knock the heads off the lot of you."

That was what I found when I drove up early that morning, after a sleepless night: Andy on guard, Bessie on the ground, the side door open, and Reynolds keeping the servants back. Andy would not even let my car pass, or allow me to get out of it. "Stay where you are," he said. "We've maybe some tire prints around here."

"But what's wrong?" I asked, bewildered. "Is she—"

"Aye, she's dead," he said. "I never liked her, God forgive me. But she's been murdered, and the law comes first."

I felt very sick. Like Andy I had not liked her, but she had loved living. Her very faults had been due to that, her greed to get all she could out of life. Now she was only a flame-colored heap at the foot of the west wing steps. Not even covered. Just lying there.

Not that I was thinking all this. There was no time to think. I heard a car behind me and saw the men from the radio patrol car pass me. I saw Reynolds hand out a rug to cover her, and Andy wave him back. Also I saw Jim arrive and stoop over her. But none of it was real. It became real only when Tony pushed aside the gaping servants inside the door and came out.

It was bitterly cold. The men, including Tony, stood over her, looking down. Jim snapped an order, and Reynolds handed him the rug. The house door was closed, leaving only the five men, including Andy, standing there. I could not see Tony's face. Jim walked about, looking at the ground. Thomas brought Tony an overcoat and put it on him. In doing so he half turned and saw me. He spoke to Jim, and the two men came over to my car. Tony looked the way I felt, sick. It was Jim who spoke. "Go on back home, Pat," he said. "You can't do anything. You're only in the way."

"Can't you take her inside? It's so cold."

"We're waiting for Bill Sterling."

I shivered. Tony reached into the car and turned on the heater. He had not spoken at all until then. "It won't help to have you get pneumonia," he said quietly. "Go on down and get some hot coffee. Better put a little brandy in it."

They did not want me there. I felt lost in a world of men, men who could handle such matters, men who did not want a girl sitting in a car to watch them, men who were waiting for another man, calmly and unexcitedly, while Bessie lay on the frozen ground.

I turned my car around. There were more men on the road—the stablemen, the chauffeurs, some of the gardeners. They had been kept at a distance by Andy, but there they were, twenty or more of them. Murder was a man's business. What had Amy said? Everything comes in threes. But the men were not in threes. The men—

"Gus!" Tony called sharply. "Drive Miss Abbott down to the village. Tell Miss Mattie Sprague to put her to bed."

I was fully conscious, but I was shaking all over. I moved and Gus climbed into the driver's seat and started the car. We passed Bill at the gate. He did not even notice us. Gus looked at me. "If you feel weak, miss, put your head down on your knees."

I put my head down, and Gus steadied me with one hand. "That's the ticket," he said. "Have you home in a jiffy. Car looks kind of loaded up this morning."

"Trimmings for the Christmas tree," I told him. Then I burst into tears, which was probably the best thing I could have done. I could feel his big hand patting my back. "Take it easy, miss. It's shock. Miss Mattie got any liquor?"

"I don't think so. I don't want any."

"I'll send some around from Nelson's," said Gus the efficient. "You take it. Maybe you won't want it. Take it anyhow."

Man's cure-all, I thought, drying my eyes. Bessie dead on the ground, and Tony and Gus suggesting a drink. I began to laugh, and suddenly Gus's pat became a good hard slap. I was so astonished that I stopped laughing and stared at him.

"Sorry, but I had to do it," he said, his face a brilliant red. "Can't have you getting hysterical, miss. I hope you'll forget it. I'm kind of excited myself."

"Thanks, Gus. I needed it."

That is all I know myself of that morning. Miss Mattie put me to bed. I lay there shivering until Gus brought around a bottle of brandy. Miss Mattie stood over me while I drank a little, and gradually I began to relax. I think I even escaped into sleep. I had to escape somewhere.

It was weeks before I heard the full story of that morning. Bill Sterling said Bessie had been dead for hours. He did not move the body, but from what he could see it looked as though her skull had been fractured. She had probably either died at once or been unconscious. There was no evidence that she had been shot.

I believe Jim picked up the revolver then, using a pencil in the barrel to do it and wrapping it carefully in a clean handkerchief. After that they re-covered the body and waited for the coroner. Reynolds had brought out hot coffee. Some of them drank it, but Tony did not. When a young deputy coroner arrived he found the immediate group still there. The others had dispersed at Jim's order to search the grounds for the weapon.

The deputy coroner's examination was a short one. He turned the body over, and Tony looked away. In the sharp morning light Bessie's rouge and lipstick were hideous against the blue-white pallor of her face; but she looked calm, quite peaceful. "Probably never knew what hit her," said the deputy coroner, getting up and shaking down his trouser legs. "I'll want a better examination before I talk."

The homicide men arrived then, piling out of their car with their equipment. There was a long interval when, the ground cleared, they took photographs and examined everything in the vicinity. Then they allowed the body to be carried into the house.

By that time O'Brien had appeared. His cocksure manner was gone, but he had nothing of importance to tell them. He had left at seven in the morning as usual, going out by the kitchen door. Having no car, he had taken the short cut to the village by way of the country club, and so had not seen the body, hidden from the rear of the property by a screen of evergreens.

As for the night before, he stoutly maintained that he had examined the west wing door after the house had settled down, and that the chain was on it then. He had heard no noise, nor had anything suspicious happened, so far as he knew.

"Except that Mr. Wainwright and the missus had a fight at dinner," he said. "The help was talking about it."

"What kind of a fight?" said Hopper.

"I don't know," said O'Brien, looking uneasily at Tony. "Just knocking chairs around. You know."

The deputy coroner had followed Bessie's body upstairs. When he came down he said it looked like murder to him, and could he have some breakfast? He had been up since daylight. Case of gas poisoning. "One of these stoves with a rubber tube," he said. "Death machine, of course. The tube slipped, so—" He shrugged his shoulders. "Hell of a job this is," he said.

They brought him a tray to the library. Hopper was there, Jim, Tony, and Bill Sterling. While the deputy coroner ate bacon and eggs Hopper questioned Tony.

"We quarreled, of course. Pat Abbott was there. She'll tell you about it."

"What did you quarrel about?"

Tony hesitated. "She's dead now," he said. "I don't want to

discuss her. She'd pulled some pretty dirty work, and I told her so. But I didn't kill her."

Hopper said nothing. He went out to the servants' hall and questioned the servants there. Reynolds, as I have said, was non-committal, but the other men, Thomas and Stevens, were easier prey. A chair had been overturned, and Mr. Wainwright had slammed the door when he went out. No, they hadn't been getting along very well. They had separate rooms, and they hardly spoke when they met. Stevens had even overheard Tony's last words before he banged out of the room. "It's over and you're through. Get that and get it right. You're through."

Hopper was hot on the trail by now. He sat in the comfortable servants' hall and went on plugging. He called poor silly old Partridge, and Hilda and Nora. And he called Ethel, the housemaid who cared for Bessie's rooms, and smiled at her pleasantly. "Now tell me, Ethel, did Mrs. Wainwright have a gun of her own?"

"Why, yes, sir, she did. She slept with it under her pillow."

"Isn't that rather unusual? Did the rest of the family do that?"

"Oh, no, sir."

"Why do you think she did it, Ethel? You seem to be an observing young woman. She didn't look as though she would be afraid of much."

"Well, that's just it," said Ethel, succumbing at last. "She *was* afraid of something. In this house too. Else why did she keep her doors locked?"

"She did that, did she?"

"Yes, sir. Day and night for weeks on end."

Hopper went back to the library. "Let's have that story of last night again, Wainwright," he said. "What did you do after dinner?"

"I had some work to do. I stayed in the study until eleven. At ten-thirty Reynolds brought me in some whiskey."

"Where was your wife then?"

"Reynolds said she was in the library, reading. I told him to lock up when she went to bed. I didn't see her myself."

"When did Miss Abbott leave?"

"Immediately after dinner, I believe."

"You went to bed at eleven."

"About then. You can ask O'Brien. I met him on the second floor."

"You didn't leave your room after you went up?"

"No. Absolutely not."

Hopper sat still. When he spoke again his voice was dry. "I'll put it to you this way, Wainwright. You hated your wife. You wanted her out of the way. I have an idea you've been checking up on her past. As a matter of fact, I know you have. And you probably didn't like what you found."

"I didn't. That doesn't mean I killed her."

"I've not said that," said Hopper. "I do say this. You're in love with another woman, and your wife wouldn't give you a divorce. Maybe she was holding out for a larger settlement. Maybe things just happened to suit her as they are. It doesn't look too good, Wainwright. You threatened her, and—"

"I never threatened her. Not with bodily harm."

"All right. Admit that for a minute. We've had three deaths here, all of them violent. I'll grant that a dozen people might have wanted to kill Don Morgan. Who wanted to kill your mother? Sorry, but we've got to go back to that. Look at her will. Who profited by it? The servants got a little. Elliott gets twenty thousand which is chicken feed to him. Pat Abbott got five thousand dollars and a bracelet, but she didn't know she was to get them. Charity got a lot, but we can't claim that the rector of St. Mark's committed a crime to get a new organ for the church. I don't mean to be flippant.

"All right. Your wife got a dollar, but she had you to draw on. And you got the whole estate."

"So I killed my mother," Tony said thickly. "My mother and my wife! By God—"

He made a lunge at the detective, but Jim caught him in time. "Stop it, Tony," he said. "What's the use? You're not helping anything, including yourself."

Hopper remained undisturbed. "I'm going to ask you a question," he said. "If you'll tell the truth you'll save yourself a lot of trouble later. Did your wife know anything that made her afraid of being killed?" He grinned. "I'm leaving you out for a minute," he said, not unkindly. "Suppose she wasn't afraid of you, but of somebody else. Have you any idea who, or why?"

"No. Except that we'd had two crimes here. That would scare any woman."

They left him there, Jim Conway to go back to his office to wait for the cablegram which had not come, and Hopper to face an irate district attorney.

"Looks as though your case against Stoddard has got another hole in it, chief," he finished, after detailing the facts. "I passed the attorneys for the defense on the road, hellbent for Beverly. What do you bet they'll move to quash the indictment?"

"What's this murder got to do with Stoddard? Tony Wainwright wants to get rid of his wife, and does it. That's easy."

"Poor place to do it, chief. On his own doorstep. Lots of other places would have been better."

"A cemetery, I suppose," Stewart sneered.

CHAPTER THIRTY-SEVEN

I HAD no idea what was going on that day. Tony called twice, to ask Miss Mattie how I was; but I knew nothing of the conference at the Cloisters between Dwight Elliott, Brander Jones, and Tony; or of the autopsy, which showed that Bessie had been killed, as had been suspected, by a blow on the head. The little revolver, fingerprinted, showed no prints but her own. It had not been fired. The doorknob to the west wing door showed her prints, but also those of Reynolds. It looked as though she had simply stepped through it and had been immediately attacked.

What I knew by six o'clock that night was only from the newspapers. They spread themselves, of course. *Third Murder At Cloisters. Wife of Young Millionaire Killed* was typical of them all. None of them openly accused Tony, but practically all of them spoke of an estrangement. I learned later that Jim Conway had called the reporters into his office and laid his cards on his desk face up.

"This is straight," he said. "We don't know who did it. I'll swear that I don't, and that goes for the district attorney's men too. We haven't got the weapon. You can say we hope to make an arrest soon, but I'm damned if I know who it will be. You needn't put that in, unless you want Beverly to have a new chief of police; but that's how it is."

He took them over to the hotel and ordered ginger ale, which made their faces fall until he produced a bottle. After that they cheered up.

"Straight goods, chief. Not a clue?"

"Not a clue. Why don't you fellows look for the weapon? Whoever did it wouldn't carry it far."

The net result of which was a rather hilarious crowd of young newspapermen searching the woods and ditches, and even the grounds of the country club. Just before dark one of them went back to Jim's office. He had a package carefully wrapped in yellow paper. He unrolled it and stood back.

"Ditch behind that playhouse affair. Looks like it, doesn't it?"

It did, although it had been carefully wiped. Jim looked at it. It was a bronze Buddha, very heavy, and he had a good idea where it came from. He kept an impassive face, however.

"Ever see it before?" the reporter inquired, watching him.

Jim smiled. "Dozens of them around, boy," he said. "What home without a fat Buddha these days?"

"What d'you bet it comes from the Cloisters itself? There's a Chinese room, isn't there?"

"You don't have to have a Chinese room to have one of them. I've got a pair myself. Book ends," he added, seeing the boy's grin. "Go and look if you like. They're both still there."

When he was alone he telephoned Reynolds, and Reynolds called the parlormaid. He came back, his voice strained.

"There is one missing, sir," he said. "She doesn't know when it went. She says she hasn't seen it for two or three weeks. The room's full of stuff, you see, sir, and sometimes things get moved about."

Jim was pretty low that night. He had the story. He was certain he was on the right track, but Bessie's murder did not fit in anywhere that he could see. He even began to wonder if he had two types of crime on his hands, one and probably two coldly premeditated, and Bessie's on impulse, out of deep rage and resentment. But he could not conceal the Buddha; not with a fresh-faced young reporter already writing a story about it.

He called Hopper and told him. "No doubt about where it came from," he said. "I've had the butler and one of the maids down here. They identify it."

"Anything on it?"

"No. Clean as a whistle."

Hopper conferred with somebody for a moment or two. Then he came back to the telephone. "Better bring Wainwright in," he said. "The D.A. would like to talk to him. Bring the what-you-call-it too, but don't tell him."

It was the same thing all over again; first Bill, then Julian, now Tony. The same strong light, the same smoke-filled air, the same group of men questioning him in relays. Tony was tired. He asked for his lawyer, but they told him that they merely wanted to clear up some points. When at last they set the Buddha before him he hardly looked at it.

"Ever see this before, Mr. Wainwright?"

He glanced at it then. "It looks like one from the house. I wouldn't know."

"From what part of the house?"

"I suppose from the Chinese room. It might have been anywhere."

"It wasn't in your hand last night, when your wife stepped outside the door to where she was found?"

He stiffened then. "Is that what killed her?"

"We're asking the questions, Mr. Wainwright."

If they had hoped he would break they were disappointed. They made him admit that his marriage had been a mistake. He admitted too that he had put a New York firm of private detectives on Bessie's track. He hadn't wanted to do it, but she had claimed to know something to his mother's discredit. He had had to fight fire with fire.

"What was this thing she knew about your mother?"

"What could she know? Anybody who knew my mother would know she had never done a wrong thing in her life."

They would not hold him, even as a material witness. They knew they could not hold him for any length of time, so they let him go that night. Rather it was morning when he and Jim drove out to Beverly; one of our rare clear winter dawns, with the air light and crisp. Tony slept part of the way, out of sheer exhaustion. He roused when Jim turned in at the Cloisters and slowed the car.

"See here, Tony," he said. "You must have some idea of what Bessie knew."

"I haven't. She may have thought I did."

"So she locked herself up?"

"So she locked herself up," said Tony, and got wearily out of the car.

I went back to the Cloisters that morning. Tony and Dwight Elliott were there, but I did not see them. I was glad I had gone, however. The morale of the entire staff was badly shattered. Mrs. Partridge had retired to her bed. In the kitchen Pierre had threatened the kitchen-maids with a knife and they had fled, screaming. The silver was unpolished, the ashes still in the grates, and a general air of uncertainty and demoralization permeated the entire place.

In the emergency I called the household together and gave them a plain-spoken talk. Do your work or pack and get out was the gist of it, and to my surprise it seemed to help them. They needed orders, and I was giving them. But anyone who without any authority has faced twenty-odd servants and read the riot act to them will know that I felt weak when it was over.

I remember that Pierre sent me a fat little quail on my lunch tray that day. I took it as it was meant, an overture toward peace, and I ate it, although the mere thought of food choked me.

Nobody could have told me then that we were close to the end of our mystery, or that Jim Conway was that day to receive a cable and set a trap. That a body in the city morgue was to play its own part in our solution. That I was to have a talk with Margery Stoddard late that very night. Or that only an hour or two after it I was to shoot O'Brien and nearly kill him.

I was busy that day. Rather than give up the Christmas party I called Dr. Leland and asked him if he would transfer it to the parish house. That meant gathering gifts and tree trimmings and sending them down in the station wagon. It made a number of trips, but at last the ballroom was clear. I went to the powder room to wash before I started for home. Mr. Elliott was in the west hall when I came out. He was as dapper as ever, but he looked tired. I asked him if I couldn't order a drink for him.

"I think perhaps I will have one," he said. "All this excitement—Better take one yourself, Miss Abbott. You look all in."

"Aren't we all?" I said.

We sat down by the fire in the library, and he told me something of Tony's situation. He seemed worried, although his voice was as dry as usual. It didn't look well for Tony, he said. The quarrel was bad. Then there was the question of the Buddha, and—

"What Buddha?"

My heart sank when he told me. I knew it well. It had stood on top of a cabinet in the Chinese room, where an angry man could find it ready to his hand. But I went down fighting.

"Why on earth would she take a revolver and go outside to meet him? He was in the house all evening."

"The police are not sure she was outside when she was struck."

It was horrible. I had a queer ringing in my ears. They thought Tony had waited for her, struck her down and then carried her out into the winter night; had left her there, gone over to the playhouse, wiped the Buddha and left it where it might not be found until spring, if ever.

"But why?" I asked. "What reason had he? He meant to divorce her. He didn't have to kill her."

He hesitated. "He was angry, of course. Aside from that— well, you'll hear it soon enough. She told me, and I don't doubt she told him, that she knew something about his mother. He had endured a great deal. He wouldn't take that easily."

Neither he nor Tony knew what it was, he said. It was Bessie's secret, and she had kept it to the end. "Probably only something in her own unhealthy mind," he observed, and got up to go. "I gather she was not on confidential terms with you."

"No. She told me she was afraid, but not why."

"I've been over her papers," he said. "She has left a number of bills but nothing important. Whatever it was, if anything, it died with her."

I went out with him. He looked better, certainly for the whisky and perhaps for the talk. But before he stepped on the gas he asked me to regard our conversation as strictly private.

"I needn't tell you that the police would jump at it."

I nodded, and I can still see him, neat, distinguished, important, starting that big car of his and giving me a dignified wave of the hand as the car got under way.

I never saw him again alive.

That was on Friday, the twenty-second of December. Bessie had been killed on Wednesday night, and the inquest, delayed a day by request of the police, was set for Saturday morning. Down in his office in Beverly, Jim Conway was still waiting for a cablegram. He was not idle, however. He was in touch with Hopper at the detective bureau in town; and as a result, an inconspicuous individual with a small load of Christmas trees had unloaded them on an empty lot across from Lydia's house, and the little man who had tailed Bill Sterling was back again, to Mrs. Watkins's indignation.

"What do you want here?"

"I'm waiting for the doc. Got a cold. How've you been lately?"

"I've been a sight better since you went away. If you're back here on any of your dirty work you can get out. We don't want you."

But he remained. Once he went back to the kitchen. "That wouldn't be mince pies I smell, would it?" he inquired wistfully.

"It would," said Mrs. Watkins tartly. "Take a good smell. It's all you'll get."

About six o'clock that evening there was a conference, not at Jim's office but at his house. Men left their cars at a distance and went in, by ones and twos. Jim was there, Tony, and O'Brien. Even Hopper came, stayed for a short time, and went away, leaving behind him the box of keys found in the trunk room. At seven they separated, still stealthily, walking lightly over the hard-frozen ground, and in their various cars went up the Hill Road. Only Tony went on to the Cloisters, however. The rest left their cars, one or two in the country club grounds, others at the Stoddard place but away from the house, and at the Earles'.

I knew nothing of all this. If I had, perhaps one life would have been saved, and certainly little O'Brien would not have spent the rest of the winter in the hospital.

CHAPTER THIRTY-EIGHT

I WAS ready to leave that afternoon, as I have said. I had seen Mr. Elliott off and gone back to get my coat and hat when the library telephone rang. To my surprise it was Margery Stoddard. "Is that you, Pat? Thank goodness you're still there. I only have a minute. The nurse is downstairs having tea. Pat, I must see you."

"When? I can come over now."

"Not now. I don't want anybody to know. Tonight. You must come. I'm almost crazy. And don't bring your car. Walk over. I don't want anyone to know."

"What about your night nurse?"

"She's gone. I fired her. Don't come early. Wait until the house is quiet, will you? Not before eleven. Later if you can."

"I wasn't very lucky the last time I did that!"

"You'll be all right, I promise. That was a mistake."

"Good heavens, are you telling me—"

"I'll explain it all tonight," she said feverishly. "Here's the nurse coming. I'll be down in the sun room. The door will be open." She hung up abruptly.

I remember standing by the telephone, uncertain and uneasy. After what had happened to Bessie I did not care to drive up the Hill alone late at night. And my previous experience at the Farm was not cheering. So Margery knew about it, and it was a mistake! But if she knew that she might know something else; something that ought to be known. After all, she was in this thing up the neck, with Julian awaiting trial; sitting in a cell in town, seeing his lawyers, trying to tear a way out of the spider-web of circumstantial evidence the district attorney's office had woven around him.

It was then that I had the bright idea of not going home at all that night; of merely staying in my former rooms upstairs until it was time to see Margery. It was entirely possible. My rooms were closed but in order. It meant doing without dinner, but I had not been hungry for days. And it meant telling Gus about my car.

I unlocked the west wing door and went to the garage. One of the men was on duty, but Gus was not in sight. I told him I was staying at the Cloisters overnight, and I managed to get the automatic from my car without his seeing it. With the gun under my coat I felt safer. I was almost cheerful as I went back. The house servants would think I had gone, the garage that I was staying.

No one saw me when I returned. It was supper hour in the servants' hall, and the front of the house was deserted. I got upstairs easily and into my sitting room. But I had not counted on the long hours there until eleven o'clock. To add to my troubles there seemed to be small unusual noises all about me, and at one time I was so sure of this that I opened the door and looked out. It was only O'Brien moving toward the stairs, and he did not see me.

By ten o'clock I had run out of cigarettes. I did not dare go down for any, or even for a book to read. I was too nervous to sit still. I paced the floor for the last hour, ready to bite my nails out of sheer desperation.

Once outside the house, however, it was better. I did not need my pocket flash. In the faint starlight the path was a thin yellow thread under the leafless trees. I carried the gun in my coat pocket, but nothing whatever occurred. The house at the Farm was dark, and Margery was in the sun room waiting. She opened the door and I slid in, to have her put her arms around me and hold to me as if I was her last hope on earth.

"I'm not crying," she said. "I'm beyond tears, Pat."

"Sit down. You're shaking. What's it all about, Margery?"

"It's about my father. My stepfather, really. Pat, I don't know what to do."

"Your stepfather?" I said stupidly. "What about him? Who is he?"

"Evans," she said. "Evan Evans. And I think he has lost his mind."

I sat very still. I was too startled to speak. Was Evans our murderer, after all? Certainly Margery thought so. She sat there in the dark, huddled in a blanket from her bed, and told me, in a voice husky with strain.

"He hated Don," she said. "After I ran away with him he said he would kill him if he ever saw him again."

"But Maud? And now Bessie? You don't know what you're saying, Margery."

"Oh, yes, I do," she said obstinately. "He's been queer ever since Don's death. At first I thought it was because he believed Julian had killed him. But now——"

Evans, she said, had never forgiven Don for what he had done to her. Even when she came back, safely married to Julian, the resentment still held. He was still fond of her, however, and when she and Julian had tried to get him to leave the Cloisters he had refused. Julian had paid him a hundred and fifty dollars a month ever since. But he had not cared for money. He had put it in the bank for the girls.

"I wasn't ashamed of him," she said. "He had been good to me after Mother's death, although I did not live at home. But to recognize him might have been to bring up the old story about Don and me. He was happy—in his own way—and comfortable, so we let him alone."

He had liked the children. Now and then he saw them. They had no idea who he was, but he would buy small presents for them and hide them about the place. The little girls called them fairy gifts, and never knew where they came from.

"Then early in the summer he changed, Pat. I think he saw Don somewhere. He told me again that he would kill him if he showed up. He may even had talked to him. I don't know. They knew each other. Father had gone to Don years ago when he learned I was seeing him. He threatened him at that time. That's one reason we went abroad."

But with Don's return to Beverly things had become serious with them. Julian could not sleep. He took to walking around at night, wondering what to do. Then came the murder, and Julian was convinced Evans had done it.

"He denied it. He even said Julian had killed Don, and good riddance to bad rubbish! It was dreadful."

However that may be, after Don's murder it had been necessary to get him away. Julian had got him out of the hospital at night and to a house he owned across the river. He withdrew money from the bank—three thousand dollars in cash—and urged Evans to go away. But he did not go. Now and then he telephoned her, but he didn't sound like himself. He told her once that if she heard of a lunatic loose not to worry.

"That was the cemetery, Pat," she said, and shuddered. "It was his idea of throwing suspicion away from Julian."

They did their best for him. He didn't want a car. He wanted a bicycle as less conspicuous, and Julian took one to him. By that time both she and Julian were sure he had murdered Don, but they could not turn him over to the police. Maud's death, however, confused them. "He had been fond of her, in his way," she said. "He would never have done that, Pat. And now, Bessie!"

At first they had succeeded in keeping him hidden. The cemetery incident had convinced them that he was unbalanced. "And what good would it have done to arrest him? He would have died, and he had been good to me."

But the search at last began to catch up with him. One day he saw the storekeeper where he got his groceries looking at him hard. That night he got away. He wasn't young. It must have been dreadful for him. He came over here and borrowed Andy McDonald's car, and the state policeman chased him. He ran into him and took his clothes, to gain time.

"He brought them here that night, Pat," she said. "They're buried somewhere behind the kennels."

But at least he was safe now, she thought. He had never admitted killing Don, of course, although he might if Julian's case went against him. But he insisted that it had been Don who knocked him out in the playhouse and took his keys.

"Is he where you can find him if you need him?" I asked.

"Yes. I got old Connor down and told her the whole story. He has a room where she lives. He's supposed to be her brother."

I had hardly recovered from that when she told me about my being attacked the night I had sat with her beside the empty pool. Evans had been in the grounds that night, and he had overheard what I told her.

"That's when I began to think he had lost his mind," she said. "I hadn't known he was there, but he admitted it later. You see, if you ever told what you knew about me, either Julian or he would go to the chair. I really think he meant to kill you."

It was Bessie's death, however, that had forced her to send for me.

He would come over at night, she said; would bicycle to the river after dark, row across, and walk up to the Farm. He knew the back roads. What terrified her was that once when he came she had told him about Bessie and her extortion.

"I was afraid he would have a stroke," she said. "The veins on his forehead swelled up, and his face was purple. 'That little bitch,' he said. 'If she makes trouble for you it will be the end of her.'"

"He couldn't have done it, Margery. Not unless he could get into the house."

I told her about the Buddha, but she was not convinced. He knew the Cloisters from top to bottom. He might have had ways of his own for getting in.

We had been sitting in the dark. Once she lit a cigarette, however, and by its light I saw her face. It was thin and despairing, as though she had not a hope left in the world.

"My husband or my father, Pat," she said. "What am I to do?"

"Julian never did it. You can be sure of that."

"I can't prove anything. If my father is crazy—and he must be—even a confession from him wouldn't be much good, would it?"

The only thing I could think of was to tell Jim Conway the

whole story. He had never believed Julian guilty. He might be able to find some way out. She promised to think it over.

Going home that night I carried my automatic in my hand, with the safety catch off. I had no desire to meet a half-crazed Evans on my way back. It was a hideous trip. The sky had become overcast and I had to use the flash. It was like walking through a black tunnel in which the light bored a faint yellowish hole. That half mile or so was one of pure agony, for I had not gone a third of the way before I knew I was being followed. There was someone behind me.

There was no doubt whatever. Someone—perhaps in rubber-soled shoes—was following me. There was no sharp impact of leather on frozen ground, but a soft regular beat. Like a trapped rat I turned suddenly and threw the light back along the path. Whoever it was dodged among the trees, but that was all I needed. I ran the rest of the way as I never ran before, and if I had had any doubts they were settled when I left the trail and struck the grass lawn of the Cloisters. Whoever it was was still running along the path, and running fast.

I think he stopped there, however. I made the east wing door, where I had left the chain off, in nothing flat. Somehow I unlocked the door and got inside. I put up the chain and then, completely breathless and shaken, I sat on a chair in the hall and struggled for breath. Everything was quiet. Only my own noisy breathing broke the silence. There was the usual dim light in the main hall, and at last I forced myself to my feet. I was still trembling. I was cold and I had had a shock.

It must have been then that I remembered the thermos of hot coffee left at night for O'Brien, and using the flash I went back to the kitchen. It was in its usual immaculate order; the range, long enough to serve a hotel, was bright, and Pierre's brass kettles were shining around the walls. O'Brien's lunch tray was there, and I poured a cup of coffee from the thermos jug. I was still holding it when I saw that the door to the servants' hall was open and a light burning there. I walked over and glanced in. To my amazement O'Brien was asleep on the couch.

I went over, prepared to pour hot coffee on him, waken him to his job, and send him out to search for the man who had followed me. But it was not O'Brien. It was a dummy made of blankets and covered with one, its head buried in pillows, and a pair of shoes at the other end. My first reaction was one of pure rage. I hadn't a doubt that he was out of the house on some business of his own. He would turn up toward morning, cocky as usual, confronting me.

"Well, maybe I did take a little nap, miss. Try it yourself some night. This place gets you after a bit."

"You weren't here at all, O'Brien."

"I just went outside to look around. That's an old gag, that blanket stuff. Crook looks in, sees me there, and goes away."

Nevertheless, he might be about somewhere. I took the flash and went over the lower floor, room by room. I did not find him, but there were small sounds that made me jumpy. I tried to think they were the creakings and crackings of the house itself on a cold night, but at last they were too much for me. I shot up the staircase and stood in my room, panting and divided between a desire to stand there and yell my head off, to waken Tony, to call the police, or to rush out of the house, go down the hill, and crawl into bed with Miss Mattie. To do anything but stand still in my room with that horrible noise all around me, and O'Brien only a roll of blankets and a pair of shoes.

I remember getting Jim's automatic out of my pocket. I remember taking off my coat and sitting down on the edge of my bed, the gun in my hand. I remember feeling like a child who doesn't know what it is all about but is scared anyhow. And then I really heard sounds. Small and cautious as they were, they were going on, over my head in the trunk room.

It was more than I could bear. I went down the hall as quietly as I could and opened Tony's sitting-room door. The room was dark. So was his bedroom. I went straight to the bed to rouse him, and at first I thought he was there. But what looked like a human body was merely pillows under the bed clothing. Like O'Brien, I thought stupidly. Like O'Brien.

I suppose I stood there for some time, my knees sagging and my heart jumping in all directions. Then some sort of reason came to me. It was Tony up in the trunk room, perhaps Tony and O'Brien both. I went back into the hall and listened. Everything was still above. I even relaxed a little. Then I heard it. The elevator was coming up.

I was instantly in a panic. If Tony was in the trunk room I must warn him. Someone was in the dark cage, perhaps bringing death again.

I remember that. I remember running up the third floor stairs and to the trunk-room door. I remember that somebody grabbed me and put a hand over my mouth. And I remember a wild explosion, and the arms holding me letting go. I fell to the floor, but not alone, and suddenly all over the house bedlam seemed to break loose. Someone was yelling from the first floor, and what seemed like a dozen men erupted from the trunk room and ran along the hall to the elevator. A strong light went on from somewhere, and I tried to get to my feet. But I could not do it. There was a man lying there, groaning.

It was O'Brien, and I had shot him through the chest.

CHAPTER THIRTY-NINE

I WAS in bed at Miss Mattie's for three days before Jim came to see me. I knew from Tony and the newspapers that our murderer had been trapped that night, and had committed suicide in the elevator. But Tony would not talk about it.

"It's Jim's story, darling," he said. "I'm not sure yet of all of it. Wait a little."

He spent a great deal of time with me. Not that I was really ill. I had had a nervous shock which left me weak, and before it there had been long weeks of strain. Amy Richards, standing over me, said I looked like something no self-respecting cat would watch a mousehole for.

"All collarbones and ribs," she said disparagingly. "What Tony Wainwright sees in you to send him off his head I don't know. Here's your cream. Drink it."

She was filled with curiosity about that last night at the Cloisters. For it seemed that I, too, was getting my share of publicity. *Policeman Badly Hurt. Excited Girl Shoots Guard.* She read the newspaper headlines to me until Tony took her in hand.

"Shut up, Amy," he said amiably. "Let my girl alone."

"It's your girl, is it?"

"Mine, strawberry marks and all."

"Strawberry marks! She hasn't a mark on her, I'll have you know. She has as nice a skin as I've ever seen."

"Tut, tut," said Tony. "Have a few decent reserves. And speaking of this and that, how would you like to go and take a walk?"

The old Tony was coming back. He would come in grinning, bringing me things to amuse me, a cigarette box which played a tune, a pair of lovebirds which he named Bill and Coo, although neither of us ever learned which was which. He filled my room with flowers too, although none of them came from the green houses at the Cloisters. I wondered about that, until Jim explained it.

He came alone that day, looking rather smug, and reported that O'Brien was getting better.

"He'll have a long pull," he said. "That was a big gun, Pat. But he doesn't hold it against you. He understands. Just the same, if you'd done it ten minutes earlier—or maybe less than that—you would have wrecked the whole business."

It did not take long to tell the story. He'd known a lot of it after we had opened that old trunk of Maud's. He had even suspected it before, when he saw the official notice of her death. He had cut it out and studied it. *Jessica Maud Wainwright, widow of the late John C. Wainwright.* So her name had been Jessica, and there was the scar on Don Morgan's chest.

"I got to wondering. He'd had it cut out a long time before, but it might not mean a thing. Quite a few girls' names begin with a J. Then one day I got Tony talking about his father. He didn't remember him. Said he'd been killed in the war; went over early with the Canadians and never came back. I wondered if he had been killed. Maud Wainwright had married old J.C. five years later. If he was still alive, that was the mistake she made. She should have waited seven years, but she hadn't.

"It was only a chance, but look at it yourself. He'd apparently knocked Evans out and taken his keys. He had broken into the Cloisters more than once. And finally he'd been killed at the playhouse there. There had to be some reason. There was, of course. That's really the story.

"Don Morgan was Maud Wainwright's first husband. What's more, it looked as if her second marriage wasn't legal.

"I didn't know it, of course. I was still guessing until I found those letters of his to her in the trunk room, but I checked them with some tax receipts we had here on file. The writing was the same, and all at once things began to fall into a sort of pattern.

"Let's go back a bit. One day in August Maud goes to the city. Old J.C. is dead, but otherwise she's sitting pretty. She's got Tony, she has plenty of money, friends, and what have you. She drives along, and there's Morgan in the street beside the car. He sees her, and she sees him. She collapses in the car, but Morgan gets the license number from the car, goes to the license bureau and learns who she is.

"He must have had a fit, poor devil. If he was the man you saw at the playhouse window in June he was probably only trying to get a glimpse of Audrey. But his wife is now Mrs. J.C. Wainwright, and the scandal sheets are saying that Tony and Audrey are so-and-so about each other. They're half brother and sister, and they don't know it.

"Now you knew Morgan. Outside of women he wasn't a bad sort, but he's in a hell of a mess. He doesn't want to upset Maud's applecart, but he's got to see her. He tries, but first she's laid up sick, and later he finds he can't get her on the telephone and she has a secretary to open her mail.

"He stays on in the city, and he hires a drive-it-yourself car. He hangs around the Cloisters at night, but it's no good. So at last he knocks Evans out and takes his keys. You know the rest of that. He knew about the old man's job, of course. He'd eloped with his daughter!

"All right. Grant all that. Then who had killed him? I was pretty sure Tony didn't know the story, if there was one. Even if he had he wasn't the sort to kill his own father. So what? Had Maud Wainwright done it? She might. Here she was, sitting pretty with the Wainwright money, and if my guess was right she had no right to it. Nor had Tony. It was understandable too, if she'd done it and then shot herself. But I was sure her death was murder, not suicide.

"You see how it went. Here was Bessie. She liked money a lot better than she cared for her own soul. Suppose she knew the story? She'd been pretty intimate with Morgan in France. She'd almost certainly seen the scar. 'What's that?' 'Initials of my wife, my dear. Name was Jessica Maud.' You see how it could have been worked. How many Jessica Mauds are there, do you suppose? And little Bessie with her baby face—sorry, Pat, but it was a baby face—getting busy. 'What did she look like? Where is she now?' He didn't know. He hadn't seen her or heard of her for so many years. But if he mentioned how she looked and that hair of hers, Bessie could be pretty certain.

"He'd told her about Margery. All Bessie saw in her was a source of extra income by blackmail. But if Maud was still his wife, that was pretty bad news. What, lose the Wainwright money? Tear Tony away from it and where was she? You can be good and sure Bessie'd have put both Morgan and Maud out of the way before she let that happen.

"Well, you know the rest of it. I got Maud's early love letters out of the trunk. One or two came from France. They were signed Anthony, but on the back of the envelope was his full name, Anthony Donaldson Morgan. The last one said he was going to the front and didn't expect to come back.

"He didn't, of course. He got through all right, but he dropped part of his name and stayed in France.

"Here was Maud keeping his letters and grieving over him. She was that sort. But he doesn't worry about that. He gets a job in Paris, and—here's the catch—he divorces her! She doesn't know it. Nobody knows it. It took me a hell of a time to learn it from the French police. But probably that's one of the things Morgan wanted to tell her. He'd notified her, but she'd been moving around. When the notifications came back to him he'd just let it ride.

"Well, there's the picture. He gave up trying to see Maud and went back to New York. But he was still worried about Audrey and Tony. He wrote to Lydia but she sent the letter back unopened. He must have been pretty desperate by that time. Finally he had to play sick to get back, but Lydia kept a pretty cold eye on him. He could have told her about Maud and his first marriage; but I think he was still determined not to spill the beans if he could help it. What he did was smart. He sent for Tony, and Tony told him he had no intention of marrying Audrey. He had a wife already.

"It must have been a jolt to Morgan when he learned that he'd been playing around with his son's wife. Anyhow, he managed to see Bessie at least once. He got out at night and they drove around in her car. What she said then I don't know. The chances are that she told him she knew that neither Maud nor Tony had a right to the Wainwright money, and he let her think so! Why? Well, look at it. She was a bad actor, and he knew it. Probably he wanted her to leave Tony. He could have threatened to blow the works if she didn't and leave her flat.

"She looked like a pretty good suspect when I got that far. There was only one thing against it. She was scared of Tony himself.

"Now, that was curious. What she finally worked out in her crooked little mind—sorry again, Pat!—was that Tony knew the story and suspected that she knew it. She was sure Tony had shot at her the night she was hurt.

"Outside of that there was a pretty strong case against her. She wouldn't have had a scruple about putting Morgan out of the way if she could get away with it. Only thing was, I didn't believe she had done away with him by herself. Then who helped her? And again, when Maud Wainwright was killed, she'd had people to dinner that night, and Gus reported that no car had been out of the garage. She couldn't have gotten down to the village and spiked Lydia's tire.

"I was all for Bessie and an accomplice by that time.

"I began to wonder about Evans. After Haines was attacked with Andy's car I knew he was around somewhere. But we couldn't find Evans, and there was somebody else who stood to gain by Morgan's death. Hold your horses, Pat. This was murder. Tony didn't do it, but he was on the list all right.

"Of course, when I got that far I understood a lot of things. I could guess pretty well why Maud Wainwright had sent for Lydia to meet her at the playhouse the night she was killed. Look at it yourself. If her marriage to J.C. wasn't legal, then Lydia's to Don wasn't legal either. In other words, Audrey was a—well, let's say she was without a father.

"You get the picture, don't you? What had Maud Wainwright of her own? If she wasn't J.C.'s legal wife the estate wasn't hers. Maybe she got legal advice on it. I don't know. But she had done Audrey Morgan a deadly injury, as she saw it.

"Remember, she still didn't know Don had divorced her. She didn't even know that the Don Morgan who had been killed and the husband who had deserted her were the same person until a day or so after his murder. Remember the day she had the heart attack? She'd been perfectly normal. She'd eaten her breakfast and looked at her mail. She'd even read the first page of the paper about the murder. But after that, while she waited for Hilda to bring something, she turned the page and there was his photograph.

"It pretty nearly finished her.

"She must have lain in bed for weeks wondering what to do. Then one day she had an idea. She could sell her jewels and give Audrey the money. They were hers. Wife or no wife to J.C., he had given them to her. The Cloisters too.

"What else could she do? Make a big gesture, tell the truth, and ruin Audrey? I think she meant to lay her cards on the table that night at the playhouse, tell Lydia the facts, and let her decide. She never had a chance, of course. Somebody else was taking mighty good care of that.

"Who was it? Who knew she was going to be there? Or that she had taken that brown manila envelope with her? Because that's what she did. I imagine it contained her wedding certificate to Anthony Donaldson Morgan, maybe Tony's birth certificate, and perhaps some old photographs of Morgan himself. But she did one thing before she left that night that fooled nobody. She'd meant Tony to have those certificates after she died, and she'd put a sort of explanatory letter to him in with them.

"Only she wasn't going to die that night, or so she thought. So she took that letter to Tony out and hid it temporarily under her mattress. It fooled everybody for a while.

"Now let's look at our killer for a minute. When he met Don at the playhouse the night he threw him in the pool he found a bonanza. Don had Evans's keys! After that, by going down to the basement and slipping the chain he could get into the house any time he wanted. And he wanted to, all right. You never know about women. What had Maud kept, out of that past of hers? If anything, where was it?

"Finally he thinks of the trunk room, but you scare him off that night. He damned well had to get into it just the same, and the way we got him was to indicate it was there and we intended to look it over.

"Well, that's the story, sister," he said. "Maybe I was pretty slow, but even after I'd gotten the papers out of the trunk room I still didn't know that Don Morgan had divorced Maud. But if he hadn't, the one person to benefit by his death and Maud's was Bessie.

"She didn't want that story known any more than she wanted to lose a leg.

"Then she herself was killed.

"I'm not going over that again. You know all the answers. She was murdered because she knew too much, and because her price for keeping her mouth shut was too high. But there was one thing she didn't know, or you can bet she'd have had them. That was about those letters in the trunk room. As I say, they were the cheese with which we baited the trap that last night."

He got up and picked up his hat. Then he looked down at me and grinned.

"Sorry to have scared you on the footpath that night, Pat. One of our men saw you leave the house and followed you to Margery's. You carried a gun and he was damned suspicious of you. He says you beat the world's record coming back."

I sat up in bed. "Are you telling me that man on the path was a policeman?"

"Sure he was."

"It was a dirty trick," I said furiously. "I hate you, Jim Conway. I've had enough of the police to last me a lifetime."

He laughed. "Well," he said. "You haven't a thing on them, sister. I had men stationed all over the place that night. When you started making rounds of the lower floor at the Cloisters they all had to dive for cover. There wasn't a sofa that didn't have a cop behind it, cursing to beat the band."

CHAPTER FORTY

THAT IS the story, as Jim would say. Tony and I have never discussed it since it happened, but lately he has been reading it chapter by chapter as I have written it. He has been trying to pick up the loose ends for me, but also he has learned some of the things he never knew. He will look up suddenly and say, "I can't find anything about what happened to Evans, my love. Slipped up there, haven't you?"

"I'm sure it's in," I say vaguely. "About his being at Miss Connor's, and being asphyxiated by the gas stove? It's back where the deputy coroner came in when Bessie was—you know, when he said it was his second case that morning."

There is a prolonged shuffling of yellow paper, and a snort from Tony. "Here it is. According to you he says: 'One of these stoves with a rubber tube. Death machines, of course. The tube slipped, so—' He shrugged his shoulders. 'Hell of a job this is.' I suppose that explains everything."

"Well, it was Evans," I say meekly. "I just forgot to put it in."

"And was he murdered? Did the fair Miss Connor put him out of the way?"

"I don't think he was murdered," I say worriedly. "She was a nice little thing, Tony."

"Of course she killed him," he says. "Don't you know you can't leave any threads loose? He complained about the tea one day, and she up and kicked the tube off the stove. Why wasn't it in the newspapers? His death, I mean."

"He was there as Miss Connor's brother. I know I've told that. So his name had to be Connor too. That's perfectly plain, isn't it?"

"When you tell it, it is. What about Margery? Didn't the Connor woman tell her her father was dead?"

"Not right away. Margery was sick and in trouble. I think she even had him buried, Tony."

"And it was Evans in the cemetery after all?"

"That's in," I say, exasperated. "He was trying to save Julian by pretending there was a lunatic around."

Now and then he puts down the manuscript and sits thinking. For instance, the fact that Mr. Morgan and his mother could have lived for three years or so in close proximity puzzles him. "It doesn't seem possible, Pat."

"Well, Maud had lived here for eighteen years, and I saw her only once or twice in all that time."

He has other objections, of course. It is his deep conviction that I have shown him as something between an idiot and a schizophrenic, as well as a rotten lover. But his jibes are to hide deeper emotions. He knows it and so do I. There are many chapters which he reads somberly, without comment. And he has read and reread the bit about Roger's death. It has always been a sore point with him. He loved the dog.

"What did happen to him, Pat?"

"I'm sorry, Tony. I left that out on purpose. You see, Bessie—"

"All right. Go ahead."

"She had been going out at night to see Margery Stoddard. I suppose he barked or something. She might have left it about. I don't know, of course."

"I see," he says, and is silent for a long time.

Now and then he shows a light resentment, especially as to the night of his father's murder.

"I suppose you have to direct suspicion to me," he says. "Only thing I object to is that you seem to enjoy it. Why the hell all this stuff about my having no alibi for that night?"

"You hadn't," I tell him sweetly. "I suspected you myself for some time. Just what were you doing that night anyhow, Tony?"

He grins, gets up, and kisses me. "I was moving around, wondering just how long I could do without you, my darling," he says.

But later on he puts down the manuscript and looks at the fire. He has been reading something about Maud, and his mouth looks soft and tender. "She was a great woman—Mother," he says. "If only she'd told me about things. But she didn't. She—"

Over Jim's list of tangible clues he puzzles for a long time. "What about this garter?" he asks. "Roger found it in the grounds. You gave it to Jim. Then you drop it. That's no way to do."

"It wasn't really important, Tony. Jim says when he and Hopper counted the time it took to—well, to do away with your father in the playhouse and so on, it took him some time to dress. He has an idea now that no dressing was done. Just a long coat perhaps. You see"—I hesitate here—"he thinks the drowning took place earlier, before the party broke up. All that was necessary then was to strip in a hurry, get the body out, and take it away."

His mother's appointment with Lydia at the playhouse puzzles him too. "What about it?" he said. "Did Mother notify him that she and Lydia were going to meet that night?"

"How else could he have known, Tony?"

"She didn't tell Lydia why she wanted to see her?"

"No. But Lydia got the idea somehow that it was about Audrey."

Perhaps my voice is a little cool, for he looks up and smiles. "Still jealous of little Audrey?" he inquires.

"Not any more. There were times when I wanted to claw her eyes out."

But he grows serious again. "I suppose Bessie talked," he says. "She told him what she knew, or thought she knew. So she had to go."

He lets it go at that, but I have to explain a number of things which he had been too busy or too distracted at the time to notice. The possibility of slipping down the basement stairs to the wine cellars under the ballroom, and taking the chain off the door. The probability that the Buddha had been taken some time before Bessie's death and concealed outside. Even the reason why I hid in my room at the Cloisters that last night. That amuses him. He leans back and eyes me. We are in Miss Mattie's parlor, with the manuscript on the table beside him. Near it are the blueprints of my old house. Tony keeps them at hand, for we are going to live there after we are married. The Cloisters is to be a summer home for poor children.

"I recognize the hazard in marrying you," he says. "You shoot policemen, you fall down elevator shafts, and you get bopped on the head in cement pools. You jump bad fences on horses. You're the jealous type. It sticks out all over you. And you wan-

der around at night packing a gun! No wonder I tremble in terror. Look at me now. But at least," he says, considering, "you do
have a brain."

"You said last night it resembled a scrambled egg."

"Not an egg. Just scrambled, my darling. Which reminds me.
Why don't you go on and tell about some of the nice people in
the story? That's usual, isn't it? Julian out of jail and so on."

"I'm not writing a fairy tale," I scoff, "with everybody living
happily ever after. Nobody does that, Tony."

"Well, we're going to do our damnedest," he says soberly. "I've
learned a lot about living, Pat, and so have you."

He has helped me with this story too. There has been so
much talk that we both wanted it straightened out. And only a
day or two ago he told me the details of the trap which was laid
at the Cloisters. "We had about a dozen cops that night," he said.
"They scattered, and I went to the Cloisters and slipped down to
the basement. The chain was off the door there, so we guessed it
would be the elevator.

"Then you appeared! If ever anybody looked guilty as hell it
was you, my darling. You carried a gun, and you slid downstairs
and out of the house as if you were on your way to kill someone.
Hopper grabbed my arm. 'My God, the secretary!' he said. 'So
she's in it too!'

"He sent one of the men to follow you, and he was so sure
you were out for murder that he listened for a shot for the next
hour. Then when you came back I had all I could do to keep him
from strangling you. You started around with that flashlight, and
it looked as though the game was up.

"But our man was in the basement by that time. If he heard
you he thought it was O'Brien, making rounds. We heard the el-

evator going down to the cellar, and we knew it was all right. We had him. We had a half dozen cops guarding the doors of the shaft, from the top down, and he hadn't a chance in the world.

"He knew he was caught when your gun went off. That scared him. He started the car down again, but he couldn't get out. All he could do was to keep the thing moving. Then I remembered to shut off the power. It left him between floors, but he knew the game was up."

That was when Dwight Elliott shot himself.

The motive, Tony has always maintained, was perfectly clear once you knew the facts. From nothing he had built himself a strong position in the Wainwright Company. Not only wealth, but prestige. Then the day Maud has asked me to smuggle him into the house she laid her cards on the table.

She was not legally old J.C. Wainwright's wife. She had seen her husband. He was still alive, and what she wanted to do that day was to clear out, bag and baggage, to tell the truth, hand over the mills and the Cloisters to the Wainwright family where she thought they belonged, and go away.

But he managed to keep her quiet, for a time at least. "Take time to think it over," he probably said. "There's no hurry."

He must have been fairly desperate that day, however. He had never married. The business had been his wife and his child, and there was also the fifty thousand a year he drew as its counsel. But there was more at stake than that. For years he had fought the Wainwrights, fought them and hated them. Now Maud threatened to hand everything over to them.

Even then he probably had some hope. He could influence her. Given time enough he might persuade her. But then he got a letter from Don Morgan in New York: *I have just learned who*

and where Maud is. I would like to see her. In fact, it's essential to see
her. There are matters which should be settled at once.

They found that letter in his safe after his death. But it was
Don's return to Beverly that was the real blow. He had no rea-
son to believe in him, his good faith or anything else. Perhaps at
first he thought he could make an arrangement between them,
Maud and Don; meet them, secure a *modus vivendi* of some sort.
Almost certainly he never dreamed of murdering them. He tele-
phoned Don, agreeing to have Maud meet him that night, and
Don came.

What happened after that? Was there a quarrel? Did he slip
to the playhouse from his bridge game, and in some bitter anger
knock Don into the pool? Or was it more cold-blooded than
that? Elliott walking in on him in evening dress, neat and im-
peccable, and Don looking down at the water.

"Nice pool, isn't it? She's done well by herself."

And then the blow and the drowning. The lights off, the body
in the pool, the key hung on Bill Sterling's ring, and Dwight Elliott, after five minutes' absence, coming back to the bridge table.

"How'd you make out, partner?"

"Four spades."

Not a mark on him, his hands calm, his face impassive. Shuffling and dealing, bidding and playing, and his mind busy. The
body couldn't stay there. He would have to get it out, take it
away somewhere, as far as possible.

Jim Conway has always believed that after he left that night
he undressed in his car, hidden somewhere near by; that he
whipped off his coat, shirt, shoes, and trousers, and put on his
topcoat instead. And perhaps lost a garter on the way back to
the pool. But by that time he had, Jim maintains, a definite plan,

helped out by the fact that Don had not been able to dress. This plan was to drop the body in the river so that it would look like suicide. What happened to prevent it was probably the shortage of gas in Lydia's car. He had to get back up the hill and to his own car again.

In the end he could not reach the river, except where it was thickly settled. So he dropped the body out where it was found, and sped back up the hill. But here something happened which threw out all his calculations. Bill Sterling saw the car and followed it.

He went on, looking wildly for a lane, anywhere to get away from Bill and leave the car. As we know, he left it in the ravine behind the Farm. How he got back to his own car, dressed, and made the city can only be guessed.

Bad as it had been, it was only the beginning. Maud was stricken when she learned that it was Don who had been killed. Elliott tried to see her. For a long time he had wanted to marry her, to cement his own position. When he did see her he urged it again. But Maud was thinking only of Lydia and Audrey. "I can't let it go on. I must do something."

He began to see trouble ahead. Not only from Maud. Bessie was talking strangely, hinting to Tony of some secret she knew. Tony went to him. "Secret? About your mother? That's absurd, Tony. You ought to know better."

But he was worried. He tried to talk to Bessie. She only laughed at him. "I'll tell it when I'm good and ready. Not before, and not to you."

Not in those words perhaps, but something of the sort. That must have been when he tried to kill her as she drove out from town in her car.

Then at last the real blow fell. Maud telephoned him to say

she had sent for Lydia. She was to meet her that night at the playhouse. She was taking the envelope he knew about, and a list of her jewels. "I've done her a terrible injury. It's up to her to decide what to do."

Things were getting beyond his control. There was Bessie, sitting in his office and threatening even while she powdered her nose. "You can tell Tony what I know. If he does the right thing I'll keep my mouth shut. If he doesn't I'll blow the whole thing wide open. He has no legal right to the Wainwright money, and you know it." That was probably the day when she demanded a million dollars.

We will never know the details of her death. She must have suspected him by that time. But there had been the scene with Tony that night. She knew Tony was through. Her only hope was to see Dwight Elliott that night and bring pressure to bear on him. Perhaps she sent for him. What she said would have brought him in a hurry. "I'm being kicked out, but I can still keep my mouth shut—for a price."

She had her revolver with her when she saw him. She did not trust him. To avoid O'Brien she probably arranged to meet him outside the west wing door, and from the position of the body Jim thinks she was sitting on the steps there talking to him when it happened. He would have been quiet, eminently reasonable. "Give me time, Bessie. I can't raise money in a hurry."

And Bessie, fingering the gun and looking at him with her cold blue eyes. "You can raise it if you have to. So can Tony."

He must have killed her then. Perhaps he had hidden the Buddha outside for that purpose. Perhaps he invented an excuse, slipped into the house and got it. In any case, so far as we know he killed her with it.

That is all we know or guess about Bessie, lying as I saw her the next morning on the frozen ground, the bright sunlight on her pale hair and her flame-colored dress, with old Andy standing over her.

There is only one thing we have never discussed, Tony and I. That is the night of his mother's death and what happened in the playhouse. Why did Dwight kill her? He must still have hoped that Lydia would never tell the story for Audrey's sake, that Maud herself would see in time that she could make restitution without exposure. But I am quite certain I know.

She had suspected him of killing Don. Not at once. Perhaps not until that last night when he walked into the playhouse and she saw him there. She was shrewd. I think she herself led him to the pool. She was not afraid. As Tony said, she was not afraid of anything. She would have stood there with him beside her, neat and distinguished in his dinner clothes, and looked down to where Don had lain. "So this is where you killed him, Dwight. He threatened all you wanted in this world, power and place, so you killed him."

Something of that sort must have happened. Perhaps he protested, but she would not have believed him. Only the three of them knew the story, so far as she could tell. Of those three Don was dead and she was innocent. Only Dwight remained.

I think he had loved her, after his fashion. But there she stood beside him, menacing his very life. Even now I wonder if some vast anger, even jealousy, did not underlie what he did. He who had cared for her so long to die for the man who had deserted and neglected her. He may even have said it. "You always loved him, didn't you? You never forgot him."

"No. I never forgot him."

That is the story. Tony has read it to this point. Now he puts it down. He sits very still for a time, staring at the fire. Then he draws a long breath. "Let's forget it, darling. It's over, thank God. Suppose we stop remembering and plan a bit."

He has the blueprints ready. I put away the manuscript and settle myself to such things as plumbing and kitchen stoves and sunglass for a possible nursery in the future. From somewhere in the rear comes the odor of boiling cocoa, and soon Miss Mattie will rap at the door and I will slide off Tony's knee.

"I thought you might like a little something to eat," she says. "It will help you to sleep."

It is the authentic voice of Beverly, and we bow to it.

THE END

DISCUSSION QUESTIONS

- Were you able to predict any part of the solution to the case?

- After learning the solution, were there any clues you realized you had missed?

- Would the story be different if it were set in the present day? If so, how?

- Did the social context of the time play a role in the narrative? If so, how?

- What role did the geographical setting play in the narrative? Would the story have been different if it were set someplace else?

- If you were one of the main characters, would you have acted differently at any point in the story?

- Did you identify with any of the characters? If so, which?

- Did this story remind you of any other books you've read?

- If you have read other books by Mary Roberts Rinehart, how did this one compare?

MORE MARY ROBERTS RINEHART FROM
AMERICAN MYSTERY CLASSICS

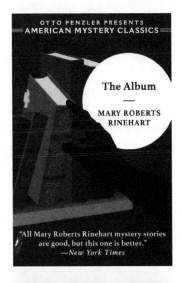

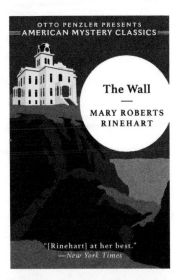

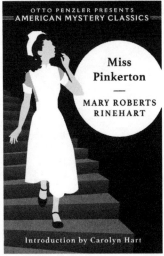

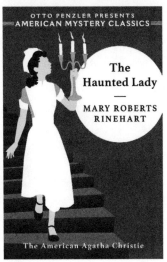

All titles are available in hardcover and in trade paperback.

Order from your favorite bookstore or from
The Mysterious Bookshop, 58 Warren Street, New York, N.Y. 10007
(www.mysteriousbookshop.com).

Charlotte Armstrong, *The Chocolate Cobweb*. When Amanda Garth was born, a mix-up caused the hospital to briefly hand her over to the prestigious Garrison family instead of to her birth parents. The error was quickly fixed, Amanda was never told, and the secret was forgotten for twenty-three years … until her aunt revealed it in casual conversation. But what if the initial switch never actually occurred? **Introduction by A. J. Finn.**

Charlotte Armstrong, *The Unsuspected*. First published in 1946, this suspenseful novel opens with a young woman who has ostensibly hanged herself, leaving a suicide note. Her friend doesn't believe it and begins an investigation that puts her own life in jeopardy. It was filmed in 1947 by Warner Brothers, starring Claude Rains and Joan Caulfield. **Introduction by Otto Penzler.**

Anthony Boucher, *The Case of the Baker Street Irregulars*. When a studio announces a new hard-boiled Sherlock Holmes film, the Baker Street Irregulars begin a campaign to discredit it. Attempting to mollify them, the producers invite members to the set, where threats are received, each referring to one of the original Holmes tales, followed by murder. Fortunately, the amateur sleuths use Holmesian lessons to solve the crime. **Introduction by Otto Penzler.**

Anthony Boucher, *Rocket to the Morgue*. Hilary Foulkes has made so many enemies that it is difficult to speculate who was responsible for stabbing him nearly to death in a room with only one door through which no one was seen entering or leaving. This classic locked room mystery is populated by such thinly disguised science fiction legends as Robert Heinlein, L. Ron Hubbard, and John W. Campbell. **Introduction by F. Paul Wilson.**

Fredric Brown, *The Fabulous Clipjoint*. Brown's outstanding mystery won an Edgar as the best first novel of the year (1947). When Wallace Hunter is found dead in an alley after a long night of drinking, the police don't really care. But his teenage son Ed and his uncle Am, the carnival worker, are convinced that some things don't add up and the crime isn't what it seems to be. **Introduction by Lawrence Block.**

John Dickson Carr, *The Crooked Hinge*. Selected by a group of mystery experts as one of the 15 best impossible crime novels ever written, this is one of Gideon Fell's greatest challenges. Estranged from his family for 25 years, Sir John Farnleigh returns to England from America to claim his inheritance but another person turns up claiming that he can prove he is the real Sir John. Inevitably, one of them is murdered. **Introduction by Charles Todd.**

John Dickson Carr, *The Eight of Swords*. When Gideon Fell arrives at a crime scene, it appears to be straightforward enough. A man has been shot to death in an unlocked room and the likely perpetrator was a recent visitor. But Fell discovers inconsistencies and his investigations are complicated by an apparent poltergeist, some American gangsters, and two meddling amateur sleuths. **Introduction by Otto Penzler.**

John Dickson Carr, *The Mad Hatter Mystery*. A prankster has been stealing top hats all around London. Gideon Fell suspects that the same person may be responsible for the theft of a manuscript of a long-lost story by Edgar Allan Poe. The hats reappear in unexpected but conspicuous places but, when one is found on the head of a corpse by the Tower of London, it is evident that the thefts are more than pranks. **Introduction by Otto Penzler.**

John Dickson Carr, *The Plague Court Murders*. When murder occurs in a locked hut on Plague Court, an estate haunted by the ghost of a hangman's assistant who died a victim of the black death, Sir Henry Merrivale seeks a logical solution to a ghostly crime. A spiritual medium employed to rid the house of his spirit is found stabbed to death in a locked stone hut on the grounds, surrounded by an untouched circle of mud. **Introduction by Michael Dirda.**

John Dickson Carr, *The Red Widow Murders*. In a "haunted" mansion, the room known as the Red Widow's Chamber proves lethal to all who spend the night. Eight people investigate and the one who draws the ace of spades must sleep in it. The room is locked from the inside and watched all night by the others. When the door is unlocked, the victim has been poisoned. Enter Sir Henry Merrivale to solve the crime. **Introduction by Tom Mead.**

Frances Crane, *The Turquoise Shop*. In an arty little New Mexico town, Mona Brandon has arrived from the East and becomes the subject of gossip about her money, her influence, and the corpse in the nearby desert who may be her husband. Pat Holly, who runs the local gift shop, is as interested as anyone in the goings on—but even more in Pat Abbott, the detective investigating the possible murder. **Introduction by Anne Hillerman.**

Todd Downing, *Vultures in the Sky*. There is no end to the series of terrifying events that befall a luxury train bound for Mexico. First, a man dies when the train passes through a dark tunnel, then it comes to an abrupt stop in the middle of the desert. More deaths occur when night falls and the passengers panic when they realize they are trapped with a murderer on the loose. **Introduction by James Sallis.**

Mignon G. Eberhart, *Murder by an Aristocrat*. Nurse Keate is called to help a man who has been "accidentally" shot in the shoulder. When he is murdered while convalescing, it is clear that there was no accident. Although a killer is loose in the mansion, the family seems more concerned that news of the murder will leave their circle. *The New Yorker* wrote than "Eberhart can weave an almost flawless mystery." **Introduction by Nancy Pickard.**

Erle Stanley Gardner, *The Case of the Baited Hook*. Perry Mason gets a phone call in the middle of the night and his potential client says it's urgent, that he has two one-thousand-dollar bills that he will give him as a retainer, with an additional ten-thousand whenever he is called on to represent him. When Mason takes the case, it is not for the caller but for a beautiful woman whose identity is hidden behind a mask. **Introduction by Otto Penzler.**

Erle Stanley Gardner, *The Case of the Borrowed Brunette*. A mysterious man named Mr. Hines has advertised a job for a woman who has to fulfill very specific physical requirements. Eva Martell, pretty but struggling in her career as a model, takes the job but her aunt smells a rat and hires Perry Mason to investigate. Her fears are realized when Hines turns up in the apartment with a bullet hole in his head. **Introduction by Otto Penzler.**

Erle Stanley Gardner, *The Case of the Careless Kitten*. Helen Kendal receives a mysterious phone call from her vanished uncle Franklin, long presumed dead, who urges her to contact Perry Mason. Soon, she finds herself the main suspect in the murder of an unfamiliar man. Her kitten has just survived a poisoning attempt—as has her aunt Matilda. What is the connection between Franklin's return and the murder attempts? **Introduction by Otto Penzler.**

Erle Stanley Gardner, *The Case of the Rolling Bones*. One of Gardner's most successful Perry Mason novels opens with a clear case of blackmail, though the person being blackmailed claims he isn't. It is not long before the police are searching for someone wanted for killing the same man in two different states—thirty-three years apart. The confounding puzzle of what happened to the dead man's toes is a challenge. **Introduction by Otto Penzler.**

Erle Stanley Gardner, *The Case of the Shoplifter's Shoe*. Most cases for Perry Mason involve murder but here he is hired because a young woman fears her aunt is a kleptomaniac. Sarah may not have been precisely the best guardian for a collection of valuable diamonds and, sure enough, they go missing. When the jeweler is found shot dead, Sarah is spotted leaving the murder scene with a bundle of gems stuffed in her purse. **Introduction by Otto Penzler.**

Erle Stanley Gardner, *The Bigger They Come*. Gardner's first novel using the pseudonym

A.A. Fair starts off a series featuring the large and loud Bertha Cool and her employee, the small and meek Donald Lam. Given the job of delivering divorce papers to an evident crook, Lam can't find him—but neither can the police. The *Los Angeles Times* called this book: "Breathlessly dramatic ... an original." **Introduction by Otto Penzler.**

Frances Noyes Hart, *The Bellamy Trial.* Inspired by the real-life Hall-Mills case, the most sensational trial of its day, this is the story of Stephen Bellamy and Susan Ives, accused of murdering Bellamy's wife Madeleine. Eight days of dynamic testimony, some true, some not, make headlines for an enthralled public. Rex Stout called this historic courtroom thriller one of the ten best mysteries of all time. **Introduction by Hank Phillippi Ryan.**

H.F. Heard, *A Taste for Honey.* The elderly Mr. Mycroft quietly keeps bees in Sussex, where he is approached by the reclusive and somewhat misanthropic Mr. Silchester, whose honey supplier was found dead, stung to death by her bees. Mycroft, who shares many traits with Sherlock Holmes, sets out to find the vicious killer. Rex Stout described it as "sinister ... a tale well and truly told." **Introduction by Otto Penzler.**

Dolores Hitchens, *The Alarm of the Black Cat.* Detective fiction aficionado Rachel Murdock has a peculiar meeting with a little girl and a dead toad, sparking her curiosity about a love triangle that has sparked anger. When the girl's great grandmother is found dead, Rachel and her cat Samantha work with a friend in the Los Angeles Police Department to get to the bottom of things. **Introduction by David Handler.**

Dolores Hitchens, *The Cat Saw Murder.* Miss Rachel Murdock, the highly intelligent 70-year-old amateur sleuth, is not entirely heartbroken when her slovenly, unattractive, bridge-cheating niece is murdered. Miss Rachel is happy to help the socially maladroit and somewhat bumbling Detective Lieutenant Stephen Mayhew, retaining her composure when a second brutal murder occurs. **Introduction by Joyce Carol Oates.**

Dorothy B. Hughes, *Dread Journey.* A big-shot Hollywood producer has worked on his magnum opus for years, hiring and firing one beautiful starlet after another. But Kitten Agnew's contract won't allow her to be fired, so she fears she might be terminated more permanently. Together with the producer on a train journey from Hollywood to Chicago, Kitten becomes more terrified with each passing mile. **Introduction by Sarah Weinman.**

Dorothy B. Hughes, *Ride the Pink Horse.* When Sailor met Willis Douglass, he was just a poor kid who Douglass groomed to work as a confidential secretary. As the senator became increasingly corrupt, he knew he could count on Sailor to clean up his messes. No longer a senator, Douglass flees Chicago for Santa Fe, leaving behind a murder rap and Sailor as the prime suspect. Seeking vengeance, Sailor follows. **Introduction by Sara Paretsky.**

Dorothy B. Hughes, *The So Blue Marble.* Set in the glamorous world of New York high society, this novel became a suspense classic as twins from Europe try to steal a rare and beautiful gem owned by an aristocrat whose sister is an even more menacing presence. *The New Yorker* called it "Extraordinary ... [Hughes'] brilliant descriptive powers make and unmake reality." **Introduction by Otto Penzler.**

W. Bolingbroke Johnson, *The Widening Stain.* After a cocktail party, the attractive Lucie Coindreau, a "black-eyed, black-haired Frenchwoman" visits the rare books wing of the library and apparently takes a head-first fall from an upper gallery. Dismissed as a horrible accident, it seems dubious when Professor Hyett is strangled while reading a priceless 12th-century manuscript, which has gone missing. **Introduction by Nicholas A. Basbanes**

Baynard Kendrick, *Blind Man's Bluff.* Blinded in World War II, Duncan Maclain forms a successful private detective agency, aided by his two dogs. Here, he is called on to solve the case of a blind man who plummets from the top of an eight-story building, apparently with no one present except his dead-drunk son. **Introduction by Otto Penzler.**

Baynard Kendrick, *The Odor of Violets.* Duncan Maclain, a blind former intelligence officer, is asked to investigate the murder of an actor in his Greenwich Village apartment.

This would cause a stir at any time but, when the actor possesses secret government plans that then go missing, it's enough to interest the local police as well as the American government and Maclain, who suspects a German spy plot. **Introduction by Otto Penzler.**

C. Daly King, *Obelists at Sea*. On a cruise ship traveling from New York to Paris, the lights of the smoking room briefly go out, a gunshot crashes through the night, and a man is dead. Two detectives are on board but so are four psychiatrists who believe their professional knowledge can solve the case by understanding the psyche of the killer—each with a different theory. **Introduction by Martin Edwards.**

Jonathan Latimer, *Headed for a Hearse*. Featuring Bill Crane, the booze-soaked Chicago private detective, this humorous hard-boiled novel was filmed as *The Westland Case* in 1937 starring Preston Foster. Robert Westland has been framed for the grisly murder of his wife in a room with doors and windows locked from the inside. As the day of his execution nears, he relies on Crane to find the real murderer. **Introduction by Max Allan Collins**

Lange Lewis, *The Birthday Murder*. Victoria is a successful novelist and screenwriter and her husband is a movie director so their marriage seems almost too good to be true. Then, on her birthday, her happy new life comes crashing down when her husband is murdered using a method of poisoning that was described in one of her books. She quickly becomes the leading suspect. **Introduction by Randal S. Brandt.**

Frances and Richard Lockridge, *Death on the Aisle*. In one of the most beloved books to feature Mr. and Mrs. North, the body of a wealthy backer of a play is found dead in a seat of the 45th Street Theater. Pam is thrilled to engage in her favorite pastime—playing amateur sleuth—much to the annoyance of Jerry, her publisher husband. The Norths inspired a stage play, a film, and long-running radio and TV series. **Introduction by Otto Penzler.**

John P. Marquand, *Your Turn, Mr. Moto*. The first novel about Mr. Moto, originally titled *No Hero*, is the story of a World War I hero pilot who finds himself jobless during the De-

pression. In Tokyo for a big opportunity that falls apart, he meets a Japanese agent and his Russian colleague and the pilot suddenly finds himself caught in a web of intrigue. Peter Lorre played Mr. Moto in a series of popular films. **Introduction by Lawrence Block.**

Stuart Palmer, *The Penguin Pool Murder*. The first adventure of schoolteacher and dedicated amateur sleuth Hildegarde Withers occurs at the New York Aquarium when she and her young students notice a corpse in one of the tanks. It was published in 1931 and filmed the next year, starring Edna May Oliver as the American Miss Marple—though much funnier than her English counterpart. **Introduction by Otto Penzler.**

Stuart Palmer, *The Puzzle of the Happy Hooligan*. New York City schoolteacher Hildegarde Withers cannot resist "assisting" homicide detective Oliver Piper. In this novel, she is on vacation in Hollywood and on the set of a movie about Lizzie Borden when the screenwriter is found dead. Six comic films about Withers appeared in the 1930s, most successfully starring Edna May Oliver. **Introduction by Otto Penzler.**

Otto Penzler, ed., *Golden Age Bibliomysteries*. Stories of murder, theft, and suspense occur with alarming regularity in the unlikely world of books and bibliophiles, including bookshops, libraries, and private rare book collections, written by such giants of the mystery genre as Ellery Queen, Cornell Woolrich, Lawrence G. Blochman, Vincent Starrett, and Anthony Boucher. **Introduction by Otto Penzler.**

Otto Penzler, ed., *Golden Age Detective Stories*. The history of American mystery fiction has its pantheon of authors who have influenced and entertained readers for nearly a century, reaching its peak during the Golden Age, and this collection pays homage to the work of the most acclaimed: Cornell Woolrich, Erle Stanley Gardner, Craig Rice, Ellery Queen, Dorothy B. Hughes, Mary Roberts Rinehart, and more. **Introduction by Otto Penzler.**

Otto Penzler, ed., *Golden Age Locked Room Mysteries*. The so-called impossible crime category reached its zenith during the 1920s, 1930s, and 1940s, and this volume includes the greatest of the great authors who mastered the form: John Dickson Carr, Ellery Queen, C. Daly King, Clayton Rawson, and Erle Stanley Gardner. Like great magicians, these literary conjurors will baffle and delight readers. **Introduction by Otto Penzler.**

Ellery Queen, *The Adventures of Ellery Queen.* These stories are the earliest short works to feature Queen as a detective and are among the best of the author's fair-play mysteries. So many of the elements that comprise the gestalt of Queen may be found in these tales: alternate solutions, the dying clue, a bizarre crime, and the author's ability to find fresh variations of works by other authors. **Introduction by Otto Penzler.**

Ellery Queen, *The American Gun Mystery.* A rodeo comes to New York City at the Colosseum. The headliner is Buck Horne, the once popular film cowboy who opens the show leading a charge of forty whooping cowboys until they pull out their guns and fire into the air. Buck falls to the ground, shot dead. The police instantly lock the doors to search everyone but the offending weapon has completely vanished. **Introduction by Otto Penzler.**

Ellery Queen, *The Chinese Orange Mystery.* The offices of publisher Donald Kirk have seen strange events but nothing like this. A strange man is found dead with two long spears alongside his back. And, though no one was seen entering or leaving the room, everything has been turned backwards or upside down: pictures face the wall, the victim's clothes are worn backwards, the rug upside down. Why in the world? **Introduction by Otto Penzler.**

Ellery Queen, *The Dutch Shoe Mystery.* Millionaire philanthropist Abagail Doorn falls into a coma and she is rushed to the hospital she funds for an emergency operation by one of the leading surgeons on the East Coast. When she is wheeled into the operating theater, the sheet covering her body is pulled back to reveal her garroted corpse—the first of a series of murders **Introduction by Otto Penzler.**

Ellery Queen, *The Egyptian Cross Mystery.* A small-town schoolteacher is found dead, headed, and tied to a T-shaped cross on December 25th, inspiring such sensational headlines as "Crucifixion on Christmas Day." Amateur sleuth Ellery Queen is so intrigued he travels to Virginia but fails to solve the crime. Then a similar murder takes place on New York's Long Island—and then another. **Introduction by Otto Penzler.**

Ellery Queen, *The Siamese Twin Mystery.* When Ellery and his father encounter a raging forest fire on a mountain, their only hope is to drive up to an isolated hillside manor owned by a secretive surgeon and his strange guests. While playing solitaire in the middle of the night, the doctor is shot. The only clue is a torn playing card. Suspects include a society beauty, a valet, and conjoined twins. **Introduction by Otto Penzler.**

Ellery Queen, *The Spanish Cape Mystery.* Amateur detective Ellery Queen arrives in the resort town of Spanish Cape soon after a young woman and her uncle are abducted by a gun-toting, one-eyed giant. The next day, the woman's somewhat dicey boyfriend is found murdered—totally naked under a black fedora and opera cloak. **Introduction by Otto Penzler.**

Patrick Quentin, *A Puzzle for Fools.* Broadway producer Peter Duluth takes to the bottle when his wife dies but enters a sanitarium to dry out. Malevolent events plague the hospital, including when Peter hears his own voice intone, "There will be murder." And there is. He investigates, aided by a young woman who is also a patient. This is the first of nine mysteries featuring Peter and Iris Duluth. **Introduction by Otto Penzler.**

Clayton Rawson, *Death from a Top Hat.* When the New York City Police Department is baffled by an apparently impossible crime, they call on The Great Merlini, a retired stage magician who now runs a Times Square magic shop. In his first case, two occultists have been murdered in a room locked from the inside, their bodies positioned to form a pentagram. **Introduction by Otto Penzler.**

Craig Rice, *Eight Faces at Three.* Gin-soaked John J. Malone, defender of the guilty, is notorious for getting his culpable clients off. It's the innocent ones who are problems. Like Holly Inglehart, accused of piercing the black heart of her well-heeled aunt Alexandria with a lovely Florentine paper cutter. No one who knew the old battle-ax liked her, but Holly's prints were found on the murder weapon. **Introduction by Lisa Lutz.**

Craig Rice, *Home Sweet Homicide*. Known as the Dorothy Parker of mystery fiction for her memorable wit, Craig Rice was the first detective writer to appear on the cover of *Time* magazine. This comic mystery features two kids who are trying to find a husband for their widowed mother while she's engaged in sleuthing. Filmed with the same title in 1946 with Peggy Ann Garner and Randolph Scott. **Introduction by Otto Penzler.**

Mary Roberts Rinehart, *The Album*. Crescent Place is a quiet enclave of wealthy people in which nothing ever happens—until a bed-ridden old woman is attacked by an intruder with an ax. *The New York Times* stated: "All Mary Roberts Rinehart mystery stories are good, but this one is better." **Introduction by Otto Penzler.**

Mary Roberts Rinehart, *The Haunted Lady*. The arsenic in her sugar bowl was wealthy widow Eliza Fairbanks' first clue that somebody wanted her dead. Nightly visits of bats, birds, and rats, obviously aimed at scaring the dowager to death, was the second. Eliza calls the police, who send nurse Hilda Adams, the amateur sleuth they refer to as "Miss Pinkerton," to work undercover to discover the culprit. **Introduction by Otto Penzler.**

Mary Roberts Rinehart, *Miss Pinkerton*. Hilda Adams is a nurse, not a detective, but she is observant and smart and so it is common for Inspector Patton to call on her for help. Her success results in his calling her "Miss Pinkerton." *The New Republic* wrote: "From thousands of hearts and homes the cry will go up: Thank God for Mary Roberts Rinehart." **Introduction by Carolyn Hart.**

Mary Roberts Rinehart, *The Red Lamp*. Professor William Porter refuses to believe that the seaside manor he's just inherited is haunted but he has to convince his wife to move in. However, he soon sees evidence of the occult phenomena of which the townspeople speak. Whether it is a spirit or a human being, Porter accepts that there is a connection to the rash of murders that have terrorized the countryside. **Introduction by Otto Penzler.**

Mary Roberts Rinehart, *The Wall*. For two decades, Mary Roberts Rinehart was the second-best-selling author in America (only Sinclair Lewis outsold her) and was beloved for her tales of suspense. In a magnificent mansion, the ex-wife of one of the owners turns up making demands and is found dead the next day. And there are more dark secrets lying behind the walls of the estate. **Introduction by Otto Penzler.**

Joel Townsley Rogers, *The Red Right Hand*. This extraordinary whodunnit that is as puzzling as it is terrifying was identified by crime fiction scholar Jack Adrian as "one of the dozen or so finest mystery novels of the 20th century." A deranged killer sends a doctor on a quest for the truth—deep into the recesses of his own mind—when he and his bride-to-be elope but pick up a terrifying sharp-toothed hitch-hiker. **Introduction by Joe R. Lansdale.**

Roger Scarlett, *Cat's Paw*. The family of the wealthy old bachelor Martin Greenough cares far more about his money than they do about him. For his birthday, he invites all his potential heirs to his mansion to tell them what they hope to hear. Before he can disburse funds, however, he is murdered, and the Boston Police Department's big problem is that there are too many suspects. **Introduction by Curtis Evans**

Vincent Starrett, *Dead Man Inside*. 1930s Chicago is a tough town but some crimes are more bizarre than others. Customers arrive at a haberdasher to find a corpse in the window and a sign on the door: *Dead Man Inside! I am Dead. The store will not open today.* This is just one of a series of odd murders that terrorizes the city. Reluctant detective Walter Ghost leaps into action to learn what is behind the plague. **Introduction by Otto Penzler.**

Vincent Starrett, *The Great Hotel Murder*. Theater critic and amateur sleuth Riley Blackwood investigates a murder in a Chicago hotel where the dead man had changed rooms with a stranger who had registered under a fake name. *The New York Times* described it as "an ingenious plot with enough complications to keep the reader guessing." **Introduction by Lyndsay Faye.**

Vincent Starrett, *Murder on 'B' Deck*. Walter Ghost, a psychologist, scientist, explorer, and former intelligence officer, is on a cruise ship and his friend novelist Dunsten Mollock, a Nigel Bruce-like Watson whose role is to offer occasional comic relief, accommodates when he fails to leave the ship before it takes off. Although they make mistakes along the way, the amateur sleuths solve the shipboard murders. **Introduction by Ray Betzner.**

Phoebe Atwood Taylor, *The Cape Cod Mystery*. Vacationers have flocked to Cape Cod to avoid the heat wave that hit the Northeast and find their holiday unpleasant when the area is flooded with police trying to find the murderer of a muckraking journalist who took a cottage for the season. Finding a solution falls to Asey Mayo, "the Cape Cod Sherlock," known for his worldly wisdom, folksy humor, and common sense. **Introduction by Otto Penzler.**

S. S. Van Dine, *The Benson Murder Case*. The first of 12 novels to feature Philo Vance, the most popular and influential detective character of the early part of the 20th century. When wealthy stockbroker Alvin Benson is found shot to death in a locked room in his mansion, the police are baffled until the erudite flaneur and art collector arrives on the scene. Paramount filmed it in 1930 with William Powell as Vance. **Introduction by Ragnar Jónasson.**

Cornell Woolrich, *The Bride Wore Black*. The first suspense novel by one of the greatest of all noir authors opens with a bride and her new husband walking out of the church. A car speeds by, shots ring out, and he falls dead at her feet. Determined to avenge his death, she tracks down everyone in the car, concluding with a shocking surprise. It was filmed by Francois Truffaut in 1968, starring Jeanne Moreau. **Introduction by Eddie Muller.**

Cornell Woolrich, *Deadline at Dawn*. Quinn is overcome with guilt about having robbed a stranger's home. He meets Bricky, a dime-a-dance girl, and they fall for each other. When they return to the crime scene, they discover a dead body. Knowing Quinn will be accused of the crime, they race to find the true killer before he's arrested. A 1946 film starring Susan Hayward was loosely based on the plot. **Introduction by David Gordon.**

Cornell Woolrich, *Waltz into Darkness*. A New Orleans businessman successfully courts a woman through the mail but he is shocked to find when she arrives that she is not the plain brunette whose picture he'd received but a radiant blond beauty. She soon absconds with his fortune. Wracked with disappointment and loneliness, he vows to track her down. When he finds her, the real nightmare begins. **Introduction by Wallace Stroby.**